CHILD OF THE MORNING

CHILD *of the* MORNING

Pauline Gedge

CHICAGO REVIEW PRESS

Cover design: Sarah Olson
Cover illustration: Leo and Diane Dillon

Copyright © 1977 by Pauline Gedge
Foreword © 2010 by Michelle Moran
All rights reserved
Published by arrangement with the author
This unabridged edition published in 2010 by Chicago Review Press, Incorporated
814 North Franklin Street
Chicago, Illinois 60610
ISBN 978-1-56976-324-7
Printed in the United States of America
5 4 3 2

Foreword

Thousands of years ago, Egyptians believed that to speak the name of the dead was to make them live again. In our own time, few have spoken those names so eloquently as Pauline Gedge. Perhaps it fortifies us, her fans, to think that it could not have been otherwise, to think that novels like *Child of the Morning* or *The Lady of the Reeds* were not put on paper by chance alone. From her first childhood glimpse of desert sand through a ship's porthole in Suez, to the school days spent daydreaming about Egypt's greatest queens, Pauline seemed destined to bring ancient Egypt to life. She describes the almost-fated process by which her debut novel came to be:

> I forget where I had been that morning, but I vividly remember standing at the foot of those steps, looking up towards (my sister's) door, and feeling as though my life had no purpose. I began to climb. By the time I came to the top a miracle had taken place in me. I knew exactly what I was going to write about—or rather, who—an ancient Egyptian woman I had studied about and admired since I was eleven. It was an experience that every writer longs for once in a career, that flash of inspiration, and for me it happened at the moment when my future seemed darkest.

And so reading *Child of the Morning* gives one a special sense of "being present at the creation." After all, it was winning a writing competition with this very novel that launched Pauline Gedge's career as an author. Thirteen works in print and millions of loyal readers later, we can only be glad that it did.

Queen Hatshepsut, sometimes described as a consummate self-promoter, knew the value of a legacy as well as anyone. Having seen her father and brother/spouse die, she served as regent for her young nephew, Tuthmosis III. Had her role ended there, she might be little-remembered today. Yet humans have always been driven to build something of transcendent value in this, our short season above the soil. The Egyptians felt this more keenly than perhaps any other civilization. They started the process of carving a legacy in stone and hieroglyph early, almost from birth. But the very grandeur of Hatshepsut's monuments and achievements made them a target for less able rulers who were to follow. Pity the poor Egyptian whose life's work was rubbed away after their death. Across different times and cultures, the *damnatio memoriae*, the expunging from memory, has been seen as the most evil of fates. A life can be taken in the twinkling of an eye, but to rob someone of their legacy is to unmake them in an even more profound sense.

Yet fortunately, modern Egyptologists have been able to reconstitute a clear picture of Hatshepsut's singular rule, not just as symbolic *she-Pharaoh*, but as a tremendous builder and a savvy administrator. Despite the best efforts of her successors to erase all remnants of her reign, we know more about Hatshepsut than any woman alive 3,500 years ago. Her era was as ancient to Emperor Marcus Aurelius as his is to us today: that her story has been recovered now seems almost miraculous. It is a story that sings through the stones of her temple at Luxor, a masterpiece of this golden age of architecture. Her military successes and voyages of exploration are all gone now, but the perfect symmetries of her mortuary temple serve as a symbol of the confident and prosperous and peaceful society that it would have taken to produce it. It stands, still, anchored into granite cliffs that she must have known would endure until the end of the world. She has succeeded in the most profound way the Egyptians could imagine: to write her name in history, to build a legacy. Fortunately for us, a legacy can be left in pen as well as in stone, and you hold in your hand a novel that legions of readers will remember forever. Thanks to Pauline Gedge, we are able to walk alongside Queen-Pharaoh Hatshepsut, this *God's Wife*, to enter her world, hear her thoughts, and witness her extraordinary life.

MICHELLE MORAN

For my mother Airini and my father Lloyd, with love

I owe a debt of gratitude to the staff at the Extension Library of the University of Alberta at Edmonton for their excellent service, and I must also thank the authors of those works I have consulted. Their lifelong and painstaking dedication to the collation of facts on ancient Egypt has enabled me, a mere neophyte, to write this book, and I am sorry that the list is so long that I cannot name them all.

I have done this from a loving heart for my Father Amun;
I have entered into his scheme for this first jubilee;
I was wise by his excellent Spirit, and I forgot nothing of that which
he exacted.
My Majesty knoweth that he is Divine.
I did it under his command; it was he who led me.
I conceived no works without his doing; it was he who gave me
directions.
I slept not because of his temple; I erred not from that which he
commanded.
My heart was wise before my Father; I entered into the affairs of his
heart.
I turned not my back on the City of the All-Lord, but turned to it
the face.
I know that Karnak is God's dwelling upon earth; the August Ascent
of the Beginning;
The Sacred Eye of the All-Lord; the place of his heart;
Which wears his beauty, and encompasses those who follow him.

Prayer composed by King Hatshepsu I
on the occasion of Her Jubilee.

Prologue

She went to her couch early, signaling to her slave and slipping from the hall almost unnoticed while the food still steamed on the little gilded tables and the fragrance of the flowers, scattered everywhere, moved in an invisible cloud with her down the colonnaded walk. There was a flurry of clapping behind her as the musicians took their places and began a quick, lilting rhythm, but she strode on, Merire almost running to keep up with her. When she reached her own apartments, she ignored the salute of her guard, sweeping into the bedchamber and kicking off her sandals.

"Shut the doors," she said, and Merire obeyed, swinging them closed. She turned with wary eyes, trying to gauge her mistress's mood. Hatshepsut sank onto the stool before her mirror and gestured. "Take it all from me."

"Yes, Majesty."

The competent hands lifted the heavy, elaborate wig, gently removed the glowing gold and carnelian necklet and slid the jingling bracelets over nerveless hands. The room was pleasantly warmed by the two charcoal braziers in each corner, and the lamps barely flickered to disturb the shadowed depths, for at that hour the gay, color-splashed walls were muted, scarcely visible; only the odd, rapid dart of a leaping flame picked out a point of frozen movement here, licked along a spark of precious metal there. The room, unlike its taut and angry prisoner, slumbered.

Hatshepsut stood as Merire released the shoulder straps of the delicate linen sheath and drew it from her. She poured hot, scented water and began washing the kohl from the dark eyes, the red henna from the soles of the feet and the palms of the hands. The older woman continued to stare at herself in the burnished depths of the huge copper mirror.

When Merire had finished, Hatshepsut walked to the head of her couch and leaned on it, her arms folded.

When the palace was filled with the comings and goings of my court, and all night and day at my command the incense rose in the temple, then all were willing to serve me to the death. Yes, yes, but whose death? Whose? Where are they now, the brave boasters? And what have I done that it should all end like this? For the gods I have poured out gold and slaves. I have built and labored. For this country, my eternal, my beautiful Egypt, I have given of my Divine Self, sweated and lain wakeful and anxious in the night so that the people should sleep and be safe. Now even the fellahin in the fields can talk of nothing but war. War, not raids for plunder, not border skirmishes, but full battles for the acquisition of an empire. And I can do nothing but watch, impotent. This country is not a country suited to war. We laugh, we sing, we make love and build and trade and work, but war is too solemn for us and will destroy us all in the end.

Merire took away the water and returned with the sleeping robe.

But Hatshepsut waved it aside. "Not tonight. Just leave all as it is. You can tidy it in the morning. Now get out."

It was not death that she feared. She knew that the time was close, very close. Perhaps it would come the next day, and not a moment too soon, for she was weary of living and wished to rest. But she was finally lonely, and the silence of an empty room unsettled her. She slid to the couch and sat quite still. "O, my Father," she prayed, "Mighty Amun, King of all gods, it was thus, naked, that I entered this world; and it is thus, naked, that I shall be carried to the House of the Dead."

She rose and began to pace about, her bare feet making no sound on the red and blue tiled floor. She walked to the water clock and watched it drip for a moment. It lacked four hours to the rising of the sun. Four hours. And then another day of wearing frustration and enforced idleness, sitting in the garden, sailing on the river, taking her chariot round the circuit in the army's training ground to the east of the city. The same chariot that had been presented to her by her own body of troops that bright, fresh morning. How young she had been then. How her heart had fluttered with fear and excitement, and how she had clutched the burnished sides of the golden chariot as her horses thundered across the hard, sunbaked sand, cleaving the blazing, still desert air with fire and death!

Now it was winter, the month of Hathor, a month that seemed to reach back forever, although it had only just begun. In the chilly nights, the days only a little less breathlessly hot than those of summer, she began to feel a rising desperation born of inaction. And the old pain, the pain that was always new, began to tug at her so that she opened her eyes. Before her, far back in the dimness, her own image swam in the half-light, beaten silver, a huge relief that formed a portion of the wall. The haughty chin holding the Pharaonic Beard was lifted high, the eyes steady and unyielding beneath the weight of the tall and regal Double Crown of Egypt. She smiled suddenly.

So it was, and so it shall always be that I was King of Egypt, I, Daughter of Amun. And in times to come men shall know and wonder, as I have done regarding the monuments and works of marvel that my forefathers did. I am not alone. I shall, after all, live forever.

1

Although the north wall of the schoolroom opened onto the garden, the prevailing summer wind did not blow between the dazzling white, color-splashed pillars. It was suffocatingly hot. The students sat cross-legged on their papyrus mats, knee to knee, their heads bent over the pieces of broken pottery, laboriously copying out the day's lesson. Khaemwese, his arms folded, felt sleep steal into his head, and he cast a surreptitious glance in the direction of the stone water clock. Almost midday. He coughed, and a dozen little faces were turned up to him expectantly.

"Are you all finished? Who shall read back to me today's wisdom? Or should I say, who has the wisdom to read back to me today's lesson?" He beamed at his witticism, and a polite ripple of laughter ran around the room. "You, Menkh? User-amun? Now I know that Hapuseneb can do it, so I will not ask him. Who will volunteer? Thothmes, you will."

Thothmes struggled unhappily to his feet while Hatshepsut, sitting at his side, poked him and made a face. He ignored her, holding the pot in both hands and peering at it in distress.

"Begin. Hatshepsut, sit still."

"I have heard that thou—that thou—"

"Followest."

"Yes, followest. I have heard that thou followest pleasures. Turn not thy back on my words. Dost thou give thy mind to all—to all—"

"Manner of deaf things."

"Oh. To all manner of deaf things?"

Khaemwese sighed as the boy's voice droned on. It was certain that Thothmes would never make an informed and enlightened man. He had no love at all for the magic of words and seemed content to drowse through his lessons. Perhaps the One should consider putting his son into the army early. But Khaemwese shook his head at the vision of Thothmes, bow and spear in hand, marching at the head of a company of hard-bitten old campaigners. The boy was stumbling again, waiting, his finger under the offending hieroglyph, a dumb bewilderment in his eyes as he watched his teacher.

The old man felt a spark of anger. "This passage," he said waspishly, stabbing at his own scroll with petulance, "refers to the judicious and wholly deserving use of the hippopotamus whip on the posterior of a lazy boy. Perhaps the scribe is thinking of just such a boy as yourself, Thothmes? Do you need a taste of my hippopotamus whip? Bring it to me at once!"

Several of the older boys began to snigger, but Neferu-khebit put out her hand in distress. "Oh, please, Master, not again! Only yesterday he was beaten, and father was angry!"

Thothmes flushed and glared down at her. The hippopotamus whip was an old and well-worn joke, being only a slender and springy willow switch that Khaemwese carried under his arm from day to day like a general's staff of office. The real thing was for criminals and malcontents. To have a girl speak out on one's behalf was salt in an already throbbing wound, and the boy muttered under his breath as the master peremptorily motioned him to sit down.

"Very well. Neferu, seeing that you wish his sentence commuted, you may take upon yourself his task. Rise and continue."

Neferu-khebit was a year older and considerably more intelligent than Thothmes. She had just graduated from the old, fragmented pots to papyrus scrolls, and she finished the lesson with ease.

The class ended as usual with the Prayer to Amun. The students rose as Khaemwese left the room, and then a babble broke out.

"Never mind, Thothmes," Hatshepsut said brightly, rolling up her mat. "Come with me after the sleep, and see the new gazelle in the zoo. Father shot its mother, and now it has no one to love it. Will you come?"

"No," he snapped. "I do not want to go running all over the grounds with you anymore. Besides, now I have to go out to the barracks and practice with the bow and spear every afternoon with Aahmes pen-Nekheb."

They walked to the corner and laid their mats in a pile with the others while Neferu-khebit signaled to the naked slave waiting patiently by the big silver ewer. The woman drew water for them and presented it, bowing.

Hatshepsut drank deeply, smacking her lips. "Lovely, lovely water! What about you, Neferu? Would you like to do that with me?"

Neferu smiled down at her younger sister. She ran her hand over the smooth, shaved scalp and straightened the tousled youth-lock so that it hung decorously once more over the left shoulder. "You have ink on your kilt again, Hatshepsut. Will you ever grow up? Very well, I will come with you if Nozme gives permission. Just for a little while. Will that do?"

The little girl hopped in delight. "Yes! Come for me when you get up!"

The room was empty of all save the slave and the three of them. The other children were drifting home with their slaves as the heat increased to a solid weight of stifling air that seemed to bend their heads and fill them with the desire for sleep.

Thothmes yawned. "I am going to find my mother. I suppose I should thank you, Neferu-khebit, for delivering me, but I wish that you would mind your own business. The other boys find the spectacle amusing, and you humiliate me."

"Would you rather be beaten than made to look silly?" Hatshepsut snorted. "Really, Thothmes, you have too much dignity. And it's true. You are lazy."

"Hush!" said Neferu. "Thothmes, you know that I only acted out of concern for you. Here's Nozme. Behave yourselves. I will see you later, little Hat." She dropped a kiss on the top of Hatshepsut's head and drifted out into the glare of the garden.

Nozme was allowed quite as many liberties with the royal children as Khaemwese. As Royal Nurse she scolded them, wheedled them, occasionally spanked them, and always adored them. She was answerable to Pharaoh for their safety with her life. She had been hired by Second Wife Mutnefert as wet nurse when the little boy twins, Uatchmes and Amunmes, were born, and Divine Consort Aahmose had retained her for Neferu-khebit and Hatshepsut. Mutnefert herself had nursed Thothmes. He was her third son, and she watched over him like an eagle, for a son was precious, particularly a royal son, and her two little boys had died of plague. Nowadays Nozme was acid-tongued, hatchet-faced, and so emaciated that her thick, businesslike linens hung loosely on her gaunt frame and flapped around her bare ankles as she flew here and there, screaming at the slaves and admonishing the children. They no longer feared her, and only Hatshepsut still loved her, perhaps because, with the fickle selfishness of childhood, Hatshepsut was loved by everyone and so feared no check to her desires.

Seeing Nozme come sweeping in from the dimness of the hall, Hatshepsut ran to her and hugged her.

Nozme returned the hug and shrieked to the slave, "Get rid of that water now, and wash the basin. Sweep out the floor for tomorrow's lessons. Then you can go to your room and rest. Hurry up!" She glanced sharply after Neferu-khebit, but now that the young woman wore the sheath of adulthood and her head was no longer shaved but covered in shining black tresses that hung to her shoulders, Nozme's authority had almost come to an end. She contented herself with a muttered "Where is she going at this time of day?" Taking the little girl by the hand, Nozme led her gently through the maze of pillared halls and dark porticoes to the door of the children's apartment, adjacent to the women's quarters.

The palace hung in a drugged, hot silence. Even the birds were quiet. Outside, beyond the gardens, the great river flowed on, burning silver. No boat moved on its surface, and below, in the cooler, muddy depths, the fish lay waiting for evening. The whole city slept as if under a spell. Beershops were closed, markets were shuttered, and porters nodded in the shade of their little alcoves under the protecting walls of the nobles' great estates that bordered the river for mile upon mile. On the docks nothing moved except the little beggar boys who hunted for the gleanings of spilt cargoes. Over the river, in the Necropolis, the City of the Dead, the temples and empty shrines shimmered in the haze, the heat making the brown cliffs beyond dance and shake. High summer. The wheat and barley, clover, flax, and cotton standing tall for the harvest. The irrigation canals slowly drying out despite the frantic, backbreaking efforts of the fellahin to keep the shadoofs in motion. The dusty green date and doom palms, the march of trees along the riverbank, and the ripe green of the reedbeds all turning slowly brown. And always the white-hot, eye-searing glory of Ra, pouring down eternally from a cloudless and limitless deep blue sky, mighty and invincible.

In the apartment of Her Royal Highness the Princess Hatshepsut Khnum-Amun there was a stirring of air. The wind catchers on the roof funneled down whatever breezes there were out of the north, making little eddies of hot, stale air. As Nozme and her charge entered the room, the two waiting slaves sprang together into obeisance and picked up their fans. Nozme ignored them. As she removed Hatshepsut's white linen kilt, she barked an order, and another slave appeared bearing water and cloths. The nurse quickly washed the wiry little body. "Your kilt is covered in ink again," she said. "Must you be so messy?"

"I am truly sorry," the child replied, not sorry at all. She stood sleepily as the blessed water ran down her arms and trickled across her brown belly. "Neferu-khebit also frowned at me for my dirty kilt. Truly I do not know how the ink got spilled."

"Did you have a good lesson today?"

"I suppose so. I do not like school very much. There is too much to learn, and I am always waiting for Khaemwese to jump on me. I do not like being the only little girl there, either."

"There is Her Highness Neferu."

"That is quite different. Neferu cares nothing for the smirks of the boys."

Nozme sniffed. She would have liked to reply that Neferu seemed to care nothing about anything, but she remembered in time that this bright-eyed, handsome youngster, yawning copiously as she walked to the couch, was Great Pharaoh's special joy and doubtless prattled to him every word spoken in the nurseries. Nozme disapproved of any break with tradition, and the idea of girls, even royal girls, studying with boys was a continual source of irritation to her. But Pharaoh had spoken. Pharaoh wanted his daughters to be educated, and educated they were. Nozme swallowed the heresies rising on her tongue and bent to kiss the little hand. "Sleep well, Highness. Do you need anything more?"

"No. Nozme, Neferu promised to take me to see the animals afterward. Can I go?"

The request was as usual, as predictable as the child's constant appetite for sweetmeats, and Nozme flashed a rare and gentle smile. "Of course, if you take a slave and a guard with you. Now rest. I will see you presently." She signaled to the silent, stiff figures standing in the shadows and left the room.

The two women came forward, sweat shining on their black skin, and their fans began to dip and sway slowly above Hatshepsut's head, making no sound.

Small ripples of air moved over her body, and for a moment she watched the feathers quiver and swish as a feeling of security and peace stole over her. Her eyelids closed, and she turned onto her side. Life was good, even if Nozme snapped at her and Thothmes scowled a lot these days.

I don't know what he has to be so grumpy about, she thought dimly. I would like to be a soldier and learn how to shoot the bow and throw the lance. I would like to march with the other men and fight.

Above her, one of the Nubians coughed, and from beyond the doorway she heard Nozme climb heavily onto her couch with a long sigh. Hatshepsut's small ebony headrest felt smooth under her neck, and dreams began to wash her mind. She slept.

When she awoke, the sun was still high but had lost its bite. All around her the palace shook off lethargy and began to lumber to the end of another day, like a great hippopotamus rising from the mud. In the kitchens the cooks chattered, and the pots clanked; and there was laughter and the scurrying of many feet in the hallways. As she stepped outside, clean and fresh and eager, the gardeners were already back at work, their bare backs bowed, weeding and trimming the acres of exotic foreign flowers and watering the hundreds of sycamores and willows that made the royal confines a sun-dappled, sweet-smelling forest. The sudden bright flash of gay birds on the wing was everywhere, and the sky was as blue as her mother's eye paint. She began to run, slave and guard striding to keep up. Wherever she passed them, the laborers rose and bowed before her, but she hardly saw them. From the time she could toddle, the world had worshiped her, the Daughter of the God, and now, at the age of ten, the image of her destiny flowed undiluted with her blood, a natural and unselfconscious certainty of the rightness of her world and everything in it. There was the King: the God, her father. There was the Divine Consort, her mother. There was Neferu-khebit, her sister, and Thothmes, her half brother. And then there were the people, existing solely to adore her, and beautiful, beautiful Egypt somewhere beyond the towering walls of the palace, a land that she had never seen but that surrounded her and infused her with awe.

Once, a year ago, she and Menkh and Hapuseneb had hatched a plot. They would leave the palace and run into the city instead of sleeping. They would go to Menkh's house a mile upstream and play in his father's boat. But the porter, lurking in his cubbyhole by the great copper gates, had caught them. Menkh had been flogged by his father, Hapuseneb had been beaten also, but she herself had simply been reprimanded by her father. It was not time, he had said, for her to leave the safety of the palace. Her life was precious. It belonged to all the land and must be protected, he had told her. He had then taken her on his knee and given her honey cakes and sweet wine.

Now, a year later, the adventure was almost forgotten. Almost. One thing had then been brought home to her. When you are grown up, you can do anything, but you must wait. Wait.

Neferu was standing by the enclosures, alone. She turned and smiled as Hatshepsut came up panting. Neferu's face was pale, her eyes strained. She had not slept. Hatshepsut slid her hand into the older girl's, and they set off.

"Where is your slave?" Hatshepsut asked. "I had to bring mine."

"I sent her away. I like to be by myself sometimes, and I am old enough now to do almost as I please. Did you rest well?"

"Yes. Nozme sounds like a bull when she snores, but I still manage to fall asleep. I miss having you on the next couch, though. The room seems so big and empty."

Neferu laughed. "It is really a very small room, dear Hatshepsut, as you will see when you are moved into a big, echoing apartment like mine." Her voice held bitterness, but the child did not hear it.

They went through the gate and strolled down a wide, tree-lined path flanked on either side by cages, most of which were occupied by an assortment of animals: some local, such as the ibex, the family of lions, the gazelles; some brought back by their father from the foreign lands where he had campaigned in his youth. Most of the beasts were asleep, lying quietly in the shade, their smell a warm and friendly thing that enveloped the girls as they passed. The path ended right against the main wall, so close to them that it seemed to rear up and cut off the sun. At its foot was a modest, two-roomed mud-brick house where the Keeper of the Royal Zoo lived. He was waiting on his porch, watching for them. As they approached, he stepped out and went down on his knees, touching his forehead to the dust.

"Greetings, Nebanum," said Neferu. "You may rise."

"Greetings, Highness." The man struggled to his feet and stood with his head lowered.

"Greetings!" Hatshepsut said. "Come on, Nebanum, where is the baby gazelle? Is he well?"

"Very well, Highness," Nebanum replied gravely, his eyes twinkling, "but always hungry. I have him in a little pen behind my house, if you would care to follow me. He is a very noisy baby. He bawled all night long."

"Oh, the poor thing! He misses his mother. Do you think I could feed him?"

"I have prepared goat's milk if Your Highness would like to try. But I must warn Your Highness that this baby is strong and might knock Your Highness over or spill milk on Your Highness's kilt."

"Oh, that doesn't matter. You two"—she turned and looked up at the patient, perspiring attendants—"stay here. Sit under a tree or something. I won't run away." She stepped to Nebanum. "Go on!"

Neferu nodded, and the little party rounded the house. The wall was no more than ten steps away, casting a cool shadow; and beneath it was a small, temporary pen made of wooden stakes and twine. A brown head, all big, liquid eyes and long eyelashes, poked over the top. With a cry Hatshepsut ran up to it and thrust her hands through to pet it. Immediately the soft mouth opened, and a pink tongue rolled out.

The girl squealed, "Look Neferu! See how he sucks at my fingers! Oh, hurry, Nebanum, he is so hungry that I should have you whipped! Get the milk!"

Nebanum barely concealed a laugh. He bowed again and disappeared around the corner.

Neferu came and stood by the pen. "He is beautiful," she said, stroking the sleek neck. "Poor thing, to be a prisoner."

"Don't be so silly!" Hatshepsut retorted. "If father had not brought him home, he would have perished in the desert, eaten by lions or hyenas or something."

"I know that, really. But he seems pathetic in a way, so eager for love —so alone—"

Hatshepsut turned with another impatient word, but it quickly died on her lips. Neferu was crying, the tears running unchecked down her cheeks. Hatshepsut watched with astonishment. She had never seen Neferu anything but composed and dignified, and this sudden breakdown afforded her an unexpected moment of interest. She was not in the least embarrassed, and after a second or two she withdrew her hand from the fawn's mouth and began to dry it on her kilt.

"Whatever is the matter, Neferu? Are you ill or something?"

Neferu shook her head violently and turned away silently, struggling to regain some control. Presently she picked up the hem of her sheath and wiped her face. "I am sorry, Hatshepsut. I don't know what's the matter. I didn't sleep at all today, and I think I must be a little tired."

"Oh." Hatshepsut did not know what else to say, and as the moments ticked on, she began to feel uncomfortable. When Nebanum reappeared with a tall, narrow jar carried carefully in his hand, she ran to him in relief. "Let me carry it! Is it heavy? You open his mouth, and I'll pour it in."

Nebanum opened the pen, and they went in. He gently took the animal between his knees, forcing open the jaws with both hands.

Hatshepsut, her tongue between her teeth, balanced the jug close to the squirming face and began to pour. Out of the corner of one eye she saw Neferu turn and walk away. Damn Neferu! she thought angrily. She has spoiled this lovely day! Her hand shook, and the milk began to cascade down her front, pooling uncomfortably under her bare toes.

Nebanum took the jar from her as she held it out, and the fawn wobbled away, licking its lips and looking at them sleepily with one rolling eye.

"Thank you, Nebanum. It's harder than it looks, is it not? I will come back tomorrow and try it again. Good-bye."

The man's mouth twitched, and he bowed very low. "Good-bye, Highness. It is always a pleasure to see you here."

"Of course it is!" she flung back to him over her shoulder as she began to run. She caught up with Neferu just as her sister was turning out of the gate. Hatshepsut impulsively took her by the arm. "Don't be angry with me, Neferu. Have I made you angry?"

"No." The older girl's arm slid around the bony young shoulders. "Who could be angry with you? You are lovely to look at, intelligent, and kind. No one dislikes you, Hatshepsut, not even me."

"What do you mean? I don't understand you, Neferu-khebit. I love you. Don't you love me, too?"

Neferu drew her in under the trees, leaving the servants to wait in the middle of the path. "I love you, too. But lately—oh, I don't know why I should be telling you; you are far too young to understand. But I must talk to somebody."

"Do you have a secret, Neferu?" Hatshepsut cried. "You do! You do! Are you in love? Oh, please tell me all about it!" She tugged at Neferu's arm, and they sank down together onto the cool grass. "Is that why you weep? Your eyes are still all puffy."

"How can you know what it is like?" Neferu said slowly, pulling up a blade and running it back and forth over her palm. "For you life will be easy, an endless game, day after day. When you are old enough, you will be able to marry whom you please and live where you please—in the provinces, in the nomes, in the mountains. You will be free, able to travel or not; you will be able to do whatever you and your husband choose, enjoy your children. But I—" She flung the piece of grass away and clasped her hands together, leaning against the trunk of the tree. From the stress of her emotion her sallow skin took on an even yellower hue, and the muscles of her neck stood out like little knotted cords. Seen this way, she was no longer regal or dignified. Whatever prettiness she had, in her hands, in her thin nose, and in her long black hair, was overlaid by the distress that made her seem like nothing more than a collapsed and faintly fluttering white sail. "I am set apart," she continued woodenly, "fed on delicacies and clothed in the finest linen. Jewels fill my boxes and chests like hand-fuls of pebbles, and all day slaves and nobles prostrate themselves before me. All I see for days on end is the tops of people's heads. When I rise, they clothe me; when I am hungry, they feed me; when I am tired, there are a dozen hands to draw back the covers of my couch. Even in the temple when I pray and sing and shake the sistrum, they are there." She gestured wearily, her hair falling disheveled about her neck. "I do not want to be Great Royal Wife. I do not want to be Divine Consort. I do not want to marry silly, well-meaning Thothmes. I only want peace, Hatshepsut, to live as I choose." She closed her eyes and was silent. Timidly Hatshepsut put out a hand and stroked her sister's arm. They held hands while the sun began to sink, the shadows to lengthen imperceptibly.

Finally Neferu stirred. "I have had a dream," she whispered, "a horrible dream. I have it almost every time I sleep. That is why I did not go to my couch today but came out here to the gardens and lay under a tree until my eyes were burning from tiredness and the world seemed as unreal as if I had slept after all. I dream—I dream that I am dead, and my ka is standing in a huge, dark hall that smells of rotting flesh. It is very cold. At the end of the hall there is a doorway through which light streams, lovely, bright, warm sunlight. I know that Osiris waits for me there. But where my ka is, there is only the dark, the odor, and a terrible despair because between me and that door there are the scales, and behind the scales there is Anubis."

"But why should you fear Anubis, Neferu? He only wishes that the scales should balance."

"Yes, I know. All my life I have tried to do right so that when my heart is weighed, I will have nothing to fear. But in this dream something is different." She knelt, her hands trembling as she rested them on Hatshepsut's shoulders. "I approach the God. He has something in his hand, quivering and pulsing. I know that it is my heart. The Feather of Maat, so beautiful, is lying on the scales. Anubis's head is bent. He lays the heart in the other dish, and the scales begin to dip. I am frozen. Lower it falls, lower, and then with a little thud the dish containing my heart strikes the table. I know then that I am finished and will never walk that cold floor to the glory of Osiris, but I do not scream—not, that is, until the God raises his head and looks at me."

Suddenly Hatshepsut wanted to get up and run away, far away, anywhere so that she could not hear the end of this terrible dream. She began to wriggle with fear under her sister's grip, but the fingers tightened, and Neferu's eyes blazed, burning her.

"Do you know what, Hatshepsut? He looks at me, and it is not with the glittering eyes of the jackal. No. For it is you who condemns me, Hatshepsut. You in the apparel of the God but with the face of a child. It is more terrible than if Anubis had turned his dog face toward me and opened his mouth and snarled. I scream, but your face does not change. Your eyes are as cold and as dead as the wind that blows through that accursed place. I scream and scream, and I wake up screaming, my head pounding." Her voice had sunk again to a whisper, and she gathered the puzzled, frightened little girl into an embrace.

Held against her bosom, Hatshepsut could hear the uneven racing of Neferu's heart. All at once the world did not seem to be such a safe and fun-filled place anymore. She was aware for the first time of the unknown realms that lay behind the smiling eyes of friends, of those one trusts. She felt as though she herself stood in Neferu-khebit's dream—but on the other side of the door, in the benediction of Osiris, looking back into the gloomy shadows of the Hall of Judgment. She wrenched herself free and stood up, brushing off the grass that clung to the milk stains on her kilt. "You are quite right, Neferu-khebit. I don't understand. You frighten me, and I don't like it. Why don't you go and see the physicians?"

"I have seen them. They nod and smile and say that I must have patience, that young people have strange things on their minds when they are growing up. And the priests! Make more offerings, they advise. Amun-Ra has power to deliver you from all fear, they say. So I make offerings and I pray, but still I dream." Neferu rose also, and Hatshepsut clung to her arm as they started back for the path.

"Have you told mother or father?"

"Mother would only smile and offer me a new necklace. You know that more often than not father becomes very irritated with me if I am with him for too long. No, I think I will just have to wait and see whether or not this thing will leave with the passing of the months. I am sorry if I upset you. I have many acquaintances these days but no friends, little one. I often feel that there is no one at all who cares about who I am inside. I know that father does not, and if not he, then who? For he *is* the world, is he not?"

Hatshepsut sighed. Already she had lost the thread of Neferu's words. "Neferu, why will you have to marry Thothmes?"

Neferu shrugged wearily. "I do not think that you would understand that, either, and I feel too tired to begin to explain it to you now. Ask Pharaoh when you see him," she replied a little grimly. They finished the walk in silence.

When they reached the sun-splashed hall that led to the women's quarters, Neferu stopped and gently withdrew her arm. "Go in to Nozme now, and have another wash. To look at you, no one would know that you are not a dirty little street urchin who has crept in here by mistake." She laughed shakily. "I must return to my own apartment and think about what I shall wear tonight. You can go, too," she nodded to the two weary servants behind them. "Report to the Royal Nurse later." She absently patted Hatshepsut on the head and glided away, her bracelets clinking.

Hatshepsut wandered to her own rooms in a subdued frame of mind. Things had been so much simpler and happier when she and Neferu were younger and had romped and laughed their way from day to day. Now it seemed that she would have to content herself by playing with the young aristocrats and sons of nobles who filled the schoolroom each morning, letting Neferu-khebit grow up and away. Already the gulf had widened between them. After the simple, time-honored rite that had signaled Neferu's entrance into the mysterious and awesome state of womanhood, Neferu had moved into a northern wing of the palace, with her own garden and pond, her own slaves, advisers, and spokesmen, and her own personal priest to make the sacrifices for her. Hatshepsut had seen her change from a gentle, carefree girl into a stately, withdrawn adult, drifting about with her quarreling, bowing retinue, but apart, cold.

I shall not change like that, Hatshepsut vowed fervently as she turned in at the door and Nozme swept from her own room to greet her. I shall always be gay and have nice dreams and love animals. Poor Neferu.

She was uneasy and turned a deaf ear to Nozme's immediate, shrill protestations at the state of her second clean kilt of the day. She reflected on Neferu's dream in a cloud of gloom that refused to go away. Finally the woman's grumbles penetrated, and some new stubbornness in the girl rebelled. "Shut up, Nozme," she said. "Get this kilt off me, and brush my youth-lock, and shave my head, and just—shut up."

The result was surprising. There were no shouts, no splutters. After a shocked silence during which the nurse stood, her mouth tight as a trap and her hands frozen in midair, she inclined her head and turned away. "Yes, Highness," she said, knowing that the last baby was feeling its wings, surprised at its own temerity, and that her days as Royal Nurse were numbered.

The Sun was sinking at last. Ra was journeying to his rest, and the red, fiery skirts of his hot Barque trailed through the Imperial Gardens as Hatshepsut went to greet her father. Great Horus was brooding in his great chair, his belly hanging over his jeweled belt. His barrel chest was afire with gold, and atop his massive head the rearing symbols of kingship gleamed in the slanting rays of his Celestial Father.

Thothmes the First was aging. He was in his early sixties, but he still gave the impression of the enormous, bull-like strength and singleness of purpose that had caused him to snatch up the Crook and the Flail held out to him by his predecessor and to use them to bludgeon to death the last remnants of Hyksos domination. He was immensely popular with the common people of Egypt—a God, at last, of freedom and vengeance, who had made the border something more than a word. His campaigns had been tactically brilliant, bringing much booty to the temples and the people and, more importantly, security in which to till the soil and ply their trades. He had been a general in the army of Pharaoh Amunhotep, and the King had passed over his own sons to place the Double Crown on Thothmes' willing head. He was ruthless, too. He had given up a wife in order to marry Amunhotep's daughter, Aahmose, thus legitimizing his seat on the throne. His two sons by his first wife were now in his army, grown men, battle-hardened, patroling border garrisons for their father. His power and popularity were greater, perhaps, than any Pharaoh's before him, but that power had not weakened or softened him. His will was still as strong and absolute as a granite pillar, and under that will the country had licked its wounds and lived and blossomed.

Thothmes was sitting beside the lake with his wife, his scribes, and his slaves, relaxing before dinner and watching the water ripple pink in the late-afternoon breeze. As Hatshepsut, barefooted, quietly approached him over the warm grass, he was speaking to his old friend Aahmes pen-Nekheb, who stood awkwardly before him, embarrassment visible in every portly line of his body. Thothmes was obviously annoyed. He continued to gaze out over the water, and his voice rose to Hatshepsut in spurts of irritation. "Come, come, pen-Nekheb, you and I have spent enough time together both on the battlefield and off it. You have no need to fear me. I only ask you to speak your mind and stop shuffling about like a delinquent schoolboy. Have I not asked a simple question? Do I not deserve a simple answer? I wish a report on my son's progress, and I wish it now."

Pen-Nekheb cleared his throat. "Majesty, you have indeed been beneficent to your humble servant, and if your humble servant is to incur your wrath, then your humble servant apologizes beforehand—"

Thothmes brought his beringed hand down on the arm of his chair with a little slap. "Stop playing games with me, old friend. I know your pride, but I also know your ability. Will he or will he not make a soldier?"

Pen-Nekheb began to perspire beneath his short black wig. He scratched at his head surreptitiously. "Majesty, let me then say that His Royal Highness has not been in training for long. Under the circumstances his progress *might* be considered to be satisfactory—" His voice trailed off, and Thothmes at last turned his head and motioned the older man to the ground.

"Sit. Sit! What is the matter with you today? Do you think that I have put you in charge of the training of my son because you are good at gardening? Give me a report that is clear and short, or you can go home without your dinner."

Aahmose turned aside to hide a smile. If her husband loved and trusted any man, it was this big, ugly soldier perched uncomfortably on the ground a respectful distance from them. Though she thought it unfortunate that Thothmes should choose to discuss such a matter on an empty stomach, the situation did provide humor. Her life had been short of humor lately.

Pen-Nekheb seemed to have made up his mind. His shoulders squared. "Majesty, it pains me greatly to have to tell you this, but I do not think that young Thothmes has the makings of a soldier. He is clumsy and soft, although he is but in his sixteenth year. He has no love for the discipline involved. He is—" the man gulped and continued desperately, "he is lazy and afraid of the cut, the thrust of the work. Perhaps he will excel at his studies?" he concluded hopefully.

In the long silence that followed, one of the female slaves giggled hysterically and was abruptly cut off. Thothmes did not reply. As the color mounted slowly in his cheeks, his gaze wandered to the palace walls, to the lake, and to the bent head of his wife. Those about him waited in trepidation, knowing the signs. Grunting, he noticed his daughter, waiting and smiling at the edge of the crowd. He waved her forward, and all sighed with relief. The storm was reduced to a swift puff of wind.

"I will come myself to the training ground," Thothmes said. "I will come tomorrow, and you will put my son through his paces. If you are wrong, pen-Nekheb, I will have your Staff of Office. Hatshepsut, my dear, come and give me a kiss and tell me what you have been doing today."

She ran to him and climbed onto his knee, nuzzling his neck. "Oh, father, you do smell nice." She bent down and kissed Aahmose. "Mother, I saw the baby gazelle. Nebanum let me feed it. And Thothmes nearly got another thrashing at school this morning—" She sensed her mistake immediately with the swift intuition of a child. She saw her father's face darken. "Only nearly," she went on quickly. "Neferu saved him—" Pharaoh began to breathe heavily, and Hatshepsut hastily scrambled down from her father's lap, seeking refuge beside Aahmose. She decided to have one more try. Really, she thought, this day began so nicely, but it is ending like one of Nozme's horror stories. "Father," she piped, "it would be so kind of you if you would make Thothmes marry someone else. Neferu doesn't want him, and she is so unhappy—" She stopped suddenly, seeing the look of blank amazement on her father's face give way to dawning anger. Conscious of the breathless silence that surrounded her, she began to hop from one foot to the other. "I know, I know," she said. "I am too full of other people's business—"

"Hatshepsut," her mother bleated, distressed, "whatever has come over you today? Have you been drinking the servants' beer again?"

Her father rose, and the whole court rose with him. "I think it is time," he said heavily, "that you and I had a little talk, Hatshepsut. But now I am tired and hungry. I have had a bellyful of the problems of my erring children." He glared at pen-Nekheb, then at his luckless wife. "Aahmose, find out from Nozme what has been going on here; I want to know tonight. You, Hatshepsut, come to my rooms before you go to bed. And hope that you find me in better humor." He scowled at them all and swung away, his coterie drifting after him.

Pen-Nekheb got up with difficulty and began his evening stroll around the lake before dinner. The Great One's short bursts of ill humor did not distress him overmuch, but it had been a sweltering day, and his bones felt as brittle as sedge weed.

Aahmose smiled at her daughter as they walked to the royal apartments together. "You have been very tactless today," she said, "but do not worry. He is not angry with you, only with Thothmes. By tonight he will have little to say to you. He would be lost without you, Hatshepsut," she finished sadly. "He guards your welfare like a hawk. Poor Neferu."

"Mama, I, too, am tired and hungry. Nozme made me wear starched linen, and it is scratching me. Can we talk about something else?" Hatshepsut turned her large, dark eyes toward Aahmose, and the woman sighed.

Amun, she prayed silently as they entered her big, cool apartment and the slaves moved to light the lamps, she is your daughter. In truth, she is your very Incarnation. Protect her from herself.

To any lone fisherman bobbing in his little reed boat on the Nile in the dark, the palace at Thebes must have looked like a vision of the promised glories in the Paradise of Osiris. At nightfall all the thousands of lamps were lit—suddenly. It was as though a giant had flung a handful of bright, glittering stars at the ground and they had settled, singly and in clusters, upon the vast halls and many wide, paved ways of that kingdom within a kingdom, their reflections eddying and dancing upon the swift-flowing river far into the night.

The estate itself covered many acres of gardens and shrines, summer-houses and stables, granaries and servants quarters, and of course the main body of the palace itself, with its vast halls for receptions and dining and its pillared porticoes and walkways alive with color and paved with the likenesses of fish and fowl, hunters and hunted, and green things—all that made life a joy. The whole lapped right to the edge of the temple, with its frowning pylons and many dwarfing statues of the God's son, Thothmes, who was seated with his hands upon his monolithic knees, the calm faces all alike and staring over an invincible domain.

The gardens, too, were lit, dusted with glowing lamps, as the wives and the semiwives, the concubines and the nobles, the officials and the scribes strolled to and fro in the sweet-scented nights, their way lit before and behind by their naked, perfumed slaves.

On the river floated the Royal Barge, delicately crafted of gold and silver and precious woods, tied to the foot of the broad steps that led out of the water and onto a broad, paved courtyard lined on three sides with tall trees. Between those trees ran the avenues that led to the white and golden halls that held the heart of Egypt.

The fisherman would not linger on the west bank of the river. Over there the Necropolis, like the palace, also stretched for many acres, sprawled between the river and the tumbling dun cliffs that kept the desert out. The lights across the river, the lights in the homes of the priests and artisans who labored on the tombs and temples of the Osiris Ones, were subdued, more scattered. The night wind moaned softly in the deserted shrines, and the living locked their doors until Ra summoned them to another day of toil in the homes of the dead. The soaring pillars and empty houses, scattered with offerings of food and wilting flowers for those who still inhabited their last resting-places, were like an imperfect, distorted, and rather sad mirror image of the vibrant, pulsing life that was the Imperial city of Thebes.

The evening wind had dropped, and the night was still and hot as Hatshepsut, Nozme, and the nursery attendants made their way through the torchlit corridors, lined with motionless guards, to the dining hall. Tonight there were no foreign delegations to be feted, but the hall was full of guests and nobles, favored officials and friends of the royal family. The sound of their chatter and laughter echoed and swelled toward the girl long before she pattered through the doors and waited while the Chief Herald solemnly intoned her title. "The Princess Hatshepsut Khnum-Amun."

The company stopped talking for a moment, bowed, and then continued their conversations. Hatshepsut looked for her father, but he had not yet arrived. Neferu was nowhere in sight either. However, there was User-amun sitting on the floor in a corner with Menkh. She made her way over to them, dodging slaves who were pouring wine and settling the diners with cushions or little chairs. On the way she picked up a lotus flower that someone had dropped and began to wind its stem through her youth-lock. Immediately the thick, heady perfume began to fill her nostrils, and she inhaled it delightedly as she crossed her legs and sank to the floor beside the boys. "Greetings. What are you two doing here?"

Menkh nodded halfheartedly and winked at User-amun. They liked Hatshepsut, but she seemed to be everywhere and into all their schemes whether they wanted her to be or not. Since the abortive running-away episode they had done their best to keep clear of her, but she popped up in the most unlikely places. Whatever else she might be, she was not boring.

User-amun, as the son of one of the oldest and most aristocratic families in the country, treated her as an equal. His father, the Vizier of the South and one of the two most powerful men in the land under Pharaoh, was away on an inspection tour of the nomes under his care, and User-amun was living in the palace for the time being. He bowed extravagantly from the waist. "Hail, Majesty! Your beauty is more dazzling to behold than the beauty of the stars. Ah! My eyes fail, and I cannot look thereon!"

Hatshepsut giggled. "One day I will make you repeat your words with your mouth to the dust, User-amun. What were you talking about?"

"Hunting," User-amun straightened and replied promptly. "Menkh's father is taking us out tomorrow, early. We might even get a lion!"

"Pooh!" said Hatshepsut. "Even men have trouble killing a lion. You have to find one first."

"We are going into the hills," said Menkh. "We might even camp out all night."

"Can I come, too?" Hatshepsut asked eagerly.

The boys chorused, "No!"

"Why not?"

"Because you are a girl, and because the One would never let you," said User-amun reasonably. "Little princesses never hunt."

"But big princesses do. When I am big, I shall hunt every day. I shall be the best hunter in the kingdom."

Menkh smiled. Hatshepsut's love for animals would never allow her to hunt more than ducks, and she knew it. But even at the age of ten her pride insisted that she best everyone at everything. "What were you doing all day?" he asked. "I didn't see you anywhere."

"Getting into trouble," she groaned. "Ah! Here comes father and mother. Now we can eat."

Every forehead touched the floor. The Chief Herald's voice rang clearly. ". . . Mighty Bull of Maat, the Living Horus, Favorite of Two Goddesses, Shining in the Serpent Diadem . . ."

Hatshepsut whispered to Menkh, "Do you think that your mother will get drunk again tonight?"

"Oh, hush!" he whispered back fiercely. "Can't you stay quiet for one moment?"

"No, I can't! I'm hungry! I've been hungry for simply hours!"

Thothmes gestured, and the court rose and began to talk again. The guests found their seats, each at his or her own low table, and the slaves began to move among them, their platters heaped high. Hatshepsut's slave came and bowed. "Roast goose, Highness? Beef? Stuffed cucumber?"

"Something of everything!" As she ate, she looked anxiously around the room for Neferu, but there was still no sign of her. At a nod from her father the musicians filed in, a man with a tall harp and girls in long pleated skirts with cones of perfume on their heads, their instruments tucked under their arms. Hatshepsut noticed with interest that the girls were going to play the newfangled lutes brought from the wilds of the northeast. She made a mental note to get one of them to come and play for her in her room later on, but she remembered with a sinking heart that she had an appointment with Pharaoh. As the music began, she pushed her dish aside, dabbled her fingers in the water bowl, and wiped them on her kilt. She crept between the diners to her mother's side. Her father, a few feet away, was deep in conversation with Menkh's father, Ineni, his architect, but her mother smiled at her and motioned her to a cushion beside the table.

"You look very pretty tonight," Aahmose said. "You should wear flowers in your hair more often. They suit you."

Hatshepsut knelt on the cushion. "Mother, where is Neferu-khebit? If father sees that she is not here, he will be really angry. I'm the one he wants to reprimand tonight."

Her mother put down the piece of pomegranate she was raising to her lips and sighed. "Perhaps I should send someone to look for her. Was she upset today?"

"Yes, she was. She told me all about a horrible dream that she's been having. Is she going to be ill?"

Aahmose sipped her wine. The music was a muted, gentle twanging ripple over the babble of the guests, and her husband's booming laugh rang out, followed by another. It was wonderful what food would do to a man's disposition, Pharaoh not excepted, she thought. She swallowed the wine and turned to her daughter. "I do not know, dear. I think not. But yesterday she and I went down to the river, and pen-Nekheb's greyhounds were running up and down the steps—swimming, you know. One of them came to her and jumped up. She began to scream and beat at him with her fists. You know how your father hates sullen, brooding women. I did not tell him about it, but it was a nasty experience."

"She has been dreaming of Anubis."

"Oh? That would explain it. But she has also taken to wearing the Amulet of Menat. Why is she being so silly? What does the Chief Daughter of mighty Thothmes have to fear?"

Me. The word popped unexpectedly into Hatshepsut's head, and she kept very still, her heart beating wildly. Me? Bah! Neferu has given me her fear.

Aahmose signaled to Hetephras, her personal servant and companion. "Go along to the Princess Neferu's apartments, and find out why she is not here tonight," she ordered. "And go quietly. I do not want Pharaoh to have the answer before me, Hetephras, do you understand?"

The woman smiled. "Perfectly, Majesty," she answered, bowing. She slid away.

"Mama, why does Neferu have to marry Thothmes?"

Aahmose flung up her hands. "Oh, Hatshepsut, must you know everything? Very well, I will tell you. But you will not understand."

"Is it a mystery?"

"In a way. Your immortal father was only a general in my father's army until my father decided to make him the next Pharaoh. But in order that he might be Pharaoh in truth, he had to marry me because it is in us, the royal women, that the God's blood flows. We carry the royal strain, and no man can be Pharaoh unless he marries a royal woman, one whose mother has the pure blood of kingship and whose father was Pharaoh in his turn. That is the way it will always be. That is rightness, a part of Maat. Neferu-khebit is full-bloodedly royal, but Thothmes has royal blood only through your father, and Second Wife Mutnefert is only a noble's daughter." She did not speak with disparagement, but matter-of-factly, for these were the unalterable things of life. "Your father has not yet designated his heir, but it will probably be Thothmes as the only surviving royal son. If so, then Neferu must marry him to make him Pharaoh."

"But, Mama, if we women"—her mother smiled—"if we women have the blood and men have to marry us to rule, why bother with the men at all? Why can't we be Pharaohs?"

Her mother laughed at the little face screwed up in concentration. "That is also Maat. Only men can rule. No woman can ever be Pharaoh."

"I will."

Again the words came without volition, of their own accord, and Hatshepsut again felt her heart flutter. The fear of something brooding over her like a storm-filled cloud was back, and she began to tremble.

Aahmose took the cold hands in her own. "Little girls have big dreams, daughter, and you only dream. You can never be Pharaoh, and I know very well that if you thought about it, you would not want it either. But suppose that women did rule? Neferu is older than you. She would come to the throne."

"She would not want it," Hatshepsut replied slowly. "Not at all. Not ever."

"Go back to your table now." Aahmose was tired of the stream of questions. "Your food must be cold. I will tell you how Neferu is when Hetephras returns, but don't worry about her. I think that she is stronger than she looks."

I don't, Hatshepsut thought as she rose. Aahmose, still smiling, went back to her meal, and Hatshepsut wended her way to her own corner. On the way she passed Thothmes, and on an impulse she crouched beside him. "Are you still grumpy, Thothmes?"

"Leave me alone, Hatshepsut, I'm eating."

"So I see. Shall I spoil your appetite? Did you know that tomorrow your father himself will appear on the training ground to watch you trip over your feet?"

"I know. My mother told me."

"Is she here?"

Thothmes pointed. "Over there. Now go away. I have enough on my mind without your jibes."

Second Wife Mutnefert, piled in the jewels that she loved, was stuffing food into her mouth with single-minded purpose. Food had always been her weakness, and now it was her passion. The voluptuous curves that had first attracted Pharaoh to her were turning into rolls of unsightly fat. Compared with the dainty and gentle Aahmose, Mutnefert was gross, but she could still laugh, and her faculty for enjoyment was undiminished. Hatshepsut thought that Mutnefert was stupid, and she shrugged as she sat down. Men. Were they worth understanding? Her food was cold, and she pushed it away.

"Shall I get you something hot, Highness?" her slave asked.

She shook her head. "Bring me some beer."

"But Your Highness will not like it."

"I liked it before. Don't tell me what I will or will not like." Over the rim of her cup she saw Hetephras slip back into the hall and bend to whisper something in her mother's ear. Aahmose nodded and continued to eat. So, thought Hatshepsut, it can be nothing too bad.

Menkh and User-amun had finished their meal and were wrestling on the floor, rolling about among the diners, and Menkh's mother was quaffing wine like a soldier on leave. There was no singing. Pharaoh had a headache. So the music continued to be soft, and the people continued to eat and drink and laugh, and the hours dragged by. Hatshepsut finally sat with her chin in her hands, her head spinning a little from the strong beer, waiting for Nozme to look her way and nod that it was time for bed. At last her father pushed back his table and rose. All those who were able rose, too, and bowed.

He stalked over to her and offered her his arm. "Come, Hatshepsut. Time for our talk. And then you must get to your couch. There are circles under your eyes. Nozme!" The woman rushed up. "Come with us." He swept them out of the hall and down the corridor while the music began again behind them.

Pharaoh's private reception rooms and sleeping quarters were as sparsely furnished as the rest of the palace, but there was no mistaking the seat of power. At the doors two statues stood, sandstone overlaid with gold, frowning forbiddingly at all comers. Within, beyond the doors of beaten copper depicting Thothmes' coronation, was a suite whose walls, winking in the light of many golden lamps, held silver gods and golden trees and birds and whose fluted pillars soared to a ceiling inlaid with lapis lazuli. Gold was plentiful. Gold was holy, a gift of the God, and Pharaoh's couch was of gold, the feet four great lion's paws, the head a likeness of Amun himself, guarding his son with a protective smile. In the corners of the room four gods towered, frozen in midstride, their heads adorned with golden crowns, their shadows flowing across the endless floor. It was a room to inspire a little girl with fear and pride.

Thothmes sank into the gilded chair beside his couch and motioned to his daughter to sit. He eyed her for a moment in the steady yellow glow, and she stared steadily back at him, dizzy from the beer, her hands tensely pressed together between her brown knees. He was really a little frightening, this father of hers, with his bald head; his powerful, thick shoulders; and his aggressive, forward-jutting chin.

"Hatshepsut," he said at last. She jumped, startled. "I am going to teach you a lesson that I hope you will never forget, for if you do, you may be very, very sorry in the years to come." He paused for a suitable reply, but though she opened her mouth, no sound would come out, so he continued. "There is not one moment of any day that a thousand people do not know where I am, what I am doing. I speak, and they obey. I keep silent, and they tremble. My name is on everyone's lips, from the smallest acolyte in the temple to my lordly advisers, and the palace buzzes continually with rumors, conjectures, speculation as to my next action or the fruits of my mind. I am surrounded by plots, counterplots, suspicions, petty intrigues. But I am Pharaoh, and my word means death—or life. But one thing they cannot reach, any of them, and it is this which ultimately means power." He tapped his head with one ringed finger. "My thought. My thought, Hatshepsut. No word of any import do I utter without careful thought, for I know that once spoken, my words are repeated throughout the country. And this is the lesson that I wish you to remember. You must never, ever again blurt out to me or to anyone else your own hasty fears or conclusions in front of anyone who is not your most trusted friend. And believe me, in the end there is no one to whom a Pharaoh may turn. At the pinnacle of power he has only himself to commune with. Do you realize that even now your words to me this afternoon are being whispered back and forth in the kitchens, in the stables, in the cells of the temple? Neferu-khebit is unhappy. The Princess does not wish to marry young Thothmes. Does this mean that the Great One has chosen his son as his successor? And on and on. You have done harm today, daughter. Do you know that?" He leaned toward her. "The time is fast approaching when such carelessness could cost you very dearly. For I have not yet chosen Thothmes to succeed me. No, and my decision is not easy. The priests are powerful, and they press me with requests for an answer. My advisers become restless as my years lengthen. They, too, worry. But my answer is stayed. Do you know why, little one?"

Hatshepsut found her voice. "N—no, father."

Thothmes leaned back and closed his eyes, breathing deeply. When he opened them, he fixed her with his dark, level stare. "You are not like your mother, the sweet-smiling, submissive Aahmose, though I love her," he said. "Nor are you shy and pale like your sister Neferu, or lazy and ease-loving like your royal half brother. In you I see the undiluted strength of your Grandfather Amunhotep and the tenacity of his wife Aahotep. Do you remember your grandmother, Hatshepsut?"

"No, father, but I see Yuf from time to time, wandering around talking to himself. He is like a dried-up old prune. The children laugh at him."

"Your grandmother's priest was a very great and powerful man long ago. Be sure that you treat him with respect."

"I do. I like him. He gives me sweetmeats and talks about the old times."

"And do you listen?"

"Oh, yes! I love the stories about how my ancestor the God Sekhenenre led our people against the evil Hyksos and gave his life on the battlefield. It is all very exciting!" The childish, piping voice rose. "How noble he must have been!"

"Noble indeed, and brave. I think that you resemble him very much, my dear, and one day you, too, shall be as he was, able to draw men to you in power. But you have much to learn."

The makings are there, he told himself. And is it up to me?

"But, father," Hatshepsut said timidly, "I am only a girl."

"Only?" he almost shouted. "Only? What is this word? Never mind, Hatshepsut. Grow and bloom, but remember my lesson. Do not let your tongue run away with you again. And do not think," he concluded with a half smile, rising, "that Neferu's behavior escapes my notice, even though your mother would like to think that sometimes it does. I will deal with Neferu when the time comes. She shall do my will, like everyone else. Nozme!"

The nurse entered and stood waiting, eyes downcast.

"Take her to bed, and continue to guard her well. And as for you, my little firefly, meditate on the words of the Great God Imhotep. 'Do not let your tongue be as a flag, flapping in the wind of every rumor.'"

"I shall remember, father."

"See that you do." He bent and kissed her on the cheek. "Good night."

"Good night." She put her palms together and bowed. "And thank you."

"Oh?"

"For not screaming at me, even if I am a trial at times."

Pharaoh laughed. "I am glad that you listen to your teacher as well," he said. He patted her, and she ran to Nozme, the doors closing softly behind them.

2

Fourteen nights after Hatshepsut had gone to bed chastened by her father and giddy with alcohol, a young man sat on the edge of his straw pallet, unable to sleep. It was the month of Pakhon, and the air was thick and tense with heat. The river had begun to rise, to flow more swiftly. The normally placid silver water was becoming red, and the sound of its passing was a loud murmur that should have sung him to sleep like a lullaby but instead irritated and annoyed him as he tried to rest. At last he rolled onto the mud floor and perched, sweating and hungry, on the foot of his bed. His back ached. So did his knees. For a week he had done nothing but scrub floors in the apartments of the sem-priests, those men responsible for funerary arrangements, and he was angry. It was not for this that he had come to Thebes three years ago with his precious sandals and his one good kilt wrapped together in a piece of sacking. He had been excited then, anticipant, dreaming of a swift rise in the priestly ranks until perhaps Pharaoh himself would notice him and overnight he would become—what? He ran a hand over his shaved head and sighed into the dark. A mighty builder. A man who could make royal dreams a reality in stone. Ha! Those three years had been spent as a we'eb priest in training, the lowest of the low, washing, sweeping, running errands between his master here and his master two miles to the north at the temple of Luxor. The visions of wealth and recognition had faded slowly, leaving bitterness and a naked ambition that troubled his sleep and elbowed out his natural gaiety.

I will not give up, he vowed fiercely to the blank, invisible walls. There must be something more for me.

He thought of his teacher in the little village school at home where his father eked out an existence on his few acres of land. "You have a quick mind," he had said, "and a broad grasp of the essentials of a problem. Can your father not get you enrolled at a temple school somewhere? You are suited for a career, Senmut." And this when he was only eleven.

His father had left the farm with him and brought him to Thebes, where one of his mother's brothers was a sem-priest. After days of waiting and being jostled about from here to there and having his sandals stolen right from under his nose by a grinning, dirty street urchin, he and his father had at last been granted an audience with the Overseer of the We'eb Priests. Senmut did not remember that interview very well. He had been tired and afraid, wanting only to go home again and forget the whole thing. But, speaking softly, his father had pushed him forward and had shown the scroll of his progress given to them by the teacher. The great man, who was clad in dazzling white and smelt like the Goddess Hathor herself, had grunted disparagingly, with boredom, but had at last allotted Senmut a cell and a priestly linen. He had taken leave of his father with regret, embracing him tearfully and thanking him for all his care.

The older man had smiled. "When you are a great man, a vizier perhaps, you can purchase a good tomb for your mother and me so that the gods may remember us." He spoke half jokingly, half sadly. He did not believe that his son would ever do more than serve menially in the temple, eventually perhaps as a Master of Mysteries, but no more. He had no illusions about the cold and dangerous world Senmut was to inhabit. Kissing Senmut on both cheeks and admonishing him to do good to all men, he went home to his crops, not knowing which god's protection to implore for his son. He would need the care of them all.

Ah, Thebes, the young man groaned as he rubbed at his sore knees, how I was ravished by you when first I saw your golden towers winking on the horizon, beyond the great river! I remember awakening on that last morning, when Ra was a flush of red-pink glory from hilltop to desert. As I rose from the ground, I saw the flashes of light, now here, now there, between the palms and the pomegranate trees. I said to my father, "What in the world is that?"

"That is Amun-Ra, kissing the gold-tipped towers of his city," my father replied.

I was struck dumb with wonder and awe. I love you still, but I am no closer to your mysteries than I was on that faraway morning, although I no longer fear you, Senmut sighed.

He had spent the days since predictably, in hard work: in the mornings, at the temple school, doing work that he loved, and in the afternoons doing the chores that he loathed as his routine became more and more rigid.

Sometimes he wished that he had it in him to train to be a scribe, as the priest who was now his teacher wanted him to do, for a scribe never had to get down on his hands and knees. He was exempted from all physical labor and had nothing to do but follow his master about and scribble notes or sit in the markets of Thebes and wait to be hired to write letters. But Senmut knew far down in the secret places of his being that as a scribe he would shrivel up and die because he would be denying that force within him that cried out for something better, something more worthy. But what? he asked himself wearily as he rose from his pallet and groped about in the dark for his cloak. Surely not a priestly overseer, a phylarch, whose days are spent in frantic organizing.

When I first saw this city, with its lordly towers and pylons, its wide, paved avenues and innumerable statues, I thought I knew. Then I would wander in the long evenings, in and out of beershops and taverns, down to the docks, watching the fishermen curse and jockey their slim papyrus craft to the best moorings, watching the craftsmen sit before their ships, plying their trades, watching the slaves mount the auction block and the nobles being carried by on their handsome litters, watching, watching, always on the outside, always a stranger. Now I watch no more. Now I have fourteen years behind me and perhaps five times that number before me. Already I am a prisoner.

He drew his cloak about his shoulders and stepped barefoot from his cell, walking quietly past the rows of similar rooms down the long hall. There was moonlight, splashing cold between the pillars, and he could see where he was going. He paused to check the water clock outside his phylarch's door. Still five hours to sunrise. Smiling at the young man's snores, Senmut passed out of the hall and into the courtyard like a wraith. To his left the bulk of the temple now reared, still separated from him by another block of priests' cells and a plantation of sycamores. He swiftly turned away from it, knowing that there he might encounter movement. He wanted the kitchens and something to eat. His stomach drove him on, growling a protest. He reached the end of the line of rooms and turned the corner, away from the sacred precincts. A few moments of steady walking brought him to another group of buildings. He quietly slipped between the dark conical hulks of the granaries and turned in at the little doorway that heralded the kitchens. He was in a narrow passage down which the slaves passed each day, carrying grain. The darkness was absolute. He groped his way for a few more feet and was suddenly in a large, airy room with many high windows through which the moonbeams melted. Opposite him was a black hole in the wall, the beginning of the walk that took the cooks directly into the temple with the God's meals. Everything smelt faintly of grease. He moved cautiously, for the sleeping kitchen staff was not far away. On his left stood two tall stone ewers, placed so that the breeze which funneled through the passage could cool them, one containing water, the other beer. He picked up the jug that sat between them and hesitated for a moment, his thirst raging; finally he decided on the water. He quietly removed the wooden lid from one of the ewers, drew, and drank quickly and deeply, replacing the jug with scarcely a clink. He slipped among the tables, raising covers, lifting cloths, and it did not take him long to discover a couple of cold roast duck legs and a half loaf of flat barley bread. He did not think that anyone would miss such a tiny portion of the vast amount of food that was waiting to be distributed among the God's slaves in the morning. With a last glance to see that he had left nothing disturbed, he thrust his meal under the concealing folds of his cloak and crept back down the passage to the open air.

He stood for a moment, wondering whether to take it back to his cell and eat there, but his tiny room would be like an oven and dark as well, so he began to walk in the direction of the temple gardens, where there were trees and where there was less likelihood that the guards patrolling the paths that wound down to the Sacred Lake would find him. He knew the movements of them all, the changes of the watch, the routes they took, and he waited in the shelter of the first pylon while a couple of them strolled by, deep in conversation. As their backs were swallowed up by the night, he glided across the avenue and disappeared under the welcoming shadows of a grove of palms.

As he darted from tree to tree, he sniffed the air. A country boy to his very bones, he could forecast a change coming in the weather, and he did not like the feel of this change. Close to the ground the atmosphere was so thick and stifling that a breath required almost conscious effort; to move was like wading through a solid wall of water. But above the black, trembling fronds of the palms, the air was disturbed, and the stars were partially hidden by a thin mist of clouds. He knew the signs. It was not often that a khamsin blew this far south, but he felt sure his instincts spoke true. Within hours the burning, destructive wind would begin to trouble the surface of the desert. Until it blew itself out, there would be nothing to do but shut doors and cover windows. And then? He groaned aloud. More work for him to do, sweeping out the sand that would seep into every corner of every building in the precincts.

He chose a tree with a large, bellied bole and sat with his back against the side opposite to the path. In the distance there was a thin, silver, shifting line of light that was the moon on the waters of Amun's Lake, but from where he crouched, he could see nothing of the temple itself or the towers of the palace beyond it. He was in a world of peace for a while, safe in the friendly shushing of leaves that greeted one another in the dimness. He took out his leg of duck and bit into it happily, savoring each mouthful, for being worked like a slave, he was hungry all the time.

Within minutes he was tossing away the picked bones and starting on the bread, which was a trifle stale but nonetheless delicious. He had just finished the last crumb that had fallen on his cloak and was about to use the cloth to wipe his mouth, when some sense born of the long nights tending goats in the vermin-ridden hills that bordered his father's farm made him suddenly sit upright, his heart pounding. For a while he heard nothing. He had begun to relax when he heard soft footfalls on the grass and the subdued murmur of voices. He sprang to his feet lightly, noiselessly, and pressed himself tight to the rough bark of the tree, his hands folding the cloak against his body. The voices came nearer, hardly more than a whisper. He shrank farther into shadow, blending with tree and night, until even his rapid breathing had slowed and taken on the stillness of the hour. It was thus that he had trapped the big cats that came after the baby goats. It was this immediate reaction that saved him, for seconds later two hooded forms stooped beneath his tree only a few feet from where he stood. Although he dared not move to see who it was, he knew they were not guards. There was no clink of metal on metal, and besides, guards would have spoken aloud and walked without fear. These two had crept so quietly that they had almost tripped over him. He screwed his eyes shut and offered a quick prayer to Khonsu. Perhaps in a moment or two they would move on, before his trembling muscles played him false and he inadvertently made a sound. He continued to breathe quietly, shallowly, willing his lungs to operate slowly. The two faced each other, shapeless in the night, their whispers reaching him indistinctly.

"It is only a matter of time before the One speaks his mind. What other choice has he? He will not recall Wadjmose or Amun-mose. He cannot. They are soldiers. They have been away from the seat of power for too long, and they know nothing of government. Besides, what of their blood? Young Thothmes' claim overrides theirs."

"He is nothing but a placid, pleasure-loving, brainless whelp."

"But I say again, he will be the choice. He is the only one left. It is more than unfortunate that he should take after his noble mother; it is a disaster. For many years Pharaoh, may he live forever, has ruled with a heavy hand that has brought all in subjection to him. It is not only we who will suffer when the Double Crown is placed on Thothmes' head."

"You speak blasphemy!"

"I speak truth. With a worthy consort something could be salvaged, but who is there to legitimize Thothmes? Her Highness Neferu wishes nothing better than to withdraw from any hint of the pressures of an active consortship. She wants only to be left alone. The Great One broods and snarls like a cat at bay, but he can do nothing."

"We cannot poison a royal son! And the only royal son remaining! The

One would never rest until he had clubbed out our brains on Amun's floor!"

"Peace! Did I speak of such a thing? We are, above all, realists. But there is a way to purchase that which we need—time."

"Her Highness the Princess Neferu?"

"Neferu indeed. The younger Princess has some years yet between her and womanhood, but already she promises to be everything a Pharaoh needs in a consort. While she grows, Pharaoh's heart is content."

"And if Pharaoh goes to the God?"

There was a pause, during which Senmut, almost paralyzed with fear, held his breath.

"Then we can—*assist* the Young One and his new consort, who will have much to learn."

Behind the tree Senmut thought that he would faint. The food that he had consumed with so much satisfaction only moments before now sat in his belly like a rock. His head swam, but he clenched his teeth together and rammed his cheek against the bark, wincing a little at the pain. The full import of what he had heard still escaped him, but he had grasped enough of it to know that if he panicked or collapsed, it would mean instant death. He clutched tighter at his cloak while the sweat dampened his back.

"We are agreed, then?"

"We are. And I need not remind you that the utmost discretion is demanded of you."

"Naturally. When will it be?"

"Very soon. I feel sure that Pharaoh is about to announce his successor. You may leave the details to me. I expect my orders to be carried out immediately if I call upon you, but other than that I make no demands on you."

"And what if we are discovered?"

The other man laughed softly, and Senmut pricked up his ears. He felt sure that he knew the sound. In another second, as the voice rose slightly, he was certain, but he still could not place it. Floating disembodied on the night air, it was unreal, the voice of a faceless spirit. The boy feverishly cast about in his mind for flesh with which to clothe it.

"Do you think that the One is not aware of this very possibility? Do you not know that deep within himself he wishes it could be done, yet lacks the heart to do it? Do not fear. We will not fail."

The next words came from a little farther away, and Senmut realized with unutterable relief that they were leaving.

Silence claimed him again, and he slid to the earth with a gush of relief.

His eyes were still closed, and he lay in blissful gratitude, his limbs feeling as weak as water. "Thanks, many thanks, Mighty Khonsu," he said aloud. He got up and began to run, not in the direction from which he had come, but in a wide circle that took him to the very skirts of the Sacred Lake and far behind the temple to his own cell. He had no wish to meet strangers. As he ran, he repeated in his mind the words that he had heard, urgency growing in him and lending speed to his bare feet. By the time he reached the hall onto which the rooms of the we'eb priests opened, a clearer understanding of the whispers made him feel sick. Instead of turning in at his own door, he ran past it and stopped, panting, outside his phylarch's room, knocking softly. He glanced at the water clock. He was shocked to see that three hours had gone by. The moon had set, leaving duskiness and a hint of morning on the black and white stone floor.

Inside, there was a stirring. "Who is it?"

"Me, Master. Senmut. I must speak with you."

"Come, then."

Senmut pushed open the door and stepped through. The phylarch, a young man with a receding forehead and a small, thin mouth, was sitting up on his couch in the process of lighting his lamp. The flame shot yellow and steadied. Senmut went closer, bowing, uncomfortably aware now of his sweat-streaked skin, his scratched cheek.

"Well? What is it?" The phylarch rubbed at one eye with a blunt finger, regarding Senmut sleepily.

In that instant, just as Senmut took breath to reply, two fragments of knowledge flashed through his head, and for a moment the walls turned about him. He put out a hand to steady himself as his guts heaved.

The man in the bed snapped at him irritably, "Speak. Speak! Are you ill?"

Senmut knew with a certainty that went beyond thought and into the dim world of self-preservation that after all he must not confide in this man, his master, nor must he ever speak to any priestly person about the things he had heard. At that moment he knew with dread and a dulling fear why not. For now he was able to put a body to that low, husky voice —a thick, wrinkled body—and a lined, wily face. The speaker had been none other than the great High Priest of Amun himself, the mighty Menena.

Suddenly his wits returned, and he was able to speak smoothly, without betraying the tumbling, chaotic thoughts that chased each other in his mind. "Master, I am so sorry, but I have a fever, and my belly aches— here"—he rubbed his stomach—"I cannot sleep."

"It is the heat," the phylarch grumbled. "Go back to your room.

Morning cannot be far off, and if you still feel unwell, I will send a physician to you. You are excused your duties for one day."

Senmut bowed and murmured his thanks. The man was not unkind, but he was a worrier, continually fussing with details. He, too, had trouble with a stomach that often did not let him rest.

On an impulse Senmut turned back to him. "Master, if one wished to have audience with Pharaoh, how would one go about it?"

"Why?" The phylarch demanded suspiciously. "What would you have to say to the One?"

Senmut looked shocked and surprised. "Me? But I do not wish to aspire to such an exalted moment; I know that only the great in the land can commune with him. But I have seen him only once, afar off, on a royal progress, and I simply wish to know."

"Then stop wondering. It is no surprise that you have a fever if you spend your nights thinking about such things. No one of our station can ever hope to speak with him. It would be impossible. Now go away, and see me again in the morning if you feel no better."

Senmut bowed again without replying and went out, closing the door behind him. As he walked to his own cell, he was conscious of an overwhelming mental and physical exhaustion that threatened to pitch him full length on the floor before he reached his pallet. He entered his little cell with a sigh and flung himself down on the mattress.

Even if I could by some miracle find myself in his presence, what would I say? Would he welcome me even if I managed to say it without being carted off with chains on my legs? Did I not hear the High Priest say that deep within himself, Pharaoh wishes this evil thing could be done? Is such a deed justified by the safety of Egypt?

With his eyes closed and sleep at last preparing to pounce, Senmut thought of the tall and graceful Princess who came regularly to the temple with her maids. He had seen her from a distance, as he had seen her father. She was not beautiful, but there was a gentleness about her that made her seem closer to the people than her haughty attendants were. A pang of guilt held off sleep and made him open his eyes.

Should I sacrifice all? Try for the palace? He turned over. I shall be a realist and survive, even as the High Priest survives, he told himself grimly.

He wished that he could confide in someone. He thought of his best friend, Benya the Hurrian, apprenticed to an engineer of the temple. But Benya, with his dark, curly hair and flashing, white smile and quick, winning ways, was far to the south at Assuan with his master, helping to oversee the quarrying of sandstone in the broiling heat. Anyway, to Benya nothing in life was sacred or serious, and he might talk.

Senmut shrugged his cloak a little higher on his shoulders and slept, but his dreams were confused and sordid. He awoke sweating, finding that the wind had indeed risen. The sand was drifting through his one tiny window near the ceiling, the particles of gray dust hanging suspended in the fetid air. It was difficult to tell how long he had slept. He got up and looked out into the hall, but everything was quiet, other cell doors open, and he knew that his fellow we'ebs already were gone to their duties. His mouth felt foul and gritty, and he longed for a wash. He padded to the end of the block and called for a slave. He returned to his room and sat in his one chair, an uncomfortable thing made out of bundles of papyrus stems tied together. His head ached, and he wondered whether he really was in the grip of a fever that had worked on his mind and had caused him to imagine the whole episode in the garden. After all, he and those who moved on the fringes of power were constantly in the thick of a hundred rumors, and Pharaoh was gossiped about from dawn until dusk. But Senmut was possessed of a practical, calculating mind that, though perceptive, did not allow idle conjectures to interfere with the realities of day-to-day life. Besides, there was in Senmut a faculty for objective and pitiless observation, a sort of disengagement of the senses that allowed him to note and record the actions and reactions of those about him. He could not believe that a happening so clear and painful and fresh could be the tired wanderings of a heated mind.

His slave came running, and he ordered a basin of hot water and a clean linen. He asked the boy what time it was.

"Three hours after sunrise, Master."

"I thought so. And have the other priests eaten?"

"Yes. They have gone about their duties. The phylarch instructed me to bring you a physician if you required one this morning. Shall I?"

"No. No, I do not believe that will be necessary. See if you can get me some fruit from the kitchens. Then clean up in here for me. I have been excused work for today, and I think I'll go down to the river for a while."

"Better to stay indoors, Master. A khamsin has begun."

"Yes, I know."

The child went away and returned staggering under the weight of the steaming basin. He set it on its stand and left again. In a moment he was back with a dish of fruit and a clean robe. Senmut thanked him, and he bobbed his head and was gone.

With a sigh of relief Senmut plunged his head and his hands in the warm water, washing himself thoroughly all over, listening to the spasmodic moaning of the wind as it spurted puffs of sand into the room, sand that now clung to his wet body before he could dry himself. He wrapped the thick linen around his waist, pleating it in the front so that it hung in folds to the ground, and fastened it with a bronze pin. Around his upper arm he clasped the plain bronze band engraved with the words of his office.

And how grand I felt, he thought grimly, reaching for the fruit, the first time I put the bracelet on. Little did I know that it was to be a symbol of my incarceration.

He did not understand the other we'eb priests, who seemed happy in their work and who took it all quite seriously, even the older ones to whom preferment would never come. Why, he thought savagely, spitting pips onto the floor, can we not simply have more slaves to do the work? But he knew that there were certain places where a slave could not go, holy places, so priests had to do the chores that no servant in the palace would stoop to.

Senmut did not have the religious convictions that his friends did. His father was a pious man, and his mother prayed every day to the local god of his village, but part of the son stood back and smiled a little at their naïveté. His presence at the temple was a means to an end, and that end was education. If in order to achieve that precious goal, he had to chant prayers and wash four times a day and shave his head, then so be it. He knew that his destiny was in his hands and his alone. It was this that caused him such monumental frustration. He believed in himself, and he felt only impotence, walled in as he was in a dark, narrow, endless passageway that led only to errands and more scrubbing. Only in the schoolroom was he happy, studying the colossal achievements of the ancestors who were more than men. He longed to see with his own eyes the stone beauties that seemed to call to him in the night, asking for something that he knew he could give but that he knew he would never be allowed to offer.

He did not make fun of sacred things as did Benya. In Benya's country, Hurria, far to the northeast, the gods served men. But here in Egypt men served the gods, and Senmut wished only to see behind the gods to the inspirations and strivings of men. To him, Pharaoh was more of a God than Mighty Amun. Pharaoh was a visible mover, a being who caused all in the kingdom to happen. If he felt allegiance to anyone or anything, it was to the short, bull-like man whom he had seen only once, striding beneath his jeweled sun canopy on his way to make offerings at Luxor. This was Godhead. This was power. If he was ever to fulfill his destiny, Senmut knew he had somehow to come to the attention of Pharaoh.

But not this way, he said to himself as he left his room. Not with a tale of deadly intrigue and foul murder that the One himself might have a hand in. I would certainly lose my head.

3

Two days later, the wind still blew. It gusted into the royal schoolroom, billowing out the thick, heavy hangings that were painted with birds and sending sand eddying across the floor. It was a dull, gray morning, the sun riding high but hidden from the earth by clouds of whirling sand that streamed off the tops of the Theban hills straight from the desert beyond and descended with the wind into the valley below.

Khaemwese struggled to keep the lesson going, but the wind had unsettled his young charges. They wriggled and whispered as the lamps flickered, and he finally rolled up his scroll. "I can see that today we are going to get nowhere. The scribe truly says that the ear of a boy is on his back, and he hearkeneth when he is beaten, but this morning it is difficult for any of us to hearken to each other over the noise of the wind."

Hatshepsut's hand shot up. "Please, Master?"

"Yes?"

"If, as the scribe says, the ear of a boy is on his back, where is the ear of a girl?" She turned toward him, her look one of shining innocence.

If he had been younger and less experienced in the wily ways of children, he would have thought that she really wished to know; but as it was, he leaned over and tapped her on the shoulder with his scroll. "If you truly wish to know, I will show you. Stand up. Menkh, bring the hippopotamus whip. We will soon discover where a girl's ear may be."

"Now you did it," Hapuseneb whispered to her as she reluctantly rose. "And Neferu is not here to protect you."

"Stand before me!" Khaemwese ordered, and Hatshepsut went forward. Menkh grinned and handed him the willow switch, and he whipped it through the air. It whistled fiercely. "Now. Where is the ear of a girl? What do *you* think?" He hid a smile.

Hatshepsut swallowed. "I think that if you beat me, my royal father will have you flogged."

Khaemwese nodded. "Your royal father instructed me to teach you. And behold, you ask me a question. Where, you say, is the ear of a girl? I am about to show you." The corners of his mouth twitched, and Hatshepsut pounced.

"You will not beat me! I know you will not! I only asked you to make you annoyed."

"But I am not annoyed, oh, not in the least. And I will tell you that the ear of a girl is in the same place as the ear of a boy."

Hatshepsut's chin went up, and she slowly surveyed her squatting classmates. "Of course. There is no difference. And furthermore, a girl can do anything a boy can do," she said as she sat down.

Khaemwese raised a finger. "But wait. If that is so, then you will not mind being beaten, for I have beaten every boy in this class from time to time because of the failing of his ear that you say is the same as a girl's. Girls' ears must then fail, too. Why, then, have I not beaten you? Stand forth again!" He was laughing.

She smiled up at him, eyes alight. "Master, you have not yet beaten me because I am a princess, and you cannot lay hands on a princess. That is Maat."

"That is *not* Maat," Khaemwese replied sternly. "That is custom and decree, but not Maat. I beat Thothmes, and he is a prince."

Hatshepsut turned coolly and regarded her half brother, but he was sitting with his chin in his hand, drawing circles in the gathering sand. She looked back at Khaemwese. "Thothmes is only half a prince," she said, "but I am the Daughter of the God. That is Maat."

The room was suddenly still.

Khaemwese stopped laughing and dropped his gaze. "Yes," he said quietly, "that is Maat."

For a moment the only sound was the soughing of the wind.

Hatshepsut put up her hand again. "Please, Master, seeing we cannot work because of the wind, can we play ball?"

He looked at her in disbelief, expecting another sally, but she was waiting anxiously for his reply, hunching her shoulders. He rose with a groan and stretched. "Very well. Hapuseneb, get the ball. The rest of you roll up your mats and put them away. Neatly!" There was a general scramble and a hubbub of shrill voices, and his last words were, as usual, lost. He went to his chair and sat down gratefully. "Well. Get on with it. Thothmes, are you going to play, too?"

The handsome, smooth face rose to him. Thothmes shook his head. "I don't want to. The sand is making the floor too slippery."

Already the whoops and yells of the running children echoed to the roof. Hatshepsut had the ball and was determined to keep it. She fell with a squeal and tucked it under her as Menkh swooped upon her. The others tumbled after, and Khaemwese watched in a sober frame of mind.

There was something about the little princess that frightened him, lovable as she was. There was that in her which was wild and unfathomable. The older she grew, the more apparent it was that she took after her father. But which father? He did not know whether or not to believe the stories that had circulated ten years ago, that Amun-Ra had come to Great Royal Wife Aahmose in the night and bestowed on her his Divine Seed and that at the moment of conception Aahmose had cried out the name of the promised child, Hatshepsut! But he remembered that the name had been chosen before the little girl was born, and shortly afterward her father Thothmes had taken her to the temple, and she had been given the title Khnum-Amun. There had been rulers before who had claimed a closer than usual kinship with the God, but only rarely had they been sufficiently confident to take to themselves this name, She Who Is Closely Related to Amun. Its meaning was lost on no one. Surely Hatshepsut enjoyed a budding beauty, intelligence, obstinacy, and burning vitality that drew all men to her although she was not yet eleven. One wondered where it all came from. If Thothmes was strong, he was not exactly subtle; and Aahmose, loved and revered by all, had never been more than a dutiful royal wife. One must look elsewhere, Khaemwese thought, for the source of all that boundless energy and irresistible charm. He listened to the high drone of the wind and recalled how in years past Pharaoh's two little sons by Mutnefert had died, quickly. He looked at Thothmes sitting sulkily on the floor, and at Hatshepsut bouncing on one foot, giggling, and he fingered his amulet in disquiet. I thank the gods, he thought, that I am an old man and have not long to live.

The game ended early because of the weather. The young nobles hurried home, but Nozme was late to fetch her charge.

Hatshepsut sat on the floor beside Thothmes, dirty and out of breath. "How was it yesterday, Thothmes, with the horses? Do you think that you will like to handle them?" She was trying to be kind. Thothmes looked so miserable and uncomfortable that she felt sorry about teasing him all the time.

Once he and she might have been friends, but there were five years between them, too many years, and Thothmes considered it beneath his dignity to go racing about the palace grounds, up and down trees, and in and out of the lake with Hatshepsut and her madcap friends. If he only knew it, he was a little jealous.

He looked at her without smiling. "No. I know that father took me out of training and sent me to the stables because I'll never make a soldier. I'll never make a charioteer, either. I hate horses. Nasty little beasts. I wish we had kicked them out of the country with the Hyksos who brought them in."

"Father says that they are an important advance for Egyptian warfare. Now our soldiers can ride and be swift and tower over our enemies. I think that is very exciting."

"Do you? Well, you don't have to teeter in a chariot every day and have your arms nearly torn off while Aahmes pen-Nekheb shouts at you and Ra blazes angrily out of the sky at his unworthy son. I am miserable, Hatshepsut. I want only to attend to my monuments and be with my mother. Father should not push me this way!"

"But Thothmes, one day you may be Pharaoh. Egypt does not want a Pharaoh who cannot fight!"

"Why not? All the fighting has been done. Father and grandfather did it. Why can't I just learn government?"

"I expect you will in a few years. But I think you should try to enjoy your days in the stables. How the people love a Pharaoh who can control everything and everyone!"

"You don't know what you're talking about. You've never even been out of the palace." He laughed shortly. "Leave me alone. Find someone else to tell you how marvelous you are. I won't."

Hatshepsut scrambled to her feet. "All right, I'll go. I don't want to talk to you anymore anyway. I shall never be nice to you again. I hope Sebek gobbles you up. Go back and hang onto the skirts of your fat old mother!"

Before he could make an outraged protest, she was gone, running out of the room, a young gazelle.

Thothmes wearily got to his feet and walked to the door. One day she would pay for that, the conceited little she-cat. What did she know of the agonies of clumsiness, of the striving in the hope of receiving even a grudging word from a mighty father? How often he had stood with his hands behind his back, one foot on top of the other, waiting awkwardly for the One to notice him while Hatshepsut prattled on and Pharaoh laughed and grunted, his eyes always, only for her. How many times he had trembled before his father, brimming with a love that would not spill over and wash their relationship clean of resentment and misunderstanding, while Mighty Horus listened, fidgeting to be gone, the son blushing and stuttering and fighting the tears. He adored his father, and Hatshepsut, too, with a strange, helpless envy and a wounding guilt, for in his fantasies his father died holding his hand, begging for forgiveness while a cowering Hatshepsut waited for Thothmes to wreak his rage upon her as he triumphantly mounted the Horus Throne. In the hot nights of his childhood summers he lay awake, gleefully punishing her and then forgiving her; but in the harsh, pitiless light of the mornings he tasted anguish once more. Nothing changed. A new idea occurred to him one day as he watched his father and sister return from a boating expedition. They had been picking water lilies. The skiff was full of white, waxy blooms, and Hatshepsut was tearing petals from the stalks, raining them on Pharaoh's naked chest, both of them laughing like children. How much freer they would be without him! What if he should die, not his father? What if he became ill? And what if—how subtly it came—what if they were plotting to destroy him? His daydreams no longer brought him solace. Instead, they were filled with apprehension and shot through with the poison of suspicion. He could not share his chaotic thoughts with anyone, not even with his mother, and slowly the love for his father, the love that he could never express, turned inward, stagnated, and began to sour.

Outside, his guard sprang to attention, and Thothmes began the long walk to his mother's apartments. The halls were empty of life, the torches flickering in the wind that seemed able to find the remotest corners of the palace. His footfalls and those of his guard echoed forlornly as they traversed the dim reception hall, its forest of pillars robbed of color in the half-light. He took the passage to the women's wing; at its doors his guard left him, and the eunuchs bowed. He went on past where the way branched, glancing to the left, where the concubines were doubtless all asleep in their marble prison, but veering to the right and on toward his mother's rooms.

As he entered her little reception hall, there was laughter and chatter in the retiring room beyond. Mutnefert swept out to greet him, her robes afloat. "Thothmes, my dear, how did school go today? Is this wind not upsetting? Well, at least there will be no horses for you this afternoon. Come into the other room." He embraced her, and they linked arms. She led him into her bedroom, where many lights blazed and her women sat together, talking and playing board games. Mutnefert settled herself onto her couch and offered him sweetmeats from the box at her elbow, taking one after him and putting it into her mouth with relish. "Such dainties! These were a gift from Pharaoh's Sandal Bearer. He got them from the Governor Thure. It seems that Thure has better confectioners than the One himself." She patted the cushions by her ample hip, and Thothmes sank down beside her.

The wind was only a faint, faraway murmur, for Mutnefert's apartment was completely enclosed by other rooms, although she had her own private little passage behind the Hall of Audience and out to the gardens. She was not allowed access to the royal family unless invited, but seeing that all dined together in the evenings, this was no hardship. She would not have liked the strain of the continual presence of the One anyway. She liked her position. She had far more freedom than Pharaoh's foreign women, the beautiful slaves brought back by him from campaign after campaign or presented to him by foreign delegations. They spent their lives behind closed doors, far from the sight of all men save their master. He came to her occasionally in the middle of the night, a little drunk from the feasting, a little amorous. He was always kind to her as the mother of the only surviving royal son, but his visits became fewer as he aged, and she knew that he preferred the company of soothing Aahmose. She did not resent it. She had Thothmes, her darling, and she pampered him, proud of her achievement, an achievement that Aahmose had been unable to duplicate. She was not a fool, and she was well aware that if Thothmes succeeded to the Horus Throne, her own position would rapidly become more exalted. But any ambitions she may have had in the years of her first passion for the father were now overlaid by a pleasant laziness, and she spent her time in lurid gossip with her companions. Her face had begun to sag with the rich living in which she indulged, the chin to fold, the cheeks to become pendulous, but the eyes still sparked green with a love of life that she had not, unfortunately, passed on to her son. He had, however, a need for physical pleasures and an urge for indulgence, but not the vein of joyousness that had swept her into Pharaoh's bed. She felt a twinge of concern as she looked at her son, already a little overweight, his good looks masked by bad temper.

"I have not yet asked you how you like the chariot."

"You are the only one who has not. My royal father asked me yesterday, and today Hatshepsut asked me, and now you. Well, I hate it. As long as I can stand in the thing, why should I know how to drive it? Kings do not handle their own vehicles."

"Hush! Kings must be able to do a great many things, and you, dearest, will be King." She picked at her teeth with one long fingernail and reached for another sweet. "The palace is buzzing with rumors. I have heard that the One is about to make an announcement, and we both know what that will be. Her Highness Neferu is of age to marry. So are you."

"I suppose so. Neferu wasn't in class today. She is not well. Every night she dines in her own apartment and won't come out, even though father went and talked with her. I don't want to marry her. She's too thin and bony."

"But you will, won't you? And you will try very hard to please your royal father?"

Thothmes' lip stuck out mutinously. "I do try to please him, but it's hard work. I think I disappoint him. I am no warrior, as he was. I am not clever, as Hatshepsut is. When I am Pharaoh and have sons of my own, they shall do as they please."

"Don't talk such silly rubbish! You have a lot to learn, and you had better hurry up and learn it. For as soon as the One announces his heir, your time will be strictly limited, and your freedoms will be over. You will not be able to afford to make too many mistakes then, my son, so make them now, and profit from them. Would you like to play dominoes with me, or draughts?"

"I want to sleep. It's too hot for games. I wish that infernal wind would drop." He rose, and she took his hand affectionately.

"Go then. I will see you tonight. Now give your mother a kiss." She puckered up her red lips as he bent and brushed them with his own.

The ladies rose, too, and bowed, extending their arms; and Thothmes went out again, through the dark reception room to the passage beyond. Sometimes the palace seemed to be a sinister place, full of odd shadows and disembodied whispers, particularly at night or when, as today, the khamsin blew. Thothmes hurried along, his head down. As he passed the silent guards flanking the walls, they seemed to be giant, leather-clad djinn of the desert in grotesque human form, each assuming the likeness of his mighty father before they dissolved behind him into the dust that swirled about his ankles and drove him on. By the time he reached his own rooms and his waiting servant, he was out of breath and sweating, not with the heat, but with fear.

The day dragged to a close. By dinnertime the wind had increased in intensity. The meal was eaten to the accompaniment of its steady screaming as the burning air hit the guard posts atop the main wall and swooped down to flay buildings and garden alike. Sand was everywhere, in the food, in hair, between linen and skin, and underfoot. No one had much appetite. Hatshepsut ate beside her mother and was soon finished. Pharaoh did not eat at all but sat drinking, his eyes red-rimmed under the kohl, his gaze vacant, covering his thoughts. Ineni had retired to his estates for the night, and the hall was half empty. But the faithful Aahmes pen-Nekheb sat beside Thothmes, his aching leg propped up on cushions, his cloak wound tight around his body to keep out the sand. Pharaoh did not speak to him. Neferu was absent, too, pleading illness, as she had that morning, and Pharaoh swilled his wine and wondered darkly what he was going to do with her. She had always been so easy to cow, but this time something in her had revolted, and she stubbornly refused to have anything more to do with any of them. She would come around eventually, he thought, watching Hatshepsut roll her marbles across the streaked floor. Either that, or. . . . He shifted restless on his chair. "Go home, pen-Nekheb," he said harshly. "This is no night to be away from your own hearth. I did not give you land so that you could squat here and share mine. I will see that you have an escort."

"Majesty," pen-Nekheb replied, "I am too old to be sent running home by a desert wind. Do you remember the night we fell upon the Rethennu, and the wind blew so hard that in the murk we knew not which men were ours and which the enemy?"

Thothmes nodded. "I remember," he said. He held out his cup to be refilled and went back to his brooding, watching the bloodred liquid slop back and forth as his hand moved. His rings and his black eyes glittered. Tonight he was a dangerous man in the grip of a foul mood. Even Aahmose was careful to avoid his glance.

The meal ended, and still Pharaoh sat, motionless. Aahmes pen-Nekheb dozed in his chair, and the assembly grew restless, conversations dropping to a whisper. Still Thothmes did not move.

Finally, in desperation, Aahmose beckoned Hatshepsut to her. "Go to your father," she said in a low voice, "and ask him if you may go to bed. Be sure to prostrate yourself tonight, and do not smile at him or look in his eye. Do you understand?"

The girl nodded. She picked up her marbles and tucked them in the belt of her kilt, then walked across the floor and went down on her knees, resting her forehead on the ground beside his feet. She stayed thus, the film of sand digging into her elbows and legs and getting into her mouth. All eyes swiveled in her direction. The room held white-hot tension as a crucible holds molten metal.

Thothmes drained his cup and set it down before he saw her. "Rise!" he said. "What is it?"

She stood up, brushing her knees, her eyes averted. "Mighty Horus," she said to his jewel-encrusted sandals, "may I have your permission to go to bed?"

He leaned forward, his lips drawn back from his protruding teeth, and in spite of her mother's warning she could not help looking into his face. His eyes were bloodshot and expressionless, and she had a pang of fear. This man was a stranger.

"Bed? Of course you can go to bed. What is the matter with you?" He sat back, a gesture of dismissal, but he did not rise.

A sigh like the flutter of birds' wings ran around the hall, and Hatshepsut lingered, not quite knowing what to do. The slave again bent and filled Pharaoh's cup, and again he lifted it and drank. The girl turned her head. Her mother's face was drawn as she nodded, and Hatshepsut took a deep breath. Stepping forward she placed a knee between Thothmes' thigh and the edge of his chair and hoisted herself up so that she could whisper in his ear. "Father, the night is bad, and the guests are tired, too. Could you not rise so that they may leave?"

He stirred. "Tired, are they? Tired, yes, tired. I am tired, too, but I

cannot rest. I am oppressed. This wind howls like the kas of the damned."
His words were slurred. When he did rise, he swayed. "Go to bed, all of
you!" he shouted. "I, Mighty Bull, Beloved of Horus, order you to bed!
There!" he said to her, slumping once more into his seat. "Does that
satisfy you, little one?"

She reached up and kissed the cheek that reeked of perfume and wine.
"Perfectly, thank you, father," she replied. She scurried to Aahmose
before he could speak again. Her legs were trembling.

One by one the guests slipped out, and Aahmose beckoned to Nozme
to put her to bed. "Thank you, Hatshepsut," she said, kissing the warm
mouth. "He will be better in the morning." They, too, left the hall, and
pen-Nekheb slumbered on. Pharaoh went back to the wine.

At some hour late in the night Hatshepsut awoke from a deep sleep.
She had been dreaming of Neferu—Neferu with the body of the little
motherless fawn, locked up in a cage. Outside the cage stood Nebanum,
swinging a key on a long golden chain. But as she dreamed, it was not
Nebanum but her father who stood before the cage, his red eyes glowing
balefully as she crept closer. Poor Neferu opened her fawn's mouth and
began to baa, "Hatshe-e-epsut!, Hatshe-e-epsut."

Hatshepsut sat up in bed with a start, her heart beating painfully against
her ribs as she heard Neferu call again. "Hatshepsut!" Her night-light
glowed softly on the table beside her, and behind her head the wind
moaned in the wind catchers. They were now closed, but nevertheless the
wind butted at the stoppers with an eerie persistence, and her couch was
covered with a thin film of dust. She sat for a moment, listening, still half
in her dream, but the high, panic-filled voice did not call again. She lay
down and closed her eyes. Nozme did not snore tonight, or if she did, the
sound was drowned by the gusting of the wind; and in a corner the slave
was curled on her mat, fast asleep. Hatshepsut watched the flame of the
night-light broaden and blur. She was almost asleep again when she heard
low voices outside her door. They were real, human voices, her guard's and
another. She strained to hear them but detected only the stealthy footsteps that faded in the direction of Neferu's quarters. Hatshepsut,
bemused by sleep and dream, slid off her couch and, naked, ran to the
door. The guard, startled, came to attention. Quietly closing the door
behind her, she asked him what was going on.

He looked uncomfortable, but had to answer. "I do not really know,
Highness, but something is happening in the apartment of Her Highness
Neferu, and the Royal Steward just asked me if any had entered your
rooms this night."

Her mouth went dry, and the vision of Neferu the fawn rose unbidden, a face contorted in fear, the soft mouth open, calling her in desperation. Without another word she spun on her heel and began to run down the hall. Behind her the guard sputtered, "Highness! Princess!" He stood irresolute, not knowing whether to run after her or to rouse the sleeping attendants. He chose to run and pounded after her, but she was fleet. He followed only her shadow, which snaked along the walls, lengthening between the torches only to snap to her again as she rounded corners and fled under the flames. It seemed a long way to go in the night, with the wind screaming and the darkness reaching out to her from the entrances of branching passages, but she ran on, calling to Neferu under her breath as her arms pumped and her legs carried her.

She burst past the Imperial Guards who thronged the entrance to Neferu's rooms and came up, panting, into the older girl's ornate reception hall. It was empty. From beyond, in the bedroom, she heard the sound of chanting and saw incense, thick and gray, drifting through the open door. With a sob Hatshepsut forced her body to go forward. She fell into the other room and stopped abruptly, her heart beating so violently that it seemed about to tear her throat.

The room was full of people. The priests clustered around the couch like dim, white birds, the High Priest chanting and his assistants holding incense burners that glowed gold in their hands, the smoke rising in a cloud that made the air, already close and hot, a choking haze. At the head stood her father in his simple sleeping kilt, his big body naked. As she skidded to a halt, her hands at her throat, he glanced up but seemed not to recognize her. All at once he was an old man, his face seamed, his eyes sunken. Aahmose sat in a corner on a small stool, wrapped in a transparent cloak that floated about her on the floor. She held Neferu's little silver crown surmounted with the likeness of Mut, absently turning it over and over in her hands, her lips moving in prayer. The Chief Steward and other members of Pharaoh's suite stood together by the door, whispering anxiously.

None of them paid the slightest attention to Hatshepsut as she crept closer to the couch. She elbowed her way past the acolytes and past Menena until she could reach out and touch the cold fingers that hung over the edge. "Neferu," she called softly, standing silent, an ache of love and a seed of fear building inside her.

The Royal Physician had placed a square of linen over the thin breast of the girl on the couch, and on it he had placed powerful amulets. His pots and pestles and jars lay beside him on the table, but now he knew that only the gods had the skill to heal. He knelt by Neferu, gently tying the magic cord around her wet forehead and preparing the incantations that would drive the demon from her slight body. But he knew in his heart that nothing would avail, that Neferu had been poisoned, and he glanced up at his royal master. Pharaoh's gaze was fixed on his daughter's face, and only his fierce grip on the gilded headboard betrayed any emotion. The physician went back to his spells, distressed. He had not been able to make Her Highness vomit. If she had, there would have been a chance. But the doer of this deed knew his work well, and the pain ate away at Neferu's life with fiery inevitability, despite half a night spent in feverish attempts to save her. She was sinking fast, and the mood in the room had changed. The wind continued to howl.

Suddenly, Neferu opened her eyes, and the physician sat back on his heels, startled. Hatshepsut could see the sweat-streaked face, gray in the lamplight, and she flung herself down beside her sister and buried her head in the pillow. Neferu moaned and motioned weakly.

Thothmes spoke into the new stillness. "Raise her. Place a cushion beneath her head."

As the physician lifted the lolling head and settled another pillow on the couch, Hatshepsut looked up, trembling. "I heard you calling me, Neferu, and I came. Oh, Neferu, are you going to die?" Neferu closed her eyes as a spasm of agony gripped her, and Hatshepsut began to cry. "Don't die. Please don't. What about the fawn? What about me?"

Neferu turned her head, and her eyes opened again. When she spoke, it was with great effort, and a line of scum gathered about her mouth. Her pupils were dilated, and in their depths Hatshepsut read panic and a great sadness. "Do you remember Uatchmes and Amun-mes, who died, Hatshepsut?" She was whispering, her voice a thin flutter, like the wind in winter reeds along the marshes.

Hatshepsut shook her head dumbly.

"Do you remember grandmother, who died?"

Hatshepsut did not stir. She held Neferu's hand, afraid that if she replied, the sobs welling in her throat would break out and fill the room. She concentrated on holding down, holding on.

Neferu paused, her breath hot and quick on Hatshepsut's cheek as she roused herself for a last effort. Already the gloom of the Judgment Hall was seeping into her mind, and its cold winds tugged at her limbs. "You will remember me, Hatshepsut. You will remember this night, and you will learn. My dream spoke true. Anubis waits for me beside the scales, and I am not ready. I am not ready!" Her eyes bored into the little girl's head with a feverish intensity, and the sobs died in Hatshepsut's chest as she tried to read their message. "Take this that I give you, Hatshepsut, and make it worthwhile." Her gaze left Hatshepsut and ranged the room until it found Menena. "I did not ask a destiny. I did not want it. You take it, Hatshepsut, and use it. I want only—peace—"

The last words were a sigh, and Hatshepsut found herself looking into eyes that no longer saw her but were glazed with some far vision, filling her with grief. She took the cold arm and shook it, shouting, "I do not understand, Neferu. I never understand! I love you!"

Neferu's head began to thrash on the pillow amid its welter of sticky black hair, and the broken murmurings were unintelligible.

"She dreams," Thothmes said, his voice low but even. "She is near the end."

Hatshepsut got up and thrust a fist under his chin, the tears pouring down her face. "No!" she shrieked at him. "Neferu will never die!" She turned and fled the room in terror. At the door to the apartment her guard waited, but she turned from him, taking Neferu's own passage to the gardens, running with the speed of a hunted leopard. Before her guard had crossed the hall to the passage entrance, she was out of the palace and tearing down the avenue in the darkness.

4

The wind caught her as she left the lee of the wall, and she staggered, striking her shin against the rough reliefs and grazing her elbow, but she hardly felt the pain that shot up her ankle. The paving continued broad and flat to the river, so she soon turned aside into the comforting secrecy of the trees, following winding paths that showed up as pale ribbons, even in the driving blackness of wind and sand, taking her deeper, away from the formality of flower beds and waterfalls and into a rougher, lonelier part of the estate. Even under the protecting arms of the sycamores the wind found her and buffeted her, so that she soon had to slow down. Her eyes, nostrils, and panting mouth were all full of sand; but she struggled on, the fury within her a physical force that drove her until she could run no more. Just when the stabbing pain in her side and the whistling of her lungs grew so great that she was ready to drop to the ground, she burst out of the trees and found herself at the feet of one of the lowering statues of her God-Father that fronted the pylons at the entrance to the temple. She knew that straight ahead of her now, beyond the great temple gates and the other pylon and another belt of trees, was the Sacred Lake of Amun, the lake on which his Boat was moored. After a moment she stumbled on, thinking only of the water. Whether to drink, or to purify herself, or to fling herself in she did not know, but she ran on, the rage smouldering now, being replaced by a slow-rising wave of sorrow. Neferu! Neferu! Neferu! In all the pampered years, the adoring, worshiping years, she had never faced an emotion such as this one that drove straight to the center of her being and stayed there, leaving her open to the pain.

She was at the lake before she knew it, and her knees buckled as she fell from the edge, her arms outstretched, the water closing over her head. Immediately the wind noise ceased, and the calm was stupendous. The sand and grit fell quietly from her body, the water wound itself around her in coolness, and she floated, her eyes closed, the singing in her head now reduced to a hum. O Amun, my Father, she thought blissfully. She felt him come close to her as her breathing slowed, and she began to drift. The wind was tearing whitecaps on the lake, and her body rocked gently under the swell as though she herself was the Sacred Barque, waiting for the God to make his journey. She let out her breath until only her face rose above the water. I could stay here forever, and never have to go back, she thought. At those words her dream came back to her, and she began to cry again, softly this time, not only for her own loneliness to come but in genuine grief for Neferu herself, for the years of sunlight and happiness lost.

The next moment she felt her shoulder gripped by a strong hand. She gasped and went under, losing her breath and choking as she rose again to the surface. She began to struggle, but the hand tightened its hold and, coughing and fighting, she was towed inexorably to the bank. She felt two hands encircle her, and she found herself dumped unceremoniously on the grass. Catching her breath at last, she began to shiver. She could not see her assailant in the darkness and was tensing herself for flight when her arm was gripped again and he spoke.

"Do you know what could happen to you if the priests caught you in the Sacred Lake? What were you doing?" He was only a vague black shadow against the deeper shadows of the cloud-covered sky and the black bulk of the temple. His voice was young but stern. She began to be afraid, and she wrenched free her arm. She turned to run, but he grabbed her once more and swung her over his shoulder in one quick movement, stunning her. "No you don't," he said. By the time she had recovered her wits, he was striding along toward the west side of the temple, bouncing her around like a sack of grain.

They skirted the lake, and soon Hatshepsut lost all sense of direction. She had never been behind the temple to the maze of servants quarters, granaries, kitchens, and storerooms; and as she was carried through trees, down alleys, and through cramped doorways, she was utterly lost. She knew by the way the grass turned into paving and then into a beaten dirt track, and by the way the wind was suddenly cut off only to hit her again, that they moved between buildings. Once she saw painted paving stones that rushed dizzily beneath her, seeming familiar. By the time he set her on her feet in a narrow, dark hallway fronted by many closed doors, she was utterly lost and trembling with apprehension and the aftereffects of her dousing. He took her by the hand and quickly led her down the corridor, surefooted in the moonless passage. He pushed open a door near the end and pulled her inside, closing it and locking it after her. He left her, and she heard him fumbling about until suddenly a light sprang up, revealing a small, whitewashed cell, a pallet on the floor, a rude chair, and an unfinished wooden trunk that obviously served as table as well as clothes box, for the man placed the lamp on it.

He turned to look at her, and she stared back, her fear evaporating. He was not a man after all, at least not a full-grown man, but rather young, about Neferu's age, with strong, even features and a penetrating gaze. His shaved head told her something, and the muddy, stained, white linen that stuck to his long legs told her the rest. This was a young priest, so she must be somewhere within the temple precincts. She began to feel better. It was not nice to be snatched from the familiar and suddenly find one's self in a strange and menacing world of rough hands and disrespectful words, especially on a night that was dreadful and unreal enough without the added strain of being lost.

"You are shivering still," he said, his voice deep with the tones of a manhood half-realized. "The air is very hot, but the wind can kill." He took a tattered woollen blanket from the pallet, and before she could protest, he had gone down on one knee and was rubbing her vigorously just as Nozme used to do.

The shock of this brisk and businesslike handling knocked the last vestiges of dream from her, and as her skin began to glow and her teeth stopped chattering, she was able to look at the events of the night clearly and without the dregs of the merciful waking sleep that had carried her to Neferu's side and out again into the wildness of the night. Neferu was dying. Neferu was probably dead, and Hatshepsut, standing limply as this extraordinary young man brought new life to her limbs, looked into the black and gaping hole of the future. Along with the certainty of Neferu's death came another grim thought. She shuddered involuntarily so that the boy stopped rubbing and looked up at her. Now she, Hatshepsut, was the only royal girl left. The implications were too fine for her mind to grasp as yet, but she remembered her mother's patient words: "It is in us, the royal women, that the God's blood flows. . . . no man can be Pharaoh unless he marries a royal woman." The words of Neferu, spoken such a short while ago, were still jumbled in the girl's thoughts, but she recalled the homely face drawn in pain, the big eyes. Again, unbidden, the tears began to flow.

Senmut gently wrapped the blanket around her heaving shoulders and pushed her down on the pallet. "There," he said, drawing up the chair and sitting so that the light fell across his face, outlining its planes, the hollows and highlights flitting and changing as he spoke. "Now do not be afraid. Tell me what you were doing by the lake, or even in the temple grounds for that matter. Did you fall in by accident?" She did not reply but sat still, looking at the plain floor, her face tearstained atop a huddle of brown blanket. Senmut regarded her with impatience and pity. "Come. You must talk to me. If you do not tell me how you came to be in Mighty Amun's Lake in the middle of a foul night, then you will have to tell the

Master of Mysteries and bring disgrace or worse upon yourself and your family. If you strayed there by accident and fell in, then I can take you to your home and say no more about it, though how you managed to pass all the guards between here and the city is quite beyond me. Now will you speak? Or will I send for my phylarch? Was it an accident?"

Hatshepsut could not stop the flow of tears, and her nose was running as well. Bending her head, she wiped her face on the old blanket and blew her nose. She began to cry afresh and could not find her voice.

The young man waited. "You need not be afraid," he repeated. "I am not going to hurt you. For Set's sake, stop crying!" He did not know why, but something about her made him feel uneasy. The fine-boned little face with its square, stubborn chin; its wide forehead; and its thin, aristocratic nose reminded him of someone—not in the actual features, but in the way she held her head on its long neck and in the way she lifted her chin, looking at him with solemnity. Strange child, he thought. Perhaps she had not been about to drown after all. He lifted the wet robes away from his calves and suddenly remembered the flagon of wine he had filched from the kitchen the night before. Breathing a prayer of thanks, he moved the lamp and, after rummaging in his chest, brought out a crude wooden cup. He replaced the lamp, reached behind his chair, and brought out the flagon, filling the cup and holding it out to the girl. "Here, drink some wine. It will make you feel better."

She stopped snuffling, and her hand shot out. Without a word of thanks she took it and drank, sighing and wrinkling up her nose. She handed it back. "That wine is cheap. It tastes bitter."

"Ah! So you have a voice, then?"

She wiped her face again and sat straighter, one hand clutching the blanket to her chin.

"Now for the last time, little one, did you fall in the lake by accident?"

"Yes. No! I am not sure."

"Whose house do you serve? Are your parents slaves in the city?"

"Certainly not! I live in the palace."

"So you work in the kitchens? In the Good God's harem?"

The black eyes beneath the swollen lids flared at him. "How dare you speak to me like that! If I wish to bathe in my Father's waters in the middle of the night, that is no concern of yours, priest! And what were *you* doing there, anyway?"

Senmut had in fact been on the way back to his cell after one of his frequent forays to the kitchens, having consumed cold beef and honey cakes in the lee of the outer court of the temple. To avoid the guards, he had been walking around the lake. It was only by the merest chance that he had heard the splash as she fell. He looked at her more closely, an awful doubt growing in his mind. For the first time he noticed the bedraggled youth-lock hanging from her shaved head, still wound with ribbons of white and blue, the colors of the Imperial family. He closed his eyes. "O merciful Isis, no," he breathed. "Please, no."

The tiny mouth was tight when he opened his eyes again. "Do you not know, then, who I am?"

He shook his head slowly. "I thought you were drowning. I thought you were a slave who had wandered where she should not. I wished only to save you from disgrace."

She smiled suddenly, and her whole face lightened. It was an infectious smile, full of humor and friendliness, but he could not smile back. He knew that she could mean his death. He had laid coercive hands on royalty, and his life was forfeit. "That was kind," she mocked. "You, a little we'eb priest, wished to save me, the Princess Hatshepsut, from disgrace." She settled back, leaning against the wall with eyes alight. "How exciting! Did you really think I was about to drown?"

He swallowed. "Yes, Highness."

"Then I pardon you." She waved a hand airily. "You are a true son of Maat." Her eyes narrowed shrewdly. "But now what will you do with me? The guards will be searching, for they know I ran away. My father will be roaring, and Nozme will be crying because she knows she will be beaten for not staying with me. But it was not her fault. I crept out of bed while she slept."

Senmut's heart sank even farther. So this is what you brought me to, O my father, when you and I made the long journey to the holy city, he thought. An ignominious death for me and disgrace for you. He said aloud, "Highness, may I be permitted to ask one question?"

"I should think," she retorted waspishly, "that after laying hands on me in the lake and tossing me over your shoulder, after trotting me all over the estate and rubbing the skin off me with your nasty old blanket, you would not hesitate to put to me *another* question. Well," she finished admiringly, "you do have strong shoulders." She sobered. "I ran because —because dear Neferu—" she started to cry quietly, looking away, and Senmut watched in helpless anxiety. "A poison—my lovely Neferu is dying."

Premonition and horror crawled over his skin and up and down his spine like the soft, hairy feet of deadly spiders. His hands clenched on the arms of his chair. So it had come. And so soon. And he had done nothing after all but bury his head in the sand of his own security like one of those foolish Nubian ostriches while out there in the white-gold purity of the palace a girl choked toward death, her body wracked and tortured by the poison that he, Senmut, might just as well have administered himself. How fitting, Mighty Amun, is your judgment, he thought. I am to die, and I deserve to die, but not for the crime of which I shall be accused. He suppressed a wild desire to burst into hysterical laughter.

The little princess was curled into the wall, her head on her arms, sobbing aloud now as if the ugliness could be washed away with her tears. "She called me—in my dreams—and I went, and there she was, so sick —she will die—oh, Neferu, Neferu—" Finally she sat up, holding out her hands to him. "Please, priest, could you hold my hand? I am so afraid, and no one understands, no one."

What difference can it possibly make? he thought grimly as he slid from his chair and sat beside her on the pallet. I have touched her once already, and I am a dead man. He put his arms around her and held her close, soothing her, feeling the shoulders, fragile as a bird's wings, heave with her sobs. She buried her wet face in his neck and clung to him as though she really was drowning and he was the only rock that could save her. "Hush, little Princess," he murmured, stroking her. "Life goes on. We live, and we die, and only the gods know when. Cry out your tears." He suddenly felt the irony of his words and said no more.

She fell asleep at last, her head resting on his shoulder, and he left her in peace, watching the flutter of long eyelashes on her brown cheek. After an hour he shook her gently, and she stirred, groaning.

"Come, Highness, it is time to go. The wind is dropping, and tomorrow may be a fine and sunny day." He stood her upright and gave her more wine, which she drank without comment, swaying a little from sheer exhaustion. "I will take you back to your father. Perhaps you should keep my blanket around you." He tightened his belt and ran a hand over his shaved skull, but when he turned to go, he found her eyes on him, regarding him with speculation. Already the dim light of dawn was creeping toward them, and in the pale daylight she seemed empty but somehow older, as if the essence of childhood had flowed away with her tears and would never come again.

"What is your name?" she asked him.

"Senmut, Highness."

"Senmut. Senmut, I will return alone, as I left, and I will not take your blanket. You think I do not know what father will do to you if he knows what you did tonight? Only lead me back to the lake, and I can find my own way from there. And do not fear. My father taught me to keep my own counsel, and I believe I am just learning what he meant. I will not speak of you to anyone."

"Princess, it is right that the One should know now, before gossip and rumor tell him and not my lips."

"Nonsense! Gossip feeds on fact, or so my mother says, and the facts are known only to you and me. I will not speak, I tell you. Do you doubt my word?"

He did not. She radiated the unconscious arrogance of royalty as she unwound the blanket and let it fall. He bowed, and without another word they left the room.

Outside all was still. The last dying gasps of wind sucked at their knees as they padded silently across the courtyard and vanished into the shadow of the granaries, but above them the sky was milky white with dawn and very clear. Not even a mist hung about the obelisks and towers of the temple, and the two of them hurried through the trees and came at last to the grassy edge of the Sacred Lake, whose waters scarcely rippled in the morning hush.

They stopped and faced one another. Hatshepsut drew deep breaths. "The khamsin is over. It blew for her, for Neferu, and it has taken her. I know it. Thank you, Senmut, for risking your life for me. I know that is what you did, and when you found out who I was, you did not flinch, but comforted me like a brother. I shall not forget."

As he looked into the earnest little face, he felt no temptation to laugh. Instead he knelt and kissed the grass at her feet. "Highness," he said, "you are the bravest lady I have known, and the wisest. Long life!"

She laughed. "Get up, get up! Truly, your prostration is far more noble than the cheek of that silly User-amun. Now I had better start running before father decides to execute the guards piecemeal!"

With a wave she was gone, running like a deer toward the trees on the other side of the sphinx-lined avenue, her naked body gleaming in the new rays of the sun.

5

She was seen streaking across the grass toward the western portal of the palace, and by the time she flew in her own door, her father was waiting for her, alone. Already the slaves were at work, sweeping out the runnels and little hills of sand that had been deposited everywhere, but none sang at their labors and the waking inhabitants were quiet. A sense of doom hung in the air, although Ra danced on the golden dust raised by the sweepers and leaped across the mosaicked floors and between the white pillars. Hatshepsut sensed the oppression even before she knelt to Thothmes in apology and felt his cold gaze upon her.

He had been bathed and was girt in yellow linen. Only a simple gold and blue faience pectoral, two hawks flanking the Eye of Horus, hung on his breast, and his head was covered with a black and yellow striped leather cap whose sides rested on his shoulders and whose front band held the kingly rearing cobra, the Uraeus that gleamed on his massive forehead. He had not slept, nor had he eaten, and he looked to be an old man, his eyes rheumy and bloodshot under the fresh black kohl. He did not bid her to rise, and she stayed with her nose to the floor, trying to catch her breath. He began to pace.

"Where have you been?"

"Wandering in the gardens, father."

"Is that so? For the last four hours?"

"Yes, Mighty Horus."

"In the dark? In the wind and the sand?"

"Yes."

"You lie," he said easily, as if he were tossing off a remark to his wife in the middle of a morning walk. "The gardens have been searched time and again since you left my presence, and my captain awaits a flogging because you were not to be found there. Now answer me!" His voice hardened. "I am your father, but I am also Pharaoh. I can have you whipped, Hatshepsut. Where were you?"

She saw his feet come close and straddle her head. She was getting a crick in her neck from her awkward position, and the smell of new bread wafted about from somewhere in the room, reminding her how hungry she was, but she kept very still. "I did go to the gardens, father, but then I ran on, into the temple."

The royal foot by her left ear began to tap. "Oh? Do you not think it strange that the temple guards, who swarm the precincts like busy ants at all hours of the day and night, are still seeking you?"

"I did go to the temple, father, but not inside. I went—I went to the Sacred Barque, and I walked the ramp and lay inside, where the wind could not reach me." She was very glad now that her face was hidden from him. She had not yet learned to lie without a tremor.

"Indeed? And why did you do that?"

"I wanted to be close to my Father. I wanted to think about—about dear Neferu."

Thothmes was suddenly still. He walked quickly away from her and sat down in her low nursery chair. "Get up, Hatshepsut, and come here," he said kindly. "You have caused me moments of extreme anxiety this night, and I have heaped my anger upon soldier and servants alike. When will you learn prudence? Are you hungry?" She scrambled up and ran to her table as he twitched the linen cloth aside, revealing hot bread and smoked fish and a wet green salad that smelt of onion and papyrus shoots and set her mouth to watering. "Eat then." He did not call a slave to wash her hands, and she did not care. I have washed my whole self in the waters of my Father, she thought, and sent a guilty glance to Thothmes' face as she crossed her legs and sank onto her cushion, breaking the loaf with eager hands. He waited patiently while she ate the last scrap of fish and drank the last dribble of milk from the cup. When she had finished, he said softly, "Neferu is dead, Hatshepsut."

Her head dropped, and she nodded faintly. "I know, my father. And she was afraid, long before this night. She dreamed such terrible things. Why did it have to be her?" She looked up at him. "She only wanted to be happy."

"We must all die, Hatshepsut, some early, some late, but we all come to the feet of Osiris in the end. Neferu was not happy with her life."

"But she could have been. If you had not planned that she should marry Thothmes. If she had not been First Daughter—"

"Do you wish to alter the unalterable, my daughter?" he chided gently. "She was First Daughter. There is no other son to be Pharaoh after me. Would you have me excuse Neferu her destiny and then put Thothmes aside?"

"You have not excused Neferu her destiny," Hatshepsut replied. "Her destiny was death."

Thothmes looked into the calm, limpid eyes with a start and saw a change in their depths. He was a man with sharp perception, perfected over the years by the weight of rule. The circumstances of Neferu's death pointed, in his mind, to the one conclusion that both relieved and smote him beyond all reason. He had seen violent death many times in his career, and he knew the work of poison when he saw it. He also knew intimately the lives and aspirations of his ministers, and more than once he had overridden the subtle pressures of manipulation. He had no doubt that here was one more attempt to warp the course of his kingship or to glut the ambition of priest or official, and the knowledge had started a slow fire in him that would burn until he knew all. But there was the relief as well—relief because a decision that was tearing him apart was now taken out of his hands for the time being and could be left for a while. Though Neferu had been the second most important woman in Egypt and his own royal seed, he had never understood her and had dreaded the proclamation that would leave his beloved country in the hands of an insensitive pudding of a boy and a mooning, gutless girl. Not for this had he risked his life time without number and plotted and done his share of the plundering of ka and body. He almost wished never to know the truth of his daughter's death, for it suited his purposes very well. But the tortuous planning behind it, the extension of someone's plots into a future that might endanger his dynasty, for this he must quietly sniff about, ferret out, even though he might never accuse anyone or bring them to the Courts of Justice. He spoke in his mind to the shadowy form who had held the evil cup to Neferu's lips: I will teach you anew who is the power in Egypt. I am Maat, and my wish is the wish of the God. Now Hatshepsut, his darling, was First Daughter, and now he could breathe. In the back of his mind a new plan was gathering, dim as yet but forming rapidly.

"No," he said to the resigned face before him. "It was her destiny to be Divine Consort, but she would not. She gave that destiny to you with her own words, do you remember, Hatshepsut? 'I did not ask a destiny. I did not want it. . . . take—' "

She remembered with a sickening jolt. " 'Take it . . . and use it,' " she finished. "I still do not understand. Neferu was always saying things I could not follow, although I tried very hard."

Thothmes lifted the table away from her and drew her onto his knees. "Neferu was carried to the House of the Dead two hours ago," he said quietly, "and that is a very serious thing for you, little one. You are the last royal lady." He felt her body stiffen.

She turned her head away and finally said in a muffled voice, "Great One, will you make me marry Thothmes now?"

"You are too young to speak of marriage. Do you not like Thothmes?"

"No. He is boring."

"Hatshepsut, you have many years before you, and in those years you will come to understand the responsibilities that Neferu refused to face. Because she did so, she died, do you understand?"

"No," she replied wearily. "Of course not. I never do."

"You are cast in a different mold," he went on. "Amun himself protects you. But even so, from now on you must be very careful of all you do or say. And do not worry about the future. That is in my hands, but if I see the necessity of your marriage to Thothmes, you will obey, will you not?"

"If you order me to."

He shook her gently. "You have blatantly disobeyed my orders before! But I speak of what may come, and it is the present that must be faced. Tell me, what were you really doing tonight?"

She wriggled from his grasp and stood before him, her hands clasped demurely behind her back. "I am sorry, father, I cannot tell you. But I did not do wrong."

"Very well." He dismissed the subject, knowing that he would get nothing more from her. "Now the period of mourning begins for Neferu. There will be no school, and you will not see any of your friends. Your mother is sleeping, and I suggest that you do the same. You look very tired. And do not expect to see Nozme for some days. She will be engaged in the duties of a kitchen slave in order to learn that I, Pharaoh, who made her Royal Nurse, can now make her Royal Kitchen Assistant."

Hatshepsut smiled. "It was not her fault that I ran away."

"You were her responsibility." He clapped his hands, and Second Royal Nurse Tiyi appeared, bowed, and waited. "Put her to bed, and keep her there all morning," Thothmes ordered. "And see that you do not leave her for a moment." He bent and kissed Hatshepsut.

She suddenly wound her arms about his neck. "I love you, my father."

"I love you, too, little Hat. I am glad that you are safe."

"How could I have been anything else, with two such powerful Fathers to protect me?" she said solemnly. The ever lurking smile broke out, and she left him, placing her hand in Tiyi's and walking sedately to the door.

For seventy days, while the Inundation rose to its peak and all the land became a vast red and brown lake dotted with islanded villages and trees that seemed to float, stunted, on the calm tide, Neferu's hollow body lay in the House of the Dead being reverently prepared for its new habitation. The smooth, sallow flesh that had warmed to the sun and felt the touch of gold and human hand, now knew a very different peace from that which the girl had sought. As the sem-priests wound the thin limbs with fine linen and filled the cavities not with food or wine or love but with natron-soaked cloths, the unseeing eyes gazed upon them with blind resignation. In the temple workshops the artisans put the final touches to the coffins in which she would lie. Over the river, their tasks hampered by the water that lapped to the door and trickled between the paving stones, the painters, sculptors, and stonemasons were laboring day and night to complete the little mortuary temple begun by Neferu herself so that in afteryears, she could enjoy the offerings of the people who would bring their griefs and desires to her. But not so soon. Not yet. There was something pitiful in the half-completed biography that took rapid shape along the outer walls, the hastily laid sanctuary floor, the statues surrounded by dust and chips as the men sweated to finish all before Neferu passed on her way to the cliff behind, to the dark silence of the rock tomb whose entrance would be hidden from all eyes save her own.

It had been a good flood. Taxes would be up and crops plentiful. The fellahin, unable to work the land during these months, had slaved instead on Pharaoh's building projects. They still received their bread and onions, and they were cheerful. In the glare of the sun the country seemed full of birds, and dragonflies, their gossamer wings quivering blue and mauve, darted on the surface of the drowned fields, waiting for the mosquitoes that bred with fearsome rapidity in the still water, bringing disease to man and beast. Egypt made strong music then, the music of fecundity and rich life. But deep within the House of the Dead Neferu's cheeks were stuffed so that she appeared only to sleep, and at last the bandages fell across her eyes forever.

There was no music and no laughter in the palace. In Neferu's apartment the servants gathered together all her belongings—the clothes, the dishes, the furniture and cosmetic jars—all she had needed and would continue to use in the lonely privacy of her grave. Her gay jewels were wrapped and placed in their golden caskets, and her crowns lay empty in their lined boxes. In the nursery Nozme and Tiyi packed her old toys— the red and yellow leather balls, the spinning tops, the wooden dolls, and the little painted geese—and the tiny spoons with which she had been fed as a baby and the ribbons and kilts she had worn as a child. Her wigs were burned in a short and poignant ceremony, and at last the big rooms stood vacant and somehow transient, waiting for another occupant, another royal Heiress. The doors were locked and sealed, and the sunlight swam within, liquid gold flowing into every corner, Ra seeking his lost Daughter.

For Hatshepsut it was a time of extreme boredom interspersed with bouts of extreme grief. She spent a great deal of time in the Royal Zoo, watching the baby fawn grow, feeding the birds, and walking with Nebanum from cage to cage as he watered and fed his charges. She sat with him on his little lawn in the shadow of the walls, shredding the little white and yellow daisies that sprinkled the grass and asking him about all things that grew or flew or prowled in the land. He was a simple man, solitary and happy and full of the knowledge of natural things. His heart went out to the little girl who seemed to be suddenly adrift full of uncertainty. He spoke to her of the habits of birds and the kinds of flowers and their care. He told her of the hiding places of the desert deer, and she listened eagerly. Sometimes she would come to his door wanting only to be silent, and he would sit and watch her impassive face and restless fingers, feeling something of the pain and doubt inside her as he felt the needs of his animals, but he could offer only his company and the warm goat's milk he collected every day. Often she came alone, without guard or slave. On these occasions he prayed that the One had granted her permission to wander as she chose, but he doubted it and swallowed his fear. She needed him in an odd way. He remembered Neferu and was silent also.

There was no school. Royal Tutor Khaemwese sat in a corner of the gardens and slept in the sun. Young Thothmes spent his time with his bewildered and angry mother, and the nobles' sons, who normally would have shared the schoolroom with Hatshepsut and Thothmes, stayed home, enjoying a holiday.

Aahmose kept to her rooms, eating alone, with only Hetephras to serve her. She spoke to no one of her private grief. She had been born into palace society, her father had been Pharaoh and his father before him, and she knew well what was required of her. Royal death was like royal life, fraught with sudden changes of fortune and direction. She prayed a great deal to her beloved benefactress, Isis, kneeling before the shrine she had had set up many years ago in her bedroom. Often it was for little Hatshepsut that she prayed, not Neferu, who surely even now accompanied Amun-Ra in his Heavenly Barque and needed the prayers of no one. For her small daughter she carried anxiety like a new child in the womb, and its stirrings filled her with an uncharacteristic dismay.

As for the Mighty Bull of Maat, he took to pacing the halls and corridors of his domain in the middle of the night, discomfiting servants and startling the guards who watched over the silent, dead hours. In the day he himself went to the temple to perform the sacrifices often done by his priestly substitute. He knew now what he wanted, and it was not that Thothmes should rule. He had debated, during his nocturnal ramblings, whether or not to recall his sons Wadjmose and Amun-mose from the border and put the crown on one of their heads, but he had finally rejected that idea. Both men were in their forties and had been soldiers since their early years. Not that that mattered. A soldiering Pharaoh meant a strong and decisive rule. But he recoiled sentimentally from the necessity of marrying one of them to Hatshepsut, a girl of ten, although that solution was better than the mad scheme with which he toyed. Besides, both men had wives and families on estates outside Thebes; both men had been away from any politicking for many years; and—and—

And it is not my will, he told himself as he knelt before his God in the darkness of the great sanctuary. My will is also the will of Amun, but to will is a long way from making to be. He continued to make offerings and to measure the echoing halls of his palace with steady feet.

At last, in the middle of the month of Mesore, when the river had begun to shrink again and the rich, black land rose in its place, the funeral cortege gathered on the east bank to take Neferu home. It was a silent company that watched her coffin being hauled aboard the waiting barge along with everything that had linked her with life. The morning was fresh and sunny, and the air smelt of wet earth. The river ran fast, and already young green things were pushing through the waterlogged ground in the gardens. The priests, mourners, and family embarked for the short trip to the west with their eyes downcast, each wrapped in his or her own thoughts. On the far bank the sleds and oxen waited, motionless, and as the barges drew swiftly to their mooring, the poles of the boat slaves gleaming wet in the sun as they rose and fell, Hatshepsut began to tremble.

The days of mourning had brought her a precarious peace, and she had begun to feel at ease with life again, but the sight of the huge red beasts, held still by the unmoving and somehow sinister servants of the Necropolis, filled her with the same panic that had catapulted her from the dying Neferu's side and into the Sacred Lake. Her fingers sought the warm comfort of her mother's hand.

The boats bumped the bank gently, the ramps were run out, and Hatshepsut, Aahmose, and Pharaoh stood waiting while the coffin and chests were dragged ashore.

Mutnefert and her son stood a little apart. Hatshepsut was aware of the cautious, sidelong glances young Thothmes kept sending her way, but her anxiety deadened the stab of annoyance she felt. She deliberately turned her back on him and pressed closer to Aahmose.

Thothmes watched her sullenly. His mother had told him that now that Neferu was dead, he would have to marry Hatshepsut if he wanted to be King. He had been disgusted, but the mood of rebellion had not lasted long. As usual he had hidden it beneath the soft cushion of his sluggish thoughts, and only his sulkiness remained visible.

Mutnefert was almost unrecognizable on this day. She was swathed in voluminous folds of blue, unadorned by jewels. She watched her royal husband covertly, a glint in her eyes. She was confident that before too many days had passed her son would be Crown Prince and would easily subdue the streak of wildness in young Hatshepsut once the two were wed. The death of the Princess was not such a disaster after all, she thought, though naturally it was a pity. Mutnefert knew that Neferu would have been a far more dutiful and biddable wife than Hatshepsut was likely to be, but it could not be helped. It simply meant that they must all have patience. Nothing had been lost but time.

The funeral procession formed. First the dozen slaves, carrying on their shoulders pink alabaster jars containing food and precious unguents, then more slaves, with Neferu's clothes and jewels in long cedarwood boxes. The sledge on which the four canopic jars stood came next, the jars containing the dead girl's viscera, each stoppered with a likeness of one of the four Sons of Horus. Before it would walk a priest, chanting, and behind it would come the sledge holding the coffin itself, surrounded by priests. There was some whispering as the procession formed, and Hatshepsut went with Aahmose and Pharaoh to stand behind the coffin, still clutching tightly to her mother's reassuring hand.

Her grandmother's funeral had not been like this. She could just remember that under the mourning wails, prescribed by custom, the atmosphere had been happy—the escorting to rest of an old and noble woman who had lived long and fully and who now wished to go to her God. But here, waiting while the ladies of the harem in blue mourning dresses took their places at the end of the straggling cortege, feeling the sun gain strength, she sensed true sorrow and regret for the girl who had been little more than a child and whose days had held more than their share of misery.

Menena came and bowed before Thothmes, and Thothmes grimly gave the sign for the ceremony to commence. The oxen strained in front of Hatshepsut, and the sledge started forward with a jerk. She began to walk, hearing behind her the high, grief-filled keening as the women scooped up earth, placed it on their heads, and wept. She kept her eyes on the heels of the priest in front, not wishing to watch the swaying coffin, not wishing to think of what was within. Above them all, in the high, blue sky, two hawks wheeled, wings outstretched to catch the gliding winds, their cries the only sounds above the faint murmurs of the priests. All along the funeral route the people of the Necropolis crowded and stood silent, bowing like wheat in the wind as Thothmes passed but otherwise remaining stiff. Hatshepsut saw them from the corner of her eyes, white robes stirring in the breeze, a population of ghouls. All at once the voice of Neferu's own priest, the young and vigorous Ani, arose, clear as the notes of a trumpet on the morning air. "Cry joy for her, for she hath captured the Horizon!" There was triumph in his song, and a greater sorrow than anyone else could feel. As the others responded, "She lives; she lives forever!" Hatshepsut began to cry. She felt her other hand suddenly enfolded in her father's big fist, but she was not comforted.

At the gaping entrance to the tomb, where servants waited to assist, the procession came to a halt. The crowds had been left behind. The women fell silent but for a low, broken babble, and the coffin was lifted to the ground and stood upright. For one heart-stopping moment Hatshepsut, looking up, fancied that the golden lid would swing back on its hinges and Neferu herself would step forth, but nothing happened. The hawks screamed once more and wheeled away toward the sun, and the sem-priests gathered in a group to pour the libations. Menena came forward, Sacred Knife in hand, and the Ceremony of the Opening of the Mouth began.

For four days and nights the cortege camped outside the little temple and the raw, new hole in the cliffside. The blue and white tents flapped and tugged gently at their pegs like ungainly, tethered birds; and hour after hour the clustered priests murmured, censers cupped in their hands, the gray smoke rising in hazy columns that wavered and disappeared into the limpid desert air.

Hatshepsut sat cross-legged in the shade of her mother's canopy, her chin in her hand, gazing moodily into space or watching the red sides of the cliff for signs of animal life. At that time of the year the slopes should have yielded glimpses of young deer or ibex, crane or swallow, or even the sleek, undulating shadow of the mountain lion, but the sullen rocks remained silent and at midday began to shimmer. The girl crept away to cool herself in the river. Twice one of the hawks found her and circled slowly, warily, while she knelt and did him homage, Howatit the Mighty, Lord of the Sky.

She thought of her sister as his lazy wings beat the air in great circles. Neferu had also lain by the lake and watched the sky turn from blue to red and the birds gather in the evening. Had he come to her, too, watching her with his black, unwinking eye, waiting? Hatshepsut did not fear him, here in the dazzle of a spring day. As he screamed once and flew toward the palace, she rose and shook the water from her feet, padding through the marshy ground, bemused. It did not seem possible that anything could suffer or age or die in the clamor of spring, and she walked back to the tents and to the quiet, soft-moving people with a tired ache in her. Perhaps her father was right. Perhaps Neferu had been weak.

The coffin still stood against the rock, and the priests still sang. She went to her tent and lay down, and the tears ran down her hot cheeks. She felt altogether alone.

Finally, at sunset on the fourth day, the people gathered outside the grave, and the priests and attendants of the Necropolis took Neferu into the mountain. Thothmes, Aahmose, and Hatshepsut followed, shivering a little as the chill darkness welcomed them, their arms full of flowers, their feet bare. The narrow passage ran straight for a while and then plunged downward and began to twist. The grunts of the perspiring men, the flickering light of the torches, and the slow, reluctant grind of the coffin on the sandy floor brought a rising beat of panic to Hatshepsut's throat.

She walked last, but for a servant, and her shadow leaped and gyrated on the rough walls around her. She fixed her gaze on her mother's gently swaying hips, and when they reached the cold burial chamber at last, she was taken by surprise. Aahmose picked a petal off her linen and let it fall, turning and smiling in sympathy, but Hatshepsut was looking around with dismay. Neferu was being lifted into her stone bed, and the men stood ready to seal it shut. All around her lay her treasures, already strange, already gray with the color of death, formal and oddly untouchable, as if imbued with a hostile and jealous life of their own. The party waited, Hatshepsut not daring to move for fear that she should touch something and trigger—what? The creaking of the coffin lid? The thrusting of now-withering hands against the frail wall of the bandages?

Finally the men stepped back, and Menena intoned the last ritual, his voice losing its sonorous, weighty tone and falling flat and muffled in the solemn, waiting stillness. Aahmose felt her eyes begin to prick but dared not cry. Thothmes stood as if the magic of the tomb had turned him into the same stone from which the huge, painted guardians were carved; but his mind was ranging far and feverishly, and behind his expressionless eyes he hunted, scenting his prey. The High Priest fell silent, turned, bowed, and left them. Thothmes strode forward and laid the flowers on his daughter. Aahmose followed suit, and they went into the passage.

Hatshepsut was alone. It was her turn now. She approached Neferu, conscious all at once that the quality of the stillness had changed, become impatient, as if poised on the brink of some terrible, dumb outburst, and she was afraid. "You are not really dead, are you, Neferu?" she whispered. Behind her the slave holding the last friendly light shuffled uneasily. She flung the flowers to the floor in a shower of green and pink and ran after Pharaoh, calling his name in the pressing darkness.

6

They returned to the palace with great relief, crossing the river hurriedly and scattering to their rooms, hungry for warmth and food and diversions. Thothmes, Aahmose, and Hatshepsut dined together in Aahmose's chambers, sitting on cushions scattered around the floor, surrounded by many lamps, and eating heartily, the slaves gliding back and forth over the cool tiles with wine and roast goose and sweet, hot water. Even Thothmes himself unbent now that the mourning was over. In the morning he would send for his spies and the ferreting would begin, but now he smiled and teased them, looking upon them with the fond eyes of a simple family man.

For Hatshepsut the dark mysteries receded. Neferu was gone. It was time to look forward again, to school and her friends and to Nebanum and the animals. When the meal was over, her mother sent for the musician who had played so engagingly upon the strange new lute, and the woman came and showed the little girl how to make a melody. Hatshepsut was delighted. "I must have one for my own!" she said. "And you must come to the nursery every evening and teach me some more! I would like to learn the barbaric and marvelous songs of your country. Will that be acceptable?" She turned to Thothmes, who nodded indulgently.

"Do what you like," he replied. "As long as you are diligent in your lessons and obey Nozme, you can have a thousand interests. Go now," he said to the woman, and she bowed and blushed, walking to the door with her lute under her arm. "Fine people," Thothmes remarked to Aahmose. "In spite of the taxes my nomarchs levy, they still find time to make most marvelous music. There are northerners singing and playing in every beerhouse in Thebes now, and blind Ipuky is also taking lessons on this lute. Well, Hatshepsut"—he rose from his table, and she rose, too—"back to school tomorrow. Sleep well."

She bowed, making a face. "And back to lazy Thothmes!" she groaned. "I would rather be hunting on the marshes with you this spring, O my father, than sitting beside that grumpy, boring boy."

A look of satisfaction brushed Thothmes' face. "Is that so? And would you also rather have the reins of the chariot in your grasp than the reed pen?"

Her eyes flashed with excitement. "I would! Oh, I would! How wonderful that would be!"

"And what of the reins of government, My Little Flower?" he went on. Aahmose smothered an exclamation and sat upright. "What of a country on which to carve your name, Horus fledgling?" He was half smiling, the heavy eyes lidded, and she looked at him with astonishment.

"There are many things I do not understand, father, but this is one thing I am beginning to learn. A woman cannot rule. A woman"—here she glanced at her mother, who carefully avoided her eye—"is never Pharaoh."

"Why not?"

"Now that is something I really do not understand!" She laughed. Then she sidled up to him, stroking his arm. "May I learn to handle the horses? And cast the throwing-stick?"

"I do not see why a few simple lessons could not be tried. The throwing-stick first, for the horses need a strong wrist."

She danced to the door and to Nozme, waiting outside. "Thothmes will be angry! He will be so cross! Thank you, Mighty Horus. You will not be disappointed in me."

They listened to her excited babbling and Nozme's intermittent comments until the sounds faded. When it was quiet, Aahmose turned to her royal husband. "Great Pharaoh, I have upon occasion, because of my position, been allowed to offer you an opinion. May I do so now?"

Thothmes regarded her with wine-misted affection. He nodded. "Speak. You know how I value your words." He picked out a nut with blunt fingers and tossed it into his mouth.

Aahmose left the floor and settled herself into a chair. "I do not know your mind on this subject of the accession. True, I did not know it before, but while Neferu lived, there was no problem. Thothmes would reign, with her as his Consort, in the manner and tradition of our forefathers and in the Way of Maat. But suddenly nothing is easy. Egypt is left with a royal son but no daughter of an age to legitimize his claims, for surely little Hatshepsut is too young to marry. And while we wait, you, my dear husband, grow older." She hesitated, twisting her hands together nervously while he crunched the nut audibly and stared into space. When he made no comment, she continued, her voice high and her words hurried. "Tell me your thoughts, Noble One! I suffer! I know how you see Thothmes. I know what a disappointment it is to you to have such a one for an only son, and Wadjmose and Amun-mose grown men with lives and families far from Thebes. Will you recall one or the other? You cannot, surely, be thinking of putting the Double Crown on Hatshepsut's head! The priests would not allow it!" Suddenly she flung out her arms beseechingly, and Thothmes looked up at her. "Change nothing, Golden Horus! Do not meddle with Maat! War and murder will be the price!" Her voice rose and abruptly died, and the room fell silent.

Thothmes sipped the wine, savored the bouquet, and plunged his hands into the water bowl. He began to smile. He went to her couch and sat down heavily upon it and, with a peremptory wave of his arm, ordered her down beside him. She came, trembling, and he drew her head close to his and kissed her. "Shall we, then, make another royal daughter? Or a son? Shall I recall my sons from the desert and make them enemies one to another by cleaving them apart with the Crook and the Flail? Shall I make haste and take Thothmes and little Hat to the temple to be married?" His grip on her shoulder was no longer a caress, and his face hardened, but his anger was not directed at her. He looked to the shadowed corners of the room. "They thought to make of me a senile fool to be manipulated like a cowering Nubian eunuch.

"Well"—his grip relaxed, and he lay down, drawing her with him until they lay side by side on the golden bed—"I am Maat, gentle Aahmose, and only I. And while I live, Egypt and I are one. I have made my decision. Indeed, I made it weeks ago, while Neferu still lay in the House of the Dead. I will not have Thothmes, my brainless, soft, mother-loving son, to sit on my throne and govern my country into a shambles. And I will not put a painful, irksome bridle such as he on my little Hat. The chains she shall wear shall be golden. She is Maat. She, more than I, more than stupid Thothmes, is the Child of Amun. I will have her for Crown Prince, and I will have her tomorrow." He heaved himself up and rolled over. She quivered as she felt his weight. "The priests know what they can do with their objections. The people of Egypt love and honor me. They will do my will," he said, bringing his face close to hers.

Yes, she thought as he sought her lips again, yes, but when you are dead, Mighty One, what then?

Thothmes' announcement on the following day rocked the country as no event had done in two hundred years of occupation, war, and privation. The Royal Heralds sped north and south, dropping their news into the provincial cities and towns like human torches, igniting Memphis, Buto, Heliopolis, and sending the inhabitants running into the streets as if it were a gods' day. In the fields and on the farms, the peasants listened, shrugged, and bent to the sowing once more. The Good God did what was right, and their interest ceased at that point. South in Nubia, west in the desert, the men of Kush and the nomad Shasu heard the news with wary ears, their noses set to sniff the wind of change blowing in Egypt, whether it be the first stirrings of the death throe or a tightening of the grip of power. But in the palace the young Thothmes heard his father out in a stony silence, his handsome face betraying nothing of the unrest that now crystallized into hatred. Mutnefert, his fat mother, tore off her clothes and rolled in the dirt of the palace gardens, her hopes thwarted and her future uncertain.

Only Hatshepsut received the news without passion. She heard her father's words without expression, her wide, dark eyes on his face. She nodded coolly. "I am now the Crown Prince Hatshepsut?"

"Yes."

"I will be Pharaoh?"

"Yes."

"You have the power to make it so?"

He smiled. "Yes again."

"What of the priests?"

The question startled him. He looked down at her in her grubby kilt, the ribbon in her youth-lock undone, one tiny sandal unfastened, and felt a wave of affection mingled with awe. Sometimes she seemed unfathomable to him, not a child but one who communed directly with the God and carried his aura with her. He felt the will of her, the questing, unformed power in her, waiting for fruition, for purpose.

He answered her as if she were one of his ministers. "I spoke with Menena in the night. He is not happy. In fact he is outraged, but I pointed out to him that it is my prerogative to put another High Priest in his place."

He had done more than threaten Menena, but he knew that to tell Hatshepsut the true cause of her sister's death would be to load the small brown shoulders with more grief than they could bear. Besides, he was reluctant to expose an affair so sordid that it could easily erupt into a major scandal. He only knew that his little flower must not suffer, although he felt guilty of his own relief at Neferu's passing.

A priest of the temple had come to him in the early hours, whispering of secret meetings at night under the trees, Menena and another, and the bribery of sorcerers. Thothmes had listened with satisfaction and had sent for Menena. He had looked at the face of his one-time friend with loathing and some admiration, for Menena had not betrayed his fear by so much as the twitch of an eyebrow.

The High Priest had made his prostration and was told to rise. He had waited politely, standing with his eyes fixed on the wall somewhere beyond Thothmes' helmet, his hands hidden in his robe. For the last time Thothmes saw the man who had once been father, brother, and confidante to him, the man to whom he had given great power out of gratitude and love, the man who had been, in the end, corrupted by it. Thothmes' regret had welled up and then evaporated.

"I know all," he had said quietly, his voice the gentle purr that always sent his servants scurrying. "How clumsy of you, old friend! With Neferu-khebit dead and my son married to little Hat, great powers would come to the priests of the temple in the event of my own untimely passing." He had strode to Menena and had thrust his face so close that Menena was forced to meet his eye. "And what of my own passing, old crow?" Thothmes had hissed. "Were you ready to connive at my own death also? Speak! Speak to me if you value your life!"

Menena had stepped back and dropped his gaze. He smiled, "Mighty Bull, as the God you are all-seeing and all-knowing. What need have I of words? And if I speak, do I not bow my head to the executioner?"

Thothmes had glared at him for a moment more before exclaiming in disgust, "You priests! You scheming, glib hypocrites! And to think that you—you of all my servants—should come to this!" His voice rose, and the veins across his forehead bulged. "You were my friend! My ally in all adversity when we were young together! But you have become a snake, Menena, a foul, slimy, evil thing. You and I have no more to say to each other. Because of our former friendship, I will not have you killed and I will not have your name dishonored forever. You are exiled. In two months, be gone. I, Thothmes, Beloved of Horus, order it to be so until time is ended." He had paused and walked away, standing by his table and staring moodily out into the darkness. "Take your stinking friends with you," he muttered. Suddenly Menena chuckled. Thothmes looked up, startled, his face brick red with new rage, but Menena was already rising from his bow and sidling toward the door.

"Majesty, all that you say is true, every word. But do not think less of me than you think of yourself. For behold! Have I not unwittingly done you a great favor? My heart may be black and consumed with ambition, as you say, but what of your own? And on whose behalf do you growl and shake? On behalf of Thothmes, your son?" He had snickered again and sailed out.

Thothmes had grasped the wine jug and flung it at him as he closed the door. The cedarwood had cracked and little flakes of golden inlay had floated to the floor. He had sat down heavily, panting and trembling. I am growing old, he had thought.

Now, remembering that painful moment, anger quickened his heart-beat.

"The priests mill about, but their duty is to the God, and you are the Child of the God. Is it not so?"

She smiled, he smiled, and they held hands and walked in the garden, admiring the flowers. Thothmes felt ridiculously young again, his head lightened of its load, and for Thothmes the Younger he spared not a thought. I will give him a wife, two wives if he likes, and make him a Viceroy somewhere. But he shall not have my Hat, he told himself happily. He knew such thoughts slipped from beneath the iron discipline of statesmanship and did not belong in a Pharaoh's head, but for once he had followed his heart instead of his head, and he was glad. He would teach her to rule, and together they would go on.

He said suddenly, "Is there anything special that you desire, Hatshepsut? Any favor I may perform? I have not put a happy or an easy load upon you."

She thought for a moment, chewing a stalk of grass. Her face lightened. "A favor? Yes, father, for I owe someone a great favor and am not sure how to pay it. It would be so much easier for you to do."

"What can you possibly owe to anyone?"

"There is a young we'eb priest who did me a kindness a little while ago. Could I ask him if there is anything he needs?"

"Certainly not! What have you to do with a peasant?" He began to scowl, his foot beat a rhythm on the brown path, and the servants hovered, ready for flight or blows.

Hatshepsut spat out the mangled piece of grass and faced him, her hands on her hips, matching his frown. One of the attending girls tittered.

"You promised me a favor, and you have heard what I desire. Pharaoh does not go back on his word. Are all priests not worthy of your glance, Mighty Horus? And this little we'eb, this peasant, did me a great service, such a service that if he had been a noble in your house, you would immediately have made him an Erpa-ha Prince!"

Thothmes' foot was stilled. His eyebrows shot up. "Indeed? An Erpa-ha? Such generosity! For such an honor he must have saved the life of the Crown Prince, at least!"

She stamped her foot to hide the shock of his shrewd probing. "May I speak with him? Order him to my room? Please?"

"This is most interesting, little girl. I think by all means you may summon him. Do it tomorrow, and I shall come and grace this—this peasant with my august presence."

"No!" She swallowed, furious that now, as on that dark night when the khamsin blew, she was in dangerous and unpredictable waters. "He would be afraid if you were present, father. He would not speak, and then I should never know what desire lies closest to his heart."

Thothmes shook his head. "Do what you will!" he replied brusquely, "but you must come to me afterward and tell me all that passes. Most strange, a Prince and a we'eb priest."

He swung back to their walk, and she trotted along behind him. In truth she had forgotten all about Senmut until her father had begun to talk of favors, but now she was excited, and she began to plan her audience. Suddenly she stopped short. She could remember the voice—rough, almost manly, probing, kind—it made her feel warm to think of it, but his face was utterly gone from her mind.

7

The opposite was true for Senmut, scrubbing in the temple on his hands and knees. His days had been harried, his nights haunted and dream-ridden. It was always the Princess that he saw, pointing an accusing finger at him while the fearsome Followers of His Majesty rushed in to arrest him. But as the period of mourning for poor Neferu had continued and nothing happened, Senmut was not able to relax, for his culpability in the face of the poisoning was undeniable and kept him miserable. But at least he had begun to go about his duties without the tension of impending arrest making his spine prickle, his days running together, one like the next.

I have been a fool, he had thought, imagining that somehow I could be more than a servant in the temple. There was a time in this country when even a peasant had a chance of something better, but now only priests, princes, and nobles rule, and I must put all daydreams behind me and settle to my humble duties.

As he had told himself these sensible, calming words, ambition had stirred in him again, and he had sat back on his heels, mopping his forehead and groaning aloud. It was no good. He would never be the model of a little we'eb priest, as his father had hoped, nor could he face the thought of applying for study as a scribe. The incident with Hatshepsut had scared him, and a few days after her escapade he had almost gone to the Chief Scribe of the Temple and applied for admittance, but on the very threshold of the great man's door he had paused, then turned and run back to his cell in horror.

Keep dreaming, his heart told him. Keep hoping for the luck that only the gods can bestow. And keep hoping also that the little Princess is light of mind and will forget that a peasant presumed.

Finally, he stood with his fellows to watch the royal family return from the Necropolis. Benya was with him. That irrepressible young man had returned from Assuan the week before, knowing nothing of the tragedy that had overtaken the palace. He had been supposed to go north with the new-quarried stone, upriver to Medinet Habu, where Pharaoh was building, but nothing could move in the months of mourning for the

Princess. So he and Senmut had ranged throughout Thebes, drinking, talking to the traders and artisans in the markets, standing in the metal-works of the temple to watch the white-hot electrum being mixed and poured, observing the attendants hammering the precious metal into sheets with which to cover the vessels of the God. They could not go to the jewelers, but they spent many hours at the stonemasons' yard, both eager for knowledge. They fondled the granite and limestone that waited to be formed. They manned the huge saws and sweated happily over the jeweled drills that bit so satisfyingly to expose pink and gray marbled convolutions, crystals that sparked in the sunlight, soft alabaster that glowed like sugared honey.

The engineers knew Benya, his thirst for the heart of each rock, his ready wit, and his inexhaustible capacity for work. But Senmut asked questions they could not answer, and his intense probing tired them. They could tell him of the veins in a rock face, and where to drive the wet wooden pegs to cause a true and proper split, or which stone would stand the strain of a certain type of construction and which would crack or crumble; but of ideas, conceptions, perspective, innovations, proportions, all that followed their work or preceded it, they knew nothing.

"You need to talk to one of those," he was told by one irritated workman who indicated with a jerk of his fat elbow the group of tall, white-clad men in short wigs who were gathered in the shade at the far end of the pit, talking over a mountain of scrolls. "They'll tell you all you want to know." He laughed.

Senmut looked and turned away. Architects, the most respected, honored, and lauded men in Egypt. The great and legendary Ineni spoke with the One every day. He held so many posts that he needed his scribe to tell him what they were. But for Senmut there would be no welcoming smile, no sharing.

So he and Benya learned of Thebes. Benya sometimes went off on his own, loving the rough, pulsing night life of the brothels, but to Senmut women were still only his mother, his cousin Mut-ny, and the little beggar girls, thin as papyrus sticks, who threw mud at him in the street. He had no time to discover sexuality and not much inclination. His was a sensuous personality, his appreciation one of lines and curves, the swing of hair, sunlight on white teeth. His strivings were still introverted, obscure. He sat alone in his cell at night, thinking of the buildings he would erect: the deathless, breath-catching monuments that would say, "I, Senmut, did this," to the end of time.

Vain meanderings, he told himself. Sick and fevered dreams.

Two days after Neferu's interment, he and Benya sat under the trees beside the pylon that marked the entrance to the temple. The morning was fresh, and the smell of wet earth was in the air. Spring was slipping into summer, and in the grass around the two boys the daisies and bright cornflowers nodded together. Along the Nile the reeds rose green in the marshes, and the trees—date, pomegranate, tamarisk, the fragrant persea —showed cool green leaves to the new blue sky. Soon the granaries would be full again, and the women would pick the flax and the cotton and begin to make clothes.

Benya had come to say good-bye. Work had begun again on the temple at Medinet Habu, and he had packed his bag and sought out Senmut while the boats were being loaded with equipment and the stone was being settled and strapped to the rafts.

"How long will you be gone this time?" Senmut asked him. He was dismayed to face again his solitary round of chores.

Benya flung himself down beside his friend, the wind ruffling his shining black hair. He lay back with a sigh of satisfaction. "What a morning! It will be good on the river today, nothing to do but sit for hours and hours and watch the water. I do not know when I shall see you again. Perhaps when the construction crews move in, in a couple of months' time. There is still much cutting to do, and my master hates a job that is hurried. When the heat comes and the peasants arrive to labor, then I shall come sailing back."

Senmut looked with envy at the lean, healthy body and the contented, smiling face. "And what shall I do until then? I suppose I ought to go home for a few days and see my family," he finished doubtfully.

Benya shuddered. "What? Leave Thebes—beautiful, ravishing Thebes in the summer—for a farm? Senmut, you have a disease!"

"Thebes has not yet ravished me," Senmut retorted sourly, and, as if in instant derision, the horns atop the temple brayed rudely, signifying that it was the middle of the morning. "I wonder if I would have done better if I had stayed with my parents and Senmen and broken my back in the fields instead of on Mighty Amun's floor."

"O Mighty Amun," Benya intoned with a laugh, his eyes closed, "may Senmut get off your floor and onto your knees. Oooooh, King of Gods."

In spite of himself Senmut laughed, and his mood lightened. Dejection was not natural to him after all.

"What you need is a pretty, singing girl," Benya went on, "to amuse you and flatter you and keep your mind on something more than soap and water. I know just the one. A delicate dish belonging to that greasy Libyan

—what was his name? For a paltry fee I could arrange. . . ." He chattered on, unaware that he had lost his friend.

Senmut had had a sudden picture of the Princess Neferu and her ladies, walking to the temple, sistrums in hand, to do homage to the God. Am I never to be free of her? he wondered. As Benya stopped talking and rose in one lithe, easy motion, Senmut leaned against a tree and looked out upon the gardens toward the guarded path to the palace.

"I go," said Benya. "Embrace me." Senmut rose and hugged his friend. "May Isis protect you," Benya remarked lightly, picking up his pack. They smiled at each other, and Benya turned to go, but in an instant he was hissing in Senmut's ear, "A Follower of His Majesty and a herald! They are coming this way!"

Senmut stepped forward, his heart pounding, his palms suddenly moist. He clenched his fists behind his back, watching the tall, kilted man approach. He hardly saw the herald. His eyes were on the spear held in the huge hand, the knotted muscles of the powerful chest, the flashing gold Eye of Horus on the man's helmet. The man's face was empty. They approached Senmut, and with a soft thunk the butt of the spear hit the ground. The herald bowed, and dazedly Senmut turned to him.

"Senmut, priest to the priests of Mighty Amun?" the herald inquired gently, noting the boy's pallor.

Senmut nodded imperceptibly. It has happened, he thought. Now I am finished.

The herald saluted in the Imperial fashion, right fist to left shoulder. "I bring you a summons from the Crown Prince Hatshepsut Khnum-Amun. She orders you to appear before her in one hour on the edge of Mighty Amun's Lake. Do not be late. Do not speak to her unless she bids you do so, and keep your eyes downcast. That is all." He smiled, bowed again, and strode away, followed by the soldier.

Benya let out a trembling breath. "By Osiris, Senmut, what was all that about? What have you been up to, that the Little One should want to see you? Are you in trouble?"

Senmut turned. Excitement licked his belly, kindled and leaped in his eyes, and he began to grin. He took Benya by the shoulders and shook him. "No, no! No trouble, dear Benya! If I was to be arrested, she would not have sent a herald. I am to have an audience!"

"I can see that!" Benya stepped good-humoredly from his friend's grasp. "But why? Or is it a secret?"

"In a way. I did a service for the Princess. Or no, really I made a foolish blunder, and she—there was a mistake, Benya, and it has haunted me for weeks. I have been sick with it. And now—"

"I can see that I must go with this mystery unsolved." Benya swung his pack over his shoulder once more. "Send me word, Senmut. I must know what passes here. My curiosity is intense. Send me a coherent scroll, written by a sage and sensible scribe, or I shall not speak to you on my return." He began to leave, but turned back. "Are you sure that you are not in trouble?"

"Quite sure. I think"—Senmut spread out his arms in a gesture that was both ecstatic and free—"I think I am going to have a destiny after all."

"I hope you are right. Good-bye, Senmut."

"Good-bye, Benya."

"And send me word!"

"I will!"

Senmut waved to Benya. Before his friend was even out of sight, he began to run to his cell, shouting for a slave. There must be water and clean linen, and his head must be shaved, and all in one hour. I will, he exulted to himself as he ran, I will. But what he was saying, he did not know.

Exactly one hour later, washed and shaved and clad in rustling, starched linen, he topped the little grassy hill and paused, looking down on the western edge of the Holy Water. Far to his left, bobbing quietly, its golden masts and silver bows flashing in the late sun, lay the God's Barque. But his gaze did not stop there, for below him, on gay cushions spread over blue reed mats, his destiny waited. Two women and a little girl. Yes, it was she, he thought with an unfamiliar spurt of pleasure. She was kneeling on the ground next to a wicker basket, talking to Nozme and Tiyi who sat beside her. In that moment of hesitation she sensed his coming and looked up, at once motioning to the women, who drew away together. She rose and stood, waiting. It seemed to him that he was walking down the hill forever, but suddenly he was on his knees, his arms outstretched and his face pressed to the warm, sweet grass.

She touched him softly on the shoulder with one foot. "So, priest, you have come," she said. "You may rise."

He climbed to his feet but studiously watched his toes.

After a moment she gave an exclamation of annoyance. "Look at me! Such silly manners do not suit you, you who cared not one bit to drag me all over my own domain!"

Her voice had not changed; it was still imperious, challenging, with the high, piping treble of a child. But as he raised his head and met her wide-set black eyes and saw the firm, square chin below her large and

well-formed mouth, he was conscious of shock. She was the same and yet
not the same, still tall and thin with the flighty bones of her age, but
somewhere in the past three months she had shed total childhood. He
immediately sensed that she held within her a promise of young womanhood to come. There was that, and more. A new consciousness of blood
and history, a dim and confused power that lurked far back behind those
measuring eyes, that tiny smile.

They regarded one another for a while, after which Hatshepsut nodded,
as if satisfied, and waved him to the cushions.

"Sit here, beside me. I fear I do not have a nice, filthy old blanket, but
will my nice, filthy old reed mat do? You know, I had quite forgotten what
you looked like, but seeing you again I wonder how that could ever have
been so. You have not changed much, have you?" She leaned closer. "Are
there any other girls who have been pulled out of Amun's Lake lately?"
She laughed, and he smiled back at her. She put both hands into the
basket and drew out two kittens, one of which she put carefully in his
white lap. "Nebanum's cat had these, and he gave them to me. They are
especially holy. Their mother came from the temple of Bast and can see
demons in the night. Would you like one?"

Senmut stroked the gray fur, and the kitten mewed and pawed at him
helplessly. They were handsome animals, sleek and thin, with pointed
noses and wily, slanted eyes. He had the Egyptian's love of cats, and he
thanked her gravely for her generosity.

"I must have my phylarch's permission, but I do not think he will mind,
particularly as its mother is so distinguished a cat."

He had heard of the strange, orgiastic rituals that surrounded the
worship of the cat goddess Bast, and he looked at Hatshepsut curiously,
but she only smiled back at him, her head to one side. Bast was of the
old order, almost forgotten here in cosmopolitan Thebes where Amun,
Mut, and Khonsu reigned supreme.

"Well, priest, what have you been doing since last we met?" she asked
him.

He put the kitten on the grass and clasped his knees, looking out over
the stillness of the lake before he answered. He did not know the reason
for this audience, informal as it was, and so he could not predict the
outcome, but he knew that he must choose his words carefully. The
thought of using Hatshepsut never crossed his mind. He wished only to
get to know her better, for it seemed to him that fate had drawn them
together and somehow given him a new friend. Behind the wall of rigid
caste that separated him forever from this golden child he felt the groping
of a kindred spirit, and when he spoke, it was with ease.

"I have been attending to my duties in the temple as a good priest should, Princess."

"Scrubbing floors and running errands?"

He glanced at her sharply, but there was no malice in her face. "Yes, that is so."

"And have you no other plans than to do that until you die?"

She was looking at his long, tapered fingers interlocked around the linen and at his square, rugged shoulders. Beneath the straight, black brows his eyes were calm, and she felt at home with him, not wishing to tease or bait him as she did Thothmes. How much better than silly old Thothmes he would be at handling the chariot and the spear, she thought.

He swiftly looked into her face, but this time she did not smile. "I have dreams, Highness, but so do all men, secret dreams that have little to do with reality."

"True. But I have heard it said that a strong and willful man may make his dreams live if he but cares enough."

"I am not yet a man, Noble One."

The words said everything and nothing. Senmut, with his canny up-bringing, was no stranger to diplomacy.

She sighed and put her kitten back in the basket.

He made as if to rise, thinking the meeting had come to an end, but she put a hand on his bare arm, and he jumped.

"Do you know that I am now Crown Prince?" she said softly.

He inclined his head. "Indeed, Highness, it is Egypt's good fortune."

Benya had laughed, as usual, when he was told. "Wait until Pharaoh dies!" he had hooted. "Then we shall see who ascends the Horus Throne. I wager it will not be a slip of a girl, lovely though she may be." Senmut had agreed, though with more decorum. Now he was not so sure.

"I owe you a favor, priest, and it is my pleasure to pay it now. My father says that I may have what I like, and I want to grant you something." She looked at him anxiously. "You will not refuse?"

"Highness, you owe me nothing. I did what I thought to be my duty and nothing more. But if you feel that my duty deserves reward, then I will not refuse."

"Fine words!" she mocked kindly. "Then think. What do you wish?"

Senmut watched the swans glide by. He saw gulls wheeling and little moorhens bobbing and the two nursery attendants idly gossiping. He heard the Princess's light breaths, and from the corner of his eye he caught the flutter of her gossamer linens in the breeze. But these things were suddenly engulfed in the ensuing seconds as his long, harrowing ambition rose to drown all else. He had the instant and very clear feeling that some inner hand moved to present them all—the dreams, the hopes, the night agonies—to his unbelieving mind. He thought of his father, Ka-mes, who wished only security and anonymity for his son, and of his phylarch with the sick belly, who whined continually; but above all he thought of Pharaoh, the giant, causing all to be.

I know what I want, he thought with certainty, and I know now that I have not waited and refused all else in vain. He knelt before Hatshepsut.

"Highness, I want more than anything in the world to study architecture under the great Ineni. That, and that only, is my wish."

She pouted. "You do not want a fine house?"

"No."

"What about some land? A couple of wives? A great estate?"

He laughed, a great guffaw of release that came from his happy soul. "No, no, and no! I want only to be an architect, however insignificant. I do not know whether or not I shall be a good one, but I must find out! Highness, do you understand?"

Hatshepsut drew herself up haughtily. "You sound now like my dear dead one, Osiris-Neferu. She was always asking me whether or not I understood her, and I must confess that sometimes I found it very boring to have to try. But, yes"—she took his hand, and his own closed around hers involuntarily—"I think I do understand. I have shortened the dream, have I not?"

He bent and kissed the little palm. "Indeed," he said fervently, "you have shortened it by a lifetime!"

She withdrew her hand and got up, clapping to summon the servants. "You are sure?" she pressed.

"Very, very sure."

"Then I will speak with my father, who will speak with Ineni, who is a very grumpy, cross old man and will not like to have a new pupil one bit, and you shall then be happy. I order it!"

Senmut bent and picked up the kitten, which gave a sleepy protest.

"Carry the basket!" she said to Nozme.

Then she was gone, leaving Tiyi to fold up the mat and gather the cushions. Senmut, alone and stupefied with delight, realized that she had not even waited for his homage.

At dinner that night Thothmes had his daughter eat beside him so that she could tell him of her meeting. The whole escapade amused him greatly, and he listened carefully. When she told him what this cheeky upstart of a we'eb wanted, he let out a roar that was half laughter and half outrage. The company turned and stared at him anxiously, but he yelled at the musicians to keep on playing and sent a runner scurrying to the home of Ineni. In the meantime he made Hatshepsut tell him over again what had transpired, snorting and chuckling in between mouthfuls of grilled pigeon.

Hatshepsut was put out. He was not giving her time to eat at all, and her food kept getting cold.

At last Ineni appeared and bowed, immaculate and cool as ever despite the fact that he had left five courses and his new dancers to answer the peremptory Imperial summons. Ineni was tall, taller than most men, and still slim, although in his late sixties. His aquiline nose jutted over a straight, purposeful mouth; and his head, fantastically knobbed and planed, was shaved. He disdained the wig. If it were not for the odd, knowing twinkle in his gray eyes, his face would have been harsh and unforgiving. But he knew when and how to laugh, and he was saved from the driving pain of genius by his love of life.

"Ineni," Thothmes barked, "sit here, beside Hatshepsut. Her Highness has something to tell you." Then he began to laugh all over again.

Not one indication of the architect's bewilderment showed on his face as he bent his spare frame and accepted the wine proffered by Pharaoh's slave. He drank slowly, looked at his rings, and waited.

Hatshepsut was angry. She told her story for the third time, in quick, terse sentences. But Ineni did not laugh, as her father had done; he listened intently, his eyes on her face. When she had finished and was at last opening her mouth to stuff it with tempting barley bread, he asked, "Highness, you say this priest is nothing but a we'eb? That he is a peasant from the country?"

She had had enough. "I say that I order you to be quiet and allow me to eat my dinner. And I say that afterward I will answer all your questions, for I am famished, and even the servants have had their fill."

He waited, Thothmes waited, Aahmose waited, the slaves waited, and she ate and drank until she could swallow no more. Then she waved her table away and settled back with a sigh.

"He is a clever and most suitable young man. I like him. He is kind and respectful, and he doesn't complain like—" She had been going to say "like Thothmes" but remembered just in time what her father had told her about keeping her thoughts to herself, so she finished, "like some people. Also, I most surely owe him this favor, and I have granted it, subject to my father's permission. Oh, I hope, honored Ineni, that you will at least give him a chance to prove whether or not he has the ability. He pines for such a chance."

Thothmes said, "Hmmmm."

Ineni said nothing, but a slow, wry smile lit his cold gray eyes. He, too, liked his new Crown Prince and found her a good deal more decisive and capable than the youth who ought to have been carrying that title but who sulked in his mother's suite, refusing to come out. At last he said, "Your Highness's word is my delight to obey. Send this person to my chambers, and I shall teach him."

In truth he did not want a new pupil, not at his age. He wanted to retire soon and enjoy the blessings of long and faithful service: his wives, his son, his gardens. But he could not refuse this request.

We shall see how far the little Princess has judged a character, he thought as he walked outside, signaling for his torchbearers and his guards at the entrance to the palace. I have been too long a servant of Pharaoh to imagine that he will be anything more than a poor, frightened little scrap with more ambition than is good for him, he mused, walking home in the scented, star-strung night. He was tired.

Early the following morning Senmut was awakened by a knock on the door, and before he could get off his pallet, the room was full of people. His phylarch, bleary-eyed and put out, greeted him sharply, and behind him stood two slaves in the blue and white costume of the palace.

"You are ordered to leave your cell and go at once to the chambers of the noble Ineni," the phylarch said with irritation. "I do not know what it is all about, and I do not wish to know. Hurry and put on your linen. The men will pack your belongings." He turned and left without another word.

Senmut stood sleepily while his box was opened and his few belongings were laid disdainfully in it. There was his drinking cup, his sandals, his best linen sheath, and little else. The few scrolls he had borrowed from the temple library were placed solemnly on the pallet, already stripped of cloak and blanket, and the men vanished before he could shout for them to wait and show him the way.

He splashed hurriedly in the stone ewer and flung on his kilt from the day before. He nearly ran down the guard who was waiting to escort him into the palace. He apologized, but the man merely made a sign for him to follow, and together they left the temple. Senmut did not look back. He had nothing to regret and no affection for his fellow we'ebs. He lifted his head and sniffed the morning, pacing behind the stolid soldier along the deserted, dawn-lit paths.

In a few minutes they passed beneath the first of the royal pylons and onto pavement lined with gold-plated statues of the God Thothmes. They soon passed the groves of sycamore and stood at the western door of the palace itself. Here his companion stopped and spoke quickly to the guards, and soon they were past them, and Senmut entered the royal precincts for the first time.

Every trace of sleep had left him, and he looked about with awe and some disappointment. It was not, after all, so different from the lines of priests' cells.

He did not realize until later that he was nowhere near the royal apartments or the great audience chambers. He had entered directly into the wing that held offices and ministries, a place of functional industry and quiet efficiency. Pharaoh was an almost daily visitor, but he came here to coordinate, not to be feted, so there were no evidences of pomp. The passages were small, clean, and quiet. The tiles were decorated with little scenes from the lives of the officials—weighing grain, hearing cases in the Courts of Justice, visiting the provinces, executing floggings or deaths— and on the doors that led to more offices and more passages were the emblems of each minister's power.

I shall never find my way through all this, Senmut thought excitedly. It will take me many hentis just to get out.

His escort suddenly stopped before a door wrought delicately of cedar-wood and traced in silver. He knocked, and it was immediately opened by a young slave who bowed deeply.

"You are expected," he said, haltingly.

A new acquisition from Syria, Senmut guessed from his likeness to Benya. His guard also bowed. Senmut, cold at the prospect of an unknown future, felt that he was losing a friend. Before he could draw another breath, the one had gone and the other was bowing him into a room so filled with the bright morning sunlight that he blinked and stood stu-pefied, like an animal emerging from its burrow.

"Come forward," a cool, clear voice said. "I wish to have a good look at you."

Senmut stepped away from the closed door. In front of him stretched what seemed to be a mile of white and black tiled floor that ended at last at a very large and very heavy table on which were piled scrolls of every size and quality. On his right the wall rose straight to the ceiling, una-dorned save for a mural at the top depicting the God Imhotep construct-ing the Great Pyramids. On his left there was no wall, but a stone walkway beyond which the royal lake glittered. Between path and lake many trees and shrubs grew right up to the room, so that Senmut felt as if he was on the borders of a forest, the sun pouring in above the tops of the shrubs, able to illuminate the master's work until Ra sank below the horizon.

A man stood at the far end, beside the desk. Senmut had never seen

Ineni before, but he knew immediately that he was facing the greatest architect since the God-man who had planned the royal tombs which were picked out of the mural by the sun's rays. He was a man to respect, even to fear, Senmut knew instantly, but he was also a man to love.

Ineni waited, his arms folded, and Senmut squared his shoulders and went to meet him. He bowed, and Ineni smiled.

"I am Ineni," he said quietly, "and you are the priest Senmut, my new pupil. Is it so?"

"It is so."

"Why are you here?"

Senmut smiled back, and the other man thought, Here is no crawling priest. Ineni's eyes traveled the thick brows, the dark, challenging eyes, the high cheekbones, and the firm, sensual mouth of the boy, and he knew that here were the makings of greatness. My Princess spoke the truth, he said to himself. A young promise.

"I am here to learn how to turn royal dreams into reality. I was born for this, Noble Ineni."

"Were you? And do you believe yourself to have the purpose, the health, the power that will keep you working until you fail or succeed or die?"

"I am untried, Master, but I believe so."

Ineni unfolded his arms and pointed to the overflowing desk. "Then we will begin. You are to read all those, and you will not stop, except to eat and sleep, until you know all that is within them. Through there"— he indicated another, smaller door—"is your bed. This lad is your slave and will bring you all you need. In a day or two we will talk again, and then—" he moved away from the desk, in the direction of the door, "then we will see. I begin early, as you have seen, and I work late. I expect you to do the same. And do not worry." His voice echoed, and his hand was on the door. "I like you. The Crown Prince likes you. What more do you need?"

With a nod he was gone, and Senmut let out his breath, raised his eyebrows, and went to the scrolls. He could not see to the bottom of the pile, but he put his hand on them, conscious of the moment. Here was the key, here under his hand, smooth and inviting. "Bring me some food and a little wine," he said absently to the boy hovering behind him.

He picked up the first scroll and, sitting behind the desk, unrolled it and began to read.

After a year of grueling, eye-scorching, head-spinning reading, poring over the old plans and diagrams, learning the uses of his trade, he had at last been allowed out to some of the many building sites that Ineni oversaw. He conquered the plane, the surveyor's instruments, the draftsman's pen. His quick eye and natural gift enabled him to point out a faulty angle, smooth away a difficult problem in construction, and all the time he drank knowledge in great drafts of pleasure. He was happy, really happy for the first time in his life, and nothing existed for him outside the time he spent with Ineni.

Ineni was pleased and surprised. He grew to enjoy the company of the boy, who was swiftly turning into a handsome man with a clear and quick mind, and he increasingly allowed Senmut to voice his opinion on each project. The temple at Medinet Habu was completed. Others at Ombos, Ibrim, Semneh, and Kumneh rose year by year. Only Thothmes' pet work, the temple for Osiris at Abydos, remained closed to Senmut. On this Ineni alone was allowed to work, and when the Great One came to consult his architect, Senmut would wander out into the gardens and down to the lake.

Senmut sometimes wished that he could catch a glimpse of the little Princess, but he never did. It was as if they had never met. He met Ineni's son, the young and naughty Menkh, and from him learned of Hatshepsut's many escapades: how on her first duck hunting trip to the marshes she had flung the throwing-stick straight and sure and brought down a bird, and how after the first shout of triumph she had burst into tears and cradled the bloody body in her arms. He heard also from Menkh, who often wandered into his father's office after a morning in the schoolroom, that the Princess was doing well on the military training ground. Aahmes pen-Nekheb goaded and yelled at her as at any young recruit, but she bore it well, sallying back at him, trotting the war-horses around the circuit as if she had been born a man. Senmut liked Menkh. Menkh carried with him the languid, friendly assurance of his father's rank but approved of Senmut's wish to move up into the circles of power, and he treated Senmut with light affection. The young men found much in common beneath their separate stations.

Soon after his lessons under Ineni had begun, Senmut had gone into the marketplace of Thebes and had hired a scribe. He had dictated a letter to Benya, telling all he could as long as his money held out, for the scribe had charged by the word and the words had come pouring out. He had received an exuberant reply a month later, but Benya had not returned home until the following spring, and Senmut had found himself too busy to spend much time with his friend.

He acquired a very handsome armband of electrum with his new position emblazoned on it for all the world to see, and his linen now was bordered with golden thread. He was still a priest and would remain so, but he seldom went to the temple. The rites of worship did not interest him very much, and he often wandered among the obelisks and pylons of Karnak, dreaming of what he would do if he were able to add to the already vast sprawl of stone. Thothmes had had a roof of cedar constructed between the third and fourth pylons, and Senmut sat in the cool, echoing dimness, his back to a lotus column, listening to the daily comings and goings of the boon seekers and the dancers and gift-laden priests, his mind full of the figures and the ideals of his chosen profession. He enjoyed the homage he received from those who had so recently passed him by without a glance, and it gave him a comfortable, secure feeling to stand in the quarries with the other architects, poring over plans in the shade while the stonemasons toiled in the broiling heat. But he did not become complacent. He was too busy and too hardheaded for that. He knew that it was a long way from an apprenticeship to the confidence of Pharaoh, even if his robes now shimmered in the sun and his wine came from Charu.

Neither did he forget the girl who had been responsible for the change in his fortunes. But it seemed to him that she had swiftly passed over him, her debt discharged, and was racing toward maturity with her aristocratic friends.

8

It was not entirely true that she had forgotten him. Sometimes, when she thought of it, she inquired of Ineni how his latest pupil was doing; and as long as things were going well, she saw no reason to interfere. Besides, he seemed to be paddling his own skiff with remarkable skill, and she quickly turned to other concerns.

Two years after their first meeting, at harvest time in the month of Payni, when the land was so parched and brown that it seemed about to burst into flame and the only greenness on which to rest the eye was contained, vividly and lushly, in the palace enclosure, Hatshepsut found, much to her surprise, that she had become a woman, and the rite of passage was performed. Her youth-lock was removed by her priest, Ani, the same who had mourned so for Neferu, and Nozme gathered up her toys and the small items of nursery furniture and stowed them away to be called for again by the sem-priests when they prepared her for her burial. Ani burned the hair in a silver bowl while Hatshepsut, looking on indifferently, reflected on the self she had been two years ago when Neferu went to her tomb and how in such a short time the memory had grown ever less hurtful, until Neferu seemed to belong solely to a childhood almost over now.

The acrid smoke from the burning hair hung about her bedroom on this last day of her occupancy, and the sweat ran down her back as she thought of the cool depths of the palace lake. User-amun was waiting, and Hapuseneb, and she could barely conceal her impatience while Ani droned on. When it was all over, she said a formal and lengthy good-bye to Nozme, now to be retired to the home that had been built for her just outside the grounds, and ran for the trees as soon as decency would permit, for the call of the water was greater than the call of duty. But later she regretted her rudeness and sought out the old woman.

In the early evening she was escorted to her new apartment. It was not much bigger than the nursery and not much less spartan, for she was not yet designated Heiress or Great Royal Wife. School still continued, but without Nozme to watch her with a stern, unwinking eye. She was, at twelve, relatively free. Her new attendants were more respectful and easier to order around, but her father was more in evidence, seeking her out, sending for her, arriving unannounced in the mornings before she left for the schoolroom, and he was a far more formidable guardian than Nozme had ever been. The soldiers at her door were handpicked members of the Followers of His Majesty, and she seldom managed to evade them to visit Nebanum privately or to feed the horses.

One afternoon when the air in her bedroom hung like hot syrup and she had pulled her cushions to the floor near the wind catcher in order to sleep better, her mother was announced.

Hatshepsut had seen little of Aahmose since the ceremony. They had met at dinner and talked of the progress of her studies and her prowess with the throwing-stick. They had joked of a future for the girl as a charioteer, but of her new position as Crown Prince Aahmose had said nothing, and the knowledge that her mother disapproved had driven a wedge between them. Hatshepsut was puzzled and hurt. She was still young enough to need maternal reassurance, understanding, and sympathy, and it never occurred to her that Aahmose's seeming coldness sprang from an excessive anxiety about the future of the Flower of Egypt.

The visit was a surprise, and Hatshepsut jumped up from her nest by the wall and ran to embrace her mother, who was dressed in the blue that she so loved. Aahmose hugged her and dismissed the servants, and they were alone. The palace was quiet. Aahmose smiled uncertainly and remained on her feet, but Hatshepsut flung herself down in a chair, crossing her legs.

"I was trying to get cool," she said. "The fans are annoying. They swish, and I cannot sleep. Are you not resting, mother?"

"I found sleep impossible, too. I worry about you, Hatshepsut, and I wanted to talk to you about your dress."

"My dress?" She was as unconcerned about what she put on as she had always been.

"Yes. I think that now you are almost a woman, you should be wearing a sheath instead of running about in a boy's kilt like a little wild animal. Once the youth-lock is gone, every girl wears the dress of a woman. And you, in particular, Hatshepsut, should be careful about what you put on."

"But why? I may be nearly a woman, but I am not yet. And if I wear the sheath, I shall no longer be able to climb and to race Menkh. Is it so important, Noble Mother?"

"Yes, it is." Aahmose spoke with a firmness that she did not feel. This person with the long, brown legs and slim waist, swinging a foot and regarding her with affectionate condescension, was perilously close to being a stranger. "It is not fitting for a princess to be seen in male attire."

"But I am not a princess," Hatshepsut replied evenly. "I am a prince, and not just any prince. I am Crown Prince. Father said so. One day I will be Pharaoh, and no woman can be Pharaoh; therefore I am a prince." She giggled suddenly, and Aahmose once more saw the girl beneath the layers of budding womanhood. Hatshepsut got up. "I cannot see what difference it will make, whether I continue to put on my kilts or slide into the sheath. I do not want to be a woman yet, O my mother," she finished earnestly, putting an ingratiating arm around Aahmose's ample waist. "How can I stand with steady feet in the bucking chariot or draw the bow or throw the spear if all the time I have to be careful to push my linen out of the way?"

"So it is the bow and the spear now, is it?"

"Why, yes. Pen-Nekheb is pleased with me, and father has agreed."

"And what of Thothmes? Is he still a student of pen-Nekheb's?"

"I suppose so." Hatshepsut tossed her head. "He does not speak to me anymore."

Feeling a twinge of genuine alarm, Aahmose grasped her daughter's arm tightly, pushed her down onto the couch, and stood over her. "Listen to me, Hatshepsut. I have lived on the earth far longer than you, and I know that between the wish and its fulfillment is a pit, and the pit is dark and full of the snakes of disappointment and despair."

Hatshepsut looked up at her with astonishment. The tone was authoritative, commanding, and most unlike the gentle woman who was renowned for her sweetness and good humor. She sat straighter as Aahmose went on.

"Your father has appointed you Crown Prince, and Crown Prince you are. The future seems to you to be an unending field of green, delightful and vast as the paradise of the gods. But your father will go to the God before too many years have flown, and then you will be at the mercy of the priests—and Thothmes."

The girl blinked and stirred. All flippancy had left her, and she was frowning. "Thothmes? But he is a weak and silly boy."

"That may be so, but he is the royal son on whom the Double Crown will rest one day, no matter what your father does in his lifetime to prevent it. And you will have to marry him, Hatshepsut. There is no doubt in my mind about that."

"But the priests serve Amun, and I am the Incarnation of Amun here on earth. What can Thothmes do about that?" Her chin shot up, and her eyes flashed.

"There are many in the temple who would wish a weak and simple

Pharaoh so that their riches may increase, and moreover, no one is going to believe that a young and untried girl could shoulder the weight of a country, nay, an empire such as this, built on war and maintained by eternal vigilance."

"But by the time my father ascends to the Barque of Ra, I shall not be an untried girl. I shall be a woman."

"I thought that you did not want to be a woman," Aahmose said craftily.

The girl's jaw dropped. She returned her mother's smile with whimsical ruefulness. "I think that I do want to be Pharaoh," she answered, "but I do not want to be a woman just yet."

"All the same," Aahmose said, returning to soberness, "you will shed the garb of youth and array yourself properly, as befits your station."

"I will not!" Hatshepsut sprang to her feet again. "I will wear what I please!"

Aahmose rose, too, and, regally gathering her robes about her, walked to the door. No breath of air stirred at her passing. "I can see that Khaemwese is becoming too old to tutor the royal children. He has not been teaching you the proper respect due to your mother. Therefore I shall consult your immortal father. You are a spoiled and willful child, Hatshepsut, and it is time that you settled down to the responsibilities of your position. We will see." She floated out, her back rigid under the transparent blue linen.

Hatshepsut made a face and sank back onto her cushions mutinously. Never! she thought. And though the afternoon wore on and she was tired, she could not sleep.

Thothmes did not force the sheath upon her. When Aahmose had broached the subject, he had snapped brusquely, "Let the child wear what she pleases. It is not yet time to smother her in the trappings of adulthood, and I do not want her studies made irksome for her. I have spoken." So Aahmose, rebuffed, had retired to her suite with an aching head, and had not beseeched Isis for guidance. The Goddess must have better things to do, else she would have answered the petitions a long time ago, she had thought.

Hatshepsut continued to run, half-naked and disheveled, through the palace and all the gardens, growing like one of the beautiful blue lotus flowers she so loved, wild and exotic. In the classroom together with Menkh, User-amun, Hapuseneb, Thothmes, and the others, she began to assimilate wisdom of a sort. But on the training ground she learned other lessons: how to hit a target while balancing in the chariot, how to aim for the heart, how to feint, how to anticipate the enemy. She loved to stand under her canopy in the broiling heat and watch the drill: the dust swirling; the leather-clad troops answering the hoarse, barked commands of the Drill Commander and wheeling in fascinating precision; the sun glinting off the tips of spears; the gold-tooled shields. She was so much a part of the scene, straight and eager in her little kilt and bare feet, that from a distance she did indeed look like a little prince reviewing the men, taking the salute of raised spears with grave importance.

Life was sweet to her. Every nerve in her perfect body was keyed to the task at hand, even when the targets blurred or the men murmured or shouted encouragement. And she knew that somewhere close by her father stood, his feet apart, his hands on his mighty hips, waiting to approve. The days rolled by, the God's feast days came and went, the Night of the Tear produced without fail the turgid floods, and Egypt sang for her month after month its song of homage.

One morning in the month of Thoth, in the chill, predawn darkness when she was deeply asleep, curled under blankets and warmed by braziers, her father woke her. She felt his hand on her shoulder, shaking her gently, and she was instantly awake. She saw him vaguely, a great muffled hulk against the tiny glow of her night-light, and she sat up, shivering. He put a finger to her lips and motioned for her to get out of her couch, and she obeyed, her mind still full of warm dreams. Her slave had unaccountably disappeared, and she fumbled for something to wear. He thrust a thick woollen cloak and a pair of sandals at her, and she put her feet into the shoes, tying the leather thongs with stiff fingers, then tightly wrapping the cloak about her against the morning's bite. He left, and she followed him, wondering at last what it was all about. When they had tiptoed down the passage and out the private door into her little walled garden, he paused. The stars still shone in the black sky, and the palm trees lining the river some way off were only smudges of a darker darkness. The wind sought her skin with its cold, probing fingers as she waited patiently for the explanation.

Pharaoh bent and whispered, "We are going on a little trip—you, me, your mother, and Ineni—and none must know where. We are going to cross the river."

"To the dead?" She thought she felt them in the eternal brooding hush of the hours before daylight, watching in the shadows.

"Beyond them. It is not far, but we must pole our own boat and walk without our Canopy Bearers, so it is best that we go in the cool and return in the late morning." He turned abruptly and struck through the shrubs on the path, and she followed after, silent and smooth as a stalking cat.

They were challenged once, and Thothmes impatiently pushed aside the spear that barred their way and threw back his hood, exposing his blunt features. The soldier bowed in confusion, and they elbowed past him and glided on. The avenue soon swung to the right, and they came to the landing stairs, lapped by water that surged slowly, silkenly in the waning moon's light. Two hooded figures waited motionless, rising and falling with the little skiff that waited there. Thothmes picked up Hatshepsut and swung her unceremoniously to them. Aahmose caught her and settled her on a wooden plank laid rudely across the middle of the vessel.

I am always having adventures on water! Hatshepsut thought as Thothmes took the pole from Ineni's grasp and pushed off with one powerful thrust. He took off his cloak and flung it onto the bottom of the boat. He began to work the pole again, and Hatshepsut watched in awe, for she had never before seen her father do anything that a slave should. She heard his deep, regular breaths and saw the rhythmic rippling of his muscles with something like alarm.

What are we doing out here in the middle of the rising river? What has gone wrong? Are we running away? Has Egypt been invaded?

But she knew that if that was the case, Thothmes would never have run but would have marched out to fight. As she began to doze with the rocking and the swish of the passing water, her father got out of the boat and pulled them to the Stairs of the Dead. It was here that Neferu had disembarked, and her grandmother, and the little princes. Hatshepsut felt a quiver of superstitious fear as she was lifted free and put down on the cold, gray stone. Her mother followed. Ineni handed Thothmes his cloak and stepped smoothly after them, tying the trailing rope to the mooring post. Then without a word he took the lead. They turned south, following the line of white foam that lay beside their feet. Over the river they could see the many lights of Thebes, warm and friendly, reaching out to them over the deep-flowing Nile.

They did not look to their right. The temples and empty, white ribbons of road exuded a desolation, a warning, a listening, brooding atmosphere of hostility that hurried them along, their eyes averted. Once in a while Ineni would pause and stand, looking to the cliffs behind, muttering to himself. He would then shake his head, and they would trudge on, each islanded in the thoughts that accompany such a trek in the cold darkness. Hatshepsut was just beginning to wonder whether perhaps the Mighty Bull had gone mad when Ineni stopped short with an exclamation of satisfaction, and they gathered around him. The sky was a little lighter. They still could not see each other's faces, but the temples no longer straggled above them to the west, and the edge of the tumbled cliffs could be made out, hazy but discernible. The city across the river had been left behind, but a solitary, high light farther south proclaimed Luxor and Amun's other home.

Ineni pointed to the ground and then to the western cliffs. "The path is here, Majesty," he said, his voice somehow tiny and private and rather lost. "We must turn inland. There will be stones in the sand and rough places. Perhaps the Prince should walk behind her mother, and you follow me." Thothmes nodded, and they started off once more.

There was indeed a path, a wandering goat track through the stunted acacia and straggling fig trees. Hatshepsut, bringing up the rear, began to watch her feet in concentration. Sharp rocks abounded, some lightly covered with sand, and the path wound and swerved as though made by the staggerings of a drunken man. Hatshepsut was warmer now with the walking, and the blood began to flow faster through her veins. As daylight slowly found them, she hummed under her breath, hopping and dashing after Aahmose in little spurts; and when Thothmes called a short halt to ask her if they were going too fast for her, she shook her head vigorously, panting, her eyes alight with adventure. It was for Aahmose that they went more cautiously. As the colorless, flat light-without-Ra showed them their surroundings with that strange early-morning clarity, Hatshepsut was amazed at how far they had come. Beyond Ineni's striding, gaunt form she could see the track winding up the long, low hill and disappearing abruptly as it veered to the left and was lost in the bulk of the range that separated Egypt from the desert. As she lowered her gaze to her feet once more, Thothmes raised a hand, and Ineni stood still as if at the reading of his master's thought. The two women waited.

"Ra springs forth once more," Thothmes said. "Here we must wait, and do him homage."

The plain that swept to their left and their right was full of the gray, dull light that was the wash of the Immortal Barque, and the air held an expectant, anxious hush. The little company stood unmoving, all eyes riveted on the ragged teeth of the cliffs that seemed to spring out of the ground at their very feet. The wind suddenly dropped. The rocks and the sand and the bushes and they themselves waited breathlessly for the touch of warmth and life. Hatshepsut stood as if frozen, caught up in the solemn glory of the moment. The minutes seemed to slow to a sonorous importance, to become silently marching golden vanguards for the golden God.

All at once, when the stillness and quiet and waiting could be borne no longer, the tops of the cliffs began to flush pink, and together the four people sank to their knees. Suddenly Thothmes uttered a cry, and Ra lifted, shimmering, over the horizon, heavy and red. The blood of his hand fell upon the rocks, and they leaped into startled color, red, red, their shadows sharp blue-black. As the great orb mounted higher, the color ran all over the worshipers and thundered on to the river, leaving a wake of sizzling yellows, greens, blues. Far back, the mists of night still hung over Thebes, waiting to be royally dismissed.

It was then, for the first time, that Hatshepsut knew what it really felt to be the Daughter of the God, his perfect Incarnation. She rose from the ground and turned, holding her arms out over the city and the river, her outline still limned in fire, her body taut with ecstasy. Her Father mounted higher and higher, and they smiled on one another in understanding, the great Sun and his little daughter.

Thothmes sighed. "Even so did I see him, the Mighty Amun-Ra, rising ever new, when I stood on the towers of Thebes on my coronation morning," he said. "I do not think it will be long before I, too, join him as he sails across the sky. Now we must go on. There is much to be done today, and we have had the blessing of the God this morning."

They turned and began to plod on as the morning grew warm and the birds that nested in the mud alongside the Nile came out and rose in clouds, whistling and piping to the new day.

It did not take them long to reach the part of the path that had seemed to disappear into the cliff. They followed it as it twisted sharply to the left, and they were immediately in shadow. The cliffs loomed on both sides of them, and the way became rockier. The sand was left behind, but they were not hemmed in for long. They veered to the right as a valley began to open out, wider and wider, a valley that burst into view not half a mile from the other side of the cliff and the broad plain through which they had picked their way.

It was a place of utter silence. The sun beat into it, and nothing moved. The floor of the valley ran straight to a towering cliff face that rose, almost sheer, to the sky. To the right and the left the cliff swept toward them, and the path they were to follow wound up the northern face and once more vanished tantalizingly at the summit. To the south, on the valley floor and under the embrace of the farthest cliff, a small pyramid nestled, seeming too sharp with angles, too thrusting to belong to this calm place of wide sweeps and massive, soaring curves. Its white limestone sides glistened in the sun, and around about it lay rubble—gigantic stone blocks, crumbling pillars whose stumps looked like rotten, uneven teeth.

Thothmes spoke of it sadly. "The mortuary temple of Osiris-Mentu-hotep-hapet-Ra," he said, "long forgotten, lying ruined in this place." The atmosphere seemed to oppress him, and he raised his shoulders and shook himself, turning to the path once more.

Ineni and Aahmose straggled after him, but Hatshepsut could not tear herself away from the dreaming quietness. A sense of destiny took hold of her, and she stood gazing at the rock walls, the little pyramid, the yellow and gray sand running from her feet to meet the cliff.

This valley is yours, she said to herself. You are in a holy place. Her eyes slowly traveled again the lordly rising of the cliff, reaching to the vivid blue above. I will build here one day, her mind ran on, but what shall it be? I do not yet know. All I know is that here is peace and a fitting place for the Daughter of Amun. She felt the consecration, as if the God had rushed to her in assent.

When her mother called to her anxiously, it was as if she, too, were stone. Hatshepsut could lift her feet only with difficulty. The valley called back to her mutely, and she wanted to begin the long walk to the temple of her ancestor, but she shook her head in denial and trudged after the others. Yet the magic of the place stayed with her, and she did not hum or scuff at the stones that lay in her path.

They soon reached the top of the rise, and the track followed its crest before dropping suddenly into the long, snaking defile that presented itself to their view. As they slithered to the bottom, they found that they had at last reached Ineni's destination.

"This is the place of which I spoke," he said to Thothmes. "Only the most curious of travelers would dare to venture here, and as you can see, a hundred royal tombs could be cut throughout the defile, their entrances forever screened from prying eyes by the great rocks that lie everywhere. Besides"—he mopped his brow and pointed—"there is She."

Hatshepsut looked to where he pointed and saw, rising far at the end of the uptilting valley, a huge natural triangle of rock, aloof, setting a seal of unattainability on the place.

Aahmose felt for her amulet. "Beware the Goddess of the Western Peak," she muttered, "for she strikes suddenly and without warning."

"Meres-Ger, Meres-Ger," Thothmes said. "Lover of Silence. Truly she is a formidable guardian."

They stood in an uneasy silence until a jerboa sprang up from the shadow of a rock at Hatshepsut's feet. She jumped as it dashed away in a shower of sand, Thothmes, Aahmose, and Ineni laughing at her startled expression.

Thothmes braced himself and tightened his belt. "Come, Ineni, show me exactly the place you have chosen. Aahmose, Hatshepsut, stay here. Find shelter beneath a rock, out of the sun." And he and Ineni strode away, farther up the vale, and in a moment had disappeared from sight.

The silence was oppressive. Hatshepsut felt the Goddess's inquiring, jealous gaze upon them, and she began to whisper protecting incantations under her breath. Aahmose had sunk onto the ground and closed her eyes. She seemed very breathless and panted softly. After a while Hatshepsut looked about her, but there was not much to see, only rock. She was glad when her father and Ineni reappeared, both sticky with sweat and very thirsty.

"I approve the place," Thothmes said, "and I suggest to you, Hatshepsut, that you accept the tomb that Ineni has chosen for you, far above us. It is a fitting place for a queen to lie."

"Or a Pharaoh?"

Thothmes did not smile. He was tired, and now that the business had drawn to a successful close, he wanted his wine and his breakfast. "It suffices for me and therefore is good enough for any," he answered her sharply. "Ineni, you will have to build the workmen's village on the desert and level and widen this accursed sheep's track as you can. Choose your engineers wisely, and do not hire too many men. This time they must all die when the work is complete. I must rest safe from grave robbers, and so must my family. The first to die will be offered to Amun as a thanksgiving from his dutiful Son; and the second, to Meres-Ger. Now we will go. This silence has ears, and I am uncomfortable."

As if his words had unleashed the gates of panic within them, they hurried out of the valley with many glances over their shoulders, and Hatshepsut, again following behind, fancied that she could feel the Serpent Goddess's cold, hissing breath on her neck. Meres-Ger loved no one, and certainly she had no fear of Amun. With great relief they found themselves on the floor of Hatshepsut's sun-drenched valley, and from there to the river was but a few minutes' steady tramping. The boat rocked invitingly, the water sparkled, and on the other side the pennants of the Imperial city fluttered gaily and bravely in the breeze. They clambered aboard and cast off, Hatshepsut thinking of her valley and the scents of flowers drifting to them over the river.

9

Senmut was eighteen and bored. He had been bored for the better part of a year, ever since his master had suspended all work in the office and gone off to some vast secret project in the Theban hills, taking Benya and several other young engineers with him. For a week or two Senmut had amused himself by drawing up grandiose plans for his future tomb, but the game soon palled, and he locked the plans away. Spring had come again. This year the flood had been small, and an air of anxiousness hung over Thebes. But the marshes still abounded with wildfowl, and from water to palace and temple the gardeners still coaxed masses of blooms from the wet soil.

In a short letter from his father he learned that the sowing had been good but that a great deal of land, untouched because of the low level of the water, could not be cultivated. Could Senmut send them help later on? There had been bad years before, but now his mother was unwell, his brother had broken an arm yoking recalcitrant oxen, and the ensuing months looked bleak. Senmut wondered grimly just what his father expected him to do. He lived well, although he was paid little; but he supposed that his family had visions of him as a great lord now, a lolling, sought-after architect. In reality he was still very much an apprentice. He knew that if Ineni had been there, he would have agreed to send something, perhaps even a slave or two; but as it was, Senmut could do nothing but dispatch promises and explain the situation. He was worried, and worry and boredom together are bad company.

On this day, the third day of the month of Paopi, he wrapped his smoked fish, some bread and cheese, and a handful of figs together with a flask full of wine and set out for the river. His body longed for exercise and was often denied it, but on this sunny, crisp morning he could find nothing better to do than to walk. He chose a path that began on the outskirts of the city and ran beside the river, skirting the marshes and winding among the head-high reeds and brilliant green waterweeds. It was a path for little boys who sought the adventure of a morning's fantasy, but Senmut sought only escape from the monotony that threatened to make him slothful. He had laid aside his gold-bordered, floor-length linen and wore the short, heavy kilt of a peasant in order to move more freely, and the air felt good on his naked legs. He also went sandalless, and his toes sank most satisfyingly into the wet earth and padded gratefully on the grass. Once the city was behind him, he struck out in better spirits. At that time of the year the sun was far from its summer heat, and it was pleasant to stride along, watching the fellahin drive the oxen through the sodden ground or swing to the sowing. Often the path ran out of the reeds and took him beside fields whose canals lay full of still water and whose shadoofs, for once, stood motionless. Beyond the fields, sharp in the clear air, the hills and cliffs, the ramparts of Egypt's security, marched, keeping the desert and war out and the green fertility in. The palms that grew everywhere, following the lines of water whether it be the canal or the river itself, nodded jerkily; and Senmut strolled happily along, dappled in shade and squinting in sun.

At noon he found himself almost at the water's edge, surrounded by rustling papyrus and marsh to right and left but with a fairly clear view of the Nile and the cluster of mud huts on the other side. He sat down under a date palm and unwrapped his meal. The walk had given him an appetite, and he ate heartily, remembering how, such a short time ago— it seemed hentis past—he had stolen from his cell to raid the God's kitchens. What a vast, gaping hole his stomach had seemed to him then. It was still a hole, but the ease of his life had mitigated the appetite. He munched contentedly, throwing crumbs to the curious birds that hopped just out of reach; and when he had finished, he lay back with his hands across his stomach and drowsily counted the palm branches above his head. Soon his eyes closed. There was plenty of time to take a rest and be back in his room before night fell. He began to doze.

Suddenly something hit him in the chest with such force that he found himself on his feet and doubled over, gasping for breath. He fell to his knees, shaking, his arms rigid before him, his mind a confused whirl of bright colors and blood. For a moment, in an idiotic spasm of fear, he thought that the blood was his own. But then his mind cleared, the pain in his chest eased, and he found himself looking down at a slain duck, its feathers green and blue in the high sunlight, its head a limp mass of pulp and blood. Beside it lay a white and silver throwing-stick, stained brown. Unthinking, he picked it up with trembling fingers and rose to his feet, still shocked. As he gazed down at it, there was a rustle in the long grasses. Before he could turn, they parted, and a girl stood there, one hand on the stem of a bending reed and the other on her hip.

She was slim, as slim as the stick he held in his grasp, and almost as tall as he. Her little feet were shod with sandals whose straps were as thin as thread, and blue jewels shone where each strap met between her toes. Her toes and fingernails were painted red, as was her large mouth, now parted in surprise. Her eyes seemed huge, ringed as they were in black kohl that swept to her temples, forming a triangle at the edge of each eye. Above the kohl and below her straight, winged eyebrows there was a dusting of blue. Her hair was cut severely, straight across the forehead, forming a fringe of blue black above her eyes. The same wealth of shining hair fell straight in a cap of black that swung between her ears and her shoulders. A band of thick gold encircled her head, and gold ringed her arms; but on her breast, cascading to her tight, flat navel, lay a thick-woven mat of linked electrum studded in seeming disorder with uncut turquoises that glittered at him tauntingly as she breathed. She wore only the short kilt of a boy, but it was fastened with a gold belt from which an ankh hung. He could see nothing of her breasts under the pectoral but a slight and tantalizing swell. Her chin was up; those great, black eyes blazed at him from the deep tan of her face; the aristocratic nostrils flared; the lips closed tight. He was completely dazzled. He had no eyes for the slave who glided swiftly to his mistress's side or for the young noble in leather who had followed close behind her, his winged helmet framing a gentle, quizzical face.

"Down on your face!" the vision spat in tones of surprised outrage, and Senmut's knees buckled. Still clutching the throwing-stick, he sank to the ground, but he was smiling. He could not mistake the voice, even though it had deepened a little and acquired that melody in the four years that had passed. It was she, his little benefactress, but how changed! Her power beat down upon his head.

"Peasant, my duck is at your feet and my throwing-stick in your hand. Only the noble may hold the throwing-stick. Let it go."

Slowly his cramped fingers opened, and the slave bent and whisked the stick away.

He felt it tapping his neck.

"And my duck," she went on, "what were you going to do with my duck?" The tone was soft now, a purr. "How long have you been skulking in the reeds, waiting your chance to run away with my duck? Shall I let him speak, Hapuseneb?"

"That is up to you, Prince," the young man replied gravely. "But since you ask me, then I should say, what is a peasant doing with the badge of the architect upon his arm and the shaved skull of the priest upon his head?"

There was a long silence, during which a water beetle, drunk with sun, rolled past Senmut's nose and fell with a plop into the marsh. Then in a voice perfectly calm she said, "Stand up, priest. It is you, is it not? But of course it is! I know of no other mad priest masquerading as an architect and a peasant all at the same time."

He rose, brushing his knees. This time he did not avert his eyes but looked full into her face. She returned his smile in a sudden flash of white teeth, and with a swift gesture of affection she stepped to his side.

"We seem fated to meet in embarrassing circumstances," she laughed. "Am I never to be rid of you? What are you doing so far from Thebes? There are eels aplenty for a peasant to catch. Were you eeling, priest?"

The tone was bantering, and as she spoke, the slave picked up the duck, its head dangling limply to the ground, its eyes glazed, and went back to his place.

Senmut could see her escort, standing with his arms folded across his broad chest. His own throwing-stick hung from a thong at his belt, and his yellow linen was held to his waist by a leather belt studded in gold. He was still smiling faintly, his steady eyes questioning, appraising the scantily clad, muddy youth.

"I needed to walk," Senmut said at last, "and after I had rested here and eaten, I fell asleep. Your duck, Prince, fell upon me as a bolt from heaven." Gingerly he fingered the scratches on his stomach.

"But what of your duties?" she asked him.

"I have none at the present time. Noble Ineni is gone, and I know not how to occupy my time."

She let out a sigh. "Of course. Ineni is busy on a project for my father. Well, would you care to join us at hunting, priest? I am sure that I can find much to fill your time." Impulsively she turned to the patient Hapuseneb. "This is the priest who did me a service," she said, "and behold, he trails after me like a puppy." The impish sparkle in her eyes spoke of a will still not subdued by womanhood and of the undiminished love of a joke.

Senmut solemnly bowed to the son of Lower Egypt's Vizier, over-whelmed for a moment by the company he was in. Hapuseneb inclined his head.

Only a year older than Senmut himself, he, like Menkh, had the unconscious arrogance of his position in his bearing and manner; but, unlike Menkh, he was thoughtful, a solid planner and already a man able to take his father's office and administer with authority. Hatshepsut had always trusted him, for he was a man of his word. They had often played and hunted together, as they had worked together in the schoolroom, vying with each other for the approval of Khaemwese, in competition at the bow, racing against each other in the chariots.

"Greetings, priest," he said. "You are indeed fortunate to have been able to render service to Egypt's Hope."

Hatshepsut snorted. "Egypt's Hope!" she chortled. "Egypt's Flower! Well, let us go back to the boat, for the day advances, and one duck is a sorry showing."

She turned quickly and disappeared into the reeds, Hapuseneb following. Senmut grabbed the sack that had held his little meal and hastened after them, his head in a whirl. In a few moments the reeds gave way to open water and a small skiff, its bright blue and white flags fluttering in the afternoon breeze. It was painted red and yellow, and its cabin was hung with gold damask curtains that billowed, giving Senmut a glimpse of cushions and a low table, on which sat a small flagon and a basket of fruit. Up on the bow a sailor perched, a pole in his hand; before him a little gold mast reared, its sail folded neatly and tied. Aft, a canopy had been run out, and a group of young men and women lounged carelessly, the girls in shimmering linen, thin and fine as a bee's wings, the same that graced Hatshepsut's supple waist. Above them the ostrich feather fans waved slowly, downy white and soft against the deep blue of the sky. A small ramp ran from the doorway of the cabin to the shore, and a soldier was stationed at the foot of it, waiting patiently.

Chatter and bursts of laughter floated to Senmut long before he broke through the tall river growth, and he wished suddenly to be somewhere else, somewhere safe, in Ineni's office, perhaps, or still asleep under the palm tree. Here he was out of his depth, a gasping fish. He had no wish to be gaped at and patronized by these lordly young beings, so superior in their jewels and fine dress, but it was too late to run away.

The guard sprang to attention, the conversation became a spasmodic bubble that abruptly burst, and Hatshepsut ran up the ramp to the lowered heads, Hapuseneb striding imperturbably after her. Senmut trailed last, acutely aware of his coarse peasant linen, his lack of a wig, his dirty knees, and his humble brown sack clutched under one arm. He felt the stare of the guard hot on his back, and then he was over the top and walking past the door of the cabin, into whose cool, dim depths he wished to run and hide. He steeled himself for the first hostile shaft let loose from the cold eyes that turned upon him. Behind him two servants hauled in the ramp, and Hatshepsut waved to the man with the pole. They slid easily into the current once more, and to his surprise Senmut felt Hapuseneb take his arm and draw him in under the shade of the canopy. Hatshepsut had flung herself down on the cushions and was drinking water furiously, smacking her lips, the offending throwing-stick clattering to the deck beside her. There was a silence. All eyes were on Senmut, as he had feared, and he swallowed, glaring defiantly. Hapuseneb put a hand to his back.

"This is the priest—what is your name?" he whispered.

Senmut spoke out. "I am Senmut, priest of Amun and architect under the great Ineni." He found that he had almost shouted the words, so that they filled the boat and echoed against the swiftly passing trees on the bank.

The company sat up. Hapuseneb nodded approvingly, and Hatshepsut patted the cushions beside her.

Unbelieving, he walked to her and sank, cross-legged, taking the cup she offered. As he drank, he felt the gust of a great sigh, as if the strings that held the people stiff were suddenly cut. Talk began again, and Senmut felt sweat trickle down his temples. By all the gods, he thought shakily, is this I sitting here, enveloped in the finest satin, next to the most favored and powerful woman in the country?

"That was good," Hapuseneb said approvingly. "All respect a man who can speak for himself. Tell me, Senmut, how do you like working for Ineni? I always feared him as a boy. He had such a long arm, and when he visited my father, he would look at us as if we were scullions. 'Away!' he would call, and father would laugh."

Senmut turned to him gratefully, knowing that he spoke to put him at his ease, and he answered Hapuseneb as carefully as he could. The other's face was open, sympathetic, and all of a sudden Senmut sensed an ally. Why, he did not know. The young noble was certainly handsome, with a square jaw and deep-set eyes that invited every confidence. Senmut found himself babbling away like the river in flood, but at the same time a part of him sat back and watched with caution, saying, Tell nothing of consequence, for you sail in a fairy ship with immortal beings, and your words must be of things that do not matter. All at once he felt a touch on his shoulder. Turning, he found a brown, impish face grinning into his own.

"Menkh!" he cried with relief, and the young man slid down beside him, tucking in his feet.

"This is an odd place for a little we'eb priest," Menkh said, his smile broadening. "Wait until my august father hears! Is he to lose his favored pupil?"

"No, indeed! And truly, I am twice favored—for a little we'eb priest," Senmut responded happily.

And they glided on, the boat cutting the water silently as a gilded swan, the sun glittering on the widening wash. Hatshepsut left them, taking her stick to the side of the boat, where she knelt, sometimes trailing a braceleted hand in the limpid water, sometimes looking up to the sun.

Senmut found his gaze often straying to her wind-strewn hair, her pure, satisfying profile, as he talked. He was drawn to her. He felt the stirrings of passion, and he was ashamed and fascinated. She seemed remote, a Goddess. It was not right for him, he thought, to feel for her as he felt for any slave in the beershops. And, yet, it was not only that. Between them there was an unspoken fondness, an acknowledging of the hand of fate, the same hand that had put the seeds of ambition in his heart and kept them growing through the years of hard labor in the temple. He knew that as the son of a peasant, he had no right to be in such company. Yet he realized that the same hand of fate had placed him there on the Royal Barge.

He felt the eyes of the women on him in speculation, but he did not sense their admiration. He did not yet see what they saw: a tall young man with the grace of the legendary panther and a face that beckoned in sensual invitation. A man, moreover, with the stamp of a power all his own in his broad forehead and in his swift, capable hands. So they whispered and giggled, and Senmut, oblivious, listened to Hapuseneb and Menkh talk of things that he only dimly understood, answering diffidently but without evasion when they spoke to him.

Once Hatshepsut gave a shout, and they all left the cushions and crowded to the side of the boat. Senmut was enveloped for one delicious moment in a cloud of perfume and the touch of soft, bare female flesh as the women gathered behind him. They watched as a great crocodile waddled swiftly from the shelter of the reeds and slid with scarcely a splash into the water, floating past them, its horrible grinning snout inches from their hands.

As the gray form drew away, Menkh reached for his bow. "Shall I slay it, Highness?" he asked.

But Hatshepsut shook her head. "No. It is holy, a companion of the gods, and I believe it to be an omen. Let it live."

As she spoke, she glanced quickly at Senmut and quickly away again. But he had caught the puzzled, almost anxious look, and he stood with the others as the crocodile vanished from sight, his heart tripping within him. How she had changed! he thought to himself. Where was the endearing, infuriating child of the lake?

Toward late afternoon they started up a flock of white geese that rose screaming from the marshes, and she handed him her throwing-stick without a word. It was a challenge.

In an instant the days on his father's farm came back to him, the mock fights with Senmen, both huffing under the weight of wooden staves. This noble's toy was light and cunningly balanced in his hand, and he raised it, aimed, and threw. It sped straight to its target, and the bird dropped like a stone. Senmut heard the mutter of approval. Menkh clapped him on the back. Hapuseneb raised his eyebrows.

"You throw well for a priest, priest," Hatshepsut said, her eyes narrowed.

He turned to her more abruptly than he had intended, anger flaring in him. "My father is a peasant," he said. "Peasants do not teach their sons to hunt with throwing-sticks."

"I know," she said simply, and his anger died.

The boat was poled to the shore, and the ramp run out, but neither of them moved. It was Menkh who ran to the fallen bird and presented it, bowing delightedly.

Hatshepsut stroked the white feathers. "You may take it," she told Senmut. "Have the cooks prepare it, and perhaps we shall eat it together."

He took it gingerly, wordlessly, but then she laughed, tossing her head, and they sailed back to Thebes standing side by side in the windy, golden evening.

When they disembarked, he felt the way he had as a child. He and his father would visit the village marketplace to barter the corn and the flax, the beans, the melons, and the vegetables. There was the happiness and the weariness that the unexpected brings, and a sadness that it was all over.

He stood at the top of the water steps, facing the yellow, blue, and red sun-splashed pillars, feeling lost. Menkh and Hapuseneb farewelled him good-naturedly and got into their own little skiffs, their servants waiting to pole them home. The clustering attendants began to move up the avenue of sycamores in the direction of the palace. Already Ra was low in the sky, westering slowly, no longer white-hot but softly bronze, tinging all with gold. Senmut lifted his face and closed his eyes, suddenly and uncharacteristically loving the God who had given him this day.

"Would you like to meet my father?"

Her voice was close, and he turned to her in some confusion, imagining for a wild moment that she was inviting him to sail in the Heavenly Barque. Her skin was flushed the color of copper, on fire with the sun, and her hair glowed. She was so close that he could smell her perfume, the holy perfume, myrrh.

"You have been quiet today, priest," she went on. "Has it been an auspicious day for you?"

"I do not know," he said awkwardly, "but it has been a day to remember." He still clutched the goose, but he had lost his food sack somewhere.

"Give me the bird," she said, "and I shall have it broiled especially for you, and you and I and my father shall eat it together. Go and rest, and I will send for you. Or perhaps you would prefer to leave all as it is and go back to the architect's reed?"

He knew that she was speaking of something other than dinner with Pharaoh, but he shook his head. "No, Most Beautiful One," he said softly. "And thank you for this day."

"A day of beginnings? I am glad that you have enjoyed it."

He bowed, and she left him, her women gathering behind her like a cluster of irridescent bubbles, and he made his way slowly back to Ineni's office and his little room.

He was called for promptly at the hour of dinner, and he followed the slave through the deepening dusk. The gardens lay in warm, thoughtful darkness, but in the palace the lamps shone out and the halls were full of the smell of food and the brisk clapping of busy, sandaled feet. The slave left him at the double doors to the banqueting chamber, and the Chief Herald stood ready to open them and announce him. Senmut began to stutter forth his name, but the man held up a hand, swung back the doors, and intoned, "Senmut, priest of Mighty Amun, architect," and Senmut found himself walking into the throng. The hall seemed vast to him, as big as the outer court of the temple itself, its ceiling stretching away into darkness even though hundreds of lamps shone brightly around the cavernous walls. People drifted in and out among the tall, fluted lotus columns that marched across the white tiled floor or stood in expectant groups, drinking wine and talking aimlessly. At the farther end there was no wall, only a forest of columns giving way to the encroaching night that spilled over from the garden. A slight wind blew in his face, mingling with the odor of perfume and oils. Because it was still spring, the tiny tables that were scattered haphazardly, waiting for the diners, were piled with blossoms from the trees—white sycamore, orange pomegranate, the fragrant yellow-green persea—and an ocean of blue and pink lotus flowers lay amid the cushions and cloaks.

A little slave girl, naked and timid, scarcely more than a child, approached him and, bowing, fastened upon his head a wax cone filled with perfume. Immediately another slave appeared, also bowing low.

"Be pleased to follow me, Noble Senmut," he said respectfully. Senmut, suddenly tempted to laugh at himself and the servant and the unearned title, padded after him in his very best leather sandals. They threaded their way through the crowd until they reached a small dais halfway between the door and the colonnade of the garden. The servant indicated a group of four little gold tables, their surfaces full of flowers, their smooth legs buried under cushions. Close about the dais were other such tables, but the servant, seeing Senmut's hesitation, waved him up. "You are to dine with Pharaoh tonight," he said, and when Senmut rather self-consciously mounted the two steps and stood irresolute, the man added, "Would you like wine?"

Senmut nodded, and the servant disappeared, melting into the crowd. The heat of the night and the warmth of the bodies were already melting the brown cones on the heads of the guests, and the perfume had begun to trickle down their necks. Senmut, waiting for his wine with a dry throat and jumping nerves, felt himself enveloped in the same thick miasma, but it was not unpleasant. He put up a hand and dabbled his fingers under his ear, then rubbed his hands together and raised them to his nose. His wine arrived, presented in a flagon of gold beaten so thin that he fancied he could see the outline of his hands through it as he took it and drank. Out of the corner of his eye, over the bobbing heads of the people, he saw both doors at last flung wide and a glitter of precious stones in the dimness beyond. Conversation ceased. The breeze played fitfully.

The Chief Herald took a deep breath and raised his voice. "Horus, the Mighty Bull, Beloved of Maat, Lord of Nekhbet and per-Uarchet, He Who Is Diademed with the Fiery Uraeus, Making Hearts to Live, Son of the Sun, Thothmes, Living Forever. Great Royal Wife Aahmose, Lady of the Two Lands, the Great Lady, Royal Sister, Beloved of Pharaoh. Crown Prince Hatshepsut Khnum-Amun, Beloved of Amun, Daughter of Amun."

Knees were bent, arms were extended, foreheads went down, and the floor of the hall became fluid, rising and falling like the waves of a lake.

Senmut, exposed on the dais, went down also. He felt a little sick. What if Pharaoh did not like him? What if he said the wrong thing and was ordered ignominiously out of the chamber? The thought of disgrace was worse than the thought of death. All this flashed through his mind as his head met a cushion and rose again, and he was on his feet once more, watching the royal entourage thread its way through the adoring people.

In close quarters Pharaoh exuded authority in far greater measure than the short, squat figure Senmut had seen striding down the avenue to Luxor. Up close his shoulders were more markedly broad, his legs more muscled, his head more bull-like and belligerent, his eyes sharper, always flicking to and fro, missing nothing. Tonight he was wearing yellow, one of his favorite colors. His kilt was yellow and dusted with gold leaf, and his sandals were chained gold. His pectoral was of two crystal hands, the fingers outlined in gold, holding the blue turquoise Eye of Horus inlaid with amethyst and the blue faience glass that his Vizier of Lower Egypt had brought him that very afternoon. Thothmes' leather cap was yellow, its two wings falling nearly to his waist; and above his shining forehead the Cobra and the Vulture reared, their cold crystal eyes staring at the crowd.

Senmut looked at Aahmose with frank interest. He had never seen Hatshepsut's mother and was a little disappointed, for there was little resemblance between them. Aahmose was comfortably plump and smiling, but though he knew that all loved her for her sweetness, there was nothing of the fire, the dart, the spark of the daughter.

At last, when the Fan Bearer at the Right Hand of the King and the other officials clearing a path were almost upon him, Senmut saw Hatshepsut. She was still in a boy's garb, the kilt swaying inches above her knees, but tonight no one could mistake her sex. The black eyes were lidded in heavy green, and the kohl gleamed around them. The full mouth was red, and white buds were entwined in the dully shining tresses, surmounted by a delicate, filigreed crown of silver that seemed to weave in and out of her hair and about her ears. Silver clung to her throat and caressed her shoulders, and silver snakes crawled around both arms, their tails and flat heads carved of deep chalcedony. Her belt was silver, also, as were her sandals, and while in the afternoon brightness she had glittered and flashed like the Sun Himself, tonight she glowed dully, coldly, the moon at the full. Senmut, utterly out of his depth, was afraid.

Pharaoh's emblems were laid at the foot of the dais, and the officials melted away. Thothmes mounted heavily and settled himself on the cushions, Aahmose beside him, and Hatshepsut came to sit beside Senmut, a glad smile lighting her face. Pharaoh bellowed for food, and the diners sank to the floor to eat.

"I am glad that you are here," Hatshepsut said to Senmut. "I am also lamentably hungry. Your goose will appear before long, and then we shall know whether or not you have an eye for tender flesh! Do you like my bracelets?" She extended both arms in a rush of perfume. "The Vizier brought them home for me. Now"—she leaned over her mother and tapped Thothmes on the knee—"father, this is the priest I told you about. Do not rise again, priest. You have had enough exercise for one day."

Senmut found himself caught in the most all-embracing, searching, piercing gaze he had ever known. Ineni's slow appraisal had been as nothing compared with this sudden roasting. Thothmes' eyes trapped him and proceeded to shake him apart, bit by bit, and Senmut needed all his will just to keep his eyes fixed on the other's.

After a moment that seemed to be an eternity, Pharaoh grunted twice.

"You are elusive, young man," he said, his voice rough and deep but not unkind. "For many weeks I have heard of you from my Clerk of Works but never a shadow of you have I seen. Ineni thinks well of you. He says that you have talent and imagination. My daughter likes you. You are fortunate." He swept the blooms from the table as his slave bent with the first course, the flowers landing in Aahmose's ample lap. "Is that scruffy priest's kilt all that you have to wear? Where is your wig? Well? Where is your voice, also?"

Hatshepsut was watching, an amused little smile playing about her mouth.

Senmut answered as carefully as he had when he met Hapuseneb. "I am only an apprentice, Mighty Bull, and a we'eb priest under all priests. It is not fitting that such a one as I should be adorned as my betters."

Thothmes shot him a keen glance from beneath his lowering brows. "Well spoken. But sentiments will not buy food, as the great Imhotep once said."

"I am well fed, Mighty One. My master works me hard, but he is just."

"I know that better than you. Where do you live?"

"I have a room off my master's office."

"Indeed. Hatshepsut, do what you will with him. I like him. Now we will eat. Where is the music?"

He turned from them abruptly, and Senmut let out a sigh of relief. A slave waited patiently beside him, loaded tray in hand; and now that the interview was over, the young man discovered an overpowering appetite. The spicy smells wafting around him were making his mouth water, and he nodded at last for food. Hatshepsut was already eating with dedication, her eyes darting around the company. Senmut tucked a lotus bloom into his belt and began to eat, too. His cup was quietly refilled, and the perfumed wax dripped onto his chest. He wanted to enjoy the night, to get drunk as all the others would do, to laugh and dance and reel home with the dawn; but as always that other self stood beside him, watching all with steady, cynical eyes, cold and sober and calculating. Senmut shrugged, knowing that he would not get delightfully drunk or scream with laughter or applaud the gyrations of the dancing girls too loudly. It was not within him, such abandonment. He ate quietly, and once Hatshepsut's appetite was satisfied, she began to point out the guests to him, whispering scandals in his ear, her eyes alight.

"See over there, to the right of the fifth lotus column, beneath the lamp? The fat woman with gold hanging to her knees? That is Second Wife Mutnefert, mother of my brother Thothmes, she who refused my father entrance and locked herself in her apartments for months when I became Crown Prince. It is said that she makes love to the Chief Herald, but I do not believe it. If it were true, my father would have killed her a long time ago."

"Thothmes is not here," she replied in answer to his hesitant question. "Father has sent him with pen-Nekheb on a tour of the northern garrisons. He hopes that Thothmes will learn something, but he will be disappointed. Thothmes wanted to take his concubine, and father nearly exploded. . . . See? There, waving to you. It is Menkh!"

It was indeed the lively young man, and Senmut waved back. Menkh had a girl in his lap and ostrich feathers stuck defiantly in his wig. Hapuseneb sat below the dais, deep in conversation with his father; and though Senmut was sure he had seen him, Hapuseneb did not look his way.

As soon as the eating was over and the entertainments were to begin, the Vizier and his son rose and approached the dais. Thothmes waved them on.

"What is it, my friend?"

"I wish to be excused, Pharaoh, and to go home to my wife. I am weary with traveling."

"Then go. You, too, Hapuseneb. Be in my audience chamber one hour after dawn tomorrow with the reports." He dismissed them, and as they turned, Hapuseneb caught Senmut's eye and gave him a warm smile. They left, and Pharaoh heaved himself to his feet.

"Silence! Is Ipuky here?"

From the back of the hall the blind musician was led by one of his sons, and he stood before the dais, his new lute cradled in one scrawny arm. "I am here, Majesty," he said. Senmut looked at him in amazement, for his voice was as strong and full of melody as all the sounds of nature. Pharaoh jerked his head, and a slave helped the old man forward and left him sitting at their feet.

"Give me your lute," Thothmes commanded, and it was handed over. "The Crown Prince has been studying this instrument and wishes your opinion of her skill. We also wish to be entertained."

Hatshepsut made a face at Senmut and rose, and all at once that tiny gesture swept him back to the edge of Amun's Lake in the cool dawn, to a naked, bedraggled, and sorrowing child. How far I have come since then, he thought, not without sadness.

Hatshepsut put one foot upon her table and swung the lute across her knee. Bending her head and biting her lip in concentration, she sought the first chords of the song with her long fingers; and Senmut sat back, wine in hand. The hush deepened. Ipuky sat calmly, waiting, his fingers laced and still in his lap. Finally Hatshepsut raised her head and gazed out over the congregation. Two plaintive, running chords came from the lute, as sweet and melancholy as a winter's night. She began to sing.

> Sweet of love is the Daughter of the King!
> Black are her tresses as the blackness of the night,
> Black as the wine grapes are the clusters of her hair,
> The hearts of the women turn toward her with delight,
> Gazing on her beauty, with which none can compare.

Her voice was high, thin, and pure, the calling of the first bird in the drowsy dawn, and the song she had chosen suited her so well that Senmut was sure she had plucked it from his mind. A superstitious awe began to steal over him. Indeed she was the Daughter of the God!

> Sweet of love is the Daughter of the King!
> Fair are her arms in the softly swaying dance,
> Fairer by far is her bosom's rounded swell!
> The hearts of the men are as water at her glance,
> Fairer is her beauty than mortal tongue can tell.

No one moved. The song was well known, a love song of antiquity, usually sung in a lewd manner when the guests were far gone with wine and usually accompanied with suitable suggestive postures. But Hatshepsut gave it a treatment unequaled in its daring and its simplicity, singing it in innocence. The captivated people forgot their intrigues and dalliances and were once more in the throes of young love.

> Sweet of love is the Daughter of the King!
> Rose are her cheeks as the jasper's ruddy hue.
> Rose as the henna which stains her slender hands!
> The heart of the King is filled with love anew,
> When in all her beauty before his throne she stands.

There was a moment of stunned silence, and then the entire company was on its feet, stamping and clapping, crying her praises. Hatshepsut handed the lute coolly back to Ipuky and sat down firmly, ignoring the storm.

"The fools!" she snapped to Senmut. "They know not what they applaud, but shout because I am beautiful and sing of beauty. The tune is easy, and I do not have a great voice. Yet for the sweet and powerful Ipuky, who can fill the temple with his music, for him they clap tepidly and turn away to what they think are better things. Fools!"

When the tumult had died down, Thothmes asked the great musician's opinion.

Ipuky considered for a moment, then made his pronouncement. "The song is easy to sing, but Her Highness has arranged it well to hide the fact that her voice does not yet have its full range and depth. Her skill with the lute is well known."

Hatshepsut applauded loudly, whispering again to Senmut, "You see!"

Thothmes thanked the old man. The tables were removed, a space was cleared, and from far down the hall came the click of castanets and the rattle of the tambourines. Aahmose was asleep, snoring gently, lying among her cushions. Thothmes abruptly stepped off the dais and went to a chair that had been abandoned at the edge of the throng.

"Now we shall see the dancing," Hatshepsut said. "Let's sit on the floor over there by Menkh so that we may see the feet of the girls better." She hopped off her cushions, Senmut following, his wine flagon still in his hand.

Seven girls ran in, Syrians, Senmut judged by their swarthy skins and hawk noses, their black hair tumbling loose to their knees. Each carried a tambourine and a bell. They were naked, but for jangling bracelets of copper and a multitude of rings on their toes, and their bodies glistened with the oil that flowed from their perfume cones. Their eyes spoke of natures untamed. Senmut remembered little of the dance, if dance it was. He was heady with wine and rich odors and the nearness of the Prince. The full breasts and red-painted nipples of the girls roused him until he could think of nothing else. With a clashing of rattles and a twinkle of castanets they were gone, and the jugglers took their place, with balls and hoops and wooden sticks. After them came a magician who showered gold dust upon them and turned flowers into balls of fire.

Pharaoh was in a fine humor. He laughed and drank, slapping his massive thigh and clapping vigorously, but Aahmose slumbered on. At last, when the water clock had almost drained and in the east the sky grew gray, he rose, shouting, "To bed! All of you!" and lumbered out the doors.

The music ceased. The slaves began to carry out those guests too drunk to walk, and the rest drifted away, slipping into the garden and down to the water steps or into the passages, tired, silent wraiths.

Senmut blinked and got to his feet, weary and satiated, longing for his couch yet heated with strange fire.

Hatshepsut, cloaked and hooded now, touched his arm. "Come to the training grounds tomorrow before noon, and before we hunt again, you can earn your own throwing-stick," she said. While he was still bowing, she walked the long floor to the colonnade and the dim garden beyond.

He stumbled after her, knowing the way back to his cell better from the outside, but the same slave who had brought him beckoned him to the door, and he followed gratefully, soaked in perfume and sweat, every limb exhausted.

In the same year, in the height of summer, when human, animal, and plant were beaten to the ground by the scorching anger of Ra, Aahmose died. She had awakened in the hot night, calling for water, and Hetephras had brought her a drink from the stone jar that stood cooling in the hall. Aahmose had drained the cup and asked for more, complaining of the heat and her aching arms, clutching her heart with a shaking hand. She had curled up and gone back to sleep, only to awaken once more, this time calling in great fear for Thothmes. Her agitation was so violent that Hetephras had gone herself to rouse Pharaoh, but by the time they had returned, Thothmes sending for the Physician on his way, she was dead.

Hatshepsut had been sleeping soundly, stirred this time by no premonition. They came for her and she walked the long halls and stood looking down on her mother as if still in a dream. Aahmose looked to be a part of that dream, smiling faintly, gentle in death as she had been in life, a peace in the dulled eyes that spoke of a favorable weighing. Sebek would go hungry again.

"You are young again forever," Hatshepsut quoted softly from the Rite of Burial. "How beautiful she must have been, father! I feel no sorrow for her. She loved to live for us all, and even now she walks the blessed fields of Osiris."

Thothmes was not surprised. Aahmose had prayed more to the consort of Osiris than to Mighty Amun and would be justly rewarded for her faithfulness, but his daughter's intuition often amazed him. "The tomb in the valley is almost completed," he said. "She will lie safe." His own thoughts, as always, were hidden behind the mask of his kingship; but he sat heavily upon Aahmose's little retiring stool, his eyes on her quiet form, and after a while Hatshepsut went back to her couch and left him alone.

During the seventy days of mourning a great peace settled over Thebes. It was as if Aahmose was presenting the essence of herself as a final gift to the city she loved, and somehow all passion and all strife sank out of sight, and the life of Thebes slowed, became gentler. Thothmes went about his business silently, and Hatshepsut spent much time with the animals and Nebanum, as she had before. But this time the quiet of the park, the trusting, uncomplaining beasts, the love of Nebanum—all seemed to fuse into a long, deepening sense of contentment. She realized that she had been heading for her fifteenth year in an increasingly wild mood, gulping at life instead of biting it daintily, and the absence of feasts and dancing and chariot racing did not irk her as it would have done only weeks ago. She suddenly remembered her valley one parching, violet evening as she sat on the roof, and an idea came floating into her mind, waiting to take form. A temple. Not rising to compete foolishly with the unconquerable cliffs, but somehow complementing them, finishing them, expressing her own royal invincibility and beauty. She frowned restlessly over the vision, blind to the blood of the setting sun. She needed an architect, one who knew her quicksilver mind, her dreams, and it was not of Ineni that she thought. She scrambled up, went quickly down the stairs, and sent a passing guard to fetch Senmut.

She went back onto the roof and waited impatiently, aware that the long twilight had begun. Presently she could see him striding through the trees, following the soldier. He must have been bathing. He had on only a small kilt, and even his architect's badge was missing. She thought critically how wide his shoulders were, how long and supple his legs, how inviting his breast to an admiring hand. The soldier pointed, and as he looked up, she read eagerness in his face. Suddenly he was before her, bowing, the face that had shown such joy now a mask of polite expectancy, the servant called for some reason by his master. She noticed how brown he was, how high the cheekbones, how sensuous the mouth under an uncompromising nose. She met his eyes and turned abruptly away. "Greetings, priest. Your shoulders are still wet. Were you bathing? Come and sit with me here on the edge, and watch the last of the sun."

Obediently, he folded his body and sat next to her, watching the darkening sky. He had been swimming in the Nile, back and forth, back and forth, an exercise recommended by his shooting instructor, and his arms and legs were healthily tired.

His body had grown more muscular since the night of the feast, and his voice had deepened. But he had become silent, and the slaves who served Ineni, cleaning and tending the offices, had begun to fear him, though he was still a boy.

He rested next to her, his arms folded on his knees. He gazed calmly before him, seeming so self-contained, so apart, that for the first time in her life Hatshepsut did not want to break the silence, but night was hurrying to meet them.

"I went to the stables today and gave the black one, the one you like so much, some oats. He languishes for lack of exercise," she said.

"The slaves should walk him about," Senmut responded. "When the Great Royal Wife is laid to rest, he will be skittish and unmanageable."

"I do not yet miss my target practice. Do you?"

"No."

"Are you glad that I arranged for you to shoot and ride the chariots? Is life full for you?"

"Yes, I am glad, but I must confess, Prince, that I miss my lessons with Ineni." He shifted restlessly. "I did not thank you for my little apartment or for the slaves and the grain that you caused to be sent to my family."

"I did not give you the time. And then my mother died, and I have been wandering abroad of late, busy with my own company. Is your family well?"

"Very well, and they offer you their eternal worship. My brother's arm is healed, and my mother improves, though she is still weak. Highness," he turned to her, troubled, "you have been so good to me, far above the payment of a debt. May I ask why?"

"You may ask," she retorted, "but I may not answer you. In truth, I do not know why. I think because I see in you what I would like to see in my brother, and it angers me. Why should that pudding receive the benefits of the best education and training, and someone such as yourself be condemned to serve forever in the temple while your family hungers?"

She spoke with extraordinary vehemence, and he did not know what to say.

In her heart she feared Thothmes, and she, like Aahmose, was beginning to wonder whether perhaps on the death of her father she would find herself married to him in spite of Pharaoh's assertions to the contrary. She was discovering that death can change much—that it can change all. And she was becoming wary and cautious as a mountain goat on unfamiliar ground.

Senmut knew nothing of this. Alone with her, the gathering gloom isolating them, turning the rooftop into an island for private communion, she unpainted and without jewels, he was relaxed.

She shrugged. "I do not know, and you have no right to ask, my friend. May a Crown Prince not do as he wishes? But I summoned you for a reason. There is a place I wish you to see, a place that is holy to me. I have had a vision of what I want to do there, but I need your help. Will you come with me and see it?"

"Of course, Highness! Where is this place?" She pointed west, across the river.

"It is there, hidden, a valley, the resting-place of the great Mentu-hotep-hapet-Ra. I can tell you no more until you have seen it. We will go tomorrow. Be at the water steps an hour after dawn, and bring your sandals, for the way is sometimes rocky."

"I shall be there. But why me, Highness? How can I help you?"

"You will hear my dream, and you will understand. Ineni would hear, but he would not understand, though he would try. You and I, priest, have tried each other, though we have met not ten times. You know me. Is it not so?"

"I reverence you, Prince, but I believe that no one will ever know you. I think you trust me, and that is what you wish to say. You have no fear of me because I am nothing, a little we'eb priest."

"You ceased to be a little we'eb priest from the time you walked into Ineni's presence," she replied. "But what are you now?"

Below them the lights of the sentries moved fitfully, crisscrossing the tree-lined paths. Hatshepsut's escort and Senmut's slave waited at the foot of the stairs, but the two on the roof sat quite still, each wrapped in his own thoughts. They could hardly see each other, it was so dark.

When the horns were blown for dinner, she was the first to stir. "Tonight I do not wish to eat. Go now, priest, and I will see you tomorrow."

It was a command. He got up awkwardly and bowed, but she was no longer looking at him. She was gazing over the gardens as if with the effort of her will she could pierce the darkness and reveal her valley. He ran down the stairs. He no longer wondered at fate. He was ready now to accept his destiny.

The next day he hurried to the water steps and found her waiting for him, standing on the deck of her little hunting skiff, her Fan Bearer beside her. She was wrapped in dazzling white linen to protect her from the heat, but her Fan Bearer was a Nubian, black as night. Senmut was reminded of an illustration he had seen once in one of Ineni's precious scrolls: "The soul begins its journey to the Underworld." He made his obeisance and scrambled aboard, and the sweating sailors cast off.

"Let us sit under the canopy," she said. "It is already too hot for comfort. My father said that I may go but warned me not to walk farther into the hills than I need. In this heat I may not walk at all." She indicated the litter, folded against the side of the boat, and the parasol tossed on top of it. Then she regarded him critically. "You should wear kohl to shield your eyes from the glare," she said. "Ta-kha'et!"

From within the cabin a slave appeared and stood waiting, squinting in the white light. "Bring the cosmetic box and the brushes!" Hatshepsut ordered, and the girl went, walking down the deck with a curious swaying, gliding motion that kept Senmut's eyes riveted on her arching back. "That is my newest slave, Ta-kha'et," Hatshepsut remarked, noting Senmut's approving glance. "She is willing and very biddable, but she does not say much. Now, Ta-kha'et," she said when the girl had returned, "bring out the kohl, and anoint this priest." She chose a brush, handing it to the slave. "Do not apply too much, and hurry. We are almost at the Necropolis."

Ta-kha'et knelt before Senmut, opening the box and placing it on the deck. Her face was expressionless, but as she dipped the brush into the black bottle, she smiled. "Master, please close your eyes," she said, and Senmut obeyed, feeling the warm hands flutter on his cheeks and the cool, wet brush sweep his eyelids. "Now open them," Ta-kha'et said. Her little oval face, with its green eyes and fringe of red hair, was so close that if he had moved forward, his nose would have touched hers. He watched her as she worked, holding her tongue between her teeth, her breath smelling of sweetmeats and aniseed. When she was finished, she sat back on her heels, surveying her handiwork, and at a word from Hatshepsut she quickly closed the box and swayed out of sight. The boat bumped the Steps of the Dead, and they rose.

"She works well," Hatshepsut said. "The kohl suits you. Now we must hurry, for it is quite a long way. I think that I shall ride. Get out the litter!" she called to the sailors.

Senmut followed her to the bank, where the litter was unfolded. The Nubian opened the parasol, casting a tiny pool of shade on the ground, and Hatshepsut got onto the litter, propping herself on one elbow so that she could talk to Senmut as they walked.

They set off, and soon she fell silent, looking ahead with a brooding face. Senmut, the Nubian, and the two bearers began to sweat in the waves of sickening heat that beat off the naked sand and rocks, causing all to shimmer, so that the path ahead danced and trembled. Before long the path turned sharply to the right, but before it did Senmut noticed another path, a newer and wider one. It left their little track and plunged straight to where the cliffs met the desert. It ran on from there. Senmut could pick out the marks of oxen and the turmoil caused by the passing of many feet. He wondered about it, but he swung to the right at a command from Hatshepsut, and they began to climb gradually, winding back and forth.

Before long his legs began to ache, but still they climbed. Just when he felt that he could not take another step unless he had water, they plunged into the shade at the foot of the cliffs, and Hatshepsut called a halt. From somewhere on the litter a flagon was produced, and they all drank. Hatshepsut ordered the sailors to wait where they were. She signaled the Nubian to bring the parasol and come with them. "He is deaf," she said matter-of-factly, "so we may say what we will." She, Senmut, and the huge black man began to walk again. They had not gone far when a deep, wide valley suddenly opened out before them, its floor running straight and flat to more cliffs that now surrounded them on three sides. They stopped together, and Hatshepsut gave a little sigh.

"Behold, the sacred resting-place of Osiris-Mentu-hotep," she said.

They fell silent, and the awe of the place began to steal over Senmut as he stood under the shade of the parasol. It was indeed a holy place, a secret, lordly place. He felt like an intruder, dwarfed and meaningless. The sun poured light into it from an ever flowing, burning cup, and no sound disturbed its sleep.

"I want to build here," Hatshepsut said, her voice barely reaching him in the oppressive quiet. "This is my holy valley, a fitting monument to my Sacred Self. Here men may come and do me homage in afteryears. But how shall I construct a temple worthy of myself? A place as beautiful as I am? I do not see a pyramid such as the mighty Mentu-hotep's, for it seems to me that the cliffs themselves frown over it and render it somehow impotent. But what? Can we together plan a right and fitting jewel to set in the crown of these great rocks?"

Senmut did not reply. Already his architect's mind was busy judging distances, assessing proportions, measuring heights. Without realizing it he began to walk forward. Hatshepsut and the Nubian followed, slowly pacing the sandy floor. The small pyramid loomed closer, but even as they crossed the halfway point and drew nearer to it, it still seemed little, out of place. Senmut stopped, frowning. Finally he turned, and she came and stood before him, the linen wrapped all around her, her black eyes seeking his face. "The greatest temple in the world could be built here," he said slowly. "You have indeed chosen wisely, Mighty One. I see something light, cool, a series of colonnades, perhaps. Angles, but no rising peaks to challenge the rock behind. I must consider it more. Have I your permission, Highness, to walk here sometimes and think?"

"Come when you please," she answered. "And when you have thought on it, we may begin. What do you think of a sanctuary, hewn in the dark roots of the cliff itself, where my likeness may sit and hear the prayers?"

"It would be possible, but I would need the help of a good engineer, one who loves the rock and has a feel for its heart." He thought immediately of Benya. Benya would know where to cut and how deep to go. He would cleave the face with a sure knowledge of what to do. But Benya was the gods knew where, with the noble Ineni, on a secret project for Pharaoh. Senmut spoke of him to Hatshepsut, and her manner changed.

"This is your friend?" Her eyes were shadowed, her eager hands withdrawn. "Is he a good engineer? But he must be, or he would not be working with Ineni." Her gaze traveled up, behind them, to the path that wound on to the top of the cliff and beyond.

Senmut sensed an unease.

"Must you have this man?"

"I know him, Highness, and I trust his judgment. We can work well together."

"It may be impossible," she replied brusquely. "He may not return." Again she glanced to the cliff top and back again.

A sudden fear came upon Senmut, communicated to him through her and magnified by the strangeness of the place, but he knew better than to ask her why.

She pulled her cloak tighter about her, folding her arms. The Nubian stood as if made of stone. They had both forgotten that he was there.

"I will see what I can do," she said abruptly, "but I can promise nothing. It is the place of my father only to recall this Benya or to let him be."

"He is most worthy," Senmut pressed quickly.

She smiled, her mood lightening. "As you are, Senmut," she said softly.

The unexpected use of his name on her lips brought a rush of gladness. "I worship you, Highness," he whispered, knowing that it was the truth. "I will serve you until I die."

Seeing that the words were wrung from his soul and did not come glibly, as from the mouth of a flattering courtier, she took his hand and laid it upon her own, holding it for a moment before gently letting it drop. "I have known this for a long time," she replied, "and I also know that whether or not I shower you with preferments or give you a prison, you are mine. Is it not so?"

Her favorite question made him smile. "It is so," he replied, and they went slowly back to the waiting litter and the dozing, heat-drugged servants.

The next morning, early, he was summoned before Pharaoh. He found Thothmes in the office of the Vizier of the South, pacing up and down, a sheaf of jumbled scrolls and dispatches in his hands. When Senmut was announced, Thothmes flung them onto the desk while User-amun's father bowed himself out.

Pharaoh was upset, and Senmut waited in trepidation, wondering what he had done wrong. This morning the Mighty Bull reminded him of his old schoolmaster, and he watched the thickly muscled back march to the end of the room, turn, the massive chest march back. At length Thothmes stopped walking.

"You want Benya the Hurrian," he barked.

"Yes, Majesty."

"Choose one of my engineers. By Set! I have enough Royal Engineers to build a temple a day for the next thousand hentis! Take one. Any one!"

"Majesty, I have known Benya for a long time. He is a good engineer and a good man. It is he I want, and no other."

"What do you know of good men?" Thothmes shouted. "You who are little more than a boy yourself!"

"I know more of both good and evil this year than I did last year," Senmut replied steadily, though his palms grew damp and his knees shook. "And I know a good engineer who is, I think, also a good man."

Thothmes suddenly guffawed, laying a heavy arm around Senmut's shoulders. "Spoken like the man you look to be! Wise is my daughter, and spoiled and willful also. 'Senmut will build for me,' she says, her little chin high. 'He will have this Hurrian. Get him for me, father, I pray.' But she does not pray; she commands, my little Prince!" He sobered, swinging away from Senmut and slumping into the chair by the Vizier's desk. His stubby fingers began to drum on its polished surface. "And yet—" he muttered to himself. "And yet—know you, Senmut, that this Benya is to die in three days' time."

The walls began to slip, and in spite of himself Senmut put out a hand. His heart began to beat in slow, steady strokes that he felt in his throat. He knew that his face had gone white, but Thothmes did not look at him.

"In three days my dear Aahmose goes to her tomb, the tomb whose whereabouts I have so carefully concealed from all save my daughter and Ineni. On that dawn the men who have dug in the secret places will be slain. The Hurrian knows all. He labors for Ineni deep in the earth and will not come home."

Senmut immediately understood Hatshepsut's sudden anxiety in the valley, and he answered Pharaoh quietly. "Majesty, I know that this secret must be kept for all time, and thus the slaves must be sacrificed. But even as you allow the great Ineni to live, trusting him, so I trust my friend. If you will, let me guarantee the keeping of the secret against my life. Benya cares nothing for comforts or rewards. He cannot be bribed. He loves only stone, and that is why I need him. The task the Crown Prince has set me is difficult, and without him it will also be slow. True, I could use another engineer, but how long would it take me to make him understand what the Flower of Egypt desires? A man reprieved from death will work with a will."

"You talk nonsense," Thothmes snapped, but his fingers were stilled. In a while he got up. "Senility approaches," he said, "and I grow soft. Twenty years ago your friend would have died, and you would have been flogged. Do not presume again!" he shouted, shaking a finger at Senmut's glad smile. "At the smallest whisper from the Courts of Justice that my beloved has been disturbed, your blood will wash the floor of the temple! Now go away. I will send the Royal Messenger into the hills, and he will bring back this most lucky young man. See that you serve my Hatshepsut with the same foolish loyalty." He waved impatiently and turned back to the dispatches.

Senmut backed out, and when he was free of the palace, he let out a whoop and tore down the avenue in the direction of the temple. For the first time he would offer formal thanks to the God whose Daughter was able to work miracles. Benya would live.

At dawn on the third day, while he and Benya sat together silently in Senmut's little reception hall, the Braves of the King, armed with knives, swept down upon the helpless workers in their tiny village on the desert and cut their throats while the captain's scribe noted each killing so that none should escape to creep back later for plunder. When it was over, the bodies were buried together in the sand. The sacrifices to Amun and to Meres-Ger had taken place the morning before, and Benya was indeed lucky to escape, for it was Meres-Ger, the Bloodless One, who had awaited him on her lonely peak in the cold darkness.

The two young men heard the funeral procession forming in the garden, and Senmut at last sent out for wine. "We will drink to your deliverance," he told Benya, "and to the Blessed Great Royal Wife Aahmose."

"And to your amazing good fortune!" Benya added fervently. "If it had not been for the beneficence of the little Crown Prince, I would even now be lying with a mouth full of sand."

Senmut laughed. "She is not so little anymore," he said. "It has been long since Thebes welcomed you, Benya, and little ones grow."

"So they do, and glad I am of it. She is most beautiful, or so you keep telling me!"

"Do I? She is my Lord. I seem to have become her servant above Pharaoh himself, though how it came about, I am not sure even now."

The wine came, and they linked arms and drank.

Benya smacked his lips. "Charu, I swear! You have indeed risen in the world. And to think that I was out in the hills sweating my guts while you sat here swilling the wine of the aristocrat!"

Senmut regarded him with affection. He had not changed. Even the threat of death had shaken him only momentarily, but he had bounced back, ever childlike, ever fresh. "The Prince has saved you in order to work," he reminded him.

"Ah, yes. This work. Just what exactly am I supposed to do? Are you my master in this, Senmut?"

"We will work together. There will be no talk of master and servant between us, you ass!" Senmut told him about the valley and of his vision and of the Prince's dream, and Benya listened carefully, his interest caught.

"It sounds like the great valley I saw once. I looked down into it from high in the hills." He suddenly stopped, aghast.

Senmut said in agitation, "No more, Benya! Tell me no more! And curb that blabbing tongue of yours, or you will kill me!"

Benya paled. "Forgive me, my friend," he said humbly. "From now on I shall never speak again of the things I have seen."

"See that you do not."

They drank some more. Then Benya said, "The temple. Draw up the plans, and then I will tell you what stone will stand and which will not take the strain. It sounds to me as if you want sandstone, but granite is the stronger."

"There must be no sense of walls, of too much that is solid, and the stone must blend with the cliff at the back so that at first glance all seems as one."

"But she wants a rock sanctuary, far in the side of the hill. How do you balance the whole?"

"That is my problem. I suggest that you and I go there soon and study the site thoroughly, and then I can make a draft together with Her Highness. Where are you staying?"

"In my old cell, next to the Overseer of Engineers."

"That is too far from me. We must work closely. I will see if I can get you a room here."

Benya looked at his friend curiously but said nothing. This assurance was new, as was the apartment, the slave, the good couch in the tiny bedroom. But the steady, measuring eyes were no different, nor the strange, slow smile. Benya wondered if he was to have a completely new life in more ways than one.

They visited the site together, poring over the rock face, viewing the valley from every angle, but as yet there was no fully formed plan in Senmut's mind, and he had not seen Hatshepsut since before her mother's funeral. He went to the valley twice on his own, roaming about and seeking inspiration, and once he saw her there, sitting on a rock in the broiling sun, swaddled from head to toe, her chin on her knees and her arms about her legs while the Nubian held the parasol over her. But if she saw him, she gave no sign. She seemed immersed in some far vision all her own, and he left quietly, not wishing to disturb her. There would be time enough for consultations and discussions. He felt the sun on his strong back, the blood coursing through his long limbs. There would be time enough for everything. He went often to the training ground with spear and bow, hoping that she would come to run a chariot around the circuit. His aim improved and his wrists grew sinewy, but still she did not appear.

10

On the last day of the month of Apap, when once more the Nile had become a lake over all the land, mirroring a winter sky, Thothmes sent for Hatshepsut. Her birthday celebrations were over, she was now fifteen, and the promise of her early years was fast coming to fruition. She still stubbornly clung to the kilts of her youth, but her hips curved gently under them, and her breasts were full and well formed beneath the jewels she loved. She wore her hair loose, scorning the many wigs that sat on their stands in her bedchamber, but she had many circlets of gold and silver and electrum with which to dress her head. She had been with Nozme when the summons came, talking of her childhood days and of her mother, sharing memories with the old woman and playing with her cats. But the messenger was solemn, and Hatshepsut knew in her bones that this was to be no ordinary audience.

The winds of change were blowing with the breath of Pharaoh, and the palace shifted uneasily. It was a bad season. The mosquitoes bit and worried, and there was sickness among the many children always underfoot. Pharaoh brooded again, and his body servants touched him warily, for he seemed all nerves and tender spots. Only the Crown Prince spread laughter, and all wished for the storm to break so that they could breathe again.

But it was no storm that Thothmes was brewing. He greeted Hatshepsut amiably, kissing her and setting warm wine and pastries before her. But she sat on the edge of her chair with her eyes on his face, and he stood over her, his hands on his hips. "The New Year approaches," he said, "and with it come changes. You have been Crown Prince for long enough, Hatshepsut. That is a title for a child, and you are no longer a child. I am tired, and I need the help that a regent gives. We are going on a journey, you and I, a royal progress. I will at last show you your kingdom, all its glories, so that you may better appreciate the gift the God gives you. And when we return, I am going to have you crowned Heiress."

"Are you to wed me, father? Is there trouble because my mother is dead and to hold the throne you need a royal woman?"

He burst out laughing, and she looked annoyed.

"It was a natural question! I have been told often enough by my tutors that to be Pharaoh one must marry the right blood, and since you, dear father, seem to be truly immortal, I assumed that you would marry me."

"Do you think that I need another wife to legitimize me? Me, who has held Egypt tight in my grasp for nearly a henti? No, my Hatshepsut, such a marriage is not necessary. I wish only to unload some of the work onto you. I promised you the Double Crown, and you shall have it, but with it goes much work. Are you ready?"

"I have been ready for months," she flashed at him, "and in that time Mighty Pharaoh has seethed like a pot that cannot boil. But I did not doubt you. Amun fathered me for just such a moment. You told me so, and deep within me I know it to be true. And I will rule well. I know that, too."

He settled himself beside her. "You were born to it, Hatshepsut, as Ineni was born to design and pen-Nekheb to fight. But I must warn you that not all will welcome you as Heiress, and if I die too soon, you may have trouble with the legalists."

"Pah! Old men who pore over books, whose blood has long since dried in their bodies. The army is yours and therefore mine, and whom else should I fear?"

"You surprise me. Of course you need not fear the army. The soldiers think well of you, the Prince who can hurl a spear from a bucking chariot and hit your mark. But what of Thothmes, your brother, and the priests of Amun?"

"What of them? Thothmes has no more ambition than a gnat. Give him his women and his food, and he will lie quiet. And you dismissed the cunning Menena long ago."

"Yes, but many priests will fear that under the rule of a woman the country will grow soft, and the borders once more will be harried, and no longer will the Keftiu and the Kushites and the Nine Bowmen pour tribute into the greedy hands of the God's servants. They would serve Thothmes until they saw that, more than any woman, he fears the heat and blood of the battlefield."

"Then what shall I do?"

"Be crowned by me, and labor beside me. Learn all you can of government, and when I die, it may be that your hold will be strong enough to quash the flutterings of revolt that will surely come."

She rose swiftly, walking around him. "Then it will not be easy. At last I understand something of Neferu's fears, though never in her darkest dreams could she have imagined that the Throne of Egypt would be mine to sit upon." She laughed, stretching forth her arms. "I will be Queen. Nay, more than Queen. I will be Pharaoh!"

"Only when I go to the God," Thothmes reminded her, amused, "and by then you may be weary of the yoke of power and seek out Thothmes, preferring a soft marriage bed to a hard royal throne." He was teasing her, but she threw him a look of such horror that he ceased to smile.

"O my father! I would rather bed with the lowest soldier in the army than with Thothmes." She shuddered. "I cannot bear a fool."

"Beware!" he said sharply. "Speak no more of your brother in this manner! Your mother feared for your light tongue, and it may be that in spite of all my decrees, there is more to him than the eye sees. He may yet sit upon the Horus Throne."

Hatshepsut's teeth bared. "Only at my death," she said. "Only then."

"So be it. We will spend the month of Mesore visiting the ancient marvels of this land, and it is your duty to do homage to the gods whose shrines await you. Then we will return, and you will have the crown. I have chosen New Year's Day, after many consultations with the astrologers. First you will go into the temple, and there await the word of Amun. Spend the rest of this month in preparation, Hatshepsut, but do not speak of this yourself, for I do not intend to make a pronouncement until we return. Examine also your doubts. You must be sure that this is what you really want. Are you sure?"

"I do not need to search my mind," she said firmly. "I have no doubts, nor will I ever have. This gift is not only yours to give, Pharaoh, and I know that from the beginning the God also intended this for me. Do not fear. I will rule well."

"I have no doubts about that!" her father snapped. "Now go back to your cats and your flowers for a few days, and enjoy the last true freedom you will ever have."

"Tush!" She kissed him on his cheek and floated to the door. "I will always be free, O my father, because all in me is subordinate to my will. So should it be with every man. But as it is not so, the strong rule the weak, like Thothmes."

She danced out, and he sent for his maps. No God must be forgotten, and shrines dotted the banks of the Nile throughout its noble length.

A week later Senmut received a scroll from one of the Royal Messengers. He took it immediately to his own rooms, for he had been eating in the engineers' rooms with Benya. He saw immediately that this was no rudely printed letter from the village of his father, and he broke the heavy seal with trembling fingers. The black hieroglyphs sprang out to meet his eye.

I am soon to embark on a voyage with my father and will be away for the month of Mesore. Do thou continue in the work which I have set thee, and when I return, I will begin to build. I give to thee the slave Ta-kha'et, to be to thee what thou wilt. Do not keep her idle.

It was signed by the Great Royal Scribe Anen himself, for Hatshepsut. Senmut had scarcely finished reading when there was a knock on his door. He called, "Enter!" Ta-kha'et glided in, closing the door behind her and prostrating herself. He looked down on the shining red head with amazement. "Get up!" She scrambled to her feet and stood before him, eyes downcast. "And what am I supposed to do with you?" he asked her. "Look at me!" Immediately the green eyes were fixed on his face, and in their depths he read mirth. She was enjoying the joke.

"The Crown Prince gave me to you so that you may not go abroad under the sun without kohl," she said. She had a high, lilting voice, heavily accented; and when she spoke, she revealed tiny white teeth. Her skin was pale, almost white, and he knew that whatever she was, she came from a country far from Egypt. "The Crown Prince also said that I was to amuse you while she was away and make the nights of winter less tedious."

Senmut grinned. "Where do you come from?" She looked at him, confused. "Where were you born?"

She raised her saffron-clad shoulders in an eloquent gesture. "I do not know, Master. I remember a great cold and the sea, but little more. I have been in the household of the son of the Vizier of the North for a long time, as a body servant."

"Then how did you come to be in the palace?"

"The Prince Hapuseneb gave me to Her Highness because I was skilled in the use of all cosmetics."

Senmut finally burst into laughter, and she smiled back at him, understanding growing between them. "You have other skills, I suppose."

She lowered her eyes, pleating the skirt of her kilt with freckled fingers. "That is for you to say, Master."

"We will see. You are indeed a most valued gift."

"I hope so. The Crown Prince told me to prove my worth as soon as possible."

He dismissed her and sat beside his couch, grinning, then went about his business, eating again with Benya in the evening. But when he returned from his meal, wrapped in his cloak, for the nights of winter were often cold, he found a brazier blazing in the corner of his bedroom and the lamps lit and incense burning sweetly before his little shrine to Amun.

Ta-kha'et bowed as he entered. She was wearing only a thin garment that seemed to halo her small figure like the smoke that rose in the crucible, and she had woven winter flowers, mauve and green, in her hair.

"Would you like hot spiced wine to warm you on this cold night?" she asked him, but her eyes spoke of a drug more heady than warm wine, more spiced than the freshest honey cakes.

He could not speak. He moved toward her, and she caught the cloak that slipped from his shoulders, dropping it behind her on the stool and turning back to him, hands already exploring his shoulders, his taut back. He put an arm around her, drawing her tightly to him, feeling the hard swell of her breasts as his lips found the warmth of her neck. She laughed softly, drawing him to his couch, and the lamps burned low and began to flutter before he spoke again.

So Senmut, peasant, priest, and architect, lost his virginity at last. He grew fond of Ta-kha'et, of her dry wit, her comfortable silences, her sudden, unarticulated passions. With her waiting for him in the security of his little room, he found that he could work with a clearer mind. Doubtless the Prince knew this, he mused, and he realized that the dedication Hatshepsut demanded of him in his capacity as architect was not to be marred by the interior tensions and strivings of an unsatisfied male. How cunning she was, and how astute! And how pitiless in her single-mindedness, her assumption that all would be as she wished if she but desired the end. He went back to the plans with renewed vigor and to his couch with an ever springing appetite.

On the evening of the last day of the month of Apap, Hatshepsut approached the temple of Amun. She was alone but for the Follower of His Majesty who escorted her through the cold, wet-smelling trees; and when she reached the first pylon that warned her of the entrance to the holy precincts, he bowed and left her.

She was dressed only in her kilt, and her father had washed her thoroughly of all cosmetics, oils, and perfumes. Her hair was bound up and fastened on top of her head with a simple copper pin, and she wore no other ornament.

The sun had set an hour ago, and the heat had rapidly drained from the land, Ra taking with him all light, all warmth, all color. Hatshepsut shivered in the cold wind that funneled past her back, through the pylon, and on into the deserted outer court of the temple. She knelt, kissed the ground, and hurried on, eager to be out of the wind; but the courtyard was as cold and deserted as the garden had been, the next pylon and the next and the next casting deep shadows onto the golden floors. No priests lingered here, and no worshipers disturbed the winter evening. The girl looked about her for a moment, wanting to run from the dark places in which the wind sighed. It was the night of her private meeting with

Amun, and no lamps had been lit. She stepped forward hesitantly, passing the holes that were only connecting passages but that gaped at her like black mouths slavering to swallow her up, and crossed the outer court as quickly as she could, muttering a prayer. Between the third and the fourth pylons the darkness was thicker, for here her father's cedar roof shut out whatever light the sky still held. She ran from pillar to towering pillar, seeking the golden doors that led to another hall and another passage, smaller, more secret, fraught with mysteries, and so to the sanctuary, and the Great God Himself.

The doors were within reach now, over twice her height and ten paces wide. She jumped and uttered a cry as a silent figure glided out of the darkness, key in hand.

It was the High Priest, who had come to escort her to the sanctuary. He was heavily cloaked and hooded, and she longed to tear the cloth from him and wrap it around her own naked shoulders. He signaled to her and unlocked the doors. They opened without a sound, and the two passed through, starting up the narrow hall together. At the far end lay other doors, ivory and electrum, and here the High Priest once more used a key, standing back this time for her to go in alone.

The air was very cold and utterly without movement, as if she stood at the heart of the temple. As the footsteps of the High Priest died away, Hatshepsut felt as if she was being slowly stifled in the middle of a vast labyrinth. I have nothing to fear, she told herself, he is my Father. But for a long time she could not turn to face the One who waited, though she felt him, his presence a freezing, palpable thing here in the holiest of holiest, where his power radiated day and night. But at last she swung around, and saw him.

He sat calmly upon his golden throne, his golden hands upon his golden knees, his feet surrounded by silver and gold dishes, his body clothed in the best linen the country could make. She could see better now, for on each side of the enormous, monolithic figure dim lamps burned and before his throne two copper censers stood, glowing and smoking forever. In the wall on each side of him were set small doors, one to the High Priest's rooms and one to Thothmes' retiring chamber, but they were shut tight and did not appear to have any handles or locks. It was a long time before Hatshepsut could look on his face. She dropped to the icy golden floor, pressing her face to it, her eyes tightly closed, but she found that she could not pray as she had intended. His presence was too near, too overpowering. It surrounded her; she was suffocated by it. She remained prone until her shivering back and aching legs and arms demanded change. When she was ready, she sat before him cross-legged and looked into his face.

It was an awesome face, yet not frightening. The golden eyes were wide and farseeing, the golden mouth slightly smiling, and upon the august forehead the beautiful golden plumes of his Godhead reared, looking as if the slightest breeze would set them swaying. So he sat, Mighty Amun of Thebes, ruling the world from his tiny, dark sanctuary, receiving daily the adoration of Pharaoh after Pharaoh. Sometimes he was borne about the city, but he preferred to work his works here, in the mysterious dimness and perpetual twilight of his throne.

Hatshepsut gazed upon him until her eyes swam and he seemed to dance. She closed her eyes again, seeing him grow and grow and tower over all things, mighty, invincible. In between bouts of shivering she touched her head to the floor in worship. But he did not speak. He did not welcome her or give her any sign, and desperation and misery grew in her as the night wore on. Far above, out in the world where there were stars and clouds and fresh winds, the horns blew midnight, and still the God did not speak to the despairing girl.

Finally she put her head to the floor and left it there despite the complaining of her back. Amun, O my Father, she thought, defeated and tired, the words echoing in the empty, barren sanctuary of her mind, where she wandered, seeking him. Her limbs loosened. Her breath slowed. Somewhere there must be a door, somewhere a crack through which she might reach out to touch him.

But now the cavernous expanse of oblivion called to her softly, hypnotically. "Hatshepsut. Hatshepsut. Hatshepsut." There was a shaft of light up which she was gliding. It grew steadily brighter, and she found herself back in the sanctuary, face to face with a young man who leaned negligently against the God's knees. He was tall and very beautiful. His hair was short and golden, and his kilt was of gold tissue. His face was painted with gold, as were his feet, and the nails of his fingers and toes glittered in the lamplight. Hatshepsut did not know later whether he carried with him the brightness of the Sun or whether he sparkled because of the lamplight on him, but the room seemed full of warmth and a breath of the spring to come. She knew that never before in her life had she seen such a handsome face. His mouth was full and arrogant, his eyes large, his jaw swept up over a long neck, and his chin was square and cleft.

As she put her hands out in worship, he laughed. "By all means bow to me," he said, his voice strong and seeming as full of gold as the rest of him. "For I am a thousand thousand times greater than you, Hatshepsut. Here you stand, a Princess of Egypt, in nothing but a coarse kilt linen, while I go clothed in the Sun Himself." He held out a hand, fanning the fingers, admiring his nails. "I am beautiful, more beautiful by far than you whom they call the Flower of Egypt."

Suddenly Hatshepsut did not like him. God or not, he was as vain as herself and very dangerous. She half turned to the door.

"Oh, by all means, leave," he said. "The door is unlocked, and no one will blame you for running demented from this place. After all, Amun is a powerful God, is he not? All men fear him and serve him, do they not? And you, you have more reason than any to do both, for he fathered you, did he not? Or did he?" The last question was asked in a derisory, sarcastic tone, and the young man put his head on one side and smiled at her knowingly.

She stepped away from the door. "No man has spoken to me in that manner before," she said coldly.

His golden eyebrows rose. "But of course not!" he agreed. "None would dare question the holy conception of the Flower of Egypt." He was sneering now, the beautiful mouth twisted. "But I am not exactly a man, and I will say what I please to you, little girl pretending to be a princess."

"Then you are a God?"

"For shame, Hatshepsut! Do you not know who I am?" He stroked Amun's leg with one shimmering finger. "I ride in the Heavenly Barque every day. I journey with Ra, the King of the Living and the Dead, and bathe in his fire whenever I please. Do you still not know me?"

"No."

"I look over your shoulder when you preen in front of your mirror. I walk beside you in the garden, by the river. I saw you in the secret valley —oh, yes, and Senmut, too! A handsome cock, but too ambitious. Watch him, Hatshepsut, though you must love him. He will serve you as long as you have breath; I know that. You know it, too, do you not? But you must give him room to move, or he will destroy himself and break your heart. Oh, Hatshepsut, lovely Hatshepsut, how many kas have you?"

"The Mighty Amun created fourteen for me!" She watched him, this rude, unpredictable youth, with wary eyes, expecting him to spring at her at any moment or to meow or to call forth more gods. Yet there was a something about him that she knew.

He tripped lightly in front of the God with never a bow, and he quickly jumped and settled himself in Amun's lap. Hatshepsut gasped, but the golden boy just laughed that silly, high-pitched, slightly inane laugh again. "Fourteen! Such a generous God is our Amun! And what sex are they?"

"Why, they are male."

"Yes!"

She ran forward suddenly. "I understand! You are one of my kas!"

He raised a finger, after glancing swiftly at its golden nail again as if thirsty for a look at himself. "I am vain, selfish, grasping, arrogant, cruel, unpredictable, and thoroughly without scruples. How can I be you? For you, little peasant, are surely meek, unselfish, kindly, sweet, loving, and good. Is it not so?"

She stamped her foot. "Go away! You are playing with me, and I will not allow it!"

He whistled. "My, how good you are at giving orders. Do you never wake in the night and fear, wondering what would happen if no one obeyed you?"

"Get out! You profane the God with your silly talking, and you are wasting my holy night with your trifles!"

He pouted, the golden lips glistening. "But this is my holy night, too. I must say that I prefer playing in the sun to being in this dark, cold, incense-ridden cell." He jumped lightly from his perch and landed in front of her, and she saw that even in his nostrils gold dust glittered. "You are to go on a journey, proud Hatshepsut. Tell me, what do you want? You must decide before you go, you know, or all the begging and incense in the world will not convince the river deities to listen to you for one moment. Old Amun only created the tools, you know."

"How dare you!"

He came closer. "Well, what do you want? Power? Might to make war? Gold running through your pretty hands like shining water? The worship of all men, particularly that hard, sober priest Senmut? What? What?"

"You know what I want!"

"I know what you think you want. How shallow you are, dear one. You think that it will be fun to rule Egypt and have all bow to you, the Daughter of the God, and you want to be adored, and you want to make the country do your will. Is it not so?"

She put her hands to her ears. "Yes!" she shouted, sobbing. "Yes, it is so! Power I want, and all the rest!"

"Well, you admit it. But there is more."

"Yes, there is more. I truly believe there is more." Her hands fell to her sides. "What is greater than the good of Pharaoh, O my vile ka?"

He skipped back to Amun. "Why, the good of Egypt."

"Then we agree on this. I want the good of Egypt. That is what I want, and that is what I shall pray for on my journey."

"But, of course, you are the good of Egypt." He smiled. "I think you are right. You do not deserve Egypt, but you will be a good Pharaoh. Now I advise." He patted his curls. "Beware of Thothmes, your brother. You know in your heart that he is the snake with the lazy eye who strikes quickly, but you do not know that it is as a father he will destroy you. Beware the priests of Amun, not the God; he cannot hurt you. Beware of yourself, of your vast ambitions. There! Now I am weary of your company, peasant, and wish to return to Ra." He yawned. "And, oh, yes, Mighty Amun is pleased with you and blesses you, Hatshepsut. Go to bed now. It is dawn." He straightened. "And there is one thing more. Before you leave Thebes, make sacrifice to Montu. Thus will your reign be free from war. Not skirmishes," he finished, shaking a languid head, "just war."

"O Mighty Amun," she said happily. "What a holy night it has been!"

And when the High Priest came to escort her home, he found her still asleep and smiling, lying on her side with one arm about the foot of the God.

11

On the first day of Mesore, Hatshepsut and Thothmes set out on their journey. While he waited in the Royal Barge, she went into the temple and sacrificed a bull to Montu, watched by his silent, fierce priests. When she had finished, she left them to burn the carcass and joined her father on the boat. It was a glorious winter day, warm but with a slight breeze; the sky had lost the hard, bronzed look it had in summer and seemed to bend to them softly, bright and light and blue. The pennants of blue and white fluttered gaily from the two masts, and the golden prow slid from the steps and dipped into the water. As they pulled away, the company on the bank burned incense to Hapi, God of the Nile, and cast flowers for him upon the water, where they lay bobbing like a red carpet in the swell left by the barge. The supply skiffs followed, all in a string, swinging with the current until they adjusted speed, and the whole flotilla moved slowly out of sight, sails of damask and gold thread slapping in the wind.

Hatshepsut and Thothmes stood together, watching the city slip by. Behind them their breakfast waited under the roof of the cabin. The cabin's sides had been rolled up so that the royal pair could eat and enjoy the view, but they were not yet hungry enough to leave the bow. The smell of the river and the rushes and the thrusting, growing things mingled delightfully with a song of birds and a flashing of bright dragonflies. One settled for a moment on Hatshepsut's arm, and she had time to admire the quivering gossamer of the wings, blue and bright red, and the long, shiny black body before it tensed and darted away after a swarm of mosquitoes that floated by. She sighed, a sigh of pure delight. Never before had she left the city, and everything she saw was new to her. Ahead lay a time of feasts and informal delights, of days with her father, watching Egypt slide by, of nights gazing at the stars while the boat rocked her to sleep. She was as excited as the child she used to be.

Thothmes felt satisfied as he watched the parted lips, the bright eyes, the brown hands grasping the rail. He was free of dispatches and lawyers and petty squabbles in the Courts of Justice for a while, and Ineni and his Viziers could sweat under the load of government. He planted his feet firmly on the deck and flung back his head, sniffing the wind. It had been a long time since he had left Thebes to make war or to visit his building sites. He was as excited as she, anxious to show her the incomparable delights of this land that was a true gift of the gods. Before they went into the cabin to eat, the city had been left behind and the river wound placidly through drowned fields and acres of sodden palms that bristled against the sky. The hills to the right and the left, five miles away, were misty in the humid air of winter, and a steam rose from the river as the sun climbed higher. They ate eagerly, laughing together over nothing and leaning back on their cushions to sip wine. By the time they moved out onto the deck to sit in their chairs under the canopy, the river was taking a long curve to the east and the cliffs had begun to march away from them, back into the desert.

"In another day they will return," Thothmes told her. "They are never far from us, and well it is so, for the cliffs take the place of many divisions of soldiers and protect us most effectively from the roaming desert tribes. In three or four days we will reach Abydos, that holiest of places, but I do not want to disembark there. We will anchor and perhaps spend a night, but then we will press on."

She did not answer, engrossed as she was in watching the panorama of her kingdom unroll like a huge scroll. The sun had gained heat, and the river ran more swiftly. She could see the movement of the current ahead, pushing aside the stiller waters of the flood. When they slowly passed small villages, whose mud huts were roofed with papyrus and shaded by trees, she often noticed animals, chickens, and goats and sometimes cattle standing disconsolately and staring over their grazing fields, now under water. But the level of the flood had already dropped, and in one or two places the fellahin were already at work, their backs bent, straining after the plough or pacing in the ankle-deep mud, strewing seed upon the fertile ground. Once they sailed past a fisherman who sat in his little skiff, his line motionless, his chin sunk on his naked chest, and his head uncovered. He did not stir as they slipped quietly by.

"A most agreeable pastime," Pharaoh remarked.

Hatshepsut agreed fervently, thinking of Senmut and of how she had met him in the marshes by the river. She tried to picture his father as one of these fellahin, working unceasingly from dawn until dark, walking home to lentils and boiled papyrus shoots and thick black bread or perhaps a piece of roasted beef if he had been successful on market day. But there seemed to her to be no connection whatsoever between Senmut and his father, and she gave up, content to let her thoughts drift with the boat, watching it cleave the water like a golden crocodile, as silent and as beautiful.

On the evening of the fourth day they came to Abydos. The sun was sinking behind the little town, and Hatshepsut could see nothing. But when Ra had gone and the sky was deep blue, dressed now in a high, white moon and a few early stars, she could see the white roofs of buildings hidden by palm trees and farther back the pylons and pillars of a temple. She huddled under her cloak in the winter chill, bemused by the silence, a silence she was unused to, being always surrounded by the noises of the living palace. The pale, ghostly buildings and black arms of the trees made her feel a little lonely. The barge tugged gently at her moorings in the reeds, and a night bird chuckled, rustling on its nest.

"This is holy Abydos, where the head of Osiris lies," Thothmes told her quietly. "As your mother cared for me, so Isis loved the God and collected the pieces of his poor, broken body from the ends of the earth. I have built here, but we will not linger. Abydos is not far from Thebes, and you will have opportunity again to explore it more. I am going to bed. In the morning we will perform the ceremonies for Osiris and then press on."

He kissed her cold forehead and strode swiftly away, but Hatshepsut had not yet drunk her fill of the night. She stayed where she was, leaning over the side and watching the reflection of the aft lights far above her twinkle on the calm, oily surface of the water below. She pondered the murder of the Sun-God's Son and the dedication of his faithful Isis, and she walked around the deck, listening to her father's snores and the talk and subdued laughter that drifted over the water from the servants' skiffs. She was utterly alone with the dark sky and the cool wind, but she did not mind. The solitude was an extension of the self-discovery that had begun after the death of Aahmose, and she paced as her father often did, her brow furrowed, her eyes on the deck beneath her feet. Not until there was silence from across the water did she go to her couch.

In the fresh, new morning the whole company gathered on the bank and solemnly sacrificed to Osiris. But the mood was gay, and when all was done, they trooped back on board and cast off quickly, men and masters glad to be under way once more. Hatshepsut had slept soundly and without dreams, waking to birdsong and the cool air that flowed like wine through her cabin. She and Thothmes sat on opposite sides of the breakfast table, eating as the sailors poled the barge to the middle of the river and hoisted the sails again. The wind was favorable, a following wind, and the sails gulped at it like a fish. From the stern the captain's voice rang out with a sharp order, and the patter of swift bare feet on the deck mingled most agreeably with the smell of fresh fish and warm goose eggs.

Hatshepsut had noticed a pile of ruins some two miles north of the town, and she remarked on it to Thothmes, who put down his bread, scowling.

"That was once the temple of Khentiamentiu, the Jackal-God of Abydos," he grunted. "Now it lies desolate, not one stone still piled upon another. The wild animals have taken it for their abode." He spat on the floor. "Filthy, heathen Hyksos! Many hentis has it been since they left Egypt, driven forth in mighty anger by your illustrious forefathers. But still the wreck and sorrow they caused lives after them." He picked up his bread again, slapping meat onto it.

"Khentiamentiu," Hatshepsut said, "surely a God of power to the people of Abydos. I will rebuild for them, I think, and for him."

Thothmes looked surprised. "Will you? Good! I have done what I can, but the empty shrines litter the land like seed husks when the fruit is gone, and the people still mourn. I will show you yet another ruin in five days time, Hatshepsut. There you must go forth to see what this God has to say, for it is Hathor, and her temple at Cusae is a tangle of weeds and dead brush."

They sailed on, and the country did not change. But in that time the river fell a few more inches, exposing a pattern of black and brown land, sometimes green with young crops and crisscrossed with dirt paths and everywhere trees and the vibrant flowers of winter that clustered or straggled in the fields and beside the river. Now and then a noble's estate hove into sight, its high walls running to the river, the paved water steps, the tethered skiffs, and the low, cool promenades and cloisters falling behind them like a dream; but this did not happen often, for they were far from any large city. They could see the blinding yellow sand between field and cliff and once in a while a lonely road that ran beyond the hills and out into the burning desert.

After five days they came to a road that seemed to run right down into the river. Pharaoh ordered the anchor run out and the litters unloaded. While they waited, he pointed inland. "Cusae lies just behind the cliffs," he said, "and this road used to bring the villagers to the river. It is not much traveled now, and I have been considering stationing a detachment of troops up there in the hills, for brigands and the desert men have begun to creep in here, and life is not safe for the villagers who remain." He and Hatshepsut climbed onto their litters, and the four-mile walk began. Before and behind marched four Followers of His Majesty, their eyes on the tops of the cliffs for any sign of movement, but the horizon remained empty of all save a few birds that wheeled high above them, too far away to be identified.

In the summer such a walk would have been torture, but at this time of the year it was a pleasant jaunt. The litter swayed along under their gold-tasseled canopies, the road running straight and true to the little pass in the rocks that slowly drew nearer. Suddenly they were traveling over rock, in deep shadow, and just as suddenly they were free to look out upon the village of Cusae. There was not much to see. A few mud huts, inhabited, for smoke rose in lazy spirals from the roofs; struggling fields marked by scraggly thorns and stunted acacia and palms; the ruins of stone houses once inhabited by the rich, who had deserted the town with the troubled times of occupation. Thothmes spoke, and they walked on, for on the edge of the settlement a little temple lay, its six pillars touching the blue sky with delicate fingers, gleaming white in the morning light. The walls of its outer court lay in ruin, the stones jutting out of the windswept grasses like the bare and broken bones of the earth itself. Within the line of the wall Hatshepsut could see what once had been a garden, now only a collection of dry sticks, and a matted brown carpet of dead lawns.

"I will wait for you here," Thothmes said. The procession came to a halt. "Go forward, for that is the temple of Hathor, and to her you owe homage."

Obediently Hatshepsut slid off her litter and left them. The sand was hot to her feet and hard to struggle through. But before long the ground grew firm, and she knew that beneath her lay an avenue, long buried. She soon passed the doors of the outer court, which lay half buried in sand, and entered the hall. The paving stones were cracked and heaved asunder, the desert thorns thrust up between them; and all around lay broken columns, the colors faded to a dirty gray or muddy yellow, chipped and eaten by the passing years. She picked her way toward the sanctuary and the white pillars, but as she drew nearer, she saw that the pillars were a mockery, a false and heartbreaking travesty of what had been, for behind them was nothing, only empty desert, shaking in the sun.

She turned, near tears, feeling the infinite, pathetic loneliness of the place. Someone shyly touched her hand. She looked down. Four children had crept after her and stood gazing at her with the wide, unblinking stare of the very young. One had a crude bow fashioned from papyrus, and another had made a spear of a thorn branch and had tipped it with wood. All were thin. Their bones stuck out of their bodies like the jagged stones that lay about them, and they were the color of the brown, withered, unidentifiable dead plants under their feet. The little girl who had touched her drew back, her finger creeping into her grubby mouth. Hatshepsut wanted to laugh in spite of herself. "What are you children doing here?" she asked them severely. "Do you not know that this is a holy place?"

They continued to watch her uncomprehendingly, until one of the boys spoke. "We come here to play," he answered defiantly. "This is our garrison, and we are defending it to the death, for Pharaoh. Have you ever seen Pharaoh?" he finished, noting the fine linen, the jeweled sandals.

Before Hatshepsut could reply, the same little girl tugged at her kilt. "I know why you are here," she whispered. "Have you come to see the pretty lady?"

Hatshepsut looked into the wide, innocent eyes and repressed an instinct to reach for her amulet. She nodded. "Yes, I have. Can you take me to her?"

The child reached up a dusty hand, and Hatshepsut's closed around it. Together they walked back to the outer court. The girl picked her way unerringly through the tangle of stone and brush and stopped at last in a corner where a portion of the wall was still standing, one stone holding up the others. "There she is," the girl lisped and ran back to her friends.

Hatshepsut bent in wonderment. At her feet lay a crude basket, containing the remains of a food offering: dry bread, wrinkled fruit, a withered lotus blossom. Against the wall, hidden by fallen masonry, was the Goddess Herself, still arrayed in blue and red and yellow, smiling fixedly into Hatshepsut's startled eyes, her cow's horns rising like wands. One was still encased in gold. Hatshepsut turned swiftly, but the children had run away. She fell to the earth and kissed the feet of Hathor, her heart warming toward the woman who came still to perform lonely homage, leaving her pitiful offerings for the gentle, smiling Goddess. She sat back and began the prayers, the words coming to her tongue with difficulty, for she had not prayed to Hathor since her childhood, when she doubted that she would grow tall and beautiful. She asked for patience and for the blessing of the Goddess on her reign. Hathor, with her soft, bovine smile, seemed to be forbidding all worry and all preoccupations. "Make me beautiful even as you are beautiful, and I will lift that which is fallen and restore the priests and bring incense again to glorify you," Hatshepsut promised. She rose, kissed the feet once more, and left the court, walking swiftly.

Beyond the outer door the children huddled, waiting, and on an impulse she stopped.

"Would you like to meet Pharaoh?" she asked.

They goggled at her, speechless. Then the boy spoke up. "You are making us to look silly!" he said. "What would Pharaoh be doing out here, far from his throne and his crown?"

"Nevertheless, he is here," she retorted, sweeping down an arm and holding him. "Come with me."

With many dubious looks and whisperings they followed her. In a matter of minutes Thothmes saw her striding toward him, accompanied by a rabble of peasant children. He got off his litter with a grunt.

"Father," she shouted, "here are the children of Cusae to meet with Pharaoh!" She came up smiling and panting, her hair in disarray and her kilt smudged. Behind her the children looked up at this short, mighty man with the black, glittering eyes, hanging back, until they saw that he did indeed wear the flaming Uraeus of royalty on his leather helmet.

"Get down. Get down!" the boy whispered fiercely to the others. "It is indeed he!" They knelt as they did in their games, faltering, not knowing quite what to do.

Hatshepsut bent and patted their heads. "Up now. This is Pharaoh. You can tell your mothers and your fathers of this day!" She was excited and flushed.

Thothmes laughed at her in spite of himself. "I send you to seek the Goddess, and you find a gaggle of Nile geese!" he growled. "Well, all of you, what say you now? Here, boy, show me your bow." With one stride he was upon the lad and had swept it out of his hand. "You made it yourself?"

The child gulped. "Yes, Mighty One."

"Hmm. Can you shoot it?"

"There is something wrong with it. I cannot get the right wood, and the arrow will not fly far."

Thothmes flung it to the ground. "Kenamun!" he barked. His captain detached himself from the group of smiling soldiers and came forward, bowing. "Give the boy your bow and your arrows."

The articles were handed over, and the child's eyes grew wide as he took them with eager, trembling fingers. The bow was as tall as he, but he plucked the string, and it hummed. "Oh, thank you, Mighty Horus, Majesty!" he stammered.

Thothmes smiled. "Remember this day," he said, "and when you grow older, you may bend that bow in my service. Now I want lunch," he said, and the litter bearers jumped forward. "Come, Hatshepsut, before the whole population rushes forth to denude my men of all they have."

They got back on the litters and set off. When Hatshepsut looked back some minutes later, she could see the children standing as she had left them, four tiny dots against a wide horizon, the pillars of Hathor gleaming white behind them.

"Today we come to the great plains of the pyramids," Thothmes said as they stood together in the bow.

Two weeks of steady sailing were behind them. The trip had begun to acquire the properties of a pleasant dream for Hatshepsut: days of sun-bathing, eating, and desultory conversation while the country slipped by; nights of deep slumber, rocked by the lapping waves in some hidden, deserted bay. It was indeed a beautiful land, her Egypt, a green and fragrant flower, a gem, more beautiful than she had ever imagined. If they had turned back now, she would have been satisfied.

Thothmes continued. "It is this plain, more than any other wonder, that I wish you to see, for only then will you feel your destiny, Hatshepsut. You will be amazed. Your ancestors built on this plain, but I will say no more. Watch the western bank, and you will see the hills draw back and become invisible."

The morning wore on, and Hatshepsut wanted to go and sit down in the shade, but her father remained immobile, his face strangely still, gazing before him and to the west.

At last she could wait no longer and turned to him with a request to have a chair brought, but at that moment one of the sailors gave a shout.

Thothmes drew in his breath with a great hiss. "See, far to the west and yet on the horizon. It is the first!"

She looked. A shape loomed, small and far away, flat-topped, yet rising startlingly from the plain that had begun to open out. There was no cultivation here, no houses; only a straggling strip of green reedbeds ran between river and sand. The pyramid was like a boulder dropped from the sky. Chairs and parasols were brought, and they sat down but did not speak; the sailors and servants were silent, too. The shape came closer, became clearer, until nothing else in view mattered in the least. Hatshepsut could see that behind and beyond it others rose, still hazy and miles away, and an excitement began to grow within her. They were abreast of it, and she saw that it was surrounded by dry causeways and broken stone, its flat top and stubby feet somehow still speaking defiance to the havoc wreaked by weather and man.

"It was not always thus," Thothmes said as they passed it slowly. "Once it was sheathed in the whitest of limestone and shone as the Sun in all his glory. None knows now what God lies buried there, but it is said that Senefru rests beneath the stone."

Another pyramid glided toward them, its peak sticking into the sky with a point like a lance. Hatshepsut held her breath. It did not seem to her that any man could build so, and the knowledge that these men who were more than men were her own ancestors stirred her profoundly. She remembered the little pyramid of Mentu-hotep-hapet-Ra, but against it these were crude giants, massive and infinitely strong.

As the boat glided past them, Thothmes said, "There is more to come.

You have seen but the beginning. From here to Memphis, a day's gentle sailing, the desert is thick with them, small and large. Quite a sight, is it not?"

He turned jocularly to his daughter, but she had not heard him. Her eyes followed the slow, majestic passing of the tombs, and her face was immobile.

They reached Memphis the same night but moored a little way upriver to sleep. By the time the anchors were cast, it was quite dark, and nothing more of the pyramids could be seen. But Hatshepsut could hear the city as she lay on her couch. The rattle of boats at the docks, the human hum, the cacophony of night sounds were becoming unaccustomed noises, and she could not sleep. Her father had told her little of the city, but she knew that it was beautiful and that it had once been the capital of Egypt when Buto, that oldest and most mysterious of cities, fell from favor. The sounds of it made her a little homesick for Thebes and her cool apartment and the faces she knew, and she turned restlessly under the warmth of her mantles. All at once she wondered how Senmut and Ta-kha'et the slave were. At that thought her mood lifted, and she laughed softly into the darkness. Her mind moved from Senmut and across the river to her valley, lying silent under the moon. She still did not know what to do there. The pyramids she had seen had jolted her into a new awareness of what could be accomplished, and she vowed that Senmut must equal the achievements of the gods for her. But how? And in what way? The sights of the day had drained her, and she wanted to sleep, for the next day she must put on royal robes once more and receive the homage of the Viceroy. But sleep escaped her.

When day dawned, she wrapped herself in her cloak and stepped out into a forest of gray-green date palms. She blinked in confusion, stepping to the side of the boat on chilled bare feet, but it was so: tree upon tree upon tree, wrapped in the mist of early morning. As she breathed the good smell of wet, growing things, the sun shook off its skirts of trailing mist and rose free, glinting on something white that she only vaguely glimpsed through the trees. Shivering, she backed into the cabin, closing the flap behind her, and stepping gratefully into the basin of hot water that her slave had prepared. She let herself be bathed. She had agreed to put on a sheath for this day, and after her bath she stood still while the girl slipped it over her head and smoothed it down her thighs. It was of white linen, stitched all over with golden leaves, and its thick border of layered gold brushed her ankles. She raised her arms, and the slave pulled the belt tight, a golden rope encrusted with large pieces of lapis lazuli and tasseled with gold thread. She sat while her makeup was applied: gold paint for her eyelids, kohl to rim her eyes, henna for her lips and for the palms of her delicate hands. Her hair was brushed, and the heavy ceremonial wig—a hundred long black braids that hung stiffly to her shoulders and brushed the back of her neck—was lifted and settled into place. She moved her head uneasily while her jewel box was brought to her. She lifted the lid and considered. She would have liked to have worn something light and pretty, the silver links perhaps, or the blue faience flowers, but she chose a golden breastplate: two royal Horus birds facing one another with the double crown on their heads, joined by serpents writhing about twin ankhs, the whole picked out in feldspar and carnelian and resting heavily on her breasts. For her arms there were bracelets of electrum, and for her head a small cap of gold tissue, covered in feathers of turquoise.

When she was dressed and her slave had put on her her sandals, she went and found Thothmes waiting for her and the boat already nearing the landing stage. He too was dressed for ceremony, in gold, soft blue, and white leather. His face was carefully made up, and he greeted her absently, his eyes on the solemn assembly of dignitaries that was ranged about the water steps. Behind them a broad avenue ran to the shining white wall enclosing the city and the bronze gate that now stood wide. Beyond that Hatshepsut could make out houses and obelisks and the gardens of a temple.

"You see the famous White Wall of Menes," Thothmes told her, "and far to the rear the pylons of the home of the God Ptah's wife. We will dine this morning with the High Priest of Memphis, but before that we must go into the temple and do homage. How happy Thothmes would be to see this!"

Happy indeed, as I am, thought Hatshepsut, for she and Thothmes, despite their mutual dislike, shared in their worship of Sekhmet, the Lion-Goddess of Memphis.

They had arrived. The ramp was run out, and the horns sounded from the wall. She and Pharaoh walked slowly down it to the assembled priests, who were on their faces. They waited while Thothmes' Chief Herald called his titles, and afterward the High Priest crawled toward them and kissed their feet.

"Rise, fortunate one," Thothmes said. The High Priest got up, bowed again, and welcomed them gravely.

Hatshepsut saw that he was a young man, plump, with a crooked nose and lively eyes. He was very nervous, the perspiration gathering on his forehead under the headdress of his office.

Thothmes answered him. "Happy is this day! All Egypt rejoices at the progress of the Flower of Egypt, who goeth abroad in the land for a vision of its delights. Happy is the city of Memphis, beloved of Ptah!" When he had finished, they followed the High Priest through the gates to a tumultuous welcome of shouts, waving arms, and kneeling people. The whole city seemed to be a festival. Children ran before them, covering the way with lotus blooms; and when Hatshepsut bent and picked one up, inhaling its scent and holding it in her hand, a great roar went up. It was a day like no other for the dwellers of the city. The God and his Daughter would be with them for two days, and in that time the shops and the school would remain shut, and everyone would keep to the streets in the hope that they might catch a glimpse of the tall, lithe Prince, whose beauty and arrogance were already the talk of Egypt, and of the man who had already become a beloved legend to his people.

The royal apartments in the temple complex had been opened and prepared, and in the banqueting chamber the sun poured onto the tables, the flowers, the carpets, the cushions, and the cups for the wine. The slaves waited anxiously to serve, and the hot water steamed in the washing bowls. A brazier had been lit to disperse the night's chill, and Hatshepsut thankfully sank onto her cushion beside it, holding out her hands to the blaze. She had scorned a cloak on the boat so that the people could see her better, and now she was cold. After more speeches and prostrations a bell was rung, and breakfast commenced. Hatshepsut was delighted to see that all her favorite dishes were brought before her: cucumbers stuffed with fish, broiled goose in sauce, and salads of all the young shoots. She complimented the High Priest on his efficiency.

"What is your name?" she asked him.

"Ptahmes, Highness. My father is Pharaoh's Viceroy and was named for him, Thothmes."

"You must serve the wife of Ptah with diligence, else you would not have become High Priest."

The full face blushed, and Ptahmes bowed. "I have done what is good in the eyes of the God, and he has rewarded me." He looked with frank curiosity upon the face that had been described to him in such detail by friends whose business took them to Thebes. While the full red mouth smiled openly at him and the eyes, blacker and more exotic than a summer night, looked into his, he thought how none of the descriptions had done her justice. There was so much of her that could only be appreciated in movement, the graceful raising of a hand, the gracious inclining of the tall neck. And when she spoke, her voice was pitched low, so that one listened more to the music than to the words.

"I have long loved Sekhmet," she told him, "and it was the greatest pleasure for me to stand before her this morning for the first time in my life. Amun is truly mighty, but Sekhmet understands the heart of a woman, as Hathor does."

She was bending to him, sharing a confidence, and Ptahmes was conquered. For to tell the truth, he had also heard from Thebes of her willfulness, her vanity, her sudden rages, and he had spent the night in an agony of apprehension, lest he should disgrace himself and his father before her and before Pharaoh.

"Sekhmet is indeed mighty!" he agreed fervently.

She smiled and returned to her food. Presently she spoke to him again. "You and I must sacrifice together tomorrow so that I may tell my brother, Thothmes," she said. "He would never forgive me if I returned to Thebes having stood only once beside the High Priest in the sanctuary. I believe that my father and I are to visit the Sacred Bull at dawn, but after breakfast I shall summon you."

"I shall be honored, Noble One," he said. "Pharaoh has business with my father and so will be busy, and if you wish, I could show you fair Memphis." He wondered immediately if he had been too bold, but she drained her cup, dabbled her fingers in the water bowl, and nodded seriously.

"That would delight me, Ptahmes. And you and your father must dine aboard the Royal Barge tomorrow night. We are traveling with little in the way of entertainments, but I have my lute, and perhaps you know of some local musicians who could play for us. I have a love of music."

"I can easily arrange something, Highness. We have waited long for a glimpse of you. The last time I saw your father, I was but a child, and since then I have heard much of the Flower of Egypt."

She glanced at him from beneath dusky eyelids. "Would you flatter me, Noble Ptahmes?" she asked pointedly.

He blushed again. "Your Highness needs no words of flattery from such as I," he replied. But before he could continue, Pharaoh rose, signaling to her, and they filed out of the hall.

The rest of the day was taken up with official acts. She and Thothmes visited Ptahmes' father Thothmes in the Viceregal palace, lunching in the gardens with him, his shy wife, and Ptahmes' sister. In the afternoon they returned to the barge to sleep. Hatshepsut, tired out with speeches and progresses and sleepy from her restless night, had no trouble losing herself though her head was pillowed on her ebony headrest to preserve her wig, not on the cushions on which she longed to sink her head. Later, as the sun westered and the evening grew cool, Thothmes went to the Hall of Justice, the Flail and the Crook in his hand, and heard cases to be settled, Hatshepsut listening with interest from a stool at his feet. When they emerged, night had fallen, and they went to dine on the barge, whose lights lit the shore and twinkled far over the water. Ptahmes was there, more relaxed now. His father and the rest of the family were also present, and Hatshepsut regaled them with tales of life at court and kept them laughing while the dishes and flagons were passed and the Viceroy's own group of musicians played their pipes and sang. As the moon rose higher, the inhabitants of Memphis crept to the shore and sat under the date palms, watching the God and his Daughter and the blessed ones dine, hearing the sweet, tinkling music float to them over the water like a premonition of paradise in the underworld. Long after they grew tired, satiated with the vision of luxury and laughter, and went home to their beds, the company sat on, joke following joke. Finally Thothmes ordered them home, and their lamps were brought. They went slowly, bemused with good food and royal company.

When the last lamp had disappeared, Hatshepsut yawned. "Thothmes the Viceroy is a pleasant man and good company," she said, "but his family gawks and gapes at us like cows in a field."

"Thothmes is well seasoned in the ways of gentle living and has traveled much in his duty to me," Thothmes replied, "but his family has seen little to relieve the boredom of the provinces, and they are merely overawed. Ptahmes is also a good man, loyal and honest. You do well to cultivate his worship, Hatshepsut."

"I suppose so. What a nose he has!"

"Share a cup of wine with me before you go to bed." Thothmes handed her his cup, and she settled herself beside him while the slaves quietly began to clear away the debris of the feast.

"How still it is!" she said. "I welcome the quiet."

"Dawn is not far off, and then we must visit the Sacred Bull," he replied, "so rest while you may. In the afternoon we will set sail once more."

Before the sun was up, they were pacing the avenue to the pen of the Sacred Bull of Memphis. Apis was worshiped throughout Egypt as the symbol of the fertility of man and of the soil so vital to the life of the country, and Thothmes regularly visited his shrine, for he himself was a symbol of the land, Egypt revering Fertility. This morning they were dressed as simply as servants—kilts, sandals, and helmets—and they wore cloaks, for at that hour the city still slept and there was none to see them.

Apis was housed in a small temple close to the White Wall and on the opposite side of the city. As Hatshepsut and Thothmes passed under the little pylon and into the outer court, they could smell him, a pungent cattle smell that rose tart in the clean morning air. His priest was waiting for them and handed them garlands to hang on the God. They could hear him shuffling and blowing, snorting in the sanctuary beyond; but as he heard them approach, he stood still, and a mighty bellow made Hatshepsut's ears ring. The priest pushed open the door of the sanctuary, and they went in, almost fainting from the strong animal smell. But as they adjusted themselves to the dimness and Hatshepsut to the smell, her nostrils quivered, and her mind ran back to Nebanum and her beloved fawn. The fawn had grown up long ago, and she and the keeper had taken him into the desert one day and set him free. All this came back to her as she knelt on the straw-strewn floor and began to crawl forward. Thothmes charged the censer, and together they began the singsong chant while the beast listened quietly, saliva dripping from his gray muzzle onto his gold-shod hoofs. When the rite was finished, Hatshepsut stepped forward to drop the flowers over his horns. As she leaned over the golden railing, the bull lifted his head and licked her on the arm. Delighted, she leaned farther, scratching him behind his ears, and he rumbled and closed his eyes. The priest murmured with astonishment, for this Apis had a reputation for sudden lunges, and many a young priest, sent to wash him, had retired bruised and afraid. At length Hatshepsut slapped him on his massive brown shoulder and stepped aside for Thothmes to present his flowers.

Outside the sanctuary the priest bowed. "While you rule, the country will enjoy great prosperity," he said. "The sign has been given. Long life and health to Your Majesty!"

It was the first time that Hatshepsut had been called Majesty, and, startled, she glanced at Thothmes. He, too, was struck by her power over the animal, and he bowed to her briefly, his face set. He took her arm and led her outside. The sun was only just above the horizon, and all the city was bathed in a pink glow.

"Now we do homage to Ptah, Creator of the World," he said, "and then to our stomachs. Do you tire of all this, Hatshepsut?"

"No. I am as strong as you, father, and you know it! But I grow weary of fine speeches."

"You have not made any yet!" he teased her, and they wended their way to the temple of Ptah.

While Thothmes held conference with the Viceroy, his son took Hatshepsut around the city in a litter. He showed her the old royal palace, seat of power in Egypt for many hundreds of years, and took her up onto the White Wall, from which they could see many miles, over the sea of date palms and to the red cliffs that now paraded far to the west. They visited the markets, the tribute houses, and the place where boats were built. She commented on everything so that the High Priest, relieved, did not have to battle any long silences. She liked the city. It seemed to dream along under the spell of past glories, not with bitterness or decay, but with a proud contentment. Its people were fair and slow-walking. She was not sorry to say good-bye to it, but she would not have missed her visit for anything in the world. She promised Ptahmes that she would return one day. "When you come to Thebes, I will show you *my* city," she told him, and she left him flushed with success, a new convert to her charm.

"Before we leave, we will trek a little way to the west of the city," Thothmes said. "I did not mention it to the good people of Memphis, for the Necropolis here is something that I want you to see unencumbered with well-meaning idiots."

So they cast off, leaving the prone, white-clad figures of their hosts. When they had rounded a bend in the river and were hidden from sight, they moored again on the west bank. Thothmes lost no time in ordering out the litters, and a tired and grumpy Hatshepsut set off once more, her head aching and her eyes rasping in their sockets for want of sleep. It was the time of day when all sensible people took to their couches, she thought angrily. Father must know that I have done enough for today. She glared across at his oblivious, leather-clad head and snapped irritably at the litter bearers when one stumbled on a rock and jolted her.

After an hour of traveling, during which her anger mounted and she sat bolt upright on the litter like an offended cat, Thothmes stopped at last. He got off his litter and held out his hand for her, but she shrugged away, standing up by herself, and smoothing down her kilt in short, abrupt pats.

He noticed her pouting mouth and sullen eyes but said nothing, taking her arm and leading her forward. "Behold the ruined City of the Dead, the Necropolis of Old Memphis," he said. "Behold the works of the Great God Imhotep himself, before your eyes."

Hatshepsut put a hand to her eyes to shade them from the sun and gazed about her, her ire forgotten. The plain flowed unendingly. It was dotted with a few lone palm trees, but churning over the sand, in towers and causeways dry as old bones, in pyramids and walls and passages leading nowhere, lay Saqqara, city of dust. It was a place of unease, and Hatshepsut, even in the full and glaring light of day, could feel the crying of old bones, the wailing of the desecrated dead. It was a place magnificent in its chaotic ruin, and she felt for Thothmes' hand as her gaze traveled over it.

"All this Imhotep did, genius and God," he said quietly. He raised an arm, and Hatshepsut saw a frowning wall, square and thick, with the gloom of a doorway in it. Beyond it was a pyramid whose sides were stepped, a stair mounting grandly to a roof long gone. "That is the tomb of Zoser, mighty King and warrior, built by the hand of Imhotep himself. Upon his own likeness the King caused to be written: 'Chancellor of the King of Lower Egypt, the First after the King of Upper Egypt, Administrator of the Great Palace, Hereditary Lord, the High Priest of Heliopolis, Imhotep, the builder, the sculptor.' Where is his palace now, and his scented gardens? Look and learn, Hatshepsut."

She shuddered. "It is a holy place, but restless," she said. "See, see there, the beauty of the lotus pillars! Where are the eyes for whom they were put forth?" She was upset, her agitation making her grip upon her father's hand tighten.

He turned away. "This, too, is your heritage," he said. "It is good for a king to remember that in the end nothing but stone remains."

Before they went back to the barge, they stood together in Imhotep's chapel as so many sick had done before them, looking into the intense, intelligent face of the man whom all Egypt worshiped as a god of healing. Hatshepsut thought of the ruins behind her and of the enormous expenditure of mind and brawn that had gone into the raising of the stones. Zoser was a mighty king, but without his architect he could do nothing. Again her thoughts flew to Senmut, and she wondered what he was doing. Playing with Ta-kha'et, perhaps, or poring over his drawings, waiting for her approval.

At length they left the chapel, lying on their litters and sapped of all emotion. While the sailors headed for open water once more, they slept, exhausted, and the pile that was Saqqara sunk slowly below the horizon.

At Giza, north of Memphis, they again got onto the litters and were carried five miles inland across indifferent cultivation and under the everlasting palm trees to see what Thothmes described as the final proof of the godhead of her ancestors.

She swayed along eagerly, keyed up now, knowing that the things she had seen and the things she had yet to see were more important to her than anything else she had ever experienced. She wanted to build for herself the greatest monument of all time, and the pyramids and temples she had seen served only to whet an already burning appetite for glory. Her father had built, and his father before him, and even sluggish Thothmes' eyes would kindle as he spoke of his current project, but as yet she had done nothing, hugging to herself her ambition, her visions, and her dreams. As they jogged on, her valley came to her mind, and she felt again the presence of destiny, the mute calling of the unfinished cliffs. Not for nothing was I born of the God to rule this land, she thought fiercely, protectively. All she had seen served to make the love in her to grow— love for the soil, the people, the laughing, fun-loving people.

"Sit up and watch," Thothmes called over to her. "Here are the three crowns of Egypt."

The horizon was suddenly filled up with them, three soaring shapes, so white that her eyes hurt from looking at them. Long before she was put on the ground and had alighted, her heart pounding, the pyramids commanded all sight and all thought. When at last she was able to walk toward them, she stumbled and would have fallen but for the swift arm of her slave, so entranced was she. She leaned against the hot limestone, craning upward, and shook her head at Thothmes, unable to speak. When she had recovered, she began to walk, wanting to pace around each one, touching them, always looking up, but after the circuit of the first she gave up and went to Thothmes in wonder. "It is not possible that these were made by men!" she said. "Surely the gods came and set them here for their own greater glory!" The symmetry of them delighted her, the swift-running rise of each side to the pinnacle. From the ground in their setting in the middle of a flat and sandy plateau they looked clean and simple, sharp as Set's teeth, sufficient to themselves, secure in their mighty superiority.

"They are indeed the works of men," Thothmes told her. "For half a henti many thousands of slaves labored here to make tombs for the kings. Khufu, Khafra, Menkaure rest here. The pyramids are a fitting cover for their holy bodies. Come and see another wonder."

He walked her south, around to the other side, and she found herself standing between two giant paws, lion's feet. "This is the likeness of King Khafra" Thothmes said. "He guards the entrance to his tomb forever. Words of magic and power are engraved on his chest. He caused himself to be carved out of the cliff that reared up here, and he crouches, ever vigilant, his royal lion body waiting to spring on all the unworthy."

Am I worthy? Hatshepsut thought breathlessly, transfixed and humbled by the vastness of the body and the stern warning in the largest stone face she had ever seen. She remained there for a long time while the shadow between the smooth feet grew, fingering the desert and the silent tombs.

She stayed at Giza for the rest of that day and well into the evening, clambering over the remains of the dead courtiers' mastabas, walking the wide avenues, feeling as though every nerve in her body ran outside her brown skin. Her eyes were always drawn back to the three gigantic tombs and their crouching guardian.

Thothmes watched her from his perch on a flat rock—the tiny, lithe figure flitting in and out of sight like a moth in the dusk, her white kilt a smudged patch of lighter light. He knew what she was thinking and feeling, for when he had seen the wonders of his forefathers for the first time, he, too, had been handed the challenge and had felt doubt at his ability to pick it up. He had answered the gods with the monument of war, but how would Hatshepsut find an answer? He knew that she would also strive and sweat and shout back in some way, but the way was not his to see. Finally, when he could no longer see her in the darkness, he sent Kenamun to bring her back, and the soldier found her sitting on one of the Sun-God's paws, her chin in her hand, gazing with troubled eyes into the night.

"How can this be equaled?" she asked, more to herself than to him. "How?" Her question went unanswered. The soldier merely bowed, and she slid to the ground wearily and followed him. Never before had she been so filled with pride in her forefathers or so tired in her soul. Once again, seeing the lights of the barge rising to meet them through a fog of tiredness, she felt the press of dreams, past and present, bearing her down, and it was with unutterable relief that she allowed herself to have the desert sand washed off her and a clean kilt put on. As she sat on her chair under the lamps with a cup of wine in her hand, the dreams receded, leaving her with the feeling of having changed again, having slipped off another skin of childhood and left it behind at the feet of Khafra as an offering and a promise.

It was but half a day's journey from Giza to Heliopolis, true heart of Egypt, and they reached the city at noon. Dignitaries came aboard, crawling over the deck to present their welcome, but the royal couple did not disembark, for here Hatshepsut was to receive her first crown in the temple of the Sun. She sat on her little chair while they kissed her feet, remote from them, gazing over their heads to the shining towers of the city. Behind her, on the west bank, more pyramids marched; and from where she sat, they seemed to be all around her head, a crown of power and invincibility. The official party withdrew, and Thothmes went to lie down. But Hatshepsut had her chair moved so that she could look down-river, back to Thebes, and she pondered her destiny.

She stayed there until evening, neither eating nor drinking, and Thothmes left her alone. He suddenly fancied a little hunting and went off in the skiff into the marshes with Kenamun and his attendants, leaving her alone, the wind lifting the skirt of her kilt, the sun warming her feet, bare on the deck, and her hands as they lay immobile in her lap. When dinner was served and Pharaoh had not returned, she ate a little, quickly, and then went to bed, waking in the night to hear loud laughter and thumping, her father returning from a successful hunt. When the sun rose, she was already on deck, sitting again in her chair. Her slave came and asked her to return to the cabin to be prepared for the ceremony, and she went meekly, still silent. She emerged an hour later wrapped in white, her head bare.

Thothmes raised his eyebrows at her, questioning, while the priests waited on the bank, solemn and unmoving.

She smiled at him briefly. "I am ready," she said.

They led her to the temple through the streets lined with quiet people, for all knew what an occasion this was, and she mounted the steps and stood waiting while the doors were opened for her. Inside all the hierarchy of Heliopolis was gathered, eager for a look at an awesome presence who turned out to be nothing more than a pale, taut-lipped girl. She paced slowly between the rows of men until she came up at last before the Sacred Stone. For a moment she looked down on it, oblivious of the crowd behind her, lost in wonder, for it was from this stone that the first sun had risen on the first day of Creation, and she knew that she was on holy ground. The stone was set on a gold pillar, and at last she turned from it, lifting her chin and surveying the strange, expectant faces with hauteur. With a swift movement she dropped the linen wraps to the floor. A sigh went up like the wind through the palms, for under the cloak she was clothed in solid gold and encrusted with jewels, and only her head was naked.

She went down on her face before the image of Amun-Ra, throned beside the Sacred Stone, and there was a flurry as the gods came forward, clouded in incense. When she rose they were there: Thoth, with his ibis head; Horus, with glittering bird eyes; her beloved Sekhmet; and Set the cold, Set the fierce, gray-limbed and wolfish. She still seemed remote from it all, hardly breathing, but as Thothmes approached to embrace her, she lifted her arms and fell against him, burying her head against his thick neck. She knew that more than the great ceremonies that would follow in Thebes, it was here that he was giving her his last gift, the gift of his throne, and she cried, unashamed, while the assembly shouted and their clamor echoed to the roof high above them. Thothmes held her tightly with one arm, begging for silence with the other.

"Blessed One!" he spoke into her hair. He shouted aloud. "Blessed One, whom I take in my arms, thou art my heir, and only thou!" He thrust her forward, and the tears poured down her cheeks, but she did not try to hide them or wipe them away. She scarcely heard the gods, who continued with the rite.

This thy daughter who liveth satisfies us in life and peace. She is the daughter of thy form, begotten of thee, and thou hast given her thy soul, thy bounty, and the magic powers of the diadem. While she was yet within her mother's body, the lands were hers, all that the heavens cover, all that the sea encircles. . . .

The voices fell upon the awed congregation, and Hatshepsut struggled for control, her lips shaking.

Thy tribute is myriads of men, the captives of thy valor, men for the temples of the Two Lands. The gods have endowed thee with years, with life and satisfaction. They praise thee, for their heart hath given understanding.

Then Thoth, God of Wisdom, spoke for them all:

Set the diadem upon his head before all gods and men.

Hatshepsut felt the hands settle upon her head the pretty, jeweled coronet that had been her mother's and all queens' before her, the Cobra, Lady of Life. The High Priest began to recite the titles that had belonged to Aahmose, but his drone was lost as Hatshepsut raised her arms in triumph and the hall exploded in a cacophony of applause and approval.

Thothmes hugged her again and then spoke to them all, his mighty voice rising above the noise like thunder. "My daughter Hatshepsut, the Loving One—I put her in my place. Let her henceforth guide you. Whoever obeys her will live, but he who speaks against her will surely die!"

They began their progress out of the building, but they could go only a step at a time, for as she passed, the men fell to the ground, reaching for her feet. By the time they at last left the temple and moved out into the streets, it was full morning, and despite the solemnity of the occasion Hatshepsut was hungry.

Big tents had been erected on the bank of the river, and a feast had been prepared. She and Thothmes feted each other while the nobles of Heliopolis ate and drank to their new ruler. Not all of them were happy. Some doubted the sanity of Pharaoh, who grew old and perhaps a little overemotional; and some looked at the small, smiling face and delicate fingers of the Regent and feared for the safety of the country, praying that Thothmes would be spared to reign a few years more.

He knew their doubts. He could read their faces, but he said nothing, watching them all with his black, expressionless eyes, possessed suddenly by a wild and protecting jealousy for Hatshepsut, his beloved. She was deep in conversation with Kenamun, nodding once in a while as she ate and he gestured over the plates and cups. Her face was intent on his words, and when Thothmes heard a scrap of their conversation he turned away, smiling and roaring for wine.

"I favor a short rein and a stiff bit," she was saying, "for how else can a horse be controlled in the heat of battle unless he is trained to these things from the start?"

Thothmes drained his cup and sucked in his lips with relish.

For three days they were entertained by the people of Heliopolis, and on the fourth day they weighed anchor, and the oars were run out.

"Thebes, beautiful Thebes," Hatshepsut sighed. "Father, I have greatly enjoyed this voyage, but I am glad to be going home." The Cobra glittered on her forehead as she turned to look at him. "I am sadly in need of some practice on the training grounds, and I am eager to begin work on my temple."

"So you know now what you wish to build?"

"I think so, but I cannot speak of it until I have consulted Senmut."

"Ah, yes, the handsome young architect. No doubt he is hard at work again, for Ineni has been chosen Mayor of Thebes and will have little time for his precious buildings."

She was astonished. "How do you know that?"

"I received word last night. The heralds ply the river, as we do."

"How lovely it has all been!" she sighed. "My mother would have loved to see me crowned in the temple!"

"I do not think so," Thothmes replied gently. "She worried always for your future, and the crown you wear is as nothing to the crown you will carry on New Year's Day." He laughed fondly. "No, she would not have approved at all."

"I suppose you are right. And now I hold her titles. Great Royal Wife. How strange it seems. I remember that title on so many lips, from the time of my birth. How they loved her, the people of Egypt." She wondered whether they would love her, too, and decided that it did not really matter. The important thing was power, power to make them do her will for their own good, and power was almost within her grasp.

12

They docked at the familiar water steps two days before New Year's Day. The river had shrunk to its proper size, and the land hummed with the industry of sowing. In the palace gardens the new blooms stood tall, and the trees and shrubs had begun to flower. To Hatshepsut's delighted nose the whole of her home seemed one long flower smell. She endured the formal welcomes, glad that her new titles were given to her. She graced Ineni with a large grin, and when he went off with her father to give him all the news, she called for her guard and her attendants and went to find Senmut.

He was lying on his back in the long grass that grew at the edge of the little pond beside the sycamores under the wall. Ta-kha'et was with him, dropping flowers onto his chest. Hatshepsut heard them laughing and found, to her surprise, that she was angry. She strode toward them, and as they heard her come, Senmut said something to Ta-kha'et that sent her walking swiftly away. He ran to meet Hatshepsut, falling on the grass at her feet.

She could no longer be angry. "Rise, priest," she said. "I can see that while I have been away, you have been putting your time to good use."

The tone was bantering, but behind the royal smile Senmut could detect irritation. He bowed again. "My time has not been wasted, Divine One, although the munificence of your gift tempted me to idleness." His clear gaze sought hers in reassurance, and she looked away, her anger gone. "I have a few drawings for your approval."

"Then let us immediately go and see them, for I am eager now to begin, and I know what I want," she replied tartly.

For a moment they smiled at each other, glad to be together again. He knew that soon she would be Regent, for although Pharaoh had made no official announcement, the rumors were flying thick and fast in Thebes, and all knew of her crowning as Divine Consort and Great Royal Wife. The Cobra perched on her brow suited her, he thought. It seemed to symbolize all the latent ability and impatient power in her that waited to be released. He also thought that the King's Double Crown would suit her even better. She was eyeing him with quiet happiness, her eyes screwed shut against the sun, her black hair whipping about her face. With the heightened awareness of woman that Ta-kha'et had brought to him, he saw not only her beauty as Queen and God but her utter fascination and mystery as woman. He wanted to brush the unruly hair from her face and tuck the strands behind her ear, but he folded his arms and awaited her signal.

"Lead the way to your rooms," she said finally, "and together we will have wine and honey cakes and study these plans."

They went to his apartment, where Ta-kha'et welcomed her mistress and fetched red wine in alabaster jars and little gold drinking cups and a silver tray of candied dates and honey cakes. When Ta-kha'et had finished, Senmut dismissed her absently, already getting out his scrolls and papyrus pads, and she passed from his mind before the doors had closed behind her.

"This is what I have in mind," he began, unrolling his work on the desk.

She bent over it, her hair and necklaces falling forward. Although she was so close to him, Senmut was already poring over the yellow sheets, oblivious of all but his neat, black lines. "As you can see, Highness, I have not attempted any height, for as you said before, no building could compete with the cliff of Gurnet and win. So I have conceived a series of terraces, one upon another, leading from the floor of the valley to the shrine that you want cut deep in the rock."

She reached for a honey cake and bit into it, chewing thoughtfully as she looked down at his work. "You have made a good beginning," she said, "but the terraces must be wider and longer so that they do not huddle against the cliff. Draw it!" Obediently he took the reed, and she exclaimed with satisfaction. "Yes! The whole must be light and delicate, even as I am."

"There will be no steps to approach it," he said. "I think a long ramp would be the best, a gradual ascent. And beneath the first and second terraces and at the entrance to the shrine must be pillars, well spaced and airy." With a few swift strokes he showed her what he meant, and her eyes kindled.

"I must have other shrines as well as the one where I may be worshiped," she said. "I want one to Hathor and another to Anubis, and of course the whole will be dedicated to my Father Amun. He must have a shrine, also."

"In the rock? All of them?"

"I think so. Make your engineer earn his bread. Now pour me some wine." He filled two cups, and they settled back to discuss the temple, drinking together, forgetting the hour of rest.

"I wish the work to begin immediately, tomorrow," she told him. "Take a destruction crew and clear the site. If you wish, you may use the remains of the temple of Mentu-hotep."

"The clearing will take a long time, Highness. There is a natural rise in the earth at the foot of the hills that must be leveled."

"That is your business. Requisition what you will. The priests have approved the site; I saw to that on the day I saw the holy place, so there is nothing to prevent an immediate beginning. I will show my brother what a Queen can do!"

All at once she seemed to sink into some dark thought of her own, and as he drank, he watched the hand holding the scrolls fall into her lap, the smooth forehead under the golden snake become furrowed. She crossed her legs and began to swing a jeweled foot back and forth. Presently she shot him a searching, cold look so like her father's that Senmut hid a tremor.

"In two days I go to the temple to be crowned Regent in Egypt," she said, but he did not respond, waiting for the new train of her mercurial thought to emerge. "Then my life will change, priest. Many who bowed to me indulgently and called me Highness will begin to veil their eyes from a King and close their thoughts off from me. I must begin to wall myself about, carefully, with those whom I can trust." Her foot stopped swinging, and she pierced him with another glare. "Those whom I can trust," she repeated slowly, musingly, her eyes on his face. "How would it suit you, priest, to become a Steward of Amun?"

In the long second of shock and surprise Senmut's thoughts flew back to his first day in Thebes, to the haughty, perfumed servant of the God who had listened with such boredom to his father's anxious recommendations in the white, gilded office. He again felt the shrinking, the embarrassment, and he smelt his father's nervous sweat. "Highness, I do not understand," he said.

She laughed shortly. "I think that you do. From the beginning you have shown discreetness. You have kept your pride and your loyalty to me and to your friend in the face of Pharaoh himself, and that was not easy. I need you in the temple, Senmut, as my guardian. I love the God, my Father, and I do homage to his servants, but I am not stupid. I am young to be King, and I am untried. There are many in the temple who will not stop at watching me and will fear for their positions. I will set you over them, as a steward, and you will serve me well. I know it. Now do you understand?"

He did, but he still could see only his father's back, bent in prostration to the man in dazzling white, and his own uncertain, work-roughened hands held out in supplication.

"I have said before that I live only to serve you," he answered, "and that I will do. Only you are worthy of my worship." He spoke with his mind still full of that first day, and his words were tinged with bitterness and a certain arrogance, his head thrown back to see her.

She noted the tone with approval. "Then it is settled. Weed out those of your new servant-priests in the temple who seem to you to be unreliable, and do not fear anyone but me. Report to me every day at the hour of audience, and you shall have a staff bearer to announce you and scribes to follow you. You shall be Steward of Amun's Cattle and Amun's Gardens, for I know your experience with both, and woe to the man who says nay to you!"

He continued to sit and look at her, but his mind was busy. The responsibility was awesome, but with her usual acumen she had seized on duties that would be within his power because of his days on the farm. He was certain that he could carry them out. Of the unspoken duties he was not so sure, but he knew that no one in the temple would spread discontent while he held the Stewardship.

"Stay in this apartment," she said, "until you know the extent of your new position. Then I will build for you a palace, and you shall have your own boat and chariot and whatever else you will."

He searched her face, but she was not joking, and in the dim coolness of the room he felt her wordlessly reaching out to him, her face still with an expression of unfathomable, quiet searching. He knew that intuitively, almost blindly, she needed the boy who had pulled her out of the lake, who had revealed dreams close to her own, who as a man was still possessed of the drive that had caused him to ask a place at Ineni's feet. He wanted to tell her that he loved her, that this temple would be not only her gift to the God and herself but also his love gift to her, all that a lowly man could do for the woman he wished to take in his arms. His eyes must have told her something of what he wished to say because she smiled a little wistfully.

"You are a great noble, Senmut, inside. I like you very much. Do you remember how angry I was when you rubbed me with that ragged old blanket? And how I fell asleep on your shoulder?"

"I remember, Highness. You were a beautiful little girl. You are a beautiful woman." He spoke matter-of-factly, but the words trailed away, and he bit his lip, looking at the floor.

"I am God," she said firmly, and the mood was broken. She rose. "It is nearly time to dine. Come with me, and we will eat and talk with Menkh and Hapuseneb. Perhaps User-amun will be there. You have not met him yet, and I want you to. I want to know what you think of all my friends, for they may soon be more than friends and your opinion is of importance to me. I wish you also to meet Thothmes, my brother, who has returned from the north for my coronation."

He rose also, and he bowed. "Highness, it has just come to my mind that my brother, Senmen, would be of great help to me in my new work. May I send for him, and perhaps replace him at home with a slave? My father needs him, but I think I need him more."

"You need not ask me for this. Assemble what staff you will. Do you like your brother?"

"Yes. We have worked together often."

"I, too, have worked often with my brother!" she retorted as she swept past him, "and I must confess that he is exceedingly boring. But you may find something in common with him, for he loves to build and has already done much beautifying in Egypt."

She waited for him to catch up, and they walked side by side through the blue dusk while the servants led the way with lamps. The night folded around them with a sweetness and poignancy heightened by the new, pale stars that pricked silver fire in the water of the lily ponds, by the scented winds, and by the nearness of each other.

On her coronation day Hatshepsut awoke to the sound of horns, and she lay listening to the harsh, copper notes. She had slept deeply, without dreaming, and when the horns had ceased, she got up. The room was full of warm pink light. She walked naked to her bathroom, where her slave had already filled the stone tub with hot, scented water, and she stepped down into it until she was submerged to her chin. "How is the day?" she asked the girl who joined her with soap and cloths, and while she was scrubbed and her hair was washed, she listened to the artless gossip.

The day was fine and hot, and already the people of Thebes lined the road to the temple, the soldiers in full regalia having already taken up positions to guard the royal progress. The Imperial flags flew all over the city, and boats from Memphis and Hermonthis, Assuan and Nubia, Buto and Heliopolis crowded the wharfs with their cargoes of dignitaries and nobles. All the apartments in the palace were full of visitors. The Viceroys and the Governors of conquered nations filled the halls with their strange slaves and odd languages, and over all expectancy hung like a cloak.

Hatshepsut nodded and left the water, standing while she was toweled dry and then lying on the table to be oiled and massaged. Her Steward Amun-hotpe arrived with her morning cup and made his report. Everything was going smoothly. Her hairdresser and her tiring-woman waited in the anteroom.

Her father was being dressed in his own chambers, and in the apartments of the wives and concubines of Pharaoh, Mutnefert fluttered here and there, eating nervously, her jewels strewn over her couch as she tried to decide what to wear. She had recovered from her disappointment. Indeed, even if she had not, this day was a festival not to be missed by anyone who was anyone, and she was ready for peace once more. Thothmes, her son, sat in his own small apartment, talking to his scribe. In the months of his enforced northern tour he had had time to think, and he had decided that no end would be gained by sulks and outraged silences. He, like his mother, had put aside bitterness; but unlike her, he was biding his time. His trip had changed him. Some of the fat had been burned from him by fiery days always on the move, and away from his mother, his women, and his fine foods he learned a dangerous patience. He had been thwarted, but it would not happen again. He would wait, for years if necessary, but he would be Pharaoh. His sister would not stop him. He brooded even on this, her coronation day, but whereas his emotions had once shown on his face, now he chatted amiably with the scribe while his thoughts ran on of their own accord.

Hatshepsut sat in her loose gown while her hair was dressed carefully, pulled back from her face and piled high so that the crown would sit on her head easily. She should have been shaved, as every pharaoh was, and received the crown bald, but she had rebelled at this, and her father had agreed to let her keep the heavy, blue-black tresses that the woman now wound about her arm. She watched herself in the burnished copper mirror as the paint was applied, and what she saw pleased her: a high, wide forehead; straight brows that were being lengthened to her temples with kohl; large, almond-shaped eyes, with a depth of calm and wisdom, staring critically back at her; a thin nose that swept straight and true; and a sensual, mobile mouth that seemed to quiver on the verge of a smile. The chin betrayed her. It was square, stubborn, a forceful, uncompromising chin that warned all of a will indomitable and a thrusting surge for power. She closed her eyes as the kohl went around them, thinking of the ancestors and the gods who had blessed her with the most beautiful face in the world. She did not smile when she opened her eyes again and saw her reflected image, golden in the copper, dark and mysterious, the fine bones revealed now that her hair was pulled away from her face. The image stared back at her, a mocking, haughty stranger.

She was carried to the temple on a great litter, sitting on a high-backed throne, her Fan Bearer standing behind her. Above the exquisite head the red ostrich plumes waved, and the breathless crowds caught a glimpse of her body, encased in molten gold, before they bent to the dusty roadside. When they rose again, they saw only the sun on her hair and the back of her throne. Behind her walked the bluest blood in the kingdom: Ineni and his son; the Vizier of the North and his son, grave, stately Hapuseneb; Thothmes; and the portly Vizier of the South, deep in conversation with waggish User-amun. The young Djehuty of Hermopolis strode along arrogantly, looking neither to right nor left, Yamu-nefru of Nefrusi behind him, the mantle of his blood pulled tightly around him, a handsome and proud youth. The wealthy landowners, the old and newly rich, paraded slowly in their jewels and fine linens. Senmut came behind them, his head covered with a long wig, his new linen falling about his ankles. Ta-kha'et had carefully made up his face and anointed him with perfumed oil, but he did not yet have the badges of his latest office, and no staff bearer paced before him. Although his head was thrown back as his gaze traveled among the crowd, he did not smile, for his thoughts were on the gleaming, painted Goddess high on the throne that moved before him. The populace took him for a young noble, so withdrawn and stern was his face.

The mighty temple doors stood open, and before them the High Priest, in leopard skin and plumes, waited with his acolytes. The litter stopped, and as Hatshepsut got down, she sparked golden light with every movement. As she watched her father approach, she was motionless as a stone. Her Father's great image towered above her, and the priests crowded beyond, in the outer court, while the smoke from the incense poured out steadily above the temple. Thothmes held out an arm. She linked hers with his, and they went in, preceded by the High Priest, the nobles swarming after to pack the inner court.

The sanctuary doors had been thrown open, and all craned for a glimpse of Amun the Mighty. Hatshepsut, watching her father walk toward the God, thought of her own cold vigil here not so long ago when the temple had been a frightening, lonely place, a place of dark secrets. Then she had worn only a peasant's linen; now, in cloth of gold that weighed her down, she shifted her shoulders and lifted her chin. None should find less than a King this day.

Thothmes was on the golden floor now, laying his Flail and his Crook at the feet of the God. His words floated back to the company.

> I am before you, King of the Gods. I prostrate myself. In return for what I have done for thee, do thou bestow Egypt and the Red Land on my daughter, Child of the Sun, Maat-Ka-Ra, Living Eternally, as thou hast done for me.

He rose and stepped aside, signaling to her with his eyes.

She fell to the floor and began to crawl toward the God. The hammered gold tiles smelt of incense and flowers and dust, and oddly she thought of her mother as the agonizing inches were covered. She wrenched her mind back to the God, to his beauty, his providence, beginning to pray under her breath as the feet drew nearer. Sweat gathered between her shoulder blades, and she struggled on. The silence of the prostrate, watching nobles was so deep that her breath could be heard, rasping into the incense-laden air. At last her questing fingers found him, and she lay on her stomach before him, her cheek to the floor, her eyes shut until she felt her strength return.

She looked up at the faint smile in an agony of pleading. "Show me your favor, Amun, King of All the World!" she cried, her voice echoing to the silver roof. She waited, her eyes on his smooth face. Out of the corner of one eye she saw her father's feet and beside him the legs of the new High Priest. The leopard draping his body hung head down, the lifeless teeth bared in a cunning grin, and Hatshepsut, her thoughts turning to Menena and the other exiles in the north, wondered how many of the priests hid just such a face under the solemn mask of ritual. She began to grow anxious. There was a deep hush throughout the hall, and no one moved. All eyes were fixed on Amun as the smoke from his mighty crucibles wreathed about his face and caressed his plumes.

Senmut was caught by the rising excitement. From his place far back in the hall he could see little but the heads of the standing Pharaoh and the High Priest. Of Hatshepsut he saw nothing, but he could see the God seated on his throne, aloof and somehow cold, and Senmut could not tear his gaze from those golden plumes. A superstitious awe crept over him, prompted not so much by the God's own presence as by the stiff, expectant people, and he wished himself far away from the influence of a God who could hold his people immobile, mindless, awaiting a whim.

Suddenly, Senmut felt his head begin to spin. A crescendoing roar left the throats of the audience as Amun slowly, regally, with infinite grace, bent his golden head. Senmut felt the palms of his hands grow sticky and his skin crawl with a shiver of cold, but everyone else was on their feet, dancing. Above the melee he heard the chuckle of castanets and the music of the sistrums. When the noise died away and he could see again, he quietly got up onto the base of a pillar, giving himself a small edge over his companions. He could see her, standing pale and triumphant at the feet of the God. Thothmes was shouting:

> My daughter who loves thee, who is united to thee, beloved, thou hast transmitted the world unto her, into her hands. Thou hast chosen her as Queen!

As Buto and Nekhbet, Goddesses of the North and South, came forward on silent feet, carrying the Double Crown between them, Hatshepsut clenched her fists, the words of her father ringing in her head. The world! The world! The world! she thought exultantly, and while the goddesses spoke to her of the Red Crown of the North and the White Crown of the South, she hardly heard them. To you, Mighty Amun, and to you, Mighty Thothmes, Beloved of Horus, I offer my thanks! She felt the weight of the Double Crown on her forehead, and as she put up a hand to steady it, she saw Senmut, higher than the rest, one long arm about a pillar, and their eyes met and locked for an instant. His face served to bring her up short, and she went through the rest of the ceremony with proper attention, trying to still the wildfire of success that raged within her.

From the depths of the sanctuary the God's voice boomed, the second wonder of the day.

> Behold ye my Daughter Hatshepsut, Living. Be ye loving toward her and be ye satisfied with her.

Again Senmut felt his heart grow cold. He did not wish to serve this God, only the Daughter of the God, and he stepped down from his pillar and sat instead, looking at the floor as the rite neared its close.

Water was sprinkled on her, cool to her straining neck and pattering, shining, onto her feet. Then the heavy, jeweled robe was put on her shoulders, and Thothmes took the Crook and the Flail and put them in her hands. She grasped them fiercely, cruelly, her knuckles white as she held them to her breast, and Thothmes, looking into her dark eyes, understood and let them go easily.

He led her to the throne, from under which peeped the Blue Lotus of the South and the Papyrus of the North, and as she sat carefully, the lovely fragrance of the lotus filled her head.

The Chief Herald began to read her titles: Divine of Diadems, Favorite of the Goddesses, Fresh in Years, Horus, Living Forever, Maat-Ka-Ra, Who Liveth Forever. And her mother's titles, given to her at Heliopolis, were again repeated, every one. He had finished and was about to bow and step away when Hatshepsut held up a glittering hand. A startled silence fell.

"All the titles are mine by right of my divine birth," she said, her voice very clear and cold. "But my name I wish to change. Hatshepsut, Chief of Noble Women, is very well for a princess, but I am queen. Now I shall be called Hatshepset, First Among the Favorite Women."

Senmut smiled to himself as she began the ritual progress around the sanctuary, straight-backed and slow-moving because of the weight of the crown and the robe that brushed the golden floor. How like her, his defiant little princess, still shouting her superiority to the winds and the gods!

He slipped from the hall and went to find Benya, who had decided to go fishing, seeing that the river would be deserted. Senmut felt as if this was the last day of his freedom, and though he was buoyed by the prospect of his new work, he looked back on a youth almost over and all the free minutes gone—gifts more precious than gold.

The feasting went on all night. Dancing in the streets and drinking, the population of the city wandered in and out of their homes and places of business until the sun rose. At the palace the guests thronging the halls overflowed into the gardens. Lamps hung in all the trees, and seats and cushions were placed on the grass so that all could enjoy the warm spring air. Hatshepsut, Thothmes, and the visiting nobles sat together on the dais, almost buried in flowers, and Senmut found himself placed with the young men, Menkh, Hapuseneb, User-amun, Djehuty, and others, who drank and called for songs, applauding and shouting raucously, eating constantly. Senmut soon finished his meal, and he sat back and watched all, that cautious other self quietly pleased with the antics of the hundreds of other diners. He had fallen into a reverie when Hapuseneb pulled his chair closer.

The young man was heavily perfumed, his cone already coating his broad chest with glistening oil, but he was not drunk. The steady gray eyes looked into Senmut's with friendly appraisal. "I hear that you have a new position, Senmut," he said.

Senmut nodded briefly. He was still not at ease with this quiet, self-contained youth, and he stirred and became alert, waiting for the next words.

"You and I must learn to work together," Hapuseneb went on softly, "for I, too, serve the Queen with devotion and have pledged her my life. My father is a dying man," he said. Senmut glanced swiftly to the high table, where the spare noble was quaffing wine. "Soon I will take up his staff as Vizier of the North, which means that I must travel for Pharaoh a good deal and will not always be at hand if there is need."

This man knows something I do not know, Senmut thought anxiously, putting down the cup he had just taken up. Hapuseneb continued to watch him, smiling, but Senmut knew he was being swiftly gauged.

"The young Thothmes has opened correspondence with Menena, he that was dismissed from his office by Pharaoh. What this means, I am not sure. Time will tell all. But to you, beloved of the Queen, I offer my household, my messengers, and my spies so that if I am away and yet needed, you may act as I would myself." He looked up at Hatshepsut, laughing under the Double Crown, and back to Senmut. "As long as Pharaoh lives, she is safe. Need I say more?"

Senmut shook his head swiftly, wondering if it had been difficult for this young aristocrat to unbend enough to make such an offer. Hapuseneb did not wait for an answer but quietly removed his chair and began talking to User-amun, and Senmut went back to his wine. He had the uneasy feeling that his life would shortly become very complicated and that he would have to walk with the utmost caution. He was suddenly tired, wanting his bed and the warmth of Ta-kha'et's body, and he left the hall before the revelry was over.

Hatshepsut saw him go, but the troop of Keftian dancers, specially invited, had begun their songs, and she did not follow him.

So Hatshepsut became Queen. Thothmes looked forward to spending his last years talking over old times and playing draughts under the trees in the garden with his old campaigner, pen-Nekheb. He also looked forward to inscribing for posterity the last injunctions of his reign on his finished works of art. He had no particular wish to linger in Egypt. He was tired, bruised by old battles and worn by the strain of government. He wished only to go to the God in peace. If his conscience smote him when he thought of the death of his elder daughter, he did not show it, nor did he bother overmuch with his one remaining son. He told himself that he had done all that he could to secure the future of his country through his able daughter and that Thothmes the Younger could content himself with the pursuits of pleasure.

For several months Hatshepsut joined her father every morning in his homage to Amun and later in the audience chamber, hearing dispatches, dictating instructions to the Governors, settling squabbles. Hatshepsut's coronation had seemed to unleash a torrent of strength in her, and she passed from duty to duty like a demon, driving herself and her servants with fanaticism, the nimbus of power about her an almost palpable thing.

Hapuseneb's father died one afternoon while out hunting, and Hapuseneb was sworn Vizier of the North and immediately left Thebes on a tour of his provinces. Senmut struggled with his new responsibilities in the temple, rushing from thence to the site in the valley, where already hundreds of slaves toiled and Benya sweated and cursed under the broiling sun, the hole in the face of the mountain growing wider—the first shrine.

Hatshepsut attended the Stretching of the Cord. She held the white-painted rope as the boundaries of her monument were paced and laid the first stone. In this first frantic year she did not forget her promise to Hathor and the other gods whose poor, broken shrines she had watched slip by on her progress up the river. She told Ineni to take the work in hand. When Hapuseneb, who had also been an architect once, returned from the north, she asked him to tunnel another tomb for her in the royal valley; the little one her father had chosen for her was no longer worthy, now that she was Queen.

But she left her valley to Senmut. Whenever she could get away from the palace, she went across the river, sitting high above it under her canopy, watching the men slaving like giant ants as the first wall of the first terrace went up, the Black Wall of Hathor. At night she dreamed of it complete, sleeping in its mysteries under a white sun.

She did not neglect her new responsibilities in the temple of Amun, either. More than ever, as she matured, she felt the God's hand upon her. She loved to dance in the temple with her priestesses, festooned in flowers, as the sacred myrrh perfumed the air, and in the dead minutes of each day, the times when nothing was required of her, she would sit on the balcony of her bedroom and pray, touched gently by Ra as he passed overhead.

She knew that there was no one like her in the whole world, and her lordly isolation of spirit awed all who served her. Thothmes watched her flowering with sleepy contentment and soon left her to govern alone, though often she would seek his advice, coming to him over the grass in the cool of the evening and sitting at his feet while they talked desultorily. She often invited Senmut to accompany her, and Thothmes, who approved of the proud young man, made him welcome.

She had refused almost hysterically to occupy Neferu's old apartment now that she was Queen. Neither did she want her mother's rooms. She was building a new palace for herself, connected to the old by many wide avenues and halls. She ordered Neferu's apartment redecorated so that Senmut could be near her.

Senmen arrived from the country, shy and confused in his coarse linens and provincial accent. Senmut put him in his old apartment, where he went to earth like a desert fox, bewildered by this brother who had become as beautiful and powerful as a god. There Senmen stayed until he became used to the palace.

Hatshepsut took to visiting Neferu's mortuary temple in the early dawns, standing alone with offerings in her hands, listening to the sighing of the morning wind about the little pillars. Now she understood her sister's painful, pathetic attempts to free herself from a burdensome existence, and for the first time Hatshepsut really mourned for the life so soon ended. Neferu's likeness regarded her with a gentle, constant forgiveness, but Hatshepsut found no peace saying the prayers to the dead over and over. Sometimes she awoke with the words already on her lips.

She saw her father become fatter, more somnolent in spite of the old glitter that could still strike fear into all. He would spend his time between long dozes playing at draughts with pen-Nekheb, usually beating him, waking to eat and drink and sleep again. She also watched the younger Thothmes. A mild, plump man now, he seemed to grow stronger, sucking the life from his father. Not that Thothmes was a cat suddenly turning into a leopard. Outwardly he was still the lazy, affable boy who rose to his sister's jibes with instant irritation. But he was everywhere—in the temple, at all feasts, riding about the city behind his charioteer. Hatshepsut could not explain the apprehension these things caused in her, especially when she caught him staring at her, his eyes blank under the slow smiles. So she redoubled her efforts to learn, to understand, to know all that passed in her kingdom.

13

Five years after her coronation, in the spring, Thothmes went to sleep and did not wake. The feast of Min had begun, and Amun had gone from his temple to become the lettuce eater at Luxor, God of all excesses of the flesh. Thebes was in a ferment night and day of drunkenness and license, and the palace lay empty while the inhabitants exhausted themselves to the south.

Ineni found the old King lying on his cushions, his eyes closed and his mouth open, the protruding teeth bared in the grin of death. For a moment he stood looking down on the man who had been his life for so long. He turned quickly, sending a servant running for the Royal Physician and the sem-priests, and made his way to Hatshepsut's rooms. He found her preoccupied, dressing for the night's rituals, her litter waiting outside to take her to Luxor. He was admitted only after he had lost his temper and shouted at the guard on the door, and the astonished man had let him push past unannounced.

The Queen came toward him, bracelets clinking, fire in her great eyes. "Ineni, have you lost your head? I am in a hurry, as you can see. I should have you arrested!" There were lines of stress in her face, and the muscles of her long neck were rigid. The feast was nearing its end, and she was tired from long nights of dancing. She snatched up the Cobra Crown, holding it tightly in nervous fingers; and her slave came after her, comb in hand.

Ineni bowed, but found he could say nothing.

The royal foot began to tap. "Speak, speak! What is it? Are you ill?"

At last he opened his mouth, afraid of the words that must fall from his lips.

She saw something of his news in his face. "My father! Is he sick?"

Ineni shook his head. "The God is dead, Majesty. He passed to the Judgment Hall in his sleep. I have called the priests and the physician. Perhaps you should send word to his son."

She stared at him for a long moment, then turned away abruptly, placing the little crown on her couch.

He filled a cup with wine and went to her, but she refused it. He stood helplessly, not knowing what to do.

Presently the naked shoulders squared, and her head came up. "It was hard for you, Noble One, to bring me this news," she said softly. "Now send for my herald, and when he has come, send him to Luxor. The God must return, and the feasting must cease. O my father!" she cried suddenly, throwing up her arms, "why did you leave me so soon? We had not done enough together, you and I!"

Ineni left her, and on his way out he ordered her Steward to summon Senmut, doing it without thought, instinctively knowing that he would hold the comfort she sought. He went swiftly in search of her herald, aware as never before of the empty, echoing passages without light or voice. Between one day and the next, Egypt was floundering in a marsh of uncertainty. Ineni's thoughts were on young Thothmes, surely even now in the arms of some priestess on the floor of the Luxor temple. He felt his throat tighten.

Senmut ran as he had never run before. The word had reached him as he, Benya, and Menkh, tipsy and exhilarated, were leaving a beerhouse on the outskirts of Luxor. He had planned to watch the dancing in the temple garden and then go home to Ta-kha'et, but at the whispering of the perspiring, frightened herald he had dropped his mug at Benya's feet and begun to run. His feet pounded out the two miles. His arms pumped and his head swam with beer fumes. Through the fog he saw pilgrims and revelers wending their way with lights and laughter on the other side of the avenue. They stopped and watched the demented youth fly past, his kilt streaming behind him. It was a cool evening, still and sweet; and the water of the Nile, flowing silently beside the road, was dark and inviting. But he ran on, cursing his chariot, which stood in its stall behind the palace, cursing his boat, which rocked at anchor beside the city wharf, cursing his litter bearers, who had left him to carouse. The heavy belt that held his seal banged against his legs. He tore it off and, without stopping, wrapped it around his arm. He flew in at the Queen's private garden entrance and slowed to a stumbling trot, coming up at last before her golden door. He paused for a moment to still his shallow breath and calm his trembling limbs before nodding to the guard and walking through the door.

She was standing in the middle of the room, wringing her hands aimlessly. When she saw who it was, she gave a cry and ran into his arms. As she fell against him, his arms went about her of their own accord. He spoke curtly to the slave, ordering her out; and when the door had closed, he led Hatshepsut to the couch, sitting her down, stroking the tumble of black hair while her tears wet his chest.

"I am sorry, so sorry, Majesty," he said softly, his lips against her head.

She went on crying, the tears giving way to great shuddering sobs that wracked her, tearing at him also. He had never before felt so helpless. In the end he was quiet, holding her tightly, while out in the passage he heard whispering and the sudden pattering of many feet. At last he gently pushed her away and went to her cosmetic table, bringing back a cloth. He dipped it in wine and wiped her face. The eyes were black-circled under swollen lids, and her tears had coursed through the kohl, sending paint down her cheeks and onto her neck. He washed her thoroughly, and she became still, watching him expressionlessly. When he had finished, he cradled her in his arms once more, holding the cup to her lips. She drank meekly, sobbing once in a while. She moaned and closed her eyes, putting her head on his shoulder.

"I cannot go out there," she said.

"You must," he replied. "There is much to do, and a queen can cry only in the privacy of her bedchamber."

"No!" she said. "He was my father, my father! O Mighty One, where are you now?" In her agitation her nails bit into his arm. "The Light of Egypt has gone out!"

"You are the Light of Egypt," he said firmly, harshly. "You are the Queen. Stand tall in your grief, and show your subjects the metal from which you were poured."

She shook her head and began to cry again. "I cannot," she repeated. It was a cry from the soul, the cry of any bereaved woman. She fumbled at her table. "Here. Here are my seals and my cartouches. Take them, Senmut. I will not leave this room until I walk with my father into the valley, to his tomb. You settle the affairs of the audience chamber."

He listened in mounting alarm. This breakdown was so unlike her. He thought of young Thothmes, even now outside her door. He pushed her away from him roughly and stood up, forcing her to raise her head to him. "Listen to me," he almost shouted at her, "and listen well. You are not some witless peasant woman cowering in the darkness of her hovel. Did your father rear you so that in one weak moment you could destroy all that he made? Do you want your enemies to say, 'See! The Queen of Egypt is broken as the frail reed we thought her to be!' " He snatched up her hands, shaking them urgently. "Stand! Stand in gratitude to your father, who gave you the world! Do not bend under the load. Outside wait the High Priest and your Governors. And Thothmes, your brother. Will you show them a fainting woman?"

She pulled her fingers from his grasp and sprang to her feet. "How dare you speak to me like this! I will drag you in chains to the prisons! I will flog you with my own hands!"

The old, cold fire from her angry eyes licked him; but he met it steadily, not flinching.

She lowered her gaze and flung herself across the room to sit before her mirror. "You are right," she said. "I forgive you your words. How often must I lean on your breast, Senmut? Open the doors, and send in my slave. When I am ready, I will speak to the others without."

"He was a great God, a great Pharaoh," Senmut told her quietly. "His memory will cover Egypt as long as Ra carries him aloft in the Holy Barque."

"Yes," she replied, smiling wanly at him. "I will not disgrace the love we had for each other. He was my father, my protector, my friend, but I will do as he would wish. Egypt is mine."

Senmut went to the door, calling for Nofret, and the girl slipped in. The officials crowded behind her, but he shut the door in their faces. He went and sat on Hatshepsut's couch until he was sure that she had recovered, and when he saw her place the crown on her head with a characteristic flourish, he left her.

It was he, not she, who staggered with weariness as he walked through the passages, now filled with silent, frightened people, to the haven of his own bed. Ta-kha'et was asleep on her mat by the door, the cat curled into the hollow of her back, and he did not wake them. He stripped and washed quickly, but before he succumbed to the tiredness that threatened to put him to sleep forever, he sent a sealed message to Hapuseneb, who was attending ceremonies at Buto. "Come back," it read tersely. "You are needed."

In all the seventy days of mourning Hatshepsut did not break down again. She went about the business of government coldly, unsmiling, hiding an intensity of grief that burned and ate at her until she felt that she could never rise to face another day. The priests who had descended the steps to the Nilometers to measure the rise of the river reported to her that the flood had been unprecedented. They told her that she could raise all taxes, but she listened absently and instructed her tax collectors to lower all tribute for one year in memory of Thothmes. She received the Viceroy of Nubia and Ethiopia, Inebny the Just, who relayed that the mines were working at full capacity and that she would have to look elsewhere for gold, but she sent him to Senmut and told him to study the problem. She felt that never again would she take an interest in weighing out the gold for her monuments, for of what use were great buildings when her father was not there to grunt his approval? A caravan arrived, bringing turquoise from Sinai, crystal and red chalcedony from the Eastern Desert. Whereas before she would have sat on her throne and eagerly watched the counting of the treasures, in her grief she cared nothing, and it was Ineni, in his capacity as Treasurer, who called the weights and values to the scribe Anen and saw to the portion for Amun. Only with Senmut could she talk of her sorrow, and into his ear it all poured, but she did not encourage any closer contact. She withdrew into her godhead, and though he ached to hold her again, she was more like a cold-gleaming star illuminating the night than a woman of flesh and blood.

She and Thothmes walked together through the Necropolis and into the desert hills on the day of the funeral. Hatshepsut fell upon the coffin, scattering the flowers she had already laid there, in a last despairing act of loss. Her mother's funeral had been peaceful, comforting. She had had her father's hand to hold on the way back to the palace. But here in the dimness of the tomb, surrounded by the things they had shared, each one carrying a message of happier days, she could not control herself any longer. Thothmes was moved in spite of himself. He bent awkwardly to help her to her feet, and she did not shrug him off but leaned on his soft arm. When she reached the sunlight again, she disengaged herself without a word and left him, striding down the winding path to the waiting mourners, leaving him to follow her like a shadow.

There was no relief for her in the palace, no quiet meal shared with a father who understood a young girl's need for a word, a game, a joke to take away the pain and formality of death. She went to her silent room and firmly shut the door.

Later I will pray to you, O my father, she thought, standing alone in a patch of stray sunlight, letting the quiet enter her. But now I want only to have all as it was.

She took off her blue mourning robe and her coronet and lay on her couch. Though she did not want to, she slept.

In the middle of the night Senmut was awakened by a messenger from the north. The man was tired, his clothes rumpled and his face drawn. As Senmut turned up the lamp and put on a kilt, he saw that there was no scroll or letter.

"There is wine on the table and bread," Senmut said to him. "Sit and eat before you give me your message."

But the other declined. "I am the first to have come from the delta," he said, his voice ragged with tiredness. "My message is short. Three weeks ago Menena left his estates, and he is even now in the chambers of Thothmes the Young. That is all."

Senmut whistled. "That is enough. Are you sure that Menena has disembarked and is in the palace?"

The man nodded emphatically. "I saw him with my own eyes."

"Then go at once to Hapuseneb the Vizier. He sleeps in his house a mile downriver. Take my guards with you and this." He searched angrily in his ivory chest until he found Hapuseneb's seal. "Tell him that he is to come to the Queen at once. I will meet him in the garden outside her doors."

Ta-kha'et was awake now, sitting up on her reed mat and listening intently. Senmut called her. "Find me a cloak and my sandals, little one."

She got up, and the cat stretched and yawned, padding to the corner, where he watched them with unblinking yellow eyes. The messenger bowed and left, taking the seal, and Ta-kha'et put a timid hand on Senmut's arm.

"Master, what is it? Are we in danger?"

He kissed the sleepy eyes while his mind raced. It was too late—and too soon. Too late for his Queen to do anything more than bow to the inevitable, and much, much too soon for her to assemble and strengthen a government that would appoint her Pharaoh. It was a bitter blow.

"Go back to bed." He pushed Ta-kha'et toward the couch. "Sleep in comfort, for I shall not return tonight. If Senmen seeks me, give him wine, and tell him I will greet him in the morning. We were to see to a consignment of calves. And do not fear! There is no danger to you, lovely one!"

She was already climbing into his bed, and the cat sprang up beside her.

Standing in the shadow of the wall and pacing feverishly, he waited for Hapuseneb. The night was fine, and the moon was at her peak, casting pale shades among the trees, but for once Senmut had no eyes for the night. At any moment he expected to hear the approach of the old High Priest and his minions, and his stomach knotted and began to ache. The night birds rustled and chattered spasmodically in the sycamores, and the fish in the little ornamental pool rose and fell, sucking the air in tiny plops. At last a darker shadow moved among the tree trunks. Hapuseneb came to him silently, his eyes showing grayer than ever under the moon's blind fingers, and Senmut quickly told him the message.

Hapuseneb listened without surprise, saying nothing. At last he shrugged. "There is nothing to be done," he said. "The time is not ripe for her. I do not think that Thothmes has any vast ambition. He wants only to be vindicated for the years spent in failure under his father's critical eye, and I think he will be satisfied with the title of Pharaoh as long as he need not do much work. Egypt will not suffer. He is after all a rather likable young man."

"The Queen does not think so."

Hapuseneb laughed softly, his teeth gleaming white. He put an arm around Senmut's shoulders. "The Queen holds the spirit of a man in her beautiful young body, and she cannot tolerate weakness in any. But Thothmes is her brother, and I think she has a small affection for him. Nevertheless, his cloying yoke will irk her."

They left the garden and waited at her door while her guard obtained her permission for them to enter. When he let them pass, they went in and bowed.

She was sitting in her low chair next to the couch, Nofret beside her. A fine gossamer cloak wreathed her. Her feet were bare, and her undressed hair fell to her shoulders. "It must be serious," she greeted them, "for never before have my two friends seen fit to disturb their Queen's slumbers. Say on. I am ready." She folded her hands.

"Thothmes has recalled Menena," Senmut said. "Even now they talk in the Prince's apartments."

She nodded. "And so?"

He looked at her disbelievingly. "Majesty, you knew?"

"I had some idea. My spies are every bit as good as yours. What are your thoughts?"

Senmut and Hapuseneb looked at each other, and Senmut spoke. "I think that Thothmes wishes to be Pharaoh and that he has offered Menena a return from exile to support his claim. I think that the priests will be behind him. Your Majesty has not ruled for long enough to prove to the people that you are in every way an excellent governor."

"And you, Hapuseneb? What of the army?"

"Majesty, if you fight this thing, then Egypt will run with blood. The generals favor Thothmes because he is a man. The army needs a man as its commander in chief, but the common soldiers love you for your skill at the bow and the chariot. The people of the country will also favor Thothmes. They worship you as the Daughter of the God, and as the mighty Queen, but they want a male on the Horus Throne."

"Well said. You have given me truth."

She sat still for so long that the two men wondered if they had been forgotten, but at last she rose, clapping her hands. "Nofret! Bring out the royal robes, the ones I wore at my coronation. Find my wig, the one with a hundred braids of gold. Get out my jewel box, and break the seal on the alabaster pot of kohl Ineni gave me." Her lip curled. "Damn Thothmes and his whining impudence! Yes, I must yield, but never shall he rule! His will be the emptiest titles in the land. Even the Steward of Amun and the Vizier of the North shall wield more power than he. Damn him!" She was white-hot with anger. "Well did my father warn me. And I did not listen! Well did my mother pray for me, beseeching Isis for my protection. But I need nothing! I am God! Thothmes shall learn who is Egypt. I shall give him a paper land, and with that he will be satisfied!"

Senmut and Hapuseneb bowed and made as if to leave, but she ordered them to stay.

"Why should you go?" she asked them. "Are you not favored men, advisers of the Queen? Stay and hear what the traitor Menena has to say!" She flung off the cloak and marched into her bathing room.

They heard her order that twenty lamps, hot food, flowers, and the best of wine be brought immediately. The slaves who slept in the little ante-room scurried past Senmut and Hapuseneb, their eyes darting here and there like frightened rabbits; and before Hatshepsut was out of the water, the lamps were being brought in and lit. The room became a dazzling cup: the silver walls, the golden floor, and the gaily painted screens lapped by a warm, liquid light.

In half an hour she was ready, sitting on her little gold-plated reed chair before a table laden with food and flowers. She was like one of the lamps herself, glowing, gold from the Cobra Coronet to the jewel-encrusted sandals.

She placed the two men beside her, one on each hand. "Do not speak," she told them, "and do not rise and bow when my brother enters. He is still but a prince and subject to me. Pour wine, Hapuseneb, but we will not drink. Not yet. We will be still and wait. Nofret, call in my Chief Herald and my stewards. Call the Royal Fan Bearer and the Seal Bearer, and have two of the Followers of His Majesty stand within, one on each side of the doors. They shall find a queen indeed!"

They did not have long to wait. Within a few minutes there were footsteps growing louder in the passage and then a surprised murmuring as those without found a door unguarded. At the knocking Hatshepsut nodded to the soldiers, and the two men flung open the doors, barring the way with their spears. The startled High Priest and the Prince looked past them into a room blazing with light and full of silent people.

"Who seeks audience with the Queen?" one of the soldiers demanded loudly.

Thothmes had to state his name and rank with the eyes of all upon him. Again Hatshepsut nodded, and the soldiers sprang back to attention, spears withdrawn.

Menena, Thothmes, and three priests shouldered their way through the crowded entrance and found themselves before a ruler surrounded by her advisers. They immediately felt disadvantaged. The golden image before them regarded them coldly, the stern faces of the men behind and around her mirroring her mild disdain. Menena and the priests went to the floor, and Thothmes bowed reluctantly, his florid face heavy with embarrassment.

Hatshepsut left Thothmes' entourage lying uncomfortably on the floor while she spoke only to her brother. "Greetings, Thothmes. This is a strange hour to be paying me a visit, and a strange and motley company you keep. Since when has a Prince of Egypt associated with one under the interdict of banishment?" Her tone dripped biting sarcasm, and the portly figure on the floor shifted slightly.

Senmut looked down at it in disgust and some fear. Menena had not changed. His body was perhaps a little more wizened, the folds of his face a little more pronounced, but his eyes had lost none of their cunning. Senmut would never forget the ghostly voices whispering by the tree, and at the fresh remembering he squirmed inside, his conscience rising up in rebuke once more. He tore his gaze from the priest's bald head and fixed his eyes on the young Prince's face. Thothmes wore an expression of acute discomfort as he stood before Hatshepsut, his hands behind his back like a recalcitrant schoolboy. Senmut felt a wave of pity for a man so unprepossessing, so out of his depth.

"I have not come to be teased, Hatshepset," the young man said sullenly. "Father is dead, and you know as well as I that Menena lost his office on a whim. Why should he not return to Thebes when I myself invited him?"

"Our father never acted on a whim in his life," Hatshepsut said coldly, "and it is not the place of the Prince to recall the exiled. It is the prerogative of the Queen."

The food steamed on the table before her, the wine standing ready in silver cups, but no one moved. All sensed the gathering of power in Hatshepsut, the will that projected into the room a presence of almost superhuman strength. They also felt the stubborn will of Thothmes, bolstered by his High Priest, and they held their breath and waited.

Thothmes nodded, looking at Menena out of the corner of his eye. He wished that Hatshepsut would give the order for the priests to stand, for he felt much abler with Menena on his feet, offering mute assistance. But she continued to sit, watching him inquiringly, making him feel that he had interrupted some important conference which would go on as soon as he left. The men with her, nobles all, people he had been to school with, met his traveling eye as if they were looking right through him. He was angry and sorry, but the words he wanted to hear did not come, and, floundering, he was forced to manage by himself.

"A queen without a king may take upon herself such prerogatives," he answered her at last, "but I have decided, sister, to relieve you of the burden of such a heavy load. I am willing to take my rightful place as Pharaoh of Egypt at once."

Though no one moved, it seemed as if the whole company had sighed and loosened. Hatshepsut began to smile at him, her eyes lighting at last.

He folded his arms and planted his feet squarely apart. "What say you?"

"I know perfectly well why you are here," she said. "I have been waiting for you. Oh, Thothmes, end this playacting! Menena get up, and your rabble with you. I do not like you. I have never liked you, but it seems that I must put up with you after all."

The High Priest rose, his oily face flushed but calm, and he bowed silently.

Hatshepsut gestured. "Sit, all of you, and we will eat and drink and discuss the matter as befits our high station. My advisers will listen and give their opinion. But you, Menena"—she stabbed the air with a long finger—"I do not wish to hear your voice!"

When they sank to the cushions and Nofret began to serve them, Hatshepsut raised her cup. "Drink now, my friends," she said to Hapuseneb and Senmut, smiling on them, her eyes watchful. She drained her cup and set it back on the table with a bang. "Well, Thothmes, let me understand you. You want to be Pharaoh. Is it so?"

"It is not a matter of wanting," he said petulantly. "It is the law. Egypt cannot have a woman on the throne."

"Oh? By what law? Is not the Ruler the law, Beloved of Maat, embodying Maat in her own person?"

"In his own person," he corrected her swiftly. "Our father was Maat, and he ruled within the law as Pharaoh. He made you a mighty queen, but it was not within his power to make you male."

She leaned toward him. "My father is Amun, King of all the gods. It was he who gave me life and prepared a throne for me in Egypt. He intended me to be Pharaoh from the time before I was born of the gentle Aahmose. He gave me the sign on the day of my coronation."

"Then why did he not make you male?"

"My kas are male, every one of them! I am female because Mighty Amun wished to have a pharaoh who was more beautiful than any other being on the earth!"

"You cannot change the law of the land," he repeated peevishly. "The people will not understand a female Horus. They want a man to rule them, to make the sacrifices for them, to lead the army into battle. Can you do these things?"

"Of course I can! As Queen I am female, but as Pharaoh I will rule as male."

"You confuse the issue with your silly arguments. The fact remains that I have a claim to the Horus Throne, and I want it. It is my birthright." A gleam came into his eye as he munched on his shat cake with relish. "Besides, Hatshepset, if you rule, who can come after you? What title will a husband have? Divine Consort? Great Royal Wife of the female Horus? And if you take no husband, Egypt will have to look outside her borders for a royal son to put on the throne. Is that what you want?"

The crafty barb had gone home. She sat back in her chair as if struck by a heavy fist.

Senmut and Hapuseneb exchanged glances. This consideration had escaped them. Hapuseneb pursed his lips and imperceptibly shook his head. Senmut knew that the Queen was beaten even before she had begun. With her love for the country she would never allow a foreign power to sit on the Horus Throne, and he watched the struggle played out on her pale face.

At length she answered Thothmes, her voice dead and cold. "Do you care about Egypt, Thothmes, or do you only think of the glory of the Double Crown upon your head? For to me Egypt is my life, and her service is my vocation. Your words are true, but they were not spoken from an unselfish heart."

"You are unjust!" he protested. "Of course I love Egypt, and it is because I love her that I am willing to marry you and ascend the Holy Throne with Steps."

"Is it so?" she whispered softly, breathing in his face. She bent almost double so that she could look right into his eyes. "Is it so? How noble of you, dear brother, how kind."

"We have never agreed," he said, dropping his gaze. "But it may be that we can work together for a common cause. Our father grew old and dreamed, but it was the dream of an old man with a favorite child, and now he is gone. Face it, Hatshepset. Egypt needs me at last."

She sat back. "And does she not need me?" Hatshepsut hissed at him. "Where were you when I rose at dawn day after day to attend to the affairs of the kingdom? Where were you in the nights when I lay sleepless because the weight of government is my blanket and the hard stone of necessity is my pillow?" Her hands were clenching the arms of her chair, and they trembled as she struggled for control.

Senmut was tense in every muscle, feeling along with her the bitter disappointment and the hard dying of the hope that she had shared with her father.

She finally slumped into a thoughtful pose. "It does not matter," she said dully. "I will make a bargain with you, Thothmes. We must bargain, for we know that neither of us is as strong as we thought we were. I will build with you and appear in public behind you. I will worship with you in the temple and share with you my royal bed so that Egypt may have an heir. Thus will the people be satisfied—having a male on the throne. But you must leave to me all government."

Menena made a half-strangled exclamation, and she swung around to face him. "Do not speak, betrayer of the trust of the God! Or in this very room I will tear from you your badge of office and grind it under my sandal!"

She turned again to Thothmes and spoke gently. "Only thus will Egypt be preserved. You must admit that you know nothing of the ways of the courts or the dictating of the dispatches, and around me I have many loyal men who give me their advice. Is it not so?"

He looked into the sweet, smiling face with bewilderment. He had expected a declaration of war, an explosion of violent, destructive anger, but he did not yet know her and the depth of her love for her country.

"Then I will be Pharaoh?" he asked.

"Of course you will. Neither of us has any choice in the matter. I can see that before long the people and the generals would have demanded it of me whether I would or no. Then I would have continued, but as Divine Consort. So let it be so. We will go together into the temple, and I will give you my blood so that you may set the Double Crown upon your head. But never forget, Thothmes, that I wore it before you!"

This needless and cruel humiliation stung him. "How could I forget!" he answered her hotly. "You think that I will not be a good Pharaoh, but my father was also your father, and our blood is the blood of royalty. Do not forget that either!"

"You always were lacking in humor, Thothmes," she said. "Well, eat and drink, and then go back to your bed. In the morning the heralds will be sent out, and we will marry. But you"—she looked at Menena—"serve him well, or this time you will be executed instead of banished, and I myself will come and applaud!"

When Thothmes and his cohorts had gone, Hatshepsut looked around the grim and silent company. "I dreamed, after all," she said sadly. "It could not have been any other way. Now drink with me, all of you, and pledge to me again your lives and your gifts. I need you all, as you need me. Duwa-eneneh!"

Her Chief Herald bowed.

"Send out the word as speedily as you can. Begin tonight, or I shall change my mind. Hapuseneb, Senmut, do you think that he will change his mind also? Will he meddle in all that I have done?"

They gathered around her and drank a trifle gloomily, each giving his opinion. When at last the sun rose free of the horizon, they accompanied her to the temple for the morning rites, sacrificing with her and to her, the Queen of Egypt.

14

On the day of the coronation a wind blew from the desert. It was not a khamsin, and the sky remained bright and clear, but it ripped at the blue and white pennants that once more fluttered from the masts lining the avenues of city and palace, lifting the skirts of priest, commoner, noble, and slave alike. Hatshepsut felt it brush her like an impatient cat as she was lifted high on her throne upon the litter, and her wig began to whip about her face. This time she had dressed with deliberate simplicity. She wore only a soft white kilt and a little silver, as befitted the Queen. The little Cobra Coronet sat on her head, held in place with bronze pins. It sparkled in the sun, for the wind was too strong for the gay canopies, and she and Thothmes were exposed above the heads of the populace. There was a pause as the procession formed behind the royal pair, and Hatshepsut sat quietly, listening to the wild cheering.

I am doing the right thing, the just thing, she thought. They want him. He makes them feel safe. To them I am mighty and beautiful, but not as mighty as a king or as beautiful as a head that bears the Double Crown. Security. That is what they applaud so enthusiastically. Well let them have him. Let the people and their chosen king make each other happy, while I pursue the path of my father and bind the country to me with the chains of power. I do not care for the crown, a shallow thing worn by a shallow man! I have cared all my life for only two things: the people and the power. And though for a time I have lost the people, I still have the power. I would not be Thothmes for all the gold in the mines of my dominions. For what is he, inside himself? Did the God conceive him?

Thothmes waved, and they set off, the sound of the drums and the pipes stolen by the wind and carried far across the water. Hatshepsut watched the bald head of her new husband bob gently up and down, a little white nob above the ornate, high-backed throne she herself had sat on on her way to her own coronation.

It seems so long ago, she mused.

But it was only five years. Five years! Now I am twenty, and once more in so few years my life is to undergo a change. Is this to be the sum of my immortal existence, Amun, my Father? Am I to be no more to you, to Egypt, than the willful wife of a soft and vacillating Pharaoh? In pride I was born, of your eternal and beautiful loins; and in pride have I lived, doing all as you have wished. Deep within her something protested fiercely that this was not the end, that she had not been born to ride behind her brother for the rest of her life. As the silver petals woven into her wig lashed at her cheeks, driven into a semblance of life by the wind, she beat down the resentment that threatened to overwhelm her. I am good at waiting, she thought, dismounting. I still have all the years of my youth before me.

She walked slowly to where Thothmes stood, weighed down by the golden garb of the King. She took his arm as her father had taken hers, and casting a withering look at Menena in his leopard skin, she turned to the first pylon as the horns blared and the sistrums held in the hands of her priestesses began to jingle.

The ceremony ended without incident, and Thothmes the Second was now also the Horus of Gold, Lord of Nekhbet and Per-Uarchet, King with Divine Sovereignty, Son of Amun, Emanation of Amun, Chosen One of Amun, Beloved of Amun, Avenger of Ra, Beautiful of Risings, Prince of Thebes, the Power that Maketh Things to Be. He and his Divine Consort were carried back to the palace amid a wave of hysteria that seemed about to engulf the royal party.

At the great feast the lords and vassals of the kingdom presented their homage as befitted their position, but the young men who had sat below the dais looking up at Thothmes the First and his daughter now thronged the honored couple. Senmut found himself between Senmen and the new Pharaoh himself. Thothmes did not seem much interested in conversation. He ate and drank immoderately, looking up only to run an experienced eye over the curves of the nubile dancers. Senmut watched his pudgy hands fondle the food, his ample waist bulging out over the jeweled belt, and he grew more and more depressed.

Hatshepsut seemed to be gay. She laughed and chatted with all who passed, elfin and somehow small beside the overblown King. But Senmut thought that there was a note of desperation in her shrill laughter. He sensed that her glib and ceaseless talk hid a feverish desire to hold the moment.

The afternoon flowed into night, and the night into deeper night. Finally, Thothmes drained his last drop and got to his feet, his Standard-Bearer and the dignitaries who would escort the couple to Hatshepsut's new palace following also. She herself stopped talking immediately and meekly took her place behind Thothmes. Only Senmut saw the spasmodic jerking of the fingers that let go the cup, the tightening of the oil-saturated shoulders. He turned to find Hapuseneb at his elbow.

"Relax, my friend," the deep, calm voice said. "Remember that it is blasphemy to think of her as anything but divine, a great and noble queen. She does not need your anxious frowns. Besides, Thothmes is well versed in the arts of the bedchamber. He has devoted the better part of his life to the proving of his manhood. The little slaves and all his concubines adore him."

Senmut could not laugh as he wanted to.

"Come to my home tonight," Hapuseneb offered, "you and your brother. We will sit in my garden and gossip about nothing more important than fishing, for a change. There will be no audiences tomorrow, and you can sleep in my guest chamber."

Senmut accepted the invitation gratefully, calling to Senmen, and they left the hall by the garden entrance. The royal couple had gone. On the way to the water steps they picked up Menkh and his young woman, and a young man, Tahuti by name, a protégé of old Ineni, who greeted Hapuseneb affably. Djehuty of Hermopolis, that haughty aristocrat, was introduced to Senmut while they waited for Hapuseneb's boat to be brought. Altogether seven or eight of them with their women sailed the mile to the estate of the Vizier of the North. They walked in his garden to the lawns, where the lamps hung, tossing in the remnants of the day's wind; and they sat or lay on the warm grass, talking agreeably and drinking for the rest of the night.

Senmut enjoyed himself. He was among minds as keen, as well-trained, as sharp as his own. They passed from fishing to fighting to the classics, and from the sayings of the God Imhotep to Hatshepsut's lovely temple without once referring to their new King. When the others had gone, he and Senmen retired to Hapuseneb's private study, and the three of them opened more wine and talked of their families and their youth. Hapuseneb listened gravely to the tales of a farmer's life, and he regaled them with stories of his father's wild youth and of his own upbringing, here under the shadow of the greatest center of power in the world. They did not go to bed at all.

Hatshepsut ushered out the last of her slaves and reluctantly closed the doors behind her. She turned to face her new husband in the dim light of the night-light burning steadily beside her couch, which was strewn with sweet lotus blooms and leaves of myrrh. He had removed the Double Crown and carefully laid it upon a table. She saw its smooth red and white surfaces complacently reflect the passing flickers of light and shadow, the symbol of all she had sought and lost. Thothmes was pouring wine, and she walked to him slowly, rubbing her wrists where the silver bracelets chafed her. She slipped them off and flung them onto her night table as he held out the cup to her. She refused it irritably, tired by the demands of the day.

"I do not wish to drink any more," she said. "I should have thought that you had had enough as well."

"I like a cup before bed, warmed in the winter," he replied. He tossed back his head and drank, licking his lips and replacing the cup while she waited and watched. Taking off his sandals and loosening his belt, he sighed. "I shall not often undress myself again." She quickly jerked her head away and, turning on her heel, marched to her cosmetic table. As she removed her coronet and her wig, the black hair, freed from its bonds, fell to her shoulders in a great wave of perfume. She ran her hands through it impatiently, and Thothmes was suddenly still, watching the sheen as it caught the light.

"When you come to me, you will have to undress yourself," she answered waspishly. "My slaves are unused to anointing the body of a man." When he did not reply, she turned. Seeing his expression, she quickly looked to her mirror again. "Do not stare at me as though you had never seen a woman before!" she snapped. "I know of your reputation in the chambers of the harem!"

"You are beautiful," he said slowly, thickly. "In the garb of a Queen you do not seem somehow touchable, but thus, as you stand with your hair down your back and your arms bare, there is none to equal your beauty in the whole of Egypt." In three strides he was beside her. Before she could speak, he had covered her mouth with his own, his hands buried in her hair, his body pressing hard against her. She felt herself respond, his mouth firmer than she had imagined it could be. Against her will, the assertion of his body woke in her a part of her that always respected a mind implacably made up, always sure of its purpose. He laughed into her mouth as he felt the stiff limbs meet him in sudden acquiescence. "Can we not have some affection for one another?" he asked softly. His hand found her breast. "We are brother and sister. Need it be such a hard thing to make an heir?" She breathed his wine-laden breath, and the smell of his sweat mingled with the oil that smeared his chest, his arms. She shook her head mutely, urging him on with little cries. Before they fell together upon the bed, she had two fleeting thoughts. One was of Senmut. With a spasm of passion she remembered his solid shoulders, the firm young flesh under her hands. The other was of Thothmes himself, his indecisions, his amiable squandering of what little ability was born in him to rule. She felt the tragedy of the man, the force and ability he was displaying now, wasted and dissipated, when it should have been exercised in the halls of power.

She would have liked to talk to him when it was all over, to get to know him better, but he quickly fell asleep, snoring gently, his loose, flabby limbs sprawled upon her dainty coverlets. A wave of rejection swept her. Getting up, she put on her robe and sat in her chair. She was more than grateful to see the darkness give way to the dawn. She sat, vacant in mind and body, until she could clearly see the paintings on her walls. Then she went to the couch and bent over Thothmes, calling his name and shaking him gently by the arm. "Wake up! The High Priest will soon be here!" she whispered.

He only groaned and turned over, pillowing his head on a hand still hennaed and beringed. As the Hymn of Praise began, he opened his eyes. They sat together on the bed, listening to the priests sing his praises while the pearly light of Ra's first greetings slid along the floor.

She saw Thothmes' eyes light at the words. They are not for you, she thought. They are eternally, always, only for me.

As the hymn ended, Thothmes kissed her and got up. "I am hunting today," he said. "Do you want to join me?"

"No, not today. I have other duties."

He shrugged. "Of course." He smiled hesitantly. "Will you welcome me tonight?"

She looked at the round cheeks, the big eyes, the wisps of brown hair still clinging to the sides of the bald head, and she felt a sympathy for him. He was handsome in a loose, unformed way and pathetic as a child.

She inclined her head. "Come tonight if you will, but not tomorrow night. By then I shall have given a full day to my duties, and I shall be tired."

"Very well." He yawned widely, padding to the door. "I suppose the nobles will have gathered to watch me bathe. Enjoy your breakfast, Hatshepset, as I have enjoyed the night."

She rose and bowed to him, Pharaoh of All Egypt. When he had gone and she had sent for her slaves to put fresh linen on the bed, she got into her bath and rested, floating, her eyes closed. She fell asleep while she was having her massage, and the nap refreshed her.

At midmorning she ate some fruit and drank a little water, ignoring the silly, knowing glances and simpering smiles of her hairdresser. Afterward she took Nofret for a walk around her garden, glad of the clean, cool grass, the dry whisperings of the trees, the open, light-filled silence. She did not try to analyze her response to Thothmes. Although she was a grown woman, she had never taken a lover. In her heart she cried for Senmut, for the sympathy and support she always found in his dark eyes, for the little, cynical half smile that would tell her of his quick understanding, but she did not send for him. She spent most of the day outside, walking aimlessly, caught in a limbo of hours that seemed to stretch into days and the days into months and years, time, slow time, taking her nowhere after all.

In the evening she reluctantly went back to her apartment to bathe again and to dress, for she knew that Thothmes would dine in a hurry and be upon her doorstep not long after the sun set. Nofret, mistaking her mistress's sighs and long silences for the anticipation of love, brought out her best robe and filled the room with incense and myrrh.

In the middle of the month of Phamenoth, when Thothmes had reigned for two months, word came north to Thebes of trouble in Nubia. Hatshepsut received the dispatch from the hand of a tired and hungry soldier who had escaped into the desert and been picked up by a caravan of nomads. Even before she had finished reading it, she was ordering her cabinet to appear in the audience chamber. She sent for Aahmes pen-Nekheb and Ineni and for Thothmes, too, hoping that he had not yet left for the hunt, and while she waited for them to assemble, she paced the floor in agitation, the scroll held tightly in both hands. She sent the soldier to the barracks for food and rest. It was a scorching day, summertime, and though the mats covering the wall to the garden had been raised, no breeze penetrated.

As she paced, she barked unceasingly at her scribe. "Get out the maps of the south and the First Cataract and the placement of the garrisons on the Nubian border. Gather the generals. Find all conscription lists; I want to know where all my troops are. Bring a plan of the garrison mentioned here"—she tapped the scroll—"and the name of the commander stationed there. Hurry!"

One by one the men came in, bowing and sitting around the large, bare table upon which the Queen spread out her correspondence every morning. Pen-Nekheb came last, limping slowly to his place. He had never before been called by Hatshepsut, and his heart sank, for he smelt war. He had marched too long, he thought, tucking his voluminous kilt around his legs. He listened to the whispered speculations around him, wondering how long it would be before he could get back to his cucumbers and his melons.

At last Hatshepsut ordered the door closed and sat at the head of the table. She wore a pleated kilt of fine linen that swished about her legs and fell gracefully to the floor. She had flowers entwined in her hair, but her expression held little that was feminine. As Anen settled on his stool at her feet and took up his reed pen, her lips were taut and her forehead lined. "I have just given audience to an officer of the Medjay, our desert police," she said. "It seems that one of our garrisons has been overrun, and a rabble of Nubians is looting inside the border."

There was a stillness in the room. Yamu-nefru spat lazily upon the floor. "It was to be expected, Majesty. Every time a Pharaoh goes to the God and a new one rises triumphant, the filthy and execrable inhabitants of Kush foment rebellion. It is almost as sure a happening as the soaring of Ra each day in the sky."

"What of the commander?" User-amun asked her. His sunny, impish face was solemn.

She shook her head. "No one knows whether he is alive or dead. Indeed, I do not even know who had command there. I have sent for the Scribe of Assemblage. He will tell us. Anen, give me the maps."

Senmut took the scrolls from the scribe's hand and spread them out on the table. They all stood and watched as Hatshepsut's brown finger slashed at the tracings.

"Here is Assuan, and here the Cataract. The desert road leaves the river at this point," she stabbed at the page, "and veers west. Two garrisons stand, the one within our border and the other here, fifty miles farther, into the land of Kush. I am told that the inland one has been taken and the men slaughtered. Even now the Kushites march on the other." She let the scroll roll up with a snap and seated herself once more, looking into each of their faces expectantly. "Hapuseneb," she said at length, "as Vizier of the North you are now appointed Minister of War. Give me your thoughts."

He leaned forward, his braceleted arms on the table. "My thoughts, Majesty, must be shared by every man present. It is necessary to gather a force immediately and leave Thebes, marching south. There is no doubt that we can speedily rout these ungrateful dogs, but it must be done before they reach the second garrison."

There was a murmur of assent, and Aahmes pen-Nekheb's voice rose above the others. The old man was clearly distressed, breathing heavily "Majesty, may I be permitted to speak?"

She inclined her head, smiling at him affectionately. "I had hoped that you would, old friend. My father never stirred from Thebes on such an expedition as this without your excellent aid. Say on."

"Then, to put it bluntly, I do not understand how the garrison fell. These places are the backbone of our borders, strongly walled, impregnable, and full of seasoned fighting men. The enemy has often run amuck up and down the borders, looting and killing and stealing good Egyptian cattle, but seldom have they penetrated a garrison. I do not like the smell of it."

They all looked at him uneasily, and it was Hapuseneb who put the question to him. "What do you fear, Revered One? Treason?"

"Perhaps. It would not be the first time that men soured from long service in the desert, far from family and home, their reason turned by the offer of gold or something else."

Hatshepsut broke in. "We do not know. We have no details. The officer who came to me had only fought the Kushites in the sand and was not present when the garrison was taken. Ah, the Scribe of Assemblage!"

The man approached, his arms full of paper, and he bowed.

"Sit here," Hatshepsut told him. He laid his burden on the table and took a stool next to Anen. He was a little man, bent with years of writing and crippled in one leg. "Now, Hapuseneb, ask your questions."

Hapuseneb asked who commanded the interior garrison, and the scribe cleared his throat, shuffling among his papers.

Menkh leaned over and whispered in Senmut's ear, "This old idiot will keep us here for the rest of the morning. He can scarce find his own nose."

The man was already answering, his voice nasal but his glance to Menkh razor-sharp. "It is captained by the noble Wadjmose. Fifty infantry were stationed there by Her Majesty's father, together with a small contingent of Shock Troops."

Hatshepsut cried out and jumped to her feet.

Thothmes, who had become increasingly uncomfortable as he sat listening to the talk, exclaimed also. "Wadjmose! My brother! Now what say you, pen-Nekheb? Will a noble of Pharaoh's blood betray his countrymen?"

Pen-Nekheb's jowls shook. "It is still possible, Majesty, that there was treason and the commander knew nothing of it. I would not dismiss the theory."

"Neither will I," retorted Hatshepsut. "Continue." But she was visibly disturbed and sat with her eyes downcast, her hands clasped tightly in her lap.

Thothmes suddenly exploded. "By Amun! This is no ordinary raid we plan! Our brother must be avenged! I will smite the Kush with the might of all my armies. I will destroy all. I will allow no male to live!" He shook with an uncharacteristic rage, his protruding teeth bared in a snarl.

As Hatshepsut looked at him, the previous night's spent passions came to her, a memory of hot, sticky darkness, his teeth on her flesh. She shifted in her chair. "I agree that these people must be taught a salutary lesson," she said to him quietly, and he retired, still glowering. "Was it not for a moment such as this, Thothmes, you argued for the throne? I am glad that you intend to do as our ancestors have done and lead your troops into battle." He did not reply to this, staring at her while his anger disappeared as suddenly as it had arisen. She smiled across at him sadly. She knew that he would never go to fight, and she nodded at Hapuseneb.

"How many soldiers do we have?" he asked the scribe. "I am not concerned with any that cannot march from Thebes within the week."

"Five thousand in the city," the man said promptly. "One hundred thousand altogether of permanent troops, and four times that number can be raised by conscription."

"One division." He thought for a moment. "Majesty, how great a force is mustered against us?"

"The numbers are inaccurate, but it cannot be more than three thousand. There are some archers, bowmen of a kind."

"Chariots?"

Her lip curled scornfully. "Not unless the Kush have stolen those used by the garrison. How many chariots there?" she fired at the scribe.

He answered her with the same imperturbable calm. "One squadron, Majesty."

"Well, if Wadjmose is the soldier my father thought him to be, he will have killed all the horses early in the battle to make sure that the Nubians could not use the chariots. Now put all together, Hapuseneb."

The Vizier sat back in his chair, summing up. "It appears that there is a horde of Kushites, probably undisciplined and poorly led, somewhere in the desert about seventy miles from the river and converging on the second garrison. In number they are about three thousand. They have bowmen and perhaps chariots. I think it will be easy to quash them. Half a division and a squadron of charioteers should be enough."

Hatshepsut agreed. "But speed is essential," she added. "Pen-Nekheb, which division is quartered in Thebes at this time?"

"The Division of Horus, Majesty. There are also a few retainers from the Division of Set, here for maneuvers."

"Thank you. I see no need to keep you any further. Hapuseneb will, of course, go into the field, and you, Yamu-nefru. Djehuty, I will need the troops from your nome. You will march also. Sen-nefer, you also return to your nome and bring troops. In this way we will take half the division from Thebes, leaving soldiers in the city if the need arises. We also take five hundred men from each of your nomes, Yamu-nefru, Djehuty, and Sen-nefer. Are you satisfied?"

They murmured, nodding, but were instantly silent as Hapuseneb's clear voice rose above their whispering. "Majesty, as Minister of War I take all this from your hands, knowing your mind. But who will command in the field? True, this is not war but a punitive expedition, and yet we need a man well-seasoned, who knows the country and has fought before."

All eyes swiveled to Aahmes pen-Nekheb, and he threw up his hands, shaking his head vigorously. "Majesty, I am old. I will go and aid in tactics, but I cannot fight."

"That is a blow to me," Hatshepsut frowned. "I had hoped to have your arm, Noble Aahmes, but if you feel you cannot fight, then perhaps you can suggest a man on whom I may rely."

He hesitated. "There is such a man, Divine One, but I do not know if he would be acceptable to you."

"You will never know unless you try me."

"Then hear. He is one Nehesi."

At the name an angry buzz broke out, and Djehuty shouted, "You cannot put us into his hands, Majesty! He is a Nubian himself!"

Thothmes waved a placatory arm, and they subsided into startled silence. They had forgotten that he was there. "Peace, all of you! Sit down, Djehuty! Do we not trust Aahmes pen-Nekheb, beloved of our father? Is his judgment not sound?"

Djehuty retired, still muttering and casting dark looks at pen-Nekheb.

The old man was unruffled. "It is true that Nehesi is black," he said, "but he is not Nubian. He was born on Egyptian soil. His mother is a servant to Pharaoh's mother, the lovely Mutnefert, and his father was a slave brought back by Ineni as plunder. Nehesi has been a soldier from his earliest years. I call him a genius. He is a silent man, not given to emotion or any excess, but his prowess with bow, ax, and spear is unexcelled, and he has a cold and farseeing mind."

Hatshepsut called for Duwa-eneneh. "Find this person, and bring him to me with all speed," she ordered.

When he had gone, they waited in silence, not daring to say any more. Sen-nefer took out a box of sweetmeats and pushed a couple into his girlish mouth. Yamu-nefru began to file his nails. But the rest of them sat awkwardly while the horns sounded for noon and their heads became dizzy from the intensifying heat.

At last the Chief Herald returned, and Nehesi stood before them. They looked at him with open curiosity. He was tall, taller than any of them, and blacker than the night of the khamsin. His kilt seemed a silly, flimsy thing, a patch of white on a colossal body whose muscles rippled and flexed as he bowed. His leather helmet, also white, framed a face magnificent in its blunt angles and smooth, shiny planes. His nose was straight, betraying some Egyptian blood somewhere far back in his family's history. His full lips were firm and cold. He ignored them all, staring at the wall over their heads. If he saw Djehuty's sneer, he made no sign.

"Come closer," Thothmes told him. He took two lithe, gliding steps, his feet bare and dusty from the training ground. Over one shoulder he still wore a leather quiver that held three arrows. "How long have you served the army?" Thothmes asked, his voice kindly.

Nehesi answered with no hesitation, his voice deep. "Fifteen years, Majesty."

"What positions do you hold?"

"Commander of the Shock Troops. I also train charioteers, and I put the Braves of the King through their paces."

The indifferent, emotionless tone provoked an awed reaction from the men around the table. Senmut looked at the Negro with new respect. The Braves of the King were the elite of the army, the handpicked men who led every assault and were directly responsible to Pharaoh himself. Even Djehuty's face lost its look of disdain.

"How much action have you seen?" User-amun asked.

The man impatiently shrugged a massive shoulder. "There has been no war since I was an apprentice in the ranks of the infantry," he said, "but I have been on raids and border skirmishes without number. My Shock Troops have never been routed." He was not boasting; he simply stated a fact.

"What of strategy?" Hatshepsut asked him.

He shook his head. "I was born for war," he said, "and I feel the rightness or the wrongness of placements in my bones, but only at the time of battle. I cannot put my thoughts upon a map."

Aahmes pen-Nekheb spoke up. He had been watching the reactions his protégé was causing with quiet amusement. He thought that it would do the young aristocrats good to have their first taste of blood and death under such a one. "Majesty, I have said that I will go to advise. Nehesi will deploy. I can confidently say that the battle is won if we two have the planning of it."

They all laughed at his little joke, and the air seemed to clear.

Thothmes yawned. "Then it is settled. Is it not?" He looked anxiously at Hatshepsut.

She nodded. "I think so. Hapuseneb, I leave the victualing and arming and gathering in to you. Pitch tents on the land south of the city, and prepare to march from there. Brief your officers well, with the help of Aahmes and Nehesi. The Scribes of Assemblage, Infantry, and Distribution await you. Nehesi, I appoint you General. You understand that this appointment is given in the trust that you will serve to the death and answer to no one but your King or myself. Do you have any doubts? This foray is against your countrymen, the people of Kush."

"I have fought them before," he said indifferently. "All enemies of Egypt are the same to me. I serve only Egypt, every day of my life."

His new appointment did not seem to mean anything to him, and Hatshepsut repressed a shudder. She had never before met a colder man.

She dismissed all but Senmut, Hapuseneb, and User-amun to work, and they filed out, glad to stretch their legs. For a moment they lingered about the door, discussing the coming march; then they scattered to their duties. They had no doubt that it was the Queen who had the ordering of the expedition. They knew that nothing they did would be overlooked.

As the three young men waited, Hatshepsut turned to Thothmes, who was on his way out into the garden. She drew him farther away from her waiting ministers. "Thothmes, are you going to lead your troops yourself?"

He looked miserable. "Why should I?" he asked her defiantly. "Egypt abounds in capable generals, and the captains fall over one another. You know as well as I do that I am no warrior. Let Hapuseneb lead my men."

"Hapuseneb has his own squadron to handle, as well as the overall campaign to plot. Thothmes, will you not ride?"

He looked mutinous. "No, I will not! It is ridiculous for the precious body of Pharaoh to be endangered without need."

"But there is a need!" she said to him urgently. "The men need to see you, glorious in your battle attire, leading them, putting heart into them!"

"You sound like my mother," he flashed back. "I will not go! I will ride on my litter as far as Assuan. There I will await the return. There I will receive the tribute and will order the fate of the captives. But I will not go!"

She turned from him in utter disgust. "Then I will go! The people of Egypt shall see and shall know that their Queen is worthy of them!"

He was appalled. "You are mad! You have never seen human blood, and you have never been in the slightest danger. Can you march and thirst for water and sleep on the ground?"

"Can you?" she lashed him. "In the name of the God, Thothmes, have you no pride? I can throw a spear and shoot a bow. I can outrun any charioteer in the army! I trust my men. They will not fail me. They love me."

"Everyone loves you, mad though you are. Even me," he grumbled.

Contrite, she put a hand on his arm. "I must ride if you do not," she said gently. "I will be in no danger. I will be surrounded by the strongest arms and the keenest eyes in Egypt. Ride with me, Thothmes! Show

Egypt and the people of Kush a glimpse of the Pharaohs of old!"

He shook off her arm and walked away. "You are mad, really mad," he flung back at her over his shoulder.

She turned on her heel and stalked to the waiting men, her cheeks red and her chest heaving. "I am going into Nubia with the troops," she told them. They looked at her in disbelief.

Senmut cried out in alarm. "Majesty, you must not! A battlefield is no place for a queen!"

She gave him a queer smile. "I am not a queen," she said, her tone chilling him. "I am God, the beginning of existence. Do not again say 'must' to me, Senmut. I want to go. I shall lead the troops of Pharaoh. My Standard-Bearer shall go before me; the Braves of the King and Nehesi, behind."

"Then let me speak another way." He was desperate now, afraid for her. He saw in her eyes the glint of waywardness. "If you perish, what of Egypt? And who shall rule while you fight?"

"I shall not perish. I know it. Amun will protect me. You, Senmut, shall govern while I am gone. User-amun, you will assist. I know you are not fitted for war." She turned quickly. "Senmut, I make you Erpa-ha." The last words were sudden, almost abrupt. They stared at her, bereft of thought and speech.

Senmut heard the words come to him from far away. Once more he felt the warm wings of destiny brush him, feathers of fate. He looked into her wide black eyes as if he were peering down into a dangerous and fathomless pit.

She touched his head, his shoulders, his heart, feeling it race unevenly under her fingers. She laughed, though her lips trembled. "I would have done it before long in any case," she said, "for you have proven yourself in my service. But it must be now, today, for I cannot have a commoner as my second while I am away. Be Erpa-ha, Hereditary Prince of Thebes and all Egypt, you and your sons after you, forever. I, Hatshepsut, Beloved of Amun, Child of Amun, Queen of Egypt, make it so."

He knelt swiftly and caught her ankles, kissing her bejeweled feet. When he rose, he was unable to speak for the lump in his throat.

All at once she embraced him, holding him tightly to her, enveloping him in perfume and hair. "Never was the title so deserved," she said. "Be happy in the love of your lord, Senmut!" She released him and turned to Hapuseneb. "And you," she said. "What can I give to you? For you have everything the heart of man could desire, and your ancestors walked Egypt with mine." She smiled into the unwavering gray eyes, and Hapuseneb smiled back slowly. "Yet I know, Hapuseneb, that the thing you seek is to be forever denied to you, though I wish it were not so."

He bowed gravely. "I know it also, Majesty, yet I am not embittered. You are my Queen, my Master. I serve you as long as I breathe."

"Then to you I offer the position of Chief of the Prophets of South and North. As a Vizier and the son of a vizier you should know what this means."

He bowed, moved. "I know indeed. Great power you put into my hands, Noble One. It shall not be abused."

"Then to work. Senmut, User-amun, we will spend the rest of the day in conference with Ineni and the others. Rely on Ineni. He knows more of government than even I. And you, Hapuseneb, be about your business. I wish to leave Thebes for Assuan in five days."

In the evening, when the Sun had gone and taken the worst of the heat with him and his fire was no more than a few wisps of purple on the rim of the hills, Hatshepsut and Senmut walked beside Amun's Lake, their reflections stirring in the ripple of the water's slow washing. A mood of quiet was on them, and they did not share their thoughts, pacing side by side, their heads down, their hands brushing loosely. When they had almost completed a circuit, Hatshepsut stopped. They sat on the grassy verge, watching the geese fly home in the warm twilight.

"Will you have the time to work more in the valley?" she asked. "It would be good to return and see the first terrace complete. Already it is a thing of beauty, my temple."

"It is a mirror," he replied, "a reflection of your own loveliness. Amun could wish for no better monument from his favored Daughter."

She inclined her head, then fell to picking the dry, crisp leaves of the willow from the drooping branches. "Tell me," she said, her head averted, "now that you are Erpa-ha and a high noble and Prince of the land, will you have sons to hold the title after you?"

He smiled at the dark, bent head, but he answered her seriously. "I do not know, Majesty, but I think not. To have sons I must first take a wife."

"There is Ta-kha'et."

"True. But I do not think that I will marry Ta-kha'et, though I am very fond of her."

"You may change your mind as the years go by. How old are you, Senmut?"

"I have been on the earth for twenty-six years."

She was still not looking at him, shredding apart the curled leaves with nervous fingers. "Most men have at least one wife," she said haltingly. "Do you not want a home full of children?"

"Majesty, you know why I cannot marry." He chided her gently, knowing that to her the future suddenly seemed uncertain, her mind full of the coming march south. "Is it not best that we pursue some other train of thought?"

She turned to him, brushing the speckles of brown leaf from her knees. "I know why indeed," she said, "but will you not tell me in words? Is it because I have loaded you with too many responsibilities?"

"You know that also." He knew what she wanted him to say. He wanted with all his heart to say it, but the Cobra glinted upon her head, and at her throat lay one of her royal cartouches. He could not separate the Queen from the woman.

She flung back her head, and holding her hands palm up in the gesture of supplication, she pressed him. "Say it to me! And do not think that I have bribed you with a title so that I could force this thing from you. I know you well enough. You never lie to yourself or to me. Say it!"

"Very well." He clasped his knees, and his eyes found the last of the light, limning the temple towers in brief color, so that they stood out as sharply as the edge of a knife. "I love you. Not only as my Queen but as the woman for whom I long I love you. You knew, and yet you have forced it from me with no thought of my pride because you are Queen and I must answer. It was a cruel thing to do."

As she drank in his calm profile, her fingers curled and clenched. "It was no weakness," she answered. "I am to go away, and I am afraid. I need your words, Senmut, to hold to me, to take with me, to warm me. As Queen I expect your homage, but as a woman—" She put a hand on his arm, light as the touch of wind on grass. "Give me a gift, Senmut."

His gaze did not leave the tops of the temple wall. "Anything," he said quietly, but she felt the muscles of his arm tense and relax.

"If I take off my coronet and my cartouche, the ankh from my arm and the seal from my waist, and lay them in the grass, will you kiss me?"

His gaze snapped to her. When he saw that she was not playing a game with him but looked up at him, her mouth quivering and her eyes shining with tears, he took her face between his hands, stroking the smooth cheeks in joyous disbelief. "No," he whispered, "no, Mighty One. I will kiss you as you are, my Divine Queen, my heart's disease, my sister. There will be no pretense." And with infinite gentleness he placed his lips on hers, tasting her sweetness and the salt of her tears, feeling her arms encircle his neck, while the last of the sun's light slipped from the towers and fell to the earth, dragging quickly through the trees and vanishing behind the mantle of the night.

15

Seven days later, in the precious cool hours of early morning, the host of Egypt made rank on the desert, a mile south of Thebes. They were two days late because Djehuty and his men had become lost while trying to take a shortcut through the hills. In those two days Hatshepsut had fretted angrily. Aahmes pen-Nekheb, ever matter-of-fact, told her that in any case they would be too late to engage the Nubians before they reached the second garrison and two days would make little difference, but she stormed and paced anyway, in a fever of impatience to be gone.

Thothmes had spent the time with his mother, who had filled his ears with advice. In the end he had gone to Hatshepsut's palace, but she had sent him away peremptorily, with short words. He had spent his last night in Thebes alone on his royal couch, looking darkly into his future.

In the morning he stood on the reviewing stand that had been set up, together with Hatshepsut, pen-Nekheb, Hapuseneb, and Nehesi. It was a fine morning, the breeze lifting the standards and fluttering the flags, the sun glinting on the ranks of spears and shouldered axes like a thousand sparks flickering on tinder. The stiff lines of infantry waited, eyes front, motionless. Far to the rear stood their tents, white cones clustered like little toy pyramids. On each side of the four thousand men stood the chariots, small and light, copper-plated, their big, spoked wheels gleaming dully. The horses waited also, tossing their brown heads, their plumes, white, yellow, and red, blowing gaily. Hatshepsut looked out over it all, the power and focal point, the stay of Egypt.

Before her stood the Division of Horus, their Standard-Bearer wearing the hooked beak and cruel eyes of the God. The generals, in full battle dress, had lined up at the foot of the dais. The Shock Troops were nearest to her, hard men with hard eyes, those who died first and who left the field last. Their officers stood among them, bows slung over their shoulders and spears butt down in the sand. The Prince of the Division of Horus was Hapuseneb. He had chosen to march with them instead of riding up front with Pharaoh. He waited also, his cold eyes never wavering from the woman on the dais. Thothmes had donned the Double Crown, but it was to Hatshepsut the men looked. She was wearing the dress of a commander, a short white kilt, a short leather helmet that hid her hair and touched her shoulders, and white leather gauntlets to shield her hands from the rub of bow and rein alike. She also wore white leather boots, and under the gloves her wrists held the thick silver bands of Commander of the Braves of the King. Only on her helmet did she bow to her true station. A little silver Cobra rose from her forehead, and even the men far back could see the sunlight catch it. Her eyes traveled the rows of foot soldiers and the blue-helmeted charioteers, rising at last above the forest of spear tips and bows to the palace standing red in the distance. She abruptly turned to Thothmes, thinking of Senmut waiting on the roof and of User-amun and Ineni gathered above the walls to watch the army leave.

"Will you speak to them, or shall I?" she asked. "Pen-Nekheb, are we ready? But where are the Braves of the King?" She swung anxiously to Nehesi, and he bowed, pointing with one leather-clad hand.

"Here they march now," he said. "They are late, but I do not apologize, Majesty. You will see why in a moment."

From around a grove of trees, by the river, her fifty men appeared, their feet leaving a cloud of dust behind them, their shields slung across their backs. Before them a chariot rolled, new, finely plated in gold, intricately tooled and worked, the plumes of Amun engraved on its high prow and the Eye of Horus on each side. Its reins and curbs were of the finest, strongest leather. The horses' bits and tackles were gold. The spinning spokes whirled golden, too, as the charioteer raised his whip and the sturdy little horses broke into a gallop. In a flurry of suffocating dust and dancing white plumes it drew up before the party on the dais, and Menkh twirled his whip and jumped to the ground, laughing. Behind him the Braves of the King came to a halt and saluted. Nehesi left the stand, leaping gracefully to the earth, and walked to them. Hatshepsut strode to the edge and looked down.

Menkh bowed, his face under the blue helmet convulsed with glee. "A gift to Her Majesty from her loyal and adoring troops!" he called up to her, waving behind him at the chariot and the restless, dancing horses. She also sprang to the ground and walked up to the chariot, touching it, automatically checking the wheel axle, bits, and curbs.

Nehesi came forward. "This is no ceremonial chariot built for a royal progress," he said. "This is a vehicle of war, fast and light, a gift from men of war to their Chief Officer."

She did not reply but leaped onto its floor, snatching up the reins and wrapping them around her gauntleted wrists. With a shout she was off, bent and tight, her face set and her legs apart for balance, while the men in her dust broke rank for a moment and cheered her on as if she were a favored contender in their annual races. Once she completed a circuit, she alighted, her eyes sparkling, as she threw the reins to Menkh.

"Are you my charioteer, presumptuous one?" she asked him in passing. He bowed, grinning. She mounted the steps and stood once more beside a discomfited Thothmes, who was now starting to sweat as the sun gained strength. Hatshepsut raised an arm, and silence fell. She turned and addressed her own troops directly. "I thank you for this display of love," she said, her voice ringing clear and high. "Do not doubt but that I shall earn it fully, as I have earned your devotion. You are beautiful to me, fighting men of Egypt. I am proud to march with you this day. Now listen to the words of Pharaoh, Living Forever!"

Thothmes stepped forward, gesturing for Menena to ascend the steps with the incense. He was impressive in the tall crown, a massive Pharaoh, a bulk of power as he held his Crook and Flail over the company. The men caught a faint, faraway echo of his father as he spoke to them of glory and reward, of dangers faced for the continued safety of Egypt, and of honorable death on the field of battle. They forgot that it was the Queen who stood garbed simply as commander. When Thothmes had finished, they cheered him, the roar drifting faintly to the men who waited quietly on the roof of the audience chamber, leaning out in the hot sun.

Menena intoned the Prayers of Blessing and Victory, and Hapuseneb took over. "Greatest of Fifty! Commanders of Hundreds, Captains, Troop Commanders, Standard-Bearers! Prepare to march! Form marching ranks!"

Hatshepsut and Thothmes left the stand. "Ride with me in my chariot," she offered, taking the reins.

"I will lead in my litter," he said. "It is too hot to stand in that thing," He left, followed by pen-Nekheb.

The men were forming new ranks now, shouldering their packs and adjusting their weapons.

Hatshepsut ordered Menkh out of the chariot. "For your folly you may march," she told him. "I want to drive myself for a while, so you can eat my dust." She snatched the whip from him and tapped him fondly on the head, clucking to her horses and trotting after Thothmes. Behind her Nehesi and her men fell in, and the vast cavalcade began to wind out upon the road south like an undulating, multicolored snake. The baggage trains straggled at the rear, for although the army was traveling light and swiftly, each man carrying his own needs, there were tents to bring, and food and water, and the royal couple's carpets, chairs, folding couches, and shrines. The men began to sing a battle hymn in time to the swinging of their feet, but the music soon died away and all fell silent, striding grimly on, for the heat was great, and Assuan was a long way away.

Senmut watched until the wind dissipated the last cloud of brown dust. He turned to Ineni. "May all the gods go with them," he said softly.

The old man smiled at his expression. "This is but a small routing to be done," he said. "Do you doubt that they will all come marching back, laden with fresh spoil for the temple and gold for the treasury?"

Senmut forced a laugh as they went down the stairs and into the shadow of the cloister. "I do not doubt," he said, his thoughts on the miles lengthening between himself and the army.

Ineni quickened his pace. "Then think no more of war," he said over his shoulder, "for the emissaries from Rethennu await us in the audience chamber, and there is much to be done, Prince." He chuckled, shaking his head.

On that first day's march the army made a scant twenty-five miles, and at sunset the tents were erected beside the Nile. Hatshepsut bathed in the river with Thothmes, lying blissfully in the shallows while the sweat and dust fell from her. She wrapped herself in a loose robe and sat before her tent, watching the smoke spiral from the hundred cooking fires. Beside her hung her standard, limp in the evening stillness. She listened to the whickering of the horses and the subdued conversation of the men as she basked in the pleasant haze of physical exhaustion. The men were tired, too. No amount of drill could take the place of forced marching along hard, rutted tracks and over stony ground. Their feet were sore, their shoulders chafed. Thothmes was already preparing for sleep in the white and blue tent next to hers, and she smiled as she thought how glad he would be to reach the city of Assuan and fall onto a royal couch once more.

Hapuseneb came, squatting easily on the earth at her feet. She asked him when they would turn into the desert.

"Tomorrow we should make thirty or even forty miles," he answered. "We will enter Assuan two days from today. Another day's march will bring us to the turning point, and we will have to fill all barrels with water. Are you weary, Majesty?"

"A little. I think I will let Menkh drive me tomorrow. But the chariot runs well, and the horses are matched to perfection. Listen to the ibex and the coughing of the hippopotami in the marsh! If we could but stay here, we should have good hunting in the morning."

"Perhaps Pharaoh will venture forth from Assuan while we are gone," he replied.

They sat in companionable silence until she yawned. It was now so dark that the fires stood out like friendly, shining eyes, and the exchanges of the sentries on the riverbank came to them reassuringly. Hapuseneb bowed his good-night and melted swiftly away. She got up and went to her camp cot, pulling the blankets up to her chin and curling under them, hearing her guard take his place beyond the tent flap. Before he had settled his spear upon the ground, she was asleep.

Two days later, in the late afternoon, they reached Assuan and spread their tents outside the city. The men were coming into their second wind, and around the fires there was laughter and the rattle of gaming dice. Hatshepsut put on her coronet and wig and went with Thothmes to the royal residence, where he relaxed and immediately ordered wine and hot pastries.

"Stay here with me tonight," he begged her. "We shall not see each other for some weeks, and I am sure that you wish to enjoy some comfort before you leave."

Looking into his soft, pleading face, she agreed. "We can rise early," he promised, "for this country has good hunting."

She smiled and went into his arms dutifully, not really caring, glad to give him her body while her mind ranged far ahead to one ruined garrison and the besieged and desperate soldiers who manned the walls of the other. She slept deeply beside him, worn out by travel and the demands of his eager body.

In the morning she said good-bye to him affectionately and lightly, with relief. It was good to be one again, to be free and alone, she thought as the horns blew and she swung herself up beside Menkh. She turned and waved to Thothmes and his courtiers, smiling back at Nehesi in his chariot. When Hapuseneb gave the signal to advance, she steadied herself for the jolt, humming a song to herself.

Assuan soon emptied, and the summer day filled the streets with silence as Thothmes got into his hunting skiff rather disconsolately.

But all around Hatshepsut was the jingle of harness, the creak of leather, and the slap-slap of sandals. She looked ahead to the jagged teeth and turbulent, fighting waters of the First Cataract with an almost delirious happiness, her skin already darkening under the fierce sun and her sinews tightening to a new strength.

In the morning, after one more night's camp, water barrels were carefully filled, harnesses checked, equipment tallied, and the horses watered. Their way would quickly turn into desert, and before them was hostility, mile upon mile of rock and sand, all burning under the full power of Ra, and the mountains that had marched with them upon their western flank would leave them to wander out into regions unknown. Their path would sometimes run over hard, baked earth; but more often than not, it would take them through cloying sand. Hatshepsut tightened the straps of her helmet, and Menkh took a last walk around the chariot, noting how already the wheels sank into the earth. Hapuseneb sent scouts before them to test the ground and to find the quickest route. It was a road used by men and soldiers on business to and from the garrisons or by caravans that went on to the oasis two hundred miles to the north, but it remained a desert track, and the men knew what was ahead. When Hapuseneb and Nehesi were finally satisfied, they set off, their feet hot, already scorched through their sandals by the hating sand, their bodies burned by copper chariots whose sides glittered malevolently.

All were glad to camp that night. No fires were lit, for at the end of another day's hard marching lay the second garrison and they did not know what they would find there. At the falling of the sun the men put on their woollen cloaks, for the desert nights were very cold. Hatshepsut sat inside her tent, her lamp hanging on the center pole. She ordered wine for herself and Hapuseneb, pen-Nekheb, and her generals.

Nehesi was there, still half-naked, scorning a cloak, for he did not feel either heat or cold. Hatshepsut, shivering a little under her white woollen robe, wondered again about the heart of the man, his thoughts, his soul.

When Menkh came, reporting that the horses had been fed and watered and that the men were at rest, she asked about the morrow.

Nehesi answered her. "After a day's march through the desert the men cannot stand and fight," he said. "I think it would be well to camp for one more night and fall upon the enemy with the dawn if they are around the garrison."

"I know this country," pen-Nekheb said quietly. He looked tired and older than his years, but his eyes were clear, and he was secretly glad to be at war again. "In half a day we come to a mass of high rock and tumbled canyons, and beyond that, back on the desert floor, lies the garrison. The rock will hide our approach, and we can camp this side of it tomorrow night, deploying secretly in the clefts. If we send the Shock Troops and the Braves of the King in the night to come up on the northern wall, then we may drive the Nubians toward the rock and the rest of the army."

"That depends on whether or not the enemy still besieges the garrison, or marches toward us, or has fled back into Kush," Hapuseneb said. "For myself, I would rather march openly in the dawn. If the garrison is taken, the enemy will be within or gone; and if it is not, we may make a swift ending to all."

"Send out more scouts," Hatshepsut said. "Keep them moving through the day, and by tomorrow night we may know what has befallen. If not, then I suggest we wait in the shadow of these rocks until we do know."

"Your Majesty speaks wisely," Nehesi said, and for the first time she saw a smile play about his mouth. "What is the use of deployment in the face of ignorance?"

Hapuseneb nodded. "Very well. Since I am Minister of War, I counsel that we march tomorrow, camp under the rocks, and wait for word from the scouts. Until we pass the first garrison, we are still on Egyptian soil. Then we shall see."

They drank their wine, and Hatshepsut dismissed them early, unable to relax. When they had gone to their own tents, she remained seated at the table, the maps under her hands, wondering how it would be when they sighted the garrison. She finally folded the maps away and lay on the carpet before her shrine, praying to Amun for a swift victory. She did not doubt that victory would be theirs, but she sorrowed at the thought of the spilling of good Egyptian blood, and she saw with a woman's intuition the futility, the senselessness of war. She knew that, unchecked, the foolish people of Kush would gain confidence and strength, and this she could not permit; but she sat long on the edge of her cot, pondering the glories and wastages of revenge and conquest. When she at last took off her clothes and got under the covers, her dreams were full of fire and blood, and she awoke the next morning heavy with oppression and a foreboding that would not go away.

The ranks formed in a businesslike silence, and they were under way before the sun rose, Hatshepsut's mood intensified by the cloud of grim anticipation that hung over the files of marching infantry. She thought with dread of Wadjmose, the garrison's commander, the brother she had never seen.

Three times a halt was called, and the men ate and drank quickly, squatting over their packs. Even Menkh was subdued and lapsed into a stony silence as the day progressed. During the breaks he and Hatshepsut sat on the ground beside the chariot, in the shade cast by its gleaming prow, eating and drinking silently. Hatshepsut's throat was swollen from thirst, and her water ration served only to make her feverish for more, but they started off again in the full blaze of noon, and she could do nothing but stand, swaying, as Menkh lashed the weary horses.

She felt as if she had been riding forever, as if she was already dead and not permitted to enter the Barque of Ra, sentenced to follow him eternally, blinded and withered by his fiery breath.

Three hours into the afternoon her Standard-Bearer turned back to her with a shout, and she saw, shimmering on the horizon, a broken and serried ridge of gray that seemed to hang, quivering, above the surface of the desert. She called a brief halt and sent Menkh to Aahmes pen-Nekheb. The young man came panting back with the news that it was indeed the pile of rock they sought and not a cunning vision of the sand. The host seemed to come to new life, and the ground was covered swiftly, all eyes greedily following the slow rise and the firming of the ground. Just before they clattered into the first gully, the scouts returned, and Hatshepsut and the other generals gathered briefly around Nehesi.

"The garrison appears to be deserted," they were told, "but all about it lie bodies and spent arrows and other evidences of combat. We rode no nearer for fear of being seen."

"Of what nation are the bodies?" Hatshepsut asked quickly.

The scout gave her a wolfish, tired grin. "Black, mostly black—and red, Majesty," he said. "I think that there has been a battle but not a victory, for the bodies are only some hundred or so, and a trail of booty and discarded pots leads on into the desert."

She looked around at them, and pen-Nekheb spoke.

"I am for going forth," he said. "It sounds to me as if the garrison was besieged but is yet intact. Though I am not a gambling man, I would stake my bow on a fort still held."

The others nodded.

"Then let us waste no more time," Hapuseneb said. "Once through the rocks let the division fan out, and put the Shock Troops to the fore, under you, Nehesi. It does not pay to be too confident."

"And let us hurry," Hatshepsut put in. "Before we get through, the sun will have begun to sink, and I do not fancy an approach in the darkness."

They walked back to their chariots, and the horn sounded advance. The way was rougher now, and the horses picked their way daintily between cliffs that reared high above, shutting out much of the light but soon giving way to lower screes, jumbles of fallen stone that narrowed the track so that the men walked warily in single file, their eyes on the heights above. The flatland was gained in a further two hours, and Hatshepsut looked for the first time on her garrison.

It was little more than a high wall ringing a wide enclosure, and the square points of a tower could be glimpsed between the sentry boxes. Great wooden gates stood firmly shut, and Menkh muttered under his breath, "Deserted indeed. By Amun! What a gloomy spot!"

Nehesi called to her, "See, Majesty! The white and blue still flutters from the pole!"

With a rush of relief she saw that indeed the Imperial flag still hung.

They left the shelter of the cliffs, and as her chariot rolled onto the sand once more, she heard the orders shouted behind her that would thin out the ranks and bring the Squadron of Chariots to the fore. The assault troops thundered past her and went into the lead, their standards filling in the evening breeze, and Nehesi brought his chariot up beside hers. They moved slowly on, and in the bloodred light of the setting sun the garrison loomed steadily nearer.

Soon they began to pass huddles in the sand, and Hatshepsut looked down on them, steeling herself for her first look at death, but the dark, sprawled figures seemed so far removed from life that she took them for carrion until, on her left, she saw two hyenas slink away, gray shapes that filled her with revulsion, dragging between them a human arm. She felt nausea churn her stomach, and she fixed her eyes on the baked mud of the garrison wall, now so close that she could see the cracks between the great blocks.

With nerves ever tightening they covered the ground, each man at the ready, holding his bow or spear warily. Hatshepsut held her breath, rigid, waiting for the doors to open and pour a screaming horde onto the plain. But the sand glided by slowly, red beneath them, and the silence went on.

Suddenly there was a shout from the wall. "Egypt! It is Egypt!" She caught a glimpse of white leather and a blurred face and a bare arm that waved wildly and disappeared. More faces ringed the walls, and the gates swung slowly open.

Nehesi called a halt and got down from his chariot. Six soldiers came from within; three wore the long, flowing robes and swathed heads of the Medjay. They were led by a tall man in the white helmet of commander. Hatshepsut also got down stiffly, surprised to find that her legs were weak and trembling. She walked with Nehesi to meet them.

The commander embraced Nehesi joyfully, but when he saw the slight woman beside him, her eyes smiling at him, the Cobra glowing red in the sunset, he fell to the ground. "Majesty! This is a great honor! We had hoped—we did not know—we saw your scouts yesterday, moving among the rocks, but we feared they were the enemy."

"Rise," she said briefly, and he sprang to his feet. "We have made what speed we could, and we thought we had come too late. What is your name?"

"Zeserkerasonb, Commander in Chief, late of the Division of Ptah."

"Lead us within, Zeserkerasonb, for night falls. Nehesi, order that food be distributed and the tents pitched, and make sure that the horses are fed. Is there water here?"

"Yes, Mighty One. The cliffs yonder are full of springs, and we have dug a well in the compound."

"Good."

Nehesi bowed and went swiftly to the ordering of the camp. Then he, pen-Nekheb, Hapuseneb, and Hatshepsut were ushered to the commander's quarters.

The garrison was bare and functional, a place of work. They walked wearily into a wide room that had no cushions or hangings. The floor also was naked, a hard earth floor and the commander's eating bowls and utensils and cot were of polished wood. Through the one window the night wind blew, stirring the flames of the new-lit torches.

Zeserkerasonb brought forward his chair for Hatshepsut and sent his servant for meat and beer. He and the other men gathered around her.

The evidences of recent combat were everywhere, even within the room. A pile of dirty linen lay beside the cot, maps littered the desk, arrows and two bows stood in a corner, and the incense before Amun's little shrine had gone out, leaving a stale smell in the room that mingled with another odor, acrid and unpleasant, that made Hatshepsut's nose twitch in disgust.

"My men are beyond the walls, burning the bodies of dead Nubians," Zeserkerasonb said apologetically. "Unfortunately, there are not many of the enemy who did not escape us."

He was a handsome man, dark, a dour man of few words, but a good soldier and a harsh commander, typical of all Pharaoh's desert men. He wondered where Pharaoh was as he spoke, his curious eyes on his Queen, but he knew better than to put any question to her. She was very beautiful, more beautiful than the picture of her that he carried in his mind, formed five years ago at her coronation. He put his musings away, walking quickly to the brazier and throwing more charcoal on it. It did not matter where Pharaoh was. His army had arrived, and that was the only thing of importance.

"Where are your men?" Hatshepsut asked him sharply.

He turned to her, noting the square, forceful jaw, the shoulders tensed, even in rest. This was no pretty, pampered palace Queen, he thought, and he answered her with a new respect. "They pursue the enemy, but I fear it is a fruitless quest. I have only a few hundred stationed here, and though we patrol the border and settle endless disputes and bloody little insurrections, we are not equipped for full engagements. I ordered the men only to harry the flanks of the men of Kush. We had had word of the burning of the first garrison. We were ready for the enemy and held them off until they saw that we would not fall. We beat them from the walls, so they have turned inland once more, whether to go around us or to retreat, I do not know. Not to retreat, I think. There were many of their chiefs and bowmen gathered, and in my opinion they wish to plunder Egypt herself."

"Vain and foolish hope!" pen-Nekheb snapped. "Why the Nubians endlessly revolt only to be endlessly crushed is quite beyond me."

"They deserve constant occupation," Hatshepsut remarked, "for they are too stupid to govern themselves. Well it is for them that Egypt is in the midst of them! We see to their welfare, we receive them in Thebes, we interest ourselves in their domains, and why? When they steal our cattle and murder our defenseless villagers and slay our soldiers, we wonder."

The servant returned with smoking meat and jugs full of cheap, bitter beer, and they ate and drank without ceremony as full night fell. When she had finished, Hatshepsut sent Nehesi to summon the other generals and commanders, Djehuty, Yamu-nefru, Sen-nefer, and the rest; he returned before long. Zeserkerasonb cleared his desk with one sweep of an arm, and they had more chairs brought and clustered around it.

The scene was becoming familiar to Hatshepsut. The serious, tired faces of the men, the flickering of the lamps, the sounds of the army settling for the night, the bare and simple place in which they sat, room or tent or open fire, and she felt a new kind of peace fill her. She tried to think of her palace—the golden floors, the chased and figured silver walls, the bright-painted tiles, the mounds of flowers, the tall lotus columns, the pools, the lovely green of the gardens, and the stars on the breast of the river—but it seemed a strange, warm, ghostly place, without reality, a place of softness and ease. She turned her thoughts to the hard faces around her, glancing at the spitting brazier and feeling the uncomfortable wooden chair in which she sat.

"Begin," she said to Hapuseneb.

They bowed to her and then settled to the discussion, but they could not ignore her, sitting quietly but alert to every word, her hands folded under her white woollen robe, her dark eyes passing from one to the other.

"At what strength do you put the Kushites?" Hapuseneb asked Zeserkerasonb.

The man smiled faintly. "This question is of course of the utmost importance to you," he said. "Know then that I number the enemy at about three thousand five hundred men, mostly infantry of a sort and armed with rude clubs and axes, but of the three thousand five hundred some eight or nine hundred also have bows."

Eyebrows were raised, and the younger generals shifted uneasily in their seats. The host set against them was larger than they had thought.

"Squadrons?" pen-Nekheb shot swiftly.

The commander lifted a sneering lip. "No chariots. And no discipline. The chiefs lead their men and make a great noise, but the rabble run here and there and kill where they please. It will be a simple matter to round them up."

"And wipe them out." Hatshepsut's words dropped icily among them, and they looked up at her. "I want you to understand, every one of you," she went on, hands clenched under the cloak, "that the order of Pharaoh will be obeyed. No man is to be spared. All will be put to the ax. I do not want to spend my reign swimming in a river of Egyptian blood, and these people must be an example to all who would defy the right and true power of Egypt. It will be a very long time before the inhabitants of this filthy and uncomfortable land again raise their unworthy hands against their lords, and I have better things to do with my gold and my soldiers than make endless war. I have no intention of letting the army go soft." She smiled briefly at Zeserkerasonb. "The numbers of the standing troops will be maintained, but war I will not have!" The last words were emphasized by her hand, which came crashing down on the table, her rings glittering wickedly at them. "My grandfather made a war of recovery, and my father made a war of survival, but I make no more war! Let Egypt live in peace while I rule. Understand, all of you. I have spoken."

Nehesi nodded. "You speak wisely, Majesty. No male shall live."

"But no women or helpless children shall die." She held up a warning hand. "I will not have my troops looting and pillaging as the heathen do. All reward shall come from my hands at the proper time."

They nodded, and she felt the cool, speculative eyes of the Negro fixed on her; but when she looked at him, he was already watching Zeserkerasonb with his unblinking, level stare.

"How far ahead is the enemy?" Djehuty asked.

The commander answered quickly. "No more than one day, and they will travel slowly, worn from fighting and harried by my men."

"Then we will march again in three hours," Hapuseneb said. "Let the men rest while they may. If Amun is with us, we may make battle in the morning."

Hatshepsut watched a slow, secret smile spread over Nehesi's face.

Pen-Nekheb grunted in satisfaction. "So be it," he said. "We will need no complex battle plan if we sweep upon them from the rear. It might be as well to put the Shock Troops way in front, together with the Braves of the King, placing a squadron of chariots on either wing and the Infantry to the rear. In this fashion they will be quickly encircled and destroyed. Majesty, will you ride well to the rear also, in the midst of the spearmen?"

It was a plea, but she tossed back her hair and shook her head. "I am Commander of the Braves of the King, and where they go, I must go also. Do not fear, Nehesi, that you will be occupied with my safety instead of smiting the enemy. As the God, I fear nothing. I order you to see only to our troops."

"As Commander of the Braves of the King you are also my officer, and I obey only you," he replied, and she read approval in his black eyes. "But as General I put the Braves of the King where it is right for them to be. They shall march behind the assault troops, and in any case it is their duty to guard you at all times."

She inclined her head. "Then let us sleep if we can, for we are all weary. I shall send your men back to you, Zeserkerasonb, when all is accomplished. Their bravery and yours shall not go unrewarded."

They rose and quickly scattered, bowing their good-nights to her.

She spent the next three hours in an uneasy sleep on the cot of the commander, dreaming that the hyenas were running with the body of Senmut and that blood stained the sand from deep gashes in his throat and his breast. He still lived and called to her desperately, but her feet would not leave the spot where she stood crying. In the end he stopped calling, and the hyenas slunk over the horizon, dragging him behind them like a limp, shapeless doll.

In the depths of the chill desert night Menkh woke her, and they prepared to begin their last march. The men stood in battle formation, and their officers moved among them with words of instruction and encouragement. On either side of them the chariots rolled, the drivers checking and rechecking harness and maneuvering in a last practice, the riding soldiers behind them adjusting their stance in the bucking vehicles and unslinging their weapons. The tents were quickly and silently taken down, and the fires were put out. Hatshepsut took leave of Zeserkerasonb outside the gates. It was still full dark, and there was no sign of the dawn.

"My brother, Wadjmose," she said. "Did you know him?"

She spoke, unconsciously, as if he was dead, and the man beside her noticed grimly.

"I met him often," he replied. "He was a fine man, a worthy and much-loved officer."

"Tell me in truth, Zeserkerasonb, as you love me, do you think that he was overpowered by might alone?"

Zeserkerasonb was silent for a long time, looking past her chariot, the shuffling horses, the shrouded figure of Menkh, to the massing host beyond. At last he shook his head reluctantly. "No," he said slowly, and Hatshepsut felt her heart turn over. "Wadjmose would have held the garrison easily, for weeks, until he and his men starved for want of supplies. But it is not of defeat through starvation that I heard. My scouts tell me that the garrison was burned to the ground and the men within slaughtered while they yet sought their weapons."

A sickening picture flashed through Hatshepsut's mind: the creeping, silent figures flowing through an open gate and spilling from room to room, the sentries overpowered and killed, and the angry flames eating hungrily, suddenly, as startled men groped for their spears and died before they could leave their dreams behind.

"Someone opened the gates?"

"Yes, I think so."

"Unhappy men!" she whispered softly, her voice venomous. The horses shifted uneasily. "I will find them, and when I do, they will wish that they had never been born. I will tear their bodies apart and give them to the jackals, and not even their names will remain so that the gods may find them."

She swung herself up behind Menkh, and her runner handed her her spear and her bow.

"Farewell, Zeserkerasonb! Have no fear that the gods will not remember you, worthy servant of Egypt!"

Menkh slapped the reins, and she was gone, the darkness swallowing her up as he bowed. He turned swiftly and walked back inside, the doors thudding shut. The army left him quickly behind, already devouring the desert miles like a giant mouth.

The trail of the enemy was not hard to follow, and as pen-Nekheb had surmised, it led the Egyptian troops away from the track that ran between the garrisons and back into the desert. The Nubians were obviously trying to make a wide detour and cross the border farther south, and the scouts skillfully led the army after them. All around them the sand was churned, and often they passed pools of shadow that turned out to be discarded and broken axes, old pots, arrowheads, or the remains of food. Twice they came upon vast, blackened heaps of wood ash, but the scouts reported that the fires were long cold, and the soldiers pressed on. Once Hatshepsut's horses reared suddenly, whinnying, and Menkh got down and ran to see a family of scorpions scuttling for the nearest rock, their stings raised. But otherwise the desert lay calm and still, a fantasy land of darkness without shadow, the sky a blaze of stars without a moon.

Dawn broke, and they camped briefly, sitting in the sand to eat. But before the light had turned from gray to pink, they were moving again, a mood of expectancy quickening their pace as they sensed their prey drawing nearer. There was a cloud on the horizon, and Menkh pointed with his whip.

"There they are, the scum. That is surely their dust, and we will catch them before the morning is out!"

Hatshepsut nodded briefly, her lips compressed, and their pace quickened. The sun was up now, riding low on their left like a great orange ball, and with its rising the air began to warm. The cloud of dust spread, grew ever closer, and orders began to be shouted. Hatshepsut felt her pulses race, as once more the assault troops passed her and fanned out. The chariots went past also, saluting, then dividing to roll beside the Shock Troops. Around her the Braves of the King gathered, and beside her Nehesi leaned over to speak tersely to his charioteer. She could not see, but she knew that behind her the infantry was spreading out. Then all at once, at a shout from Hapuseneb, the pace quickened, and her horses began to trot.

"Tighten the reins!" she shouted to Menkh. "Keep their heads up!"

For a moment she leaned over the side to watch her wheels spin, golden, in the morning sun, and she felt the wind in her face. She then unslung her bow, counted her arrows, and laid her spear beside her on the floor of the chariot. She wanted to be able to shoot unencumbered, and she hoped fleetingly that she would not have to use the spear.

Suddenly the mood of the men reached her, and she felt a fierce excitement rise. The rear guard of the rabble of Kush could be discerned now, a thick, black mass of stumbling men.

Nehesi raised an arm. "Sound the horns!" he shouted, and the hot air was cut by the hoarse braying.

Far ahead, to her left and right, Hatshepsut saw the sun catch the chariots. The assault troops dropped their spears forward and began to run. Suddenly the Nubians realized that they were pursued, and they began to mill about, shouting. She saw wave upon wave of bowmen shoulder through their ranks and ring them, and she chose an arrow with trembling fingers and fitted it to her bow.

Nehesi shouted a third time. "Full forward! Attack!" Her horses broke into a gallop as Menkh's whip whistled and fell about their ears, and they thundered across the plain as a roar went up from the Nubians like the booming of floodwater rushing down a narrow valley.

Menkh was bent nearly double now, sand from the horses' flying hoofs spraying in his face, and Hatshepsut could see the chariots running headlong at the enemy, flowing smoothly over the desert, washing up on the banks of battle. Her ankles and knees ached as she tried to keep her balance. "Mark your man," she heard the voice of her trainer come from far away, still steady and firm through the years, and she drew back the string on her bow. All at once the clean, rushing lines of the Egyptian juggernaut broke up, the chariots becoming islands in a sea of black bodies, the white and yellow and blue helmets of charioteer and spearman alike engulfed, and the tumult of war rushed to meet her. Nehesi shouted something to her, some warning that was torn from his mouth by the speed of their approach, but she had no time to heed him. She found her man; he was holding an ax, his black arm raised, his head back. Suddenly the shaking in her arms and leather-clad hands was gone, and she shot coolly. Before he dropped, screaming, to the sand, she was fitting another arrow.

They were surrounded, deafened by the violent cacophony, the horses brought to a standstill by the press of gasping, shouting, cursing bodies. Menkh desperately tried to force a way through while Hatshepsut loosed another arrow, but they were caught, and he could do little more than hold the frightened horses. On their right an opening suddenly appeared as the battle eddied and swirled, and as if in a wild dream she saw Yamu-nefru, his horses fallen and pierced by arrows, swing his ax in a glittering arc, bringing it down and burying it deep in the chest of the man below him. As she watched, he leaned out the back of his chariot and placed a booted foot on the man's belly, kicking to free his ax as the body fell under the wheels. He was singing. She heard his voice, deep and strong above the noise of the battle, but she had no time to wonder at the haughty, perfumed youth who had drifted so daintily through the palace. A rain of arrows clattered against her chariot, and she ducked quickly, picking up her spear. All at once she saw Nehesi bound from his chariot while another officer took his place. Then he was beside her, arrows spent and spear gone, swinging his ax to guard her rear while she stood and aimed her own spear.

I cannot! she suddenly thought, appalled, the first rush of exultation over, and she looked around her in a tide of panic, sweat suddenly gushing and drenching her. The spear slipped in her wet palm, and she grabbed at it frantically, wanting to scream and scream and run away. Below her a face appeared, its slavering, panting mouth and bloody hands grappling at the side of her chariot. Her head cleared, and she raised the spear again and drove it deep into the open throat. She reached for the ax that hung on Menkh's belt, tugging at it furiously. She heard Nehesi laugh behind her, but the chariot began to move and before the ax was free, he had jumped down, and the melee swallowed him up.

Menkh was thrashing at the horses now, cursing them in a high-pitched stream of foul language, and the Braves of the King, seeing their Commander begin to move, began to close ranks and follow.

"Stay! Stay and fight!" she shouted at them. "I order!" And they swung back once more.

She lost sight of them in the dust and stench that rose from the sand.

The chariot picked up speed as the ranks thinned. Then they were on the periphery, and Menkh slowed the horses.

"What are you doing?" she screamed at him furiously.

He shook his head, letting one hand go of the reins for a moment, to wipe the sweat from his brow. He grinned at the spectacle of his Queen, dirty gray dust sticking to her wet kilt, sweat running between her full breasts, her face streaked with kohl and blood, waving a white fist at him in nervous anger. Beyond them the cries and clashes of war went on, but he slacked the reins before he answered.

"Majesty, the General Nehesi told me that when your spear was gone and you could no longer use your bow, I was to drive you immediately from the field on pain of death, and so have I done." His voice was hoarse from shouting, and she looked at him for one astounded and angry moment before she attempted a smile. He smiled back.

"Wise Nehesi, to so guard the Flower of Egypt!" she said, and at the sight of his face as he tried to control himself, she burst into laughter. "I know!" she said. "Never have I looked less like a flower!"

"You look like what you are, Majesty," he said. "Commander of the Braves of the King," and he saw her eyes light up.

After a while they both suddenly realized that the sun was much higher and that the breath in their lungs was scorching.

"We cannot sit here, idle, while men die," she said. "Drive me around the battle, Menkh, for I have many arrows left, and I intend to use them all. Thus you may obey both Nehesi and myself, for we shall stay well clear of the center of the conflict."

He tightened the reins again and began to canter her in a wide circle, joining the other charioteers who were harrying the Nubians who tried to run.

Nehesi saw her little silver Cobra bobbing above the heads of the struggling men. Sometimes she was cheered as she passed the little groups, but more often she was ignored, for now the Nubians were desperate men, seeing no mercy and no quarter in the eyes of the Egyptians. Gathering the last of their strength, they fought with great savagery, using teeth and bare hands when their weapons lay broken in the dust. Hatshepsut marked many men, and many men fell with her gold-tipped arrows in their throats, their backs. Once, when a Nubian broke and ran like a rabbit over the burning sand, she galloped after him, arrow to bow and eye to arrow. There was no quiver in her fingers now as she brought him, screaming and kicking, to the ground; and before Menkh could draw rein and turn, they had run over his body, the wheels of the chariot bumping as they churned him into the sand.

At last, when the afternoon sun had passed its peak and was beginning to fall, the pace slowed, and Hatshepsut fired her last arrow and laid her bow on the floor of her chariot. She ordered Menkh to drive in search of Nehesi. She was weary, tired to the bone, throbbing in every muscle. She wanted to sink to the floor and sit, her back blissfully set against the warm gold, but she forced herself to stand tall, gripping the sides of the chariot in the effort. Everywhere she saw death and ruin. The sand was littered with bodies, sometimes piled with them. Here and there little skirmishes went on; in other places knots of tired Egyptian troops gathered around their standards and their officers, dirty and caked with blood. Blood also soaked the sand, lying in little pools or covering the ground in long spurts. She passed one officer and two of his soldiers who were going among the Nubian wounded, slitting their throats with quick, businesslike strokes. She turned her head away, hearing her own voice give the order that was now being carried out. She wished with a terrible vehemence that Thothmes was here now to see how war really was, and she rode through the stillness that followed the battle with her eyes flashing and her teeth bared, her revulsion against his soft body and womanly ways growing as she looked about her.

She found Nehesi at last with pen-Nekheb and Hapuseneb and a dozen other officers. Lying at their feet were ten dark bodies of men she at first took to be dead. She got stiffly out of the chariot and walked toward them; behind her Menkh sank gratefully to the floor, the reins looped about his arm. The men bowed, not one of them wishing to meet her eye, overwhelmed by the new awe in which they held her, the avenging Daughter of Amun.

But she confronted them, smiling faintly in spite of her weariness. "So ours is the victory," she said. "Well have you fought this day, and I will cause to be set here a stone telling of your valor."

All at once the body of one of the men on the sand twitched convulsively, and she stepped back.

"Who are they?" she asked.

Hapuseneb answered her. He, too, was tired. He had fought with his men in the thick of the battle and had taken an arrow in the arm, but the eyes that at last sought hers were as steady and calming as ever.

"If they were not naked, you would know, Majesty, that they are the Princes of Kush, chiefs of the Ten Tribes you see wasted around you."

She looked down on the slippery, bare bodies and shaved skulls with renewed interest and mounting anger. "Get up!" she shouted at them, kicking the nearest one with her foot.

They rose weakly, standing before her with downcast eyes.

"Fools!" she hissed at them, stalking around them, all the pent-up relief and madness of the day breaking forth from her. "Thrice fools! Your damnable fathers, and their fathers before them, died under the hands of the soldiers of Egypt. Do you never learn wisdom? What of your children, your wives? Will they spawn new enemies of my country, to be fed to the jackals in their turn? Egypt gives you security! Egypt gives you peace and defends you! And for what?"

She turned suddenly and spat in the face of one of the chiefs, but he did not stir, and the spittle dropped from his cheek onto the ground.

"So that you can rend and burn and loot and rape. Filth!"

She swung back to her generals. "Assemble the army," she said shortly. "When the men are together, before we march from this place to seek a tenting place for the night, bring these men and remove their heads from their bodies. Set the heads on poles, with the bodies beneath, for my anger is kindled, and I wish the whole of Kush to know what it is to defy the might of Egypt. Save one, and we will bring him to Assuan, to the feet of Pharaoh, and then he will be sacrificed to Amun—a more fitting death than he deserves!" She snarled, shaking all over as if she had been struck with a fit.

Hapuseneb went to her swiftly. "Come and rest, Majesty," he said gently. "You have fought as your ancestors today, and their glory shines on in you undiminished. Let Menkh take you to a place where you can sleep."

As he spoke, she passed a trembling hand across her eyes, and her shoulders suddenly slumped. "I am weary," she admitted. "But I cannot rest yet. Tell me, Hapuseneb, how many of our men have fallen?"

"We do not know until the count is taken," he replied, "but I think not many."

"What of the traitors? Was there any sign of Egyptians among the rebels?"

"That also we do not know, but we may soon find out."

With a long stride he was beside one of the chiefs. "Now speak," he said softly, his cool voice full of menace and his gauntleted hand at the man's neck, "and by speaking you may extend your life by a few days and die a good death before the God. How did the garrison fall?"

The man looked at him sullenly, mutinously, and with one sweep of his fist Hapuseneb knocked him to the ground, where he lay stunned, blood trickling from his mouth and gushing from his nose.

"Lift him," Hapuseneb said quietly. Hands raised the prisoner to his feet, and he stood, swaying, wiping at his nose with a black, dirty finger. "I ask you again, what of the garrison?" As Hapuseneb stepped forward again, the man quailed.

"I will tell you," he said, "and since I am to die, I say also that it gave me great pleasure to slit the throats of the soldiers. My people are tired of giving the wealth of their country to Egypt, year after year, and be assured that you beat us today and beat us tomorrow and the next year and the next, but we will never stop fighting."

Nehesi made a sound deep in his chest and swung forward. But Hatshepsut put out a hand, and he was instantly very still, his eyes boring into the Nubian as if he could set him on fire with his gaze.

"The garrison, fool!" Hapuseneb growled, and the man nodded.

His companions had not moved. They seemed to be in the last stages of the apathy that impending death creates, and they stood with their limbs hanging loosely and their heads bowed.

"The gates were opened to us by an officer, a man who had befriended us over the years and whose brother had been put to death by Pharaoh many years ago, and the rest was easy."

"His name!" Hatshepsut screamed at him, galvanized. "His name, his name, his name!"

The Nubian just looked at her with dull eyes. "I do not know his name. None of us knew it. The commander slew him as he stood outside the door."

"And the commander? What of Wadjmose?" Hapuseneb asked, but it was Hatshepsut who stepped nearer, her hands clasped in an agony of apprehension.

"He also fell. He lies somewhere within the fort."

They stood in silence, and at last Hatshepsut turned away.

"Well it is that my father did not live to see this day," she said, and she slowly got into the chariot to stand behind Menkh. "Nehesi, take your men and journey farther, to the garrison, and bring back the body of my brother if you can find it. He shall have the greatest tomb and the funeral of the Prince that he was. Hapuseneb, bring me the lists of the wounded and the dead. Menkh can pitch a tent for me away from this stinking place."

She sat down on the floor of the chariot, her head lolling back, while Menkh walked the horses away. Before he had raised her tent beside the baggage train, two miles out in the desert, the sun had sunk below the horizon.

Nehesi and half the Braves of the King left the next morning on the grim quest. While the rest of the company waited for their return, the Nubian dead were piled together and burned, and the Egyptians hurriedly embalmed and buried in the sand. Hatshepsut ordered the raising of a stone that was to be brought from beyond the desert as quickly as possible and set over the Egyptian grave. She went to the tent that held the wounded, walking from man to man with whatever comfort she could give. She found Sen-nefer, delirious from a wound in his thigh that was already festering, and she ordered his removal, placing him upon her own couch and calling her own physician to tend him. The man told her that the wound was not serious and that Sen-nefer would undoubtedly recover, but Sen-nefer's groans and constant senseless babbling upset her. She took over Nehesi's tent, sitting before it and nursing her own aching muscles while she watched the army restore order quietly and efficiently. She felt a deep sense of anticlimax, sitting idly beside her standard, seeing weapons cleaned and uniforms washed. The events of the campaign were already blurred in her mind, pushed deep into the dark places of her brain by reaction and nervous exhaustion. She felt that she had done her duty and would never again go to war with the army. She no longer needed to prove by her deeds as well as by her words that she was worthy of the Double Crown. She pondered her future darkly, in a mood of fatalism, wondering whether this was to be the last adventure in her life. The mood stayed with her through the execution of the Nubian chiefs who went to their deaths as stonily silent as they had been the day before.

Nehesi returned in the evening of the third day, bearing with him the charred and almost unrecognizable body of her brother.

Hatshepsut took one horrified, unbelieving look and ordered that he also be buried in the sand. There was nothing much left of him to preserve, but she found it hard to believe that so valiant a man had no place with the gods because of it. She would cause his name to be chiseled many times over in stones and rocks and on the faces of cliffs to give him a chance, for as long as a name remained, the gods could find a man.

She sent Zeserkerasonb's troops back to him, promising gifts to him and to them all.

In the morning they would begin the trek home, but she was not eager to go. In many ways the life of a soldier suited her very well: the freedoms, the travel, the satisfactions of the campfire and the tent. But she was careful to admit to herself that it was the prospect of Thothmes that daunted her. Sen-nefer had regained consciousness and slept with Menkh, and she found the solitude of her tent and the desert night pleasing; but her mind was racing, and she could not sleep. She was restless until she heard the horns sound. As the camp stirred and shook itself like a whistled dog, she rose reluctantly, wishing for a bath in the river and feeling nauseated by the cooking smells and the taste of her morning wine. She sat in her chair while she waited for her tent to be dismantled, watching the tassels of her standard spark in the morning sun and wishing that she could vomit.

There were not many wounded to carry, but there were enough to slow them down, and they marched at a leisurely pace, favoring pulled muscles and relaxing. Their mood was one of holiday. There was a lot of singing and laughter, and in the evenings they were entertained by the antics of Menkh and other young nobles. Yamu-nefru spent the time protesting that the desert sun had utterly dried out his skin, and he moaned for his perfumed oils. Djehuty raged at a spot on his white kilt that would not come out. Hatshepsut listened with a deep thankfulness in her heart for them all, the ones who loved her. Hapuseneb and pen-Nekheb were closeted together each night, dictating to the scribe the events of the campaign, requests for new weapons to replace those splintered and lost in the battle, and lists of men for promotion and awards.

Nehesi came to Hatshepsut and squatted at her side, his handsome black face as smooth and bland as ever, his gaze sweeping the camp with a calm superiority. He seemed to enjoy her company, though they would often sit for an hour and say nothing. She once asked him if he had a wife at home in Thebes.

He grinned swiftly, caught by surprise. "No wife, Majesty, and no concubines. I do not need women, nor do I need the love of men. Egypt and the army are my loves, and fighting is my leisure. I prefer my own company above all others—save your own. I think, and I read a great deal."

Now it was she who was surprised. "It is odd for a soldier to be able to read!"

"Yes. My mother taught me, but how she learned the characters, I shall never know. I read of the wars of your father and your ancestors and their struggles with the Hyksos, but I do not think that I shall have much more time for reading."

"Why not? Do you think that I now have a taste for war and shall keep you ever on the march?" She was laughing at him, and he smiled back.

"Perhaps. You are a soldier after the heart of your noble ancestor the great Queen Tetisheri, who plotted the downfall of the invader Hyksos, and I am proud to be a general under you."

She shook her head decisively. "War is wasteful, unless it be a war of defense or a border dispute such as this was. I want peace for my people and secure growth. But you are right when you say that from now on little of your time will be your own. I have a mind to make you Guardian of the Royal Seal."

He sat very still, and presently he looked up at her. "It is enough that you made me a General, Majesty," he began.

But she cut him short. "It is not enough! I want a strong man always at my elbow, a man from whom the Royal Seal can be wrested only through force. Pharaoh does not need the Seal, but I do. Will you wear it on your belt, Nehesi, and be with me at all times? It will still be possible for you to discharge your duties as General, and I think I will put you in charge of the Followers of His Majesty also. You are an ideal bodyguard."

"I am a rough man, unused to moving in court circles, uncouth," he replied, but a faint, sardonic smile played about his mouth. "Yet I can ask nothing more than to serve you—and Pharaoh. Truly you are the God, for only the God could assume the body of a woman and yet fight as you have fought, and all the men know it. You have put on me a great privilege."

"Such words may be lightly and easily spoken," she said, "but remember them, Nehesi, in the years that follow. I do not believe that I was born to be a Queen, and yet the future is not known to me. I may need your mighty arm raised again in my defense."

He nodded briefly, accepting her faith in him without further question. When he left she felt satisfied, sure of having made a good decision.

When they reached the river, she could bathe at last. But they did not tarry long, for Assuan lay only another day's march away and the heralds had gone ahead with the news of their victory. Hatshepsut opened her ivory traveling box and got out her wig and her crown and her golden bracelets, and when the triumphal procession formed, she took her place in the forefront, her chariot gleaming clean behind the Standard-Bearers.

They passed slowly into Assuan through a laughing, crying mob of city dwellers who pelted them with flowers and ran out to offer them wine and sweetmeats. Thothmes was waiting for them in front of the gates, sitting on his throne in full regalia. She greeted him and went and sat beside him as the generals filed past, laying their staffs of office before him and kissing his painted feet before receiving their rewards.

The Nubian chief came last, bound tightly with reins from a dead horse and stumbling with utter weariness, for throughout the march the soldiers behind him had flicked him with their whips, and his back was scored and bloody and covered with flies. Nehesi led him before Pharaoh, pushing him roughly to the ground, and he fell on his face, unable to save himself. Thothmes put out a jeweled foot and placed it on his neck, and the populace roared its approval, scenting blood.

Pen-Nekheb related the events of the past weeks, and they all listened, Thothmes smiling and nodding enthusiastically; and when the old warrior had finished, Thothmes rose, raising the glittering golden Flail and Crook in the air in a gesture of victory.

"So perish all enemies of Egypt!" he shouted, and the army saluted him, banging their spear butts on the stone paving of the courtyard. "You have all heard how my brother, the noble Wadjmose, died and how he has been avenged. Now let us give thanks to Amun and take this sacrifice to the temple at Thebes so that the God may know his trust has been rewarded!"

The Nubian was hauled to his feet and led away, and Thothmes and Hatshepsut went together to the banqueting hall, where there would be a feast for them and for all the officers before the trek back to Thebes.

"Was it very bad?" Thothmes asked her hesitantly, noting with a kind of jealous awe how the sun had turned her velvety skin almost as black as the skin of the wretched Nubian and how her legs and arms were taut with new muscle.

She smiled indulgently across at him. "It was very bad—and very good," she replied as they passed under the frowning eyes of Thothmes the First and turned toward the hall. "I am more than sorry about Wadjmose, but I am more than glad that I know my officers far better than I did before, and they me."

That was not what he meant, and she knew it, but she went on teasing him, smiling that enigmatic and infuriating smile. He shrugged his shoulders and sat, waiting impatiently for his generals to file in before he clapped his hands for the feasting to begin.

She was impossible. While she was gone, he had built up a hopeful picture of her in his mind—returning shaken and tearful, needing his comfort—but here she was as healthy and clear-eyed as a young gazelle and about as reliant on him as the stones of the temple. In between the innumerable courses, she shouted down to the men, and they sallied back respectfully but with affection, and she joked and laughed with them all as if they were her family. He had ordered three troops of musicians for her enjoyment, and four cartloads of lotus flowers had come from Thebes to delight her nostrils. She wept, not at the beauty of the dancing, but at the new song of Ipuky, composed to immortalize the men who had died in the desert. Though she caught the blossoms to her and buried her face deep into their fragrance, she did not thank him for his thoughtfulness. He wanted then to have done with her, to leave her to her palace and her governors and meet her only on state occasions. But he knew as he watched the darting eyes and the graceful, quicksilver hands, that though inwardly he might rage at her, he loved her as her men loved her, the soldiers and the nobles of the land, with a kind of helpless longing.

She turned to him, taking his hand and smiling into his eyes. "It is good to be here," she said. "Now I know how the soldiers feel when they come through battle and see their home once more."

"Good," he said awkwardly. "I have missed you, Hatshepset." He did not mean to say that, and he turned from her and picked up his wine, annoyed with himself.

"I have missed you, too," she answered lightly. "Now what is this?"

A man had entered and was bowing before them, his arms holding a drum. He was naked but for a loincloth, and around his head he wore a blue ribbon, tied at the back, its ends touching his shoulders. Behind him came a woman, and at the sight of her Thothmes sighed with satisfaction, settling back on his cushions.

While she prostrated herself, he said to Hatshepsut, "This is my new dancer, Aset. She has been working here in the home of the Governor, but I think I might take her back to Thebes with me and put her in the harem. She pleases me very much."

"Ever an eye for a pretty body!" Hatshepsut chided him, laughing, but her eye skimmed the other woman swiftly as she rose from the floor in one supple motion and stood ready while the drummer sank cross-legged, the drum between his knees. She was tall, a leggy girl, quite unlike the voluptuous, giggling servants Thothmes liked to take to his bed. As Aset waited, one long, graceful limb flexed, Hatshepsut felt an unpleasant shudder run through her, as if she had lifted her blanket and found a snake curled up on her couch.

Aset's hips were small, her waist long and tight, her breasts high, tiny, and large-nippled. Her head, too, was small under the waves of black hair that hung to her buttocks, and those watching her had the immediate impression of a sleek cat about to stretch or to spring.

The drummer began a slow rhythm, and the woman raised her arms and turned her face to them, rising on the tips of her toes. Hatshepsut was disappointed. Not that the face was plain. It was a pleasing oval, with straight brows and a wide, gold-spangled forehead, but the lips were thin and unlovely, even when parted in the ecstasy of the dance. The eyes above high cheekbones were too close together, and Hatshepsut noticed that they were suddenly narrowed in a swift and cold scrutiny of the Queen. In that split second Hatshepsut stared back in haughty challenge.

The rhythm quickened, and the men fell silent, eyes on the straining, flat belly, the taunting, rearing breasts. Aset fell back suddenly, then twisted to her feet, the hair flowing to her knees as she bent again.

Hatshepsut watched, all at once quite sober. The woman was full of a subdued and smoldering fire, a drawing, tempting, maddening promise, and Thothmes was looking at her as if bewitched, his breath coming fast and his eyes glazed with desire.

Why does she disturb me? Hatshepsut asked herself. She is not the first good dancer Thothmes has been pleased to favor for a time. But she watched the dance to its end, and the hand she laid on Thothmes' arm when the thunder of delighted applause broke out was cold.

"What did you think of her?" he asked eagerly, his full cheeks flushed and his eyes bright. "Was she not incredible? She never needs music, only the drum. Her body makes all the music a man could desire."

Hatshepsut looked at him fondly. "She is not as beautiful as I," she replied easily, "but she has a certain charm, for a common dancing girl."

"Well I like her." Thothmes was angry. "And I intend to have her at Thebes."

"I did not say that I did not like her," Hatshepsut said equably, "although in truth I find her a trifle—cold under all that fire. By all means have her if she makes you happy."

Her immediate acceptance of Aset stung him; he had had some hazy thought that his sister might show some jealousy. When she did not, continuing to drink her wine, an annoying smile on her brown face, he got up abruptly.

Aset waited to be dismissed, a lazy half-smile on her foxlike face, her eyes half-closed as she stood beneath the dais, facing the royal couple. Hatshepsut popped a piece of melon into her mouth. "Are you retiring so soon, Thothmes? Will you not come to my chambers tonight?"

"No, I will not! I—Oh, I don't know, Hatshepset. I might. Well, yes, perhaps I will if you invite me." He sank back beside her, putting a tentative arm around her, and the smile vanished from Aset's face. Thothmes tossed her a jewel and smiled upon her, but even though she bowed and walked away as respectfully as Hatshepsut could wish, there was affront and thwarted ire in every inch of her upright, naked back.

I think she is dangerous, Hatshepsut said to herself as her brother's arm went around her. I do not know how. Perhaps I have been living on the edge of danger for too long and am jumping at mere shadows. Shall I blame Thothmes because I find him a pleasant bore? But she was suddenly hungry for his body, with a great burst of unexplained passion, and she leaned heavily against him so that he slopped his wine.

"Let us leave," she whispered in his ear. "I am sick with my own desire."

Startled, he left the dregs of his cup and got to his feet. "Stay and eat and be happy!" he told the company. As they prostrated themselves, he found himself hurried out the door and down the passage by a woman who whispered words that inflamed him even as he ran with her. She did not wait to reach her rooms but led him straight into the garden, drawing him in under the thickly clustered trees, and there he had her quickly, sharply, as a soldier takes a captured slave, and they lay panting together on the grass while the music of the feast drifted faintly to them on the night air.

They returned to Thebes in two days, both riding on litters, Hatshepsut full of disgust and abhorrence toward him and herself. When they arrived, the city welcomed them with open arms. Before going into the palace, they went to do homage to Amun, and while she proceeded slowly through the great hall forested with pillars, under the roof her father had built, she caught sight of Senmut, standing with Benya and User-amun. Her eyes flew to his, and he began to smile, a smile that spread from his wide mouth to fill his dark eyes, a smile full of approval and steady, sane gladness, and she answered it, a great pool of relief and anguish welling up inside her. Lying on Amun's floor beside Thothmes, shrouded in incense, she could think of nothing but herself and Thothmes locked together under the trees and then of Senmut's open smile, and she said her prayers feverishly, beseeching her Father for his protection from she knew not what.

Afterward they sat before the golden God on their thrones. The Nubian was stretched on the floor, and in a short and savage ceremony Menena smashed out his brains with a golden club. It had been long since such a sacrifice had been made to the God, and Thothmes was clearly uneasy, but Hatshepsut and the generals watched impassively, their minds full of the blackened body of Wadjmose and the new mounds even now being pawed at by the desert jackals.

When the black body had ceased to twitch, Hatshepsut got down and stood looking at it. "Egypt will live forever!" she called, and the gathering murmured assent. She stepped over the blood already congealing under her golden sandals and strode into the sunlight.

16

She signaled for Senmut and User-amun to follow, and once in her own palace she settled gratefully into her silver chair and bade them sit beside her, holding out her hand for her Seal. Senmut handed it over, bowing. As their fingers brushed, she felt his tremble.

"Is there anything that I should know?" she asked them, laying the Seal on the table. "Has all gone well?"

"Very well," Senmut answered her. "The tribute from Rethennu arrived, and Ineni caused it to be distributed. Ahmose, the Vizier of the South, is here, bringing taxes; and beside the temple, the God's granaries are filling."

"Good. And what of my temple, Senmut?"

He smiled. "The first terrace is completed, as you wished. It is more beautiful than even I imagined it would be, and now the ground is being prepared for the second."

Her eyes lit up. "Then we must go immediately and see it. User-amun, I thank you for your help. Go to your father now, for I hear he is ill; and if he wishes to rest for a few weeks, I am sure you can take over his duties for him—I forgot! Senmut, I have appointed Nehesi, the black one, Bearer of the Royal Seal. Any documents that must be imprinted take to him. He will, of course, be subject to me and to you. Find him for me —he is probably with the men on the training ground—and take the Seal and its belt to him. Find him an apartment here somewhere. Now, allow me to bathe, and then we will cross the river and look upon my valley. How I have missed it, far away in the cursed Nubian desert!"

They boated over the Nile together, got onto canopied litters on the other side, and were carried to the site. Between river and cliffs spread the village of the slaves who were working on the temple, row upon row of mud houses fronting each other. They skirted these, coming at last to the deep defile that opened onto the holy place. As they got down, Hatshepsut drew in her breath.

"For you, Mighty Amun, a token of my love and devotion," she said. "Never have you been given such adoration!"

A quarter of the way up the cliff a terrace hung, seemingly suspended, held to the side of the rock by magic. Its lovely pillar-fronted face glowed softly, pink in the afternoon light. Two of its sides hugged the side of the valley, and the third linked to an artificial wall planned by Benya. It was not square, which would have been an affront to the valley; rather, it was an oblong that seemed to have been there all the time, having needed only a little finishing by the hand of man. But Hatshepsut knew that behind those delicate pillars lay two shrines hewn deep in the roots of the cliff, one to Hathor and the other to Anubis. In the middle of the front was a gaping, jagged hole, and around it a thousand men swarmed like flies on honey.

"That is where the next terrace will join the one completed, by a ramp such as the one we talked of," Senmut told her. "This terrace will reach the ground, and another lower one will complete the temple. Your own holy place is within, between those of the gods, but none of them is finished. Would Your Majesty like to go closer?"

"No," she replied. "I will watch from here, as I have always done. And at the last, when it is completed, then I will put my feet upon the stone. You have wrought a miracle, priest! There are many who said it was impossible, but your genius has made my dreams take form."

She was overcome, as she always was when she came to watch the work, feeling the God around her, within her. But on this day she felt ill also, faint and dizzy. He saw her pale under the desert tan and was concerned. She left him abruptly and went and lay on her litter, her eyes closed.

He felt a pang of anxiety. Was she ill? Had she fallen victim to some disease picked up from the inhospitable desert sand? He knew better than to suggest that she take to her couch and call a physician, but he told Hapuseneb and Nehesi. The next day, when she appeared in the audience chambers as usual, a trifle wan but her own vigorous self, he felt foolish. Yet, he continued to watch her with wary eyes, visions of Neferu's death by poison haunting him once more.

He himself was very tired, flogging himself between his duties in the temple and the palace and his daily visits to the building site. He found that often he had to give to Senmen the responsibilities he would have liked to have seen to himself. He disliked his work in the temple and often came face to face with Menena, those sudden moments unnerving him, but he gave the High Priest the reverences of his station and received a grudging bow in return. Senmut did not trust Menena. He could never forget how the man had betrayed the trust of one Pharaoh, and he wondered whether Thothmes the Second ever pondered the reason for the High Priest's dismissal. In the end, for his own peace of mind, Senmut placed spies in Menena's household and in the temple; but he could never rid himself of the feeling that one day the man's scheming, cunning mind would bring disaster to them all. He went to bed with Ta-kha'et and the cat each night, dreading the reports of his spies in the morning; but the days ran on, carrying him down his chosen path, and the cat sensed no demons in the dark.

Two months after Hatshepsut's return from Kush, Nofret ceased struggling to overlap the ends of the kilt that she was wrapping around the royal waist. She dropped her hands in momentary annoyance. "Majesty, forgive me, but these kilts are all too small. Perhaps you should order some larger ones."

"You mean, perhaps I should stop dipping into the sweetmeat box," Hatshepsut answered her, smiling, but all at once another possibility caused her to finger her belly with thoughtful hands.

"Nofret, send for my physician. Bring him here at once. And do not worry," she added, seeing the woman's worried frown, "I do not think that I am ill."

While she waited, she sat on her couch, her attention to the chores of the day suddenly drawn away by a tide of elation mingled with apprehensive awe. Of course it was bound to happen sooner or later, she told herself. Why did I not think of it before? I have been so busy making war that I never thought about the possibilities of making a baby.

When the physician arrived, she demanded an examination, lying on the couch tensely while he probed and prodded. At last he straightened, and she sat up eagerly.

"Well? What do you think?"

"It is a little too soon to say, Majesty—"

"Yes, yes. Caution is necessary in your profession. But can you perhaps guess?"

"I think Your Majesty is with child."

"Ah! How blind and stupid I have been! Egypt will have an heir!" She got off the couch, beaming upon them. "Nofret, go and find Pharaoh. He may have returned from the temple by now. Tell him that I need him urgently." Nofret gave her a strange, frightened look as she hurried out, but Hatshepsut was too wrapped in herself to notice.

"Your Majesty will have to give up sweetmeats and take only a little wine. Go to bed early, and rest as much as you can, and do not eat too much broiled food. You must also be careful to—" The physician followed her as she paced excitedly about the room, giving her instructions in his dry, bookish voice, but she was not listening to him. Her thoughts were turned inward, to her own body, its mysteries, its beauty, and suddenly the future seemed more precious to her than it had ever been before.

Thothmes burst in at her door. He had been watching the work going forward on his new pylons in the temple when Nofret had come to him. He had torn himself away reluctantly, but the woman's face had struck fear into him, and he strode after her with unaccustomed speed. By the time he reached Hatshepsut's palace, almost running along the cool, wind-caught cloister that joined her chambers to the great palace, he was out of breath and red in the face.

"What is the matter?" he asked, panting, noting the physician.

She ran to him, her face alight.

He sat down heavily on her little chair and mopped his brow. "It cannot be too serious. You never had a healthier glow."

She held out her arms to him, waiting to be embraced. "Thothmes, Egypt is to have an heir, and I am going to produce him!"

He got to his feet again, infected by her buoyant mood, and held her briefly before letting her go and sitting down again.

She had caught on his face a look of wariness that she did not understand.

"Are you not happy?" she demanded. "Did you not wonder whether there would ever be an heir, and can you not rejoice that no foreign prince will sit on the Horus Throne now that I am about to give Egypt the greatest gift of all?"

"That depends on the sex of the child," he grunted. "If it is female, then we still have to look for a royal prince."

"Why, I do believe that you are not happy at all! Even with all our differences, you could at least be happy for Egypt!"

"I am, I am!" he said hastily. "Of course I am. But you know I am right, Hatshepset. If you do not give birth to a boy, then we will have to start all over again."

"And that would be so hard for you," she mocked him. "Really, Thothmes, you disappoint me."

"I am sorry," he said, squirming in the little seat that barely held his bulk. "It is just that—"

"Well? What?" Her happy mood had evaporated, and she faced him, her hands on her hips. "Oh, why are the Thothmesids so difficult to understand?"

"You are one yourself," he responded waspishly. "No one in the world is as hard to fathom as you, Hatshepset. Then know that I have been brought news of the same kind, yesterday. Aset is also to have a child."

"Why should that concern me?" she asked him in surprise. "There are dozens of royal bastards running wild in the palace! One more should not upset you or worry me. My child will be fully legitimate."

He shifted uncomfortably, dropping his eyes to his knees. "Aset's child will be legitimate, too. I have decided to make her Second Wife."

Her jaw dropped, and Nofret and the physician were suddenly very still, their eyes on the rigid back of their mistress. Hatshepsut stared at Thothmes until he began to fidget, and she collapsed onto her couch in an attitude of complete unbelief.

"Let me try—*try* to understand," she choked. "You are going to marry that—that common dancer?"

"Yes," he said defiantly, his gaze still on his ample linen. "I like her very much. She is clever and affectionate and able to control all the other women. She makes me happy."

"How do you judge intelligence?" she fired at him. "Is the woman with the longest legs in the harem intelligent? How else have you trained yourself to know, Thothmes?"

She guessed in a flash of intuition where Aset's power lay. Aset could make Pharaoh feel more like a man than the other women could, and because she was cleverer than the other simpering, empty-headed slaves, Thothmes felt flattered. He straightened, his bottom lip sticking out mutinously and his brow furrowed in a frown, and Hatshepsut recognized the signs of his stubborn will, sluggish to rise but impossible to sway once aroused.

She held up her hands in exasperated submission. "Very well. It is your right to marry whom you will. But I am sorry that you did not see fit to choose a noble woman, a daughter of Ineni perhaps, or one of User-amun's beautiful sisters. This Aset is not worthy of a Pharaoh, Thothmes. She is a schemer, a petty troublemaker, and you may be sorry that you introduced such a one into your palace."

"I will not listen to you!" he flared, the quick temper of his father bursting forth. "Since when has your intuition been infallible? You are sometimes mistaken, as I am, and this time you are wrong!"

"I am seldom mistaken, Thothmes," she said.

At that very moment, she remembered the cryptic words of her ka. They rushed back to her, feeling like the cold, wet slap of drying linen on her face. "It is as a father that he will destroy you." She could see the full, derisory lips of the golden boy as he had spoken to her. It was as if the room in which she sat had dissolved and she was once again in the temple, in the cold night, facing the God and the strange visitor with tired courage. She put a hand to her eyes, rubbing them, feeling a headache begin.

"As ruler of this country I cannot afford to judge men foolishly or lightly, and I say to you that Aset is small and mean."

"Words!" he jeered, shaking with the rage that she could so often stir in him, conscious as he was of his impotence in the face of her calm capabilities. "You are jealous. You fear that with Aset and her child I can put you out of the way!"

He did not think on his words, and she laughed at them in genuine amusement, knowing, as he did, that such a thing could never happen.

"Well, anyway," he grumbled, "I cannot see why you object so strenuously. I quite love her, you know, and she is at least where I want her when I want her."

"I know, I know," she said more gently, feeling the impossibility of trying to tell him just why she knew, with her sharp faculty of discernment, heightened by years of government, that Aset was dangerous. "Marry her then, and make the child in her womb a royal child. Shall it be a boy, do you think? Or a girl?"

"It would amuse you if both of you produced girls," he said sourly. "Then there would be two royal daughters and still no son to take the Horus Throne."

"In that case," she told him, smiling, "my daughter would ascend the Holy Throne with Steps, as the only fully royal and female heir."

"Don't be silly! No woman has ever worn the Double Crown."

"I have."

"That was different. You wore it as Regent, not as Pharaoh."

"Let us not begin the same old quarrel," she said gently. "There is time enough to haggle over the accession."

He rose woodenly. "There will be no haggling," he told her. "As Pharaoh I appoint whom I will to follow after me."

"Provided that your heir marries royal female blood."

"Of course. Now I must go. I am happy for us, Hatshepset, and for Egypt." He gathered the shreds of his dignity around him, accepting the prostrations of Nofret and the physician as he walked to the door. He turned to say something more but thought better of it, shutting his mouth like a trap and stalking away.

Hatshepsut was too distrait to laugh at him. "A common dancer. I cannot believe it!" she muttered. She sent the physician away and lay down while Nofret bathed her head with cool cloths.

Before the week was out, the whole city knew first that Egypt would have an heir and second that Thothmes was preparing to take another wife; and in a month the news had trickled from the delta to the Cataracts. Egypt heaved a general sigh of relief. Thothmes was a great Pharaoh and his Queen a mighty ruler, and the country was ordered with every efficiency; but the shadow of foreign domination was too fresh in the minds of the Egyptians to accept the idea of a prince who was not of their own blood, and the birth of a royal heir would solve the problem.

One night Ineni invited Senmut, Senmen, Hapuseneb, Nehesi, and other officials to a celebration, a boating party on the river, and they were all very gay and drank a great deal. Ineni, more than any other, was relieved at the news. He had lived close to the seat of power for many years, and he had been afraid that Hatshepsut would tire of a naked head and claim the Double Crown from her brother in a burst of irritated frustration. But with the prospect of a child she could look to the time when her child would rule. She did not doubt that it would be anything less than another Thothmes the First, and she seemed content.

Senmut had received the word without comment. Hatshepsut had told him herself, watching him anxiously, and he had at last bowed deeply and offered his congratulations.

But she had sensed a sadness in him that had cut her, and she had sent him away. To her the child meant a new security for Egypt, another God to continue her work when she wearied of life and ascended to the Heavenly Barque to sit beside her Father. Yet sometimes she felt well up in her a fierce denial that her child should receive what she could not, and her temper became unpredictable.

She had a granite statue carved of Ta-urt, goddess of the childbed, and she set it in a corner of her room beside Amun's shrine. She would often stand, lost in thought, before the benevolent, smiling hippopotamus, its fat hands clasped over its ridiculously swollen body. She went to her valley more frequently, riding in her litter while the deaf Nubian ran along beside her holding her scarlet fan, and she sat as she had before, greedily drinking in the harmonious lines and sweeping ramps of her monument. The second terrace rushed toward completion, and now it was clear how the missing ramp would lead the eye, flowing up to the square entrance to the hidden shrines. But still she did not approach it. Under the soft, transparent sheaths of womanhood she had grudgingly decided to wear during her pregnancy, her lithe figure changed, grew fuller, and the season drew to a close.

Her police brought her word that in the northeast the Ha-nebu was stirring, bent on a rampage of rebellion, and she peremptorily planned another campaign. But this time her officers adamantly refused to allow her to march, and she agreed reluctantly that to do so would be foolish. But she told them that she would stay in safety at Thebes only if Pharaoh would go in her stead, and Thothmes, with many sidelong glances at the advisers who thronged the table, agreed to do so. Hatshepsut was delighted, imagining him struggling on, sweating in the sun, shaking with fear, but she was happier still to think of the joy the troops would feel being led by Pharaoh himself. It was a small and insignificant undertaking, more a necessary show of Egypt's strength than a necessary fight, and she waved him off absently and returned to her chair under the shade of the spreading sycamores to play at draughts with Nofret or to shake the dice with Senmut.

Hapuseneb had once more marched off with the army in his capacity as Minister of War, but she kept Nehesi by her, why exactly she did not know. His silent presence, the sheer physical power that daunted many, brought to her a feeling of security and peace, and when he stood behind her chair as her Chief Bodyguard or bent beside her to affix the Royal Seal to some document, she knew that she was invulnerable.

A veil seemed to have fallen between her and Senmut. She was never more a possession of Egypt and of Thothmes than she was now, large with the child; and he drew back from her tactfully, although it hurt him. He continued to see her every day, often reading to her or telling her stories in the long afternoons as she requested. He knew that she took comfort from his presence, but they were as quietly companionable as cousins, and troubled each other with no spoken or unspoken emotions.

Sometimes she sent her Steward to the apartment where Aset lived to inquire about the health of the woman, and sometimes in the evenings she saw Aset walking in the women's garden, an area that was screened from the palace gardens by a high wall, cut at intervals by windows. Aset still moved like a hunting leopard in spite of her distorted body, and Hatshepsut listened to her high, screaming laughter and watched, her face a mask of indifference that hid a jumble of speculation and dislike, as Aset ordered her slaves about.

She had asked Senmut to make sure that Aset was watched all the time, and Senmut had complied, knowing that the new Royal Wife was aware of the spies and did not care. The very recklessness of her disdain alarmed him, but Hatshepsut only laughed when he tried to express his unease.

"Let her strut, peacock that she is," she said. "One day she will trip on her own feathers." But he was not so sure, and neither was she, though she ordered him to resume reading and leaned back and closed her eyes. Aset was flighty, but she was cunning and no fool. In moments of depression Senmut did not doubt that she was more than a match for poor Thothmes.

17

In five months the army returned, laden with spoil from the wealthy delta land, and Thothmes held audience to distribute rewards, very pleased with himself. He ordered his wives to be present, and Hatshepsut claimed her throne at his side, but Aset sat on a golden stool at his feet, leaning against him brazenly. She was arrayed in the bright colors she loved: a vivid yellow sheath with a wide collar of white linen studded with turquoise; a scarlet, tasseled belt; gold sandals; and a scarlet headband whose ribbons shimmered with gold. Her arms were laden with clinking golden bracelets, and her thin face was heavily painted. Mutnefert was present also, all smiles and wobbling folds; on the death of her royal lover, she had entirely given up trying to curb her appetite and now was as round as a ball. None present failed to see the resemblance between the mother of Pharaoh and his new wife, for both had a passion for jewels and many colors. In spite of the obvious fondness Pharaoh showed for Aset, smiling down on her and resting a plump, beringed hand once or twice on her head as the ceremony progressed, the assembled generals and courtiers could more than sense the gulf of blood and station between the two blazing women and the quiet, understated regality of Hatshepsut. She wore white and silver and sat almost motionless as the treasures were handed out, her gaze regarding them all calmly, her lovely wide brow smooth and her hands still in her lap. None doubted that the invisible threads of power were still gathered within the proud, coroneted head resting on the graceful neck.

When it was over, Mutnefert and Aset burst into a flurry of chatter, sparrows in the morning, and Thothmes beamed on them, but it was Hatshepsut whom he escorted to the feasting, settling her on her cushions as though she were made of the most fragile and beautiful glass, and he filled her cup himself. He had missed Aset's bony, taut body during the months of his absence, but it was Hatshepsut who had come to him in his dreams, more lovely and ageless than the God himself, her voice echoing through his first waking moments, mingling with the hard blaring of the horns of dawn.

Aset gave birth first, loudly and triumphantly, with many screams and cries.

Thothmes, bending over the wet and wailing infant, clapped his hands. "A boy! By Amun! And a lusty one! Listen to him yell!" He took his son in eager, clumsy arms, and the child began to scream all the louder, its belligerent red face screwed up convulsively.

"Give him to his nurse," Aset said, and Thothmes placed him with the silent, hovering woman. He was carried away, still yelling, and Thothmes perched on the edge of Aset's couch, taking both her hands in his. She smiled at him, her eyes hollowed with exhaustion.

"Are you pleased with your son, Mighty Horus?"

"Very pleased! You have done well, Aset. Is there anything that you would like? Something to make you more comfortable?"

Aset was crafty. She dropped her gaze and withdrew her hands. "To know that I have your continued love, Great One. That is all I desire. To be under your protection is comfort enough."

Thothmes was flattered and pleased. He drew her to him, letting her head, with its massed tangles of black hair, rest on his shoulder as she collapsed against him as weakly and trustingly as a kitten. "All Egypt blesses you this day," he told her. "Your son will be a mighty prince."

"Perhaps even Pharaoh?"

Her voice reached him, muffled, but the tone unmistakably sharp. He suddenly felt a little tired, a little miserable, his joy in his firstborn muted by the plain avarice in Aset's words. "Perhaps," he replied. "But you know as well as I that his elevation depends a great deal on the Queen's child."

"But you are Pharaoh, mighty in power and in deeds. If you wish my son to succeed you, then you only have to say the word, and all men will obey."

"It is not as simple as that, and well you know it," he rebuked her kindly. She sat up, gripping his hands. "Do not be too greedy, Aset. Many a fine prince and handsome noble has eaten himself to death."

She blushed at these words, jolted at a perception in him she had never known was there, for she, too, tended to take him lightly. She had never seen the streak of mulishness that Hatshepsut often provoked, nor had she known him in the years when he was only a prince, going about the palace with his ears and mind open and his mouth tightly shut. She said no more about it, but determination hardened in her, and she vowed that what she could not accomplish directly, she would win by soft persuasions. Next-door in the nursery her son let out a wail and was finally silent. Grimly she turned from Thothmes, settling herself for sleep. Her son would be Pharaoh. And that was the end of the matter.

Thothmes carefully consulted the astrologers and priests concerning the name of the boy, and they told him unanimously that he should be known as Thothmes. Thothmes had hoped for such an answer, and he strutted to Hatshepsut as happy as a preening cockerel. She was dressing after her daily sleep, her eyes still heavy. Her room was still darkened, and full of hot, cloying air. She admitted him, and while he talked, Nofret slipped the sheath over her head and began to brush her hair.

"I have not yet rejoiced with you over the birth of your son," she said, "and I am sorry for that, Thothmes, but for the last two days I have been preoccupied. There seems to be some dispute over the amount and kinds of tribute you ordered to be exacted from the unhappy Ha-nebu, and the nomarch and my tax collectors have been haggling like old women in the market. How is the child?"

Thothmes pulled up a chair and sat beside her, watching the comb drawn evenly and hypnotically through the gleaming tresses. "You have had some hair cut off," he remarked.

"Yes, I have. I like it better a little above my shoulders. It is not so hot on my neck. What of the child?"

"He is very strong and vigorous in his sucking, and he resembles our father in every way. He is a true Thothmesid!"

Her lips twisted wryly. "Then you must have him brought to me so that I may judge for myself how much of him is in truth Osiris-Thothmes and how much the vain pride of a puffed-up father."

"Hatshepset," he protested in an injured tone, "even the servants exclaim on his likeness. Aset is pleased at it also."

He had said the wrong thing. Hatshepsut pulled her head sharply away from the comb and got up, swinging away from him. "I am sure that she is! Well for her that your son bears the stamp of royalty and not the muddy imprint of her baseborn family." He opened his mouth in outraged anger, but she stopped suddenly by her table, pouring wine, and told Nofret to raise the mats from the windows. As the full sunlight flooded the room and the twittering of the birds became immediately apparent, she passed a cup to him and seated herself at her cosmetic table once more. Nofret opened the rouge pot. "What of the naming?" she asked.

He leaned forward, his swift anger evaporating. "The priests tell me that he is to be called Thothmes, and that it will be a name full of power and magic. Aset—"

"I know!" she broke in impatiently. "Aset is pleased."

"No," he said. "Aset is not pleased. She wished to call him Sekhenenre."

Hatshepsut burst out laughing, gasping and choking as the wine in her mouth caught in her throat. When she could speak at last, she saw Thothmes smiling unwillingly with her, touched by her mirth. "Oh, Thothmes, imagine! Sekhenenre! Does Aset see her son smiting his enemies, a man mighty in battle, a soldier of legend and song? The name of the great and valiant Sekhenenre, my God-ancestor, is indeed a powerful name, but does poor little Aset realize that the name is clouded, and the good Sekhenenre perished in pain and defeat at the hands of the Hyksos? I think not!"

"Perhaps not. But it is a good and holy name nonetheless."

"You are right," she agreed, sobering, "but Thothmes is more suitable for the son of today's Pharaoh." She wanted to ask him of his dreams for the boy, the hopes and fears that every father shares, but they were too far apart for any real confidences. She knew without asking how Aset viewed the baby's future, knew the petty ambitions and vanity of the woman.

And yet it is not such a petty ambition, she thought to herself, looking down the years in sudden anxiety. Thothmes. The name of my soft and benevolent brother? Or the name of a forceful and driving King? But why should I ponder these things now, before my own child has seen the light of Ra?

"Come with me to the marshes this evening," Thothmes said suddenly. "I want to hunt wildfowl. It will be a slow and peaceful jaunt to Luxor and back, and you might enjoy the river breezes."

"I think I will," she nodded. "I have had little rest today, and my back aches without ceasing. I am happy for you, Thothmes, and for Egypt," she said, coming close to him. "No matter what I say, it is no small thing to father a royal son." She kissed him softly on the lips, and they linked arms and walked slowly through the garden to the water steps, where they sat on the warm stone for a while, watching their skiff glide slowly to its berth at the golden mooring post. When it had been made fast, they went aboard, sitting together in the bow and watching a crane take off with slender, hanging feet and the beating of white wings before the boatmen pushed them off into midstream and they floated quietly in the long evening light.

Three weeks later, in the early hours of the morning, the nobles and title bearers of Thebes were summoned to the Queen's audience chamber. They straggled in, half asleep still, to find Pharaoh waiting for them, quivering with impatience.

"Her Majesty has begun to give birth," he announced. "As Princes of

Egypt you are all entitled to be present, with me, in the bedchamber," and he disappeared through the door, from which a ribbon of soft yellow light streamed.

The men followed him, but Senmut hung back and would have slipped out into the darkness if Hapuseneb had not caught him by the arm, turning him roughly. Senmut shook himself free, repressing an urge to strike, and Hapuseneb saw the quick flare in the black eyes.

"Where are you going, Steward of Amun?"

Senmut balled his fists under the cover of his cloak, and his teeth were clenched as he replied. "I am going out, Vizier. I am going home to await word. Do you think that I can go in there?"

Hapuseneb's face softened. "I think that you must. Firstly you are an Erpa-ha, and as a Hereditary Prince of Egypt you must attend and place your seal beside the others' as evidence of such an important birth."

"You have not changed my mind," Senmut snapped. "I was a peasant and the son of a peasant long before the Queen bestowed any titles on me, and I have a peasant's boorish stubbornness."

"When will you cease to insult a Daughter of the God and an immortal Queen by treating her in your mind as the weakest and simplest of women? Do you think that she will acknowledge you in there, or utter one word, one cry? Do you think that a Queen gives birth like a wailing woman in the harem? Mend yourself, broken reed, mend yourself. In honors and preferments you have grown—and in stature. But here"—he tapped his head—"here there are many pockets of foolishness and pride. Would you put yourself above the Queen and Pharaoh and the law?"

"Cease!" Senmut hissed at him. "I am not an untried boy or a stupid, thickheaded scholar. I do not need your lessons, for I know far better than you the secret paths of my own mind. I do not ever, *not ever,* put myself above her or Pharaoh, and I know full well what and who is the law. Do not ride me, Hapuseneb. The days are full of new loads dropped upon my back like sacks of grain until I know not whether I shall reach the end still walking or crawling like a blind man on a dangerous path. I am a Prince, yes, even as yourself, but I am also a beast of burden!"

"You speak to one who was struggling with the weight of power long before you left your mops and soap on the floor of the temple," Hapuseneb reminded him gently. "And why do we stagger on, day after day, Senmut? Because we like to keep busy? No, my friend"—he laid a firm hand on Senmut's shoulder—"because we both know where Egypt's salvation lies and because she is all that she says she is. Come in with me. It is a marvelous occasion."

Senmut gave in suddenly, allowing Hapuseneb to pilot him into the crowded, incense-laden room. But while his companion took his place beside the couch as was his right, Senmut sat at the back, on the floor, where he could see nothing.

Hatshepsut lay with her eyes closed and her hands limp above the cover of white linen. If it had not been for an occasional flutter of the long fingers or brief movements of the head, the assembly would have thought that she was asleep. The labor had begun at noon the day before, and by sunset she had been exhausted. Her physician had given her a draft of poppy, and she had sunk into a twilight of drifting images interspersed with flashes of searing pain. Her dreams were flying, but she had moments of clarity during which she opened her eyes to see Thothmes' anxious face above her and beside her, on the wall, the shadows of many men. At last her head cleared, and she heard the midwife say, "The birth is imminent!" A spasm of agony gripped her, and she shut her lips tightly, rolling her head in a supreme effort of will not to cry out.

When the pain left her, the physician bent, putting his mouth to her ear. "I can give you no more poppy, Majesty, and in any case it would avail you nothing, for the baby comes."

She nodded weakly, once, turning from him and gathering her strength as the last wave rushed to engulf her. Sweat sprang out on her forehead, but she did no more than whimper, the pain blotted out by a cry from the midwife.

"A girl, Nobles of Egypt! A girl!"

The men surged forward to catch a glimpse of the Princess, who let out a faint wail. In the eddy Senmut saw Hatshepsut raise herself on one elbow, her eyes big from the drug and her skin pale and somehow thin, like the linen that fell, rumpled, about her.

"Sit me up!" she commanded, and the physician lifted her gently. She held out her arms for the child, cradling it to her. Thothmes went down on one knee, and she smiled at him mistily, still afloat on a poppy sea. "A girl, Thothmes. A beautiful, delicate Daughter of Amun! See how her tiny fingers curl about my own!"

"Delicate indeed, and lovely as you are, Hatshepset," he replied, smiling. "Bud of the Flower of Egypt!" He kissed her cheek and rose, but she was no longer looking at him. Her eyes had dropped to the fuzz of black down that nestled in the crook of her arm, and she ignored the nurse, who waited stolidly at the head of the couch.

Thothmes spoke to the cluster of relieved men. "The documents await your seals. The Scribe Anen will assist you at the door." They began to file out, whispering together.

"Her Majesty has come through unscathed, thanks be to Amun!"

User-amun said in a low voice to Hapuseneb, and the other nodded.

"She has great strength. Egypt will feel her hand once more before too long," he replied, sharing User-amun's secret fear and its swift dissipation. They left the room and stood waiting for Anen to take their seals.

Senmut had turned to the door, but the voice from the couch stopped him. She called him, and he went to her, bowing. Pen-Nekheb also stood with him, wheezing a little as he shifted his weight from one tired foot to the other, both waiting as she gently disengaged the tiny fingers from her sleeping robe and held the child up.

"Take my daughter, Senmut." As he hesitated, she urged him. "Take her! I appoint you Royal Nurse. From today you are responsible for her health and her safety, and I know that you will see that she grows neither too spoiled nor too harshly taught. The ordering of the nursery is yours, and the wet nurse, here, is under you."

He took the tiny bundle carefully, with infinite, wondering gentleness, looking into a face so like the one he loved that his gaze traveled between them, and Hatshepsut lay back with a sigh.

"I had to know that she was in good hands," she said to them, "for much goes on in a palace of this size, and how can I hope to know all? As for you, pen-Nekheb, to you I entrust her future education. I wish her to learn as I have done, freely in the schoolroom and freely on the training grounds, and no door of knowledge is to be closed to her. She will need the wisdom of your many years." She closed her eyes, and they saw that she was almost asleep. But she opened them again to dismiss the two men.

Pen-Nekheb went home to bed, but Senmut walked through to the nursery, and he himself placed the baby in the little golden cradle, tucking the covers around her and checking that a Follower of His Majesty stood beyond the door and another in the garden under the high, narrow window. He left and sought out Nehesi, asking that more men be taken from the ranks of the Bodyguard and posted near the nursery to guard the child. Only when he was satisfied did he walk to his little palace.

All was quiet. Ta-kha'et had said that she would await his news, but he found her asleep on the carpet beside his couch, and he went to bed without waking her. The cat was nowhere to be seen, but as he reached to snuff out the night-light, it sprang upon him from somewhere in the shadows, its back arched and its teeth bared. He sat up, his ears and eyes open, every muscle tense. But the darkness was dumb, a close, comfortable darkness that seemed to hold no breath of danger, and in the end he pushed the beast onto the floor and lay down. He was very tired.

The temple celebrations went on for days, attended by Pharaoh and all his household. Ta-kha'et had to don her finery and go on her own, for Senmut spent the time in the nursery, watching every hour of the new Princess's routine. The wet nurse seemed to have plenty of milk, and the staff were all middle-aged women who had been culled from the harem because of their years spent attending their own children. Senmut gathered them together and spoke to them all, instructing them sternly, making sure that they knew the child was to receive only love and patience at all times. He left them finally, reluctantly, to see to new pens for the cattle of Amun and to speak to Benya, who was prepared to disagree on the exact dimensions of the third pillar to go up on the second terrace. He found his mind wandering back to the baby who slept so long and so often and who seemed to be so listless. It was not uncommon for a girl child to be less demanding and noisy than a boy, but all the same Senmut decided to seek the advice of Hatshepsut's physician and perhaps to procure some helpful spells from the temple sorcerers. Not that he believed entirely in the efficacy of magic, but it did no harm.

He listened to Benya's angry explanations with only half his attention.

Benya's hand shook as he held the diagram, and he finally flung the scroll down in disgust. "You are not listening, Senmut! Why should I concern myself with this—this fraction of a mistake, this tiny edge that juts like a mountain in my mind and offends my eye when you look at the wall and dream?"

"I am sorry, my friend." He tore his gaze back to Benya's black frown. "What is wrong with the pillar?"

"O ye gods!" Benya rolled his eyes and snatched up the reed and plan once more. "See, Senmut, it cannot sit thus; it will not. The angle must be so"—he slashed at the papyrus—"or the fourth one will give us endless trouble."

"Then enlarge the foundation."

"I cannot. The pillar is up."

"Then take it down, and set it again. By Amun, Benya, can you not do your job properly the first time?"

"Can the architect not foresee a muddy angle?"

They glared angrily at one another, and Benya at last grudgingly rolled up the scroll and dropped the reed back onto the desk, acknowledging his need for a few days of diversion away from the endless heat and dust of the valley. He was concerned at the strained eyes and work-worried preoccupation of his friend.

Senmut apologized sadly. "I had thought that my measurements were exact," he said, "but perhaps I was wrong."

"No, it was I. I hurried the erection, knowing the haste the Queen has, and I should have listened to my better judgment. I will take it down, Senmut, and put it up again." He raised and lowered his hands in a gesture of weary resignation and walked away.

Senmut sat for a moment in the deserted office, overcome with the need for rest. He put his head down on the smooth wood, promising himself a few moments of peace. Almost at once he was asleep, lulled by the silence and the green shade that stretched across his chair from the trees standing motionless outside.

Hatshepsut awaited the naming of the child with anxious impatience. She was up already, scorning her couch in favor of her little bedside chair, and though she still felt weak and drained, she saw her body slowly knit itself together again as her belly flattened and tightened. One day she threw her sheaths contemptuously into a corner and called for the little kilts of manhood, delighting in the old freedom. It was as she was choosing a belt, sitting undecided while Nofret held them all on both outstretched arms, that the Second High Priest of Amun was announced. Eagerly she ordered him to be admitted, and when he came, bowing, she wasted no time on pleasantries.

"Tell me at once!" she barked. "What is the name to be?"

He smiled. "The decision was long and hard, for as a fully royal Princess her name must hold great power and offer her a full protection."

"Yes, yes! Of course!"

"The name she will carry is Neferura, Majesty."

The words hung in the air. The room suddenly seemed to be filled with a rush of cold wind, a draft of dark, evil breath from the past that drained the color from Hatshepsut's face and caused Nofret to shiver, looking quickly behind her to the statue of the God, though the priest did not seem to have felt it.

Hatshepsut beckoned him nearer, shaken. "Repeat the name to me, Ipuyemre, for I did not hear it aright."

"Neferura, Majesty. Neferura."

She pressed him. "That cannot be. The name is a name full of power, certainly, but not good power, not good magic. You have made a mistake."

He was affronted, though he did not show it. "There is no mistake, Majesty. The signs were read many times. It is Neferura."

"It is Neferura," she repeated dully. "Very well. Amun has spoken, and the child shall bear that name. You may go."

He backed to the door, bowing, and the guard opened it for him and closed it again.

Hatshepsut sat staring into space, as if in a trance, muttering the name over and over. "Send Duwa-eneneh to Pharaoh," she said at last to Nofret, "and order him to give Pharaoh the name. I cannot go. I think that for the rest of the day I will lie on my couch. Neferura," she said slowly again as Nofret held back the covers. "Evil omen for my beautiful little girl. I should send for a sorcerer and pierce the future on her behalf." But she knew that such sick strivings were foreign to her nature, and she would never summon the priests of Set.

Thothmes sent Duwa-eneneh back with a formal agreement on the name, but he did not come himself. She knew that he was with Aset in little Thothmes' nursery. She lay on her side, her head pillowed on her arm, gazing into the perfumed dimness of her room and thinking of her sister Neferu-khebit and the little fawn, both long gone.

She did not get up. Senmut brought the child to her every day, and she played with it and cuddled it and smiled upon it, but she would not leave her couch. A terrible lassitude was on her, a deadening, killing apathy. Day after day she ate and drank and slept, all in the safety of her room. In the audience chambers and ministries of the country Hapuseneb, Ineni, and Ahmose, User-amun's father, struggled desperately to hold the line against an ever increasing mountain of work while Thothmes and Aset hunted and boated and feasted, their laughter and the comings and goings of their slaves and servants an ever present taunt to the ears of the harried men who rose early and were still in their offices when the next dawn broke.

Senmut tried to speak to Hatshepsut of the great machinery of Egypt that was grinding slowly but surely to a halt without her hand to guide it, but she told him irritably to get about his business, reminding him that men did not become ministers for nothing.

He had appealed to Thothmes, going to Pharaoh because there was nowhere else to go, though his heart was sick at the prospect. He had chosen a bad time. Thothmes was about to set off on a small trip with Aset and little Thothmes, down the river to Memphis to worship Sekhmet, and Senmut had to speak to him while his hangers-on thronged the water steps and the Imperial Barge, with all flags flying, rocked, waiting.

Thothmes had brushed him aside. "I will see to it all when I return," he had snapped, his eyes on Aset as she swayed up the ramp and looked back at him, beckoning.

Senmut had retired in helpless fury. And when Thothmes returned, nothing happened, and the feasting went on.

Finally Nehesi went to her, stalking unannounced into her bedroom one hot, stifling evening to find her sitting up on her couch, naked but for a film of linen across her loins, an empty wine jug on the table beside the bed and a bunch of wilting lotus flowers under her listless hands. He bowed but came to the couch quickly, looking down at her.

"It is time to get up, Majesty," he said peremptorily. "The days fly by, and Egypt needs you."

She regarded him with lackluster eyes. "How did you get in here, Nehesi?"

"I ordered my soldier to let me pass, of course."

"What do you want?"

He leaned over her urgently. "I want nothing, Majesty, but your country is crying out for your royal hand upon it once more. Why do you lie here like an ailing child? Where is the Commander of the Braves of the King? I would not fight under you now, no, not if a thousand thousand Kushites clamored at the door!"

"That is treason!" she said with a flash of her old asperity. "Who are you, black Nehesi, to speak to your Queen of treason?"

"I am your Royal Seal Bearer, carrying at my belt a worthless piece of metal that becomes tiresome. I am your General, watching your soldiers grow fat and restless and unruly. Why do you not get up?"

She looked at the massive black arms splayed in appeal, the thick, muscled waist, the smooth face that radiated a steady, overpowering vitality, and she moved pettishly under the cool linen. "My head burns like fire," she said, "and day after day I am oppressed. Since the priest told me the name of my daughter, I have felt weak, used up, as if the name itself has drawn all strength from me. I think about it all the time, Nehesi. It haunts me."

"It is but a word," he retorted. "A name has much power, yes, but the man or woman who has the name can turn the use of it to good or ill."

"Neferu-khebit is dead," she replied slowly. "Was it an accident that caused her name to come once more into my life?"

"No," he almost shouted at her, "it was no accident! It is a good name, a royal name, a name that is loved by Amun. Will he give his Daughter's daughter a name that will harm her? Did your sister die because of a name? Would she even now curse you, one who loved her and shared all with her? Majesty, you dishonor yourself, your sister, and your Father Amun!" He did not wait to be dismissed but cast her a look of withering scorn and glided away, snapping some order to the guard as he went, his voice deep.

She lay looking after him while her heart thudded faster. His words had stirred her, made her wonder in a panic what she was doing here in this soft, dark place when outside Ra rejoiced and the green things once more pushed through the earth. But still she did not stir.

One day, in the morning, when Aset was unwell, a cold and a sore throat making her scratchy and irritable, Thothmes went to the nursery to see his daughter. She was asleep, she seemed always to be asleep; whereas little Thothmes kicked and smiled and fought against his trappings. He stared down on her in perplexity, a crease of worry furrowing his broad, placid brow.

At last he went to Hatshepsut's room and sat beside her in her chair. "Are you well today?" he asked her.

She looked at him out of the corner of her eye. "Quite well. How is the business of government going for you, Thothmes?"

"I do not know. I leave it to the ministers. What else are ministers for?"

The words were so like her own to Senmut that she sat forward, aghast. "Do you mean that you do not read the dispatches every day?"

"No, I don't. I was never very good at reading, and the droning of the scribes bores me. I have had some excellent hunting, though!"

She looked at his fatuous expression with more emotion than she had felt in weeks, wanting to reach out and slap the silly grin from his face; and as she felt her temper rise, she slipped from the couch, calling for Nofret and her robe. "I believed you to be happy to order all as you wished for a while! Has nothing been done?" She remembered Senmut's imploring face and angry lips, but she had only the vaguest remembrance of his request. "While I have rested, have you done nothing but play?"

"Play? Only children play."

"O my dear Egypt," she whispered, "what have I done to you?" He turned to her, puzzled, as she slipped the robe around her and hugged it to her.

"Hatshepset," he began, but she ordered food and milk before she looked at him again. "I wanted to talk to you about Neferura," he continued.

She heard the name impassively, wondering why on earth it had distressed her. The fog in her brain was clearing fast, though her legs shook. Already her mind was racing to the audience chambers, seeing the pile of untouched correspondence that awaited her Seal. "What about her?"

"Have you spoken to the physicians about her? She seems to be a trifle frail."

"Senmut remarked upon it, too, but the physician says that she is merely delicate and will grow as strong and healthy as the young bull in *your* pen." Her mouth turned up at the corners. "She will make a good Pharaoh."

He shot out of his chair. "That is for me to decide!"

Nofret appeared, followed by a line of slaves bearing trays of food. It would be the largest meal Hatshepsut had eaten in a long while.

She folded herself onto her cushions and sniffed expectantly. "Fish! Lovely fish!" She fixed Thothmes with a sudden, level stare. "I think not. Will you, as Pharaoh, name Neferura as your Crown Prince? Your Heir?"

"Certainly not! The idea is preposterous!"

"Your father did it, and if it had not been for you, I would now be Pharaoh! Do you call him preposterous?"

Nofret lifted the lid from a silver dish and ladled the food onto Hatshepsut's plate.

"Yes, I do. There is no longer any need to fight over the succession. I am going to declare my son Thothmes my Heir and marry him in time to Neferura to legitimize that declaration."

"No, you are not." She shoveled the food into her mouth, chewing with gusto and reaching for the water. "You can declare all you want, Thothmes, but I will not allow Neferura to marry Thothmes. I have decided to found a new dynasty—of Queens. I will change the law."

He was aghast. "You cannot change the law! Pharaoh must be male!"

"Do you mean that Pharaoh must have the hangings of a man, or that Pharaoh must be seen to govern with a man's strength of purpose and command? Who is Egypt, Thothmes, I or you? You need not answer, and please close your mouth, you are putting me off my food. I rule Egypt, and Neferura will be raised to rule after me, as Pharaoh."

"Thothmes will be Pharaoh!"

"He will not!"

He got up, wanting to put his foot under her table and send the fragrant dishes flying in her face. "As Amun is my witness, as I am Pharaoh of Egypt, he will reign!" He growled. "You are as mad as a sun-crazed cur."

"Oh, go away, Thothmes." She waved an arm at him, smiling. "And one thing more. If you do not declare for Neferura, you shall never again share my bed. That I vow and promise."

He stamped to the door in a furious rage. "That will be no loss, she-cat! Bitch! I never want to feel your claws again!" He flung back the heavy bronze doors and went out. But as he half ran, half stumbled down the hall, he was already assailed by a bitter longing for the few nights he had spent lost in her arms, and he cursed her in agony as he found himself under the sweet, spreading willows of her garden.

An hour later the men gathered in the audience chamber heard quick determined steps approaching, and they looked up. Beyond the door the soldier jumped, his spear hitting the floor in salute, and the next moment Hatshepsut burst in upon them, the Cobra on her head glittering and her brief boy's kilt swirling about her thighs. She strode the length of the quiet room in long, angry steps, her golden sandals punctuating the sudden silence with purposeful little slaps. Before she reached them, they were all prostrate. She surveyed them, one beringed hand sitting on her slim hip. "Rise, all of you. By Amun, you are in paper up to your knees. Nehesi, the Seal! Hapuseneb, we will deal with your problems first. Ineni, bring me a chair; I will sit. Inept and lazy ministers that you are, your office is in a mess!"

They rose and smiled at her, enormous relief and thanksgiving shining in their eyes.

She smiled back at them in perfect understanding. "Egypt has come to you," she said, settling herself in the chair that Ineni hastily placed before her and holding her hand out for the first scroll. "My friends, we will weld this country into the greatest of all history. We will tighten the reins until there is none in Thebes, in the whole of Egypt, who will dare to oppose us. The work we have done before will be as nothing compared to the mighty acts we will perform together from this day on, and even Pharaoh will be dumb." She sought Senmut's face, and finding it, a challenge and a message flashed between them. She bent to the reading of the letter, and Anen set his scribe's tray, his pens and inks, on his crossed legs. "Pharaoh is about to announce the succession," she said to them, her eyes on the characters in front of her. In those words all present knew the reason for her sudden recovery. "He says—" here she paused, her glance sweeping over them all keenly, "he says that the Hawk-in-the-Nest will be young Thothmes." They were silent, and she tapped her teeth musingly with the crisp scroll. "But we will go to the temple and see what Amun has to say. My Father will not wish it; I am sure."

User-amun was about to protest that as both contenders were still in infancy any discussion was futile. But Hapuseneb sent him a warning glance, and he shut his mouth and coughed instead.

"Meanwhile, to work!" Hatshepsut finished. "We must grow in peace and in strength and in every good gift of the God."

They knew that she was not referring to any of them.

By the New Year the backlog of work was cleared away, and ruthlessly Hatshepsut began to consolidate the power that had been hers since her father told her she was to be Crown Prince. She drove herself and those around her with a steady whip, conscious that she and only she was Egypt's Hope. She knew that if she wished one day to make Neferura King, she would have to close any gaps between herself and the Horus Throne. She discussed the matter fully with Senmut and Hapuseneb, and they all agreed that in Thothmes' lifetime—and thus in her lifetime, also —little could be done. But Hatshepsut wanted the throne for Neferura with an increasing appetite, and she cast about for ways to make the girl's accession safe after her own or Thothmes' death.

With wily foresight she began to replace with her own men many of the priests in the temple who held high office. But she was powerless to rid herself of Menena as long as Thothmes wanted him. The choice of High Priest fell to Pharaoh alone, and so Menena continued to advise and counsel Thothmes while Hatshepsut ringed him with spies. She made sure, unobtrusively and slowly, that all nomarchs, viceroys, and governors of the provinces belonged to her, and she spent much time in the barracks with the soldiers and on the estates of the generals, winning them all with her charm and her fire. She did not do these things selfishly. Egypt had to be strong. Amun must be seen to reign supreme. She poured out her devotion to the God and to the country that blazed like a blue, green, and brown jewel before her eyes.

She made Senmut her Chief Steward, knowing as she did so that nothing in her household would pass that was not noted by his calculating, unsleeping eye. Under his care her daughter grew, toddling about in the nursery, safe in the circle of his long arms. She often invited the young aristocrats Yamu-nefru, Djehuty, Sen-nefer to hunt or to dine with her, knowing that they came of families almost as old as her own, families steeped in the traditions and mores of their forefathers. At first she did not know how they would greet a woman who was not Queen but King. They brought her rich gifts and praised and flattered her, but their dark eyes told of the disdain with which they regarded upstarts like Senmut, though they gave him every respect. He was now a great man, the greatest in the land under the Queen herself, and they knew it.

When Egypt was finally running smoothly, due to her unceasing vigilance, she turned her attention to the School of Architects, for they were a class apart, held in reverence by royalty since time began. Her careful eye spotted the promise of the young and silent Puamra. She gave him work to do for herself as well as for Thothmes, and he acquitted himself with calm dispatch. But she found him hard to understand. He went little to the temple and seemed to have few friends. He would often go north to Bubastis and come back to Thebes silent and dissipated. None knew how he served his Goddess, Bast, the Running Cat, but all could guess. Nevertheless, he was devoted to Hatshepsut in his own quiet, intense way, and he came more and more often to the conferences of her inner circle, sitting silently and watching them all or offering a brusque, pointed comment that cleared the air, then withdrawing once again to his secret thoughts. Amunophis was another newcomer to her entourage. Hatshepsut, having fought with his father in the desert, made him Under Steward, and he soon proved his ability. He and Senmut shared the responsibility for the administration of the palace. He was a quick, good-looking man with the constitution of one of his beloved horses, and no matter how arduous the tasks of each day, he seemed always to find time to harness his chariot and spend a couple of hours racing back and forth between Luxor and Thebes. Sometimes Senmut would race with him, thundering across the desert in the orange sunsets, stirring up clouds of red dust. Amunophis invariably won, for by that time of the day Senmut was often very tired, and Amunophis would trot back to the stables with his head held high, Senmut trailing behind in grim amusement.

Hatshepsut needed such men of genius and great endurance. Her concentration, her sense of urgency never left her, and her policy makers, heralds, and scribes all prayed that they would not become ill under the choking burden she laid on them. But she, too, worked hard, not sparing herself, and gradually she saw to her satisfaction the subtle shifting of the balance of power. One by one the reins slipped into her hands.

One hot afternoon she went to see Aset's child for herself. She had thought of sending for the boy, but she decided it was better that she spend some time in the women's quarters to remind Aset and her followers whose finger it was that pressed steadily on the pulse of the palace.

She took Senmut and Hapuseneb and swept unannounced into Aset's reception room. Aset was playing at draughts with one of her maids, her thin elbows resting thoughtfully on the edge of the alabaster and ebony board. She was so engrossed that Hatshepsut approached her and stood waiting for a minute before the two players felt her presence. Aset jumped up, her knee catching the board and sending the pieces clattering to the floor, she and her servant falling with them in confusion.

Hatshepsut eyed the room. It was big and sunny and obviously not much used, for she knew that Aset and Thothmes were inseparable. But couch, tables, chairs, shrines, statues were all of gold, and the running friezes on the walls sparked dully, the smooth, willowy figures of people and animals and trees all inlaid with electrum. The evidence of a Pharaoh's indulgent hand was everywhere, and Hatshepsut made a quick mental note to ask Ineni, in his capacity as Treasurer, how much wealth Thothmes lavished on Aset. She looked down on the dark head with its hair spread in confusion over the tiles. At last she spoke. "Rise, Aset. I have come to see your little one."

Aset sprang up, smiling slyly, the close-set eyes and thin mouth still sending a wave of irritation through Hatshepsut, so that her chin rose and her own smile quickly faded. She had not seen the dancer for so long, and she had been prepared to make an effort to like the girl. But once again she felt the arrogant superiority of an upstart with bold dreams.

"Send your nurse for the boy," she said sharply. "We wait to pronounce an opinion on him. Pharaoh insists that he resembles my father."

"He does indeed!" Aset replied eagerly, turning to clap to her companion. As the other woman hurried out, Hatshepsut bit back the retort she had been about to make. How did Aset know of any such resemblance, seeing that she herself had probably never seen Thothmes the First? She could not imagine that her father would have had anything to do with this pert slip who looked like a slinky, half-starved cat. Again Hatshepsut wondered at Thothmes' monumental lack of discrimination. Perhaps Aset had been already so full of ambitions before Pharaoh conveniently stayed at Assuan, that she had put a spell on him.

While she mused, she questioned Aset closely about young Thothmes' routine: how he ate, how he slept, who his playmates were. Aset answered rapidly but with respect, her eyes often darting to the two tall, silent men who stood at each side of the Queen. They looked back at her without a word, their unwavering stares cold, challenging things. Finally the far door opened, and the nurse returned, holding by the hand a sturdy, dark youngster who, though still unsteady on his feet, struck out, unafraid of falling. As Hatshepsut watched him come to her over the polished floor, she felt her composure leave her. He was certainly a Thothmesid. His shoulders were flung back, and he carried himself straight. The round, black eyes sought her out immediately, fearlessly, questioningly. His features were strong and chunky, and his front teeth protruded beneath the little nose, still snubbed slightly with the softness of babyhood, giving him the predatory look of his grandfather.

He and the nurse came and bowed, the child bobbing confidently, a princely helmet falling over his eyes. Hatshepsut knelt as the nurse dropped his hand, beckoning him to come to her. He toddled within her reach but would not be embraced, looking from her to his mother and back again while one stubby, short finger crept into his mouth. He sucked furiously, his calm gaze on Hatshepsut's face. He suddenly uttered a garbled word out of the corner of his mouth, the comforting finger still in place.

Hatshepsut looked up. "Senmut, what do you think?"

Senmut had been thinking of the years ahead, seeing the child as a young man, a thrusting, iron-willed, abrupt Thothmes the First. He was amazed at the smooth face and steady voice of the Queen, but he answered her readily. "He indeed bears the stamp of the royal seed from whence he sprang."

"And you, Hapuseneb?"

Hapuseneb nodded slowly, his thoughts hidden, as usual, beneath an urbane, friendly exterior. "I see your father, beyond any doubt," he agreed.

As Hatshepsut got to her feet and motioned the nurse to take the child away, Aset smirked, gratified.

Hatshepsut turned to Aset when the stocky little legs were out of sight. "I do not want to see him again in the helmet," she said. Though the words were kind and spoken quietly, they all heard the undertone of warning. "My husband has proclaimed him Crown Prince, but he is yet in infancy and will go shaved and free as other children do. See that you do not fill his little head with silly and vain thoughts, Aset, or you and he will come to grief."

Aset bowed, her foxlike face a sullen mask.

Suddenly Hatshepsut smiled. "He is a beautiful boy, a true and worthy Prince of Egypt and a son for Thothmes to take pride in," she said. "See that you do not spoil him. Now go back to your game. I will not trouble you further."

Hapuseneb bent and gathered up the spilled pieces, setting them gravely back on the board. Aset prostrated herself once more, and the doors closed behind the three.

Alone again, Aset sat staring at nothing, frowning nervously, tearing at her nails with her sharp white teeth.

18

Thothmes went grudgingly to war on three more occasions in the years that followed, and Hatshepsut watched him go each time with relief. He saw no engagement, drew no blood, but at least he led his troops and was proud of the fact. His generals easily scattered the hooknosed and warlike desert tribes, the Nine Bowmen, teaching the dwellers of the Eastern Desert a salutary lesson in Egyptian military might. During the periods that he was away, the work on the ephemeral, dreamlike temple in the valley went ahead in great spurts. On every return Thothmes insisted on going to see it. It rapidly became neutral ground for him and Hatshepsut. He was fanatically interested in the matter of building, and Senmut's masterpiece intrigued and excited him. Senmut sometimes pitied the plump, wheezing young Pharaoh, who would sit with frank admiration in his eyes while before him the valley swarmed with life. Thothmes had the soul of an architect, and sympathizing, Senmut showed him the plans and listened to his comments and hesitant advice, feeling the pathetic little bursts of jealousy in the man as Hatshepsut coolly and rightly pointed out the glories of her homage to posterity. In her valley, which was cupped by the lordly cliff of Gurnet and worshiped by every stone rising under the cracking, straining muscles of the workmen, she and Thothmes were able to talk together of things other than the pinpricks that drew blood, both looking forward to the day of dedication, when they would walk together for the first time up the long, smooth ramp, bearing incense for the God.

Thothmes was building in his own right, and he shared his projects with Hatshepsut. At Medinet Habu he was beginning a small memorial temple to himself, and he asked her if she would lend him the skill of her architect. She teased him a little, wanting to know which of her servants he wanted, but in the end she gave him Senmut in a gesture of good-humored tolerance. Senmut laid out a ground plan to Thothmes' specifications, but it troubled him, and one night he took it to Hatshepsut.

She glanced at it once and burst out laughing. "Poor Thothmes! Did he draw this?"

"I drew it, Majesty, but Pharaoh told me what he wanted."

"Oh, poor Thothmes," she said again, her laughter dying away. They looked at each other for a moment before she handed the scroll back to him.

"Let him go ahead," she decided, "for he can never equal my great work in the valley, even though this plan is very similar. Medinet Habu is a very different site and will lend itself to a very different temple. How foolish he is! He has a good eye and could very well design works of great originality, but so much overlays his gift."

Senmut also helped Thothmes with his new temple to Hathor. "It will be," Thothmes told him with a sidelong glance, "an act of thanksgiving to the Goddess for my dear Aset." So Senmut found himself designing for a woman he instinctively disliked and a Pharaoh he desperately tried to respect; yet somehow he found the strength to add Thothmes' demands to the list of tasks to be done each day.

He loved the little Princess Neferura. She was as pretty and fragile as a flower, and when he played with her on the floor of the nursery or watched her as she careened drunkenly about the garden, he felt the pressures of his offices recede. After all, he thought, I have fulfilled all my ambitions, and the care of this child is the sum and proof of all my strivings. But somehow, as he listened to the deep whisperings of his heart, he knew that there was more, much more, and that he had only just begun to test his limitations. His roots began to trouble him, and he thought of his father and mother, still on the acres where he had toiled as a boy. Finally he asked for permission to visit them. Hatshepsut had taken one look at his tired face and agreed, and he and Senmen had left Thebes in Senmut's gilded barge, covering the miles in half the time that it had taken him and his father to walk the distance. He found his parents to be old but kindly strangers, bewildered by the two perfumed, painted men who spoke in cultured accents of things they only dimly understood and whose white and yellow tents billowed over the ground outside the mud house, filled with haughty, scantily clad slaves and beautiful, precious things. Hat-nefer, his mother, and Ta-kha'et liked each other, and Ta-kha'et spent much of the time perched on a wooden stool in the dingy kitchen, filling it with her sweet scent, swinging her tiny feet in their jeweled sandals as she told Hat-nefer of her life and gave the silent old woman a picture of her son's life also. But Senmut and his father found many long, embarrassing silences that could not be filled as they sat together on the edge of the river in the evenings, silences that hurt but could not be healed.

When Senmut left, he kept the promise he had made to himself many years ago, and at last he and Ka-mes were able to laugh as he told them of the splendid tomb he was preparing for them so that the gods would not forget them, but at the offer of gold and slaves to till the land, Ka-mes shook his head. "I am a peasant and the child of a peasant," he told Senmut, "and if slaves worked my land, what would I do with myself? I would grow old quickly and die before my noble tomb was ready."

The two men smiled at one another and embraced, Ka-mes crushed by the strength in the arms of his handsome son. Senmut and Senmen sailed back to Thebes rested, Senmut eased in conscience and Senmen only too happy to leave the arid, poverty-stricken farm and return to the life of the palace.

As the whole of Egypt slowly began to revolve around Hatshepsut and she was more and more satisfied that there was no corner of the land that did not do her will, she began also to cover the earth with her monuments —stelae, obelisks, pylons, stone upon stone of every kind, marble, granite, gray and pink sandstone. Everywhere she reminded the people who it was that held them under her holy feet, and Thothmes continued to feast and hunt, oblivious of her growing popularity and power. The God's feasts came and went, and he and she walked Thebes beside the golden idol, praising and worshiping Amun many times as the seasons changed and the immutable traditions were observed. Little Thothmes entered the service of Amun as a temple acolyte under the wary eye of Menena, and now Hatshepsut saw him whenever she went to perform her prostrations, a blunt-featured, belligerent chunk of a boy who watched her with interest, fingers clutching the golden incense crucible, and often she could not pray because of the intensity of his gaze. Neferura grew also, graceful and with the sweet composure of her Grandmother Aahmose, and Hatshepsut made sure that on all public occasions the little girl was dressed richly in the garb of a Princess and appeared before the people.

No more words of love had passed between her and Senmut, but the depth of their emotion for one another reached new levels, forced under as it was by the need for the maintainence of vigilance. She commissioned her personal sculptor to do a huge statue of him holding the Princess. For months Senmut sat for the work, and the sculptor knew his subject well, for when completed and uncovered for Hatshepsut's eyes, the statue smote her and all who stood to watch the moment. The artist had chosen black granite, and the Steward's serene, powerful face stared back at them with a force of protective warning and calm untouchability above the imperious little head of Neferura. The granite had been sculpted in one mighty, uncompromising block so that only the two heads, one above the other, appeared from under Senmut's long robe, where the Princess was sheltered, and the whole shone darkly, its smooth surfaces cold to the royal hands that ran gently over it. Hatshepsut was very pleased and had it set outside the nursery door so that all those who passed in and out were reminded that they if they harmed Neferura, they would do so at their peril.

Thothmes also commissioned a work, a statue in ebony of his mother, Mutnefert; and when it was finished, he stood it in the middle of his gardens. She was seated, with her hands on her knees and her eyes staring into the distance. The artist had tactfully reduced her weight and made her more beautiful than she had ever been in her youth, but Thothmes loved it and had Mutnefert present when Menena blessed it. On the pedestal he caused to be inscribed "Wife of a King, Mother of a King," and Mutnefert sailed back to her apartments on a cloud of pride. But Hatshepsut thought it a little ridiculous, and the bulky thing spoiled her walks, forcing her to ponder whether perhaps young Thothmes would one day raise another statue and carve it with the same words. Often she fancied in the twilight that it was not Mutnefert's smiling, vacant countenance that she passed under, but the thin, worldly face of Second Wife Aset.

So time passed, the Night of the Tear came and went, and four times the Barque of the God sailed forth with its garlanded burden. Hatshepsut approached her twenty-fifth birthday with indifference, seeing no change in the face that stared back at her every morning from the gleaming surface of her mirror, and the occasion came and went with the same slow, measured pace of all the days that were filled with the routine of government.

She took Neferura over the river to the shrine of her namesake. In the silent little temple, standing with Ani the priest before the statue of Neferu-khebit that had been smiling now for more than a decade, she told her daughter of the aunt who was now gone. The child made her own prayers, the black youth-lock trailing its ribbons on her thin shoulders, her aquiline, imperious nose pressed to the cold stone feet.

Hatshepsut, watching the perfect, oval face with the dark eyes and well-formed mouth that so perfectly reflected her own features, was seized by a flood of memories and a sensation of being trapped, imprisoned, that would not go away. She struggled with her depression for some weeks, burying herself in work. Then one night she seemed to make up her mind. She dressed herself and painted her face with care, sent for two Followers of His Majesty, and walked to Thothmes' bedchamber. As she waited impatiently to be announced, she heard voices within; and when she was admitted, she saw the door behind the royal couch close quietly. No doubt Aset would go to bed alone this night.

Thothmes was on the couch, wine in hand as usual, his head naked and shining. The room was full of Aset's pungent perfume, now mingled with Hatshepsut's own myrrh as she went forward and bowed. He sat bolt upright, watching her; and when she rose but did not speak, he was forced to clear his throat and ask her what she wanted. He did not trust her. This new vision of a beautiful, abject woman, clothed in yellow, waiting with eyes lowered and head bent, made him wary. He swung his legs over the edge of his couch. "What are you doing here?" he growled ungraciously, setting his cup upon the table with a click and folding his arms.

She stirred, but did not straighten. "I wish for comfort, Thothmes. I am lonely."

He grunted, taken aback, but already her perfume and her words were having their effect, and he felt the old desire stir in him.

"I do not believe you," he said flatly. "Since when have you ever needed my comfort? And if you are lonely, which I doubt, what of your flock of adoring geese?"

"Long ago you and I comforted each other," she answered calmly, her voice still quiet, "and I confess that I have begun to dream of your body, Thothmes. I awake in the night, a heat on me, and I cannot rest for thought of you."

Now she raised her head, and beneath the imploring quiver of her sensuous mouth, the pretty, eloquent gestures of her red-painted hands, he saw it, a quick gleam of mockery, quickly quelled. He got off the couch and shouted. "You lie, you lie! You do not want me at all! You are here for quite another purpose, and you cannot hide from me, Hatshepset. You banished me from your bed, and I have never known you to go back on your word."

She stepped to him, putting her hands on his shoulders; and as she replied, she kneaded them slowly, her fingers leaving them to travel to his soft belly. "But I did not exactly swear by the God."

"Yes, you did! Leave me alone!" But he did not push her away.

She moved closer, putting her mouth to his neck. "I spoke then in the heat of anger," she whispered. "Now let me speak of another fire."

With his last shred of control he grasped both her arms roughly in his and pulled her down, sitting beside her on the couch. On the door behind them came a knocking, and he shouted for whoever it was to go away. Then he looked at Hatshepsut. She was smiling at him, her hair in disarray and her cheeks flushed, panting a little, and he caught a glimpse of teeth behind the open mouth.

"I do not like to be made a fool," he said heavily. "I will kick you out of this room unless you tell me truly what you want." She smiled all the wider, knowing that he had never in his life kicked anyone. "Tell me!"

he demanded, already hoping that she would so that he could toss her on her back on the couch, and he shook her arms.

"Very well, but I did not lie to you before, Thothmes. I really do want to share your bed tonight."

"Why?"

"How astute you are becoming, brother of mine! Can you guess?"

"No, I cannot. I do not like playing games with you, Hatshepset, for I always lose."

"And you will lose again, for already you can hardly wait to make love to me. Well, I have decided that I want another child."

"Is that all?"

"All! It is a great deal, a very great deal. But in answer to your question —yes, that is all."

He watched her for any hint that she was making game with him, but she continued to regard him with wide-open, liquid, innocent eyes, and finally his shoulders slumped. "Why do you want another child? Thothmes and Neferura have secured the Horus Throne."

"In your mind, perhaps, but not in mine. I may have changed my mind about admitting you to my bed, but I still forbid you to take Neferura and marry her to Thothmes."

"In the name of all the gods, Hatshepset, why, why, why? What demon drives you? What takes place in that incomparable head of yours? Thothmes has the makings of a mighty Pharaoh, and Neferura is beautiful and will make a good consort. What is wrong with that?"

"Thothmes has the makings, but I did not make him," she said softly, her eyes narrowed, "and there will be more to my Neferura than beauty and willingness to walk behind Pharaoh every day. I want a Pharaoh of my own blood, and only mine, on the throne of Egypt."

He looked at her admiringly. "You are bewitched," he said. "So you want to make a son with me, to marry Neferura and rule."

"Exactly. My son and my daughter, gods together."

"It may be that we make a girl."

"I must take that chance. This must be done, Thothmes. No spawn of Aset will wear the Double Crown as long as I can prevent it."

"You flatter me!" he said sarcastically.

With an exclamation she touched his thigh. "I did not mean any insult to you. You and I sprang from the same royal loins."

He shrugged. "I am Pharoah, and I do not really care what you say, for you cannot deprive me of my rights." His lip stuck out.

"Dear Thothmes!" she said gently. "Have I not always given you the respect due to Pharaoh?"

"No you have not, but it does not matter. I have you in my blood, Hatshepset, like some vile poison; and in all the years we have been apart, I have not succeeded in ridding myself of the longing for you."

"Then pour me wine and lock the doors, and we will make up for all the time lost to us by my foolishness."

He picked up the gold-chased jug and did as she wanted, not wondering, in his vanity, at her eagerness. They linked arms and drank slowly. When she felt the warmth of the wine fill her veins and the giddiness in her head begin, she closed her eyes and lifted her mouth for his kiss, knowing that in a few moments her distaste for his body would disappear, engulfed in the dark tides of her own deep passions.

With agony she waited for the signs of pregnancy, harrying her physician and watching herself impatiently; and when at last she knew that once more she would give Thothmes and Egypt a child, she went immediately to the temple to beg Amun to make the seed in her male. The country rejoiced. But Aset received the news in an ominous silence, taking little Thothmes on her lap and hugging him with a ferocity that frightened the child, and she made no reference whatsoever to her royal lover of the expected birth. Thothmes himself was neither pleased nor angry, determined not to offend Hatshepsut again so that he could go on enjoying the delights of her strong body, and she received him willingly, using him gratefully as the depression lifted and left her.

As time went by and again she became lethargic, she began to wonder what she would do if the child was female. Amun had made no promises, and even in the privacy of her own room, kneeling night after night before his shrine, she had felt no glow of certainty in answer to her prayers. She ordered more sacrifices made to him, and she had Tahuti make new doors for the temple, copper and bronze inlaid with electrum, so that the God should know of her devotion to him. When they were hung, she was present to make the offerings, standing dwarfed by the enormous wings that blazed under a white-hot Ra, the flashing of the deep brown, shimmering metal easily spotted a mile and more across the river.

As her time drew nearer, her anxiety spread to those about her and from them to the whole of the city, so that Thebes and the palace and the priests in the temple all seethed with speculation. Senmut did his best to keep her mind busy with the affairs of each day, seeing his own secret strivings mirrored in her, but even in his company she could not rest. She felt bitterly that this was her last chance, that only by giving Egypt a Pharaoh who was both male and fully royal could she bear the thought of hiding her omnipotence behind Thothmes for the rest of her life.

At last it was time, and once more the Princes of the country were summoned to the royal bed. The birth was more rapid this time. Hatshepsut, pacing from couch to wall and back again between bouts of pain, in a fever of doubt and impatience, barely had time to lie down and be prepared before the baby came, wailing and thrashing, into the world.

There was a moment of breathless waiting, and then the midwife turned, smiling, and the physician began to pack his drugs away. "Another girl! And a beautiful one!"

Hatshepsut uttered one long cry of protest and buried her face in the pillows, and the men filed out silently, pleased with a new Princess and mystified by the Queen's reaction, for another girl was surely proof against the sudden death of Neferura and ensured that the Crown Prince would be legitimized when the time came.

Senmut hesitated at the door, longing to go back into the room and comfort the woman whose sobs came to him audibly though muffled, but he wisely left her alone, pressing his great seal beside the others on the paper on Anen's lap and walking home to his palace in the murmuring night.

Thothmes was not so subtle. He stood by the bed, leaning down in inarticulate sympathy and stroking the heaving shoulders. But when he tried to raise her, she shrugged from his grasp angrily, and after a helpless moment of indecision he left her. It pained him to know that she had been defeated, and it pained him to know that he would never understand her complex mind. But after all, he thought guiltily as he made his way back to his own chambers, she is in truth the Child of Amun, his true and certain likeness in Egypt, and it must be hard for a God to die without leaving another God to rule. The finer points of the situation made him tired, and he had had an early rising, so he went to bed and slept heavily.

In the nursery Neferura looked at her new sister with dubious awe, and her mother finally fell into an exhausted, grudging sleep.

Aset had made Thothmes promise to send her word the moment Hatshepsut gave birth, and before he got onto his couch with a sigh, he ordered his Herald to take her the news. He could well imagine her reaction, and he wished a little wistfully that she was not quite so spiteful, so grasping. But after all, he told himself as his slave settled the sheet over him and bowed out, even a Pharaoh cannot have everything.

Aset's reaction was indeed predictable. The Herald found her in the garden, tossing a ball for her son as he ran to and fro between the trees and tried to leap the flower beds. At the sight of the tall man striding toward her over the grass, two bodyguards flanking him like twin lions, she rose, her heart in her mouth, and the ball slipped from fingers gone suddenly cold. The Herald and the two Followers of His Majesty bowed, and Aset shaded her eyes with one shaking hand. "Well?" she snapped. "Is the Queen delivered of a boy or a girl?"

The Herald smiled faintly. "The Divine Consort, Beloved of the Two Lands, has given birth today to—a girl, Highness."

Aset's eyes narrowed and began to glow, and all at once she began to laugh. She laughed until the tears ran down her thin face, laughed until she could no longer stand upright. The three men watched her incredulously, unable to believe this show of complete disrespect. Thothmes ran to her, picking up his ball and hugging it while his eyes grew round, and still she laughed until her belly ached and she could laugh no more. Finally she straightened, gasping and wiping her eyes on her linen.

The Herald waited coldly, his face impassive. "Do you wish me to carry any message to Pharaoh?" he asked her.

At the chill in his tone, she drew herself up and met his gaze with impudence. "No. Tell him only that today I am well—and very happy."

He bowed stiffly and spun on his heel, walking away with his back rigid.

Aset went down on one knee before little Thothmes, stroking his shaved head and his strong brown arms, in a paroxysm of joy. "Did you hear, little Prince? Did you? You will be King! Pharaoh Thothmes the Third! How grand you will be, in your shining Double Crown, and how mighty! I, a humble dancer from Assuan, am the mother of a Pharaoh!"

But her expression was far from humble as she took the ball from him and threw it with all her might. It sailed up, up, and disappeared into the sun, falling neatly behind the wall that separated her domain from that of Hatshepsut. Then she laughed again, in triumph at the sign; and snatching her son's hand, she led him slowly inside.

Somehow the word was passed, and in two days all knew that Second Wife Aset had laughed loud and long at the Queen's new daughter and had even had the effrontery to send a message to Pharaoh himself, telling him how happy she was.

Yamu-nefru had sneered, discussing the matter with his friend Djehuty as they dined together one evening. "What else can be expected of a skinny upstart who fancies herself a Queen?" he said, selecting a pastry with care and nibbling at it daintily. "I have never heard of such bad manners."

Djehuty agreed, smiling. "If Pharaoh had been more like his blessed and illustrious father, the bitch would have been sent packing immediately," he observed, "but seeing we have a ruler of uncertain talents, such breaches of true breeding happen all too often."

"I am surprised that she has lasted this long." Yamu-nefru finished his pastry and dabbled his long fingers in the scented water bowl. "Thothmes has no taste in women."

"You speak of Pharaoh!" Djehuty warned him, eying the servant who silently filled their goblets. For a moment they did not speak. Then Djehuty continued. "Even so, my friend, Aset has a son by Pharaoh, and by right of law he will indeed be Pharaoh in his turn. It sticks in the gullet of the Flower of Egypt, but she knows that it will come to pass one day."

"It would stick in my gullet, too, if the son were more like his father." Yamu-nefru sipped his wine with relish. "But you know, Djehuty, I like the child. He fears nothing."

"He is not the first Pharaoh who has sprung from a commoner's body and done great deeds, yet the Queen will not see it like that."

"The Queen wishes to be King," Yamu-nefru said softly, "and I have no doubt that if anything untoward happens to Pharaoh, then Aset must guard her little princeling with her life."

They looked at each other over the rim of their goblets, in perfect understanding.

Djehuty shrugged. "It is no light matter to be the Daughter of the God," he said. "You and I, Nefrusi, must simply get about our own business and serve as well as we may."

The news finally trickled through to Hatshepsut, babbled to her by her hairdresser one morning, and with a mounting rage she kept her mask of indifference until the silly woman had gone. Then she swept her cosmetics to the floor in one violent, crashing movement and marched to Thothmes' audience chamber, pushing his guard aside with such force that the man stumbled against the wall and dropped his spear. Although her body was still sore and a little weak, she strode to the foot of his throne, where Aset perched at his feet and his courtiers gathered, and she ordered them out.

"You, too, you hussy!" she shouted at Aset, and her face held an expression of such animal ferocity that Aset jumped up and dodged past her, her customary cheeky aplomb deserting her.

Thothmes got down, aghast, and Hatshepsut strode to him, thrusting her blazing face into his so that he had to step back a pace. "Your fumblings I can stand!" she shouted, "and your blatant ineptitude and your silly posturings, but to be insulted in my own palace, under the very nose of a high official of the court, by a peasant girl dressed up as a Princess, this I will not have!" She shook her fist at him and spat upon the floor, then she whirled and began to stride up and down, her earrings swinging and her bracelets jingling angrily.

"I have put up with her, Thothmes, for your sake. Pharaoh is within the law, I have said. He may take another wife, I have said, because that it his privilege, even though his choice is a woman whose blood and profession offend the very air I breathe! She is stupid and mean, Thothmes, and will not learn the graces she cannot obtain by birth. But the crowning blow, the last trial of my patience and my full cooperation, for you have had both"—she held out a rigid finger at him, and he shrank —"is that in leaving such rudeness, such blasphemy, to go unpunished, you are saying to the whole city: 'See! My wife laughs at my wife, and I laugh, too!' " She ran out of breath and came to a halt, fists clenched and face white.

But she had not finished. "Furthermore," she said more calmly, walking toward him, "if you do not order her confined to her rooms until my anger is abated, I myself will have her whipped. I can do it, Thothmes, and you cannot stop me. Aset must be checked, and it must be done now, before her vaunting greed and ambition take her to the executioner."

Thothmes fidgeted unhappily with the rings on his fingers. Her rage did not impress him, for she had a temper speedily roused and as speedily forgotten. But he knew her words were just, and in his own cowardice he had allowed the breach of protocol and decency to go unpunished.

"I am truly sorry, Hatshepset, and you are right," he offered, seeing that she was already limp with the aftermath of her outburst. "Of course I shall punish Aset, but you must understand that she was not brought up gently, as you and I were. She has had a rough and difficult life."

"Oh, Thothmes," Hatshepsut said wearily. "Many people are born with nothing and yet can live humbly and rightly in the service of the God and their fellow creatures. There is not another woman in Thebes who would display the same hardness of heart to her worst enemy, and I am not Aset's enemy if she did but stop to think on the matter. I could have been her friend."

"She fears you," Thothmes pointed out. "She is not secure; she is ever looking over her shoulder. And the Queen is, to her, a formidable rival."

Hatshepsut laughed abruptly. "How dare she think in terms of rivalry! For I am the God, and what is she? She may look over her shoulder in vain, for she is her own enemy."

"I am sorry," Thothmes repeated. "Shall I have her flogged?"

Hatshepsut glanced at the worried, frowning face with contempt and pity. "That is not necessary. Not this time, at any rate. But if she persists in her foolishness, it may be the only answer. No, Thothmes, only lock her in her apartments, and forbid the garden to her. I do not wish to see her again for a very long time, not at dinner, not on my walks, and not on any public occasion. I am going back to my couch." She bowed briefly, absently, and went to the door. Suddenly she turned back, a wry, self-deprecating smile on her mouth. "What do you think of your new daughter?"

He shuffled uneasily. "In truth, Hatshepset, I do not know. She is certainly more robust than Neferura, but her features are indeterminate. I can see no likeness in her to either me or you or her grandparents."

Hatshepsut grimaced. "Neither can I," she said lightly. "Ah, well, it was not the will of Amun to give me a King!" And she went out, closing the door softly. Outside she paused. "Did I hurt you?" she asked the guard.

Surprised and pleased, he shook his head. "No, Majesty," he replied. "I am only sorry that I stood in your way."

"You were brave," she answered. "Not many dare to stand in my way." She touched him lightly on the forehead and went swiftly down the hall.

The child was named Meryet-Hatshepset, and Hatshepsut accepted it without a tremor. It was a good, safe name, a name that held for her no memories or premonitions, and the baby was duly carried to the temple and offered to the God. Senmut felt no fears for this daughter. She was very healthy and seemed to grow every day, but he could not warm to her as he had to the dainty Neferura, and he was glad that he had not been appointed Royal Nurse to her as well. He was relieved to see that Hatshepsut recovered quickly from the birth and within weeks was back in her offices. Once more the palace hummed like a great beehive, drawing in the nectar of gold and sending out scouts, workers, and messengers who traveled the length and breadth of Egypt on the business of the Queen.

Hatshepsut swallowed her disappointment. But like Senmut, she found that she could not warm to her second daughter. She wondered if it was perhaps because she had so desperately wanted a son or because she had refused to hold the child in its first hours of life. Whatever the reason, the tiny red face, with its thin features, did not move her at all, and she was sorry. As Meryet-Hatshepset grew toward her first birthday, Hatshepsut saw in her a dismaying likeness to Aset, not so much in appearance but in disposition. The girl was a whiner, often in tears that could have been genuine but more often than not were squeezed out to accomplish some end. Her nurses had their patience tried by her day after day. The nursery became a noisy place, and in the end Senmut requested that Neferura be moved to her own little apartment. Hatshepsut agreed, and the Princess was lodged next-door to her mother in servants' cells that were redecorated for her. So it was inevitable that Queen and future consort should grow closer while the ill-tempered baby, who screamed constantly, was left to the ministrations of hired women.

Hatshepsut did not intend to neglect Meryet. She went often to play little games with her and comfort her, but she was a busy, hard-pressed woman. She found it easier to take Neferura with her, talking with the little girl as she passed steadily from temple to office to dining chamber. The baby was left to stamp her little feet in impotent rage as she saw her mother and her sister go off together, leaving her to the nurses who gathered around her. Very early on Meryet-Hatshepset learned jealousy.

19

Early in the month of Thoth, when the river had already begun to rise and the fellahin worked desperately night and day to gather in the harvest before winter's angry waters spilled over the fields, Thothmes caught a cold. He had refused all food for some days beforehand, complaining that his head ached. When he began to sniffle and his temperature rose, he took to his couch at once. His physician prescribed hot lemon juice with honey, mingled with cassia, and Thothmes miserably drank his medicine and surrounded himself with amulets and charms. After three days the fever had not abated, though the symptoms of his cold were gone. Alarmed, the physician went to Hatshepsut. Ineni was with her, and they were going over the accounts of the temple for the last month while Neferura played with her dolls in the corner.

"How is Thothmes today?" Hatshepsut asked the man quickly, her eyes still on the scroll before her and her mind on Ineni's figures.

The physician stood awkwardly, one hand about the golden scarab hanging on his sunken breast. "Mighty Horus is not well at all," he began. When she heard his tone, Hatshepsut turned swiftly, her attention now fully on him.

"The cold has left him, but the fever will not abate. His Majesty weakens."

"Then call the magicians at once! A fever is a matter of spells and charms. What have you done for him?"

"I treated the cough and the stuffed nose, Majesty; they fled. But I can do no more. Pharaoh asks that you visit him, but I do not advise it."

"Why not?"

"His breath is full of foul humors. Forgive me for saying so, Majesty, but I do not think you should approach him."

"Nonsense! Since when have I feared an evil smell? Ineni, we are finished here for today. You can take the scrolls back to the scribe."

"Is my father very ill?" Neferura had left her dolls and crept forward, her dark eyes on the face of Pharaoh's physician. The man looked help-lessly at Hatshepsut.

She swiftly knelt, straightening the unruly youth-lock and kissing the pale cheek. "He is ill, but I do not think you should worry about him," she said gently. "Is not Pharaoh immortal?"

The child nodded solemnly. "Are you going to see him now? May I come, too?"

"No, you must take your dolls and go and find Senmut. If you like, you can go with him to see the animals while I am busy. Would you like that?"

Neferura nodded again, but she did not run to pick up her toys. Hatshepsut left her standing there, staring, while Ineni gathered together the scrolls.

In Thothmes' bedchamber the air was stifling, and it stank. He was lying on his back, moaning a little. As she bent to kiss him, his skin was fiery and dry to her touch. She drew back, alarmed.

"Hatshepset," he whispered. His head rolled toward her. "Tell these fools to bring me water. They will not let me drink."

She looked at the physician, startled, words of anger on her lips.

The old man was firm. "His Majesty can only sip," he said, "but His Majesty insists on half a heket of water. I have told him that to drink so much at once will induce great pain."

"To Set with your mumblings!" Thothmes moved restlessly under the thin linen, and his breath reached her, a stench in her nostrils.

"He can at least be bathed!" she snapped. "Bring warm water and cloths, and I will wash him. And lift the hangings from the windows! How can he sleep in this heat?" The slaves who huddled in the corner ran to do her bidding, and she sat on Thothmes' retiring stool. "Come here with that fan!" she barked.

Thothmes closed his eyes as the air over his body began to move. "I am burning up," he whispered again. He began to shiver, clutching the covers in shaking hands, his teeth chattering.

She looked at him with real fear, smoothing the pillow. "Do not worry, Thothmes," she said. "I have ordered the magicians, and soon the fever will be driven from your body."

He tossed and moaned, not answering.

A slave approached with a bowl of hot water. She bade him set it beside her as she took off her rings. She added a little wine to the water, dipped the cloth in it, and began to wash his face. He smiled faintly, his hand finding hers. She gently removed the sheet and washed him all over. His body had an unhealthy sheen that was not sweat. He seemed to be slightly swollen, and she pursed her lips as she worked. Whatever it was, she did not think that spells would be of any use.

When she had finished, she washed her hands in clean water and put on her rings, slipping each on thoughtfully. As she sat, the magicians were announced. Bending over him, she said into his ear, "Thothmes, the magicians are here. I must go now. I am expected elsewhere, but I will return as soon as I may and wash you again. Would you like that?"

He smelled her perfume, a faint and pleasant cloud. He wanted to turn and open his eyes, but the effort was beyond him, and he only nodded, once.

She rose. "Begin at once," she ordered the silent, cloaked men. "Do not stop until Pharaoh leaves his bed to go hunting!" She smiled at them briefly, and before she closed the door, the deep chanting had begun.

She sent a message to Aset, telling her that she had permission to visit Thothmes but that she must on no account take her son with her. She ordered the bodyguard who carried the message to wait and see that it was obeyed. She spent some time with Tahuti in his workshop, a large, open room that nonetheless always seemed full of the fumes of hot metal. They discussed his progress on the floors of her temple. They were all to be of gold or silver, and he was responsible for their beating and laying. While she was there, he showed her some chests of copper that he was making for the Master of Mysteries. She was impressed. They were delicately wrought and carefully, lovingly put together. She made a mental note to talk to Ineni about the solemn, humorless youth.

When she returned to Thothmes' bedchamber, the physician met her at the door. Members of Pharaoh's entourage were clustered around him. He looked frightened. "Majesty, you must not go in," he said. "Pharaoh sleeps, but it is not the sleep of health, and his skin has broken out in pustules."

"Where is Second Wife Aset?" Hatshepsut demanded.

"She was here, but I told her to go to her apartment also," the physician said.

Despite his protestations Hatshepsut pushed her way into the room. "Cease!" she said to the magicians, and their droning died away. She went to Thothmes.

He was lying on his side, asleep, his mouth open. He was breathing heavily, the labored sound filling the room. His covers had slid to his waist, and she could see that the whole of his upper body was now covered in little white lumps, the skin between them a shiny, sickly yellow.

"Is it the plague?" she whispered to the physician, who had followed her.

He shook his head, lifting his hands in a gesture of bewilderment and resignation. "One of them," he answered briefly.

They were both silent, watching the sleeping King, wrapped in their own thoughts.

"Do not leave him," she ordered, "and bring me word should there be any change." He bowed, and she went out, walking to the temple with her subdued women and her bodyguard. She went in alone to the God, but the sanctuary was shut and locked. She lay on her stomach before the door, her arms stretched above her head to touch it, and closed her eyes. O my Father, she prayed, drained of all save the wish to be held in the God's golden arms. Is Thothmes to die? If he dies—She seemed to hear the mocking echo of her own thought go whispering through the clustering pillars and the vast emptinesses of the inner court, rising with the incense.

If he dies, if he dies, if he dies, if he dies—

She screwed her eyes more tightly shut and ground her forehead into the golden floor. But she could not cry for him.

In the evening she went back to his room and sat beside him. The pustules were oozing a colorless slime that stuck to his sheets and caused him agony. He called her endlessly as he tossed to and fro, his heavy body as flabby and limp as a dead beast's. Though she leaned over him many times, she could see that he was not conscious and that it was only in his dreams that he wandered with her. He seemed to be rotting even before breath left him. The stink of his corruption filled their nostrils, making them all retch. But Hatshepsut did not move. She went on watching, watching, her perfect face a blank.

Aset crept in once, her eyes on Hatshepsut, hesitating, but since the Queen made no sound, she came to the couch, her hands to her nose. Exclaiming softly, she looked down on the moving, muttering hulk. Night had fallen, and the lamps had been lit, but even their gentle, golden glow could not mask the rot. She turned quickly away, only to find Hatshepsut's steady eyes on her.

"Do you love him now, Aset?" she said quietly. "Have you looked your fill on your royal husband? Are you running to your safe little, sweet little apartment?" She called behind her to Thothmes' Steward. "Bring a chair for the Second Wife! Set it on the other side of the couch. Now, Aset, sit. Sit!" The girl collapsed onto the chair, but she kept her face averted until Hatshepsut hissed, "Look at him! He has raised you up and given you more treasure and more love than it is any woman's privilege to receive in many lifetimes. Yet you turn your head from him as if he were a poor beggar at the gates of the temple! If he wakes, he shall find your eyes upon him in adoration, faithless one!"

Aset, white to the lips, obeyed.

But Thothmes did not wake. Toward midnight he began to whimper pitifully, like a wounded dog, the tears running down his face. Hatshepsut took the flailing hands in her own, holding them strongly, surely, and he sighed. But he went on breathing in little gasps, his eyelids fluttering. When the horns sounded the passing of midnight, he died, still crying, his tears soaking the bed and her fingers.

Long after the rattle in his throat had sounded, she sat staring at him, the fat boy she had loved to tease, the grumpy youth she had lightly despised, the Pharaoh who had been less to her than her own ministers. In his death she felt the pity for him that she had never felt in his life. For what had he ever been, Thothmes the Second? What had he ever done, save that which any man could do, father children? She wept a little for him, quietly, the man who had genially and clumsily amounted to nothing more than the stiffening corpse with an overpowering odor, the tears still glistening on his round cheeks. She opened his fingers and withdrew her hand. It seemed unbelievable that Pharaoh was dead. Only last week he had bagged thirty geese, and now the lifeless hands that had grasped the throwing-stick with such delight lay curled like claws upon his still breast.

She stood and addressed the shocked company. "Send for the sem-priests, and when they have taken him away, see that his linen is thoroughly washed, and his couch as well."

Aset was still slumped on the stool, an expression of dull unbelief on her face. Hatshepsut went to her, raising her gently. "Go to your son," she said kindly. "He loved you both, and for the time being his ban on your movements is lifted. Go where you will." Aset left the room woodenly, as if in the middle of a deep dream.

At last Hatshepsut went, too. Thothmes' death seemed unreal to her, as if tomorrow she would wake to the same round of routine while he hunted and in the evening they would dine together as usual, baiting one another good-humoredly. It was almost an affront to find that nothing outside the fetid, gilded room had changed at all.

All Egypt was stunned. It was a bad time of the year for a Pharaoh to die, particularly a young and healthy one. The harvest drew rapidly to a close, and men had nothing to do but sit and gossip and watch the river rise. It was inevitable that many conflicting rumors would begin to circulate.

Hatshepsut was aware of them all. One day toward the end of the period of mourning she sent for Thothmes' physician, bidding her judges, Aset, and little Thothmes to be present also. When they had come, she wasted no time.

"It has come to my ears," she said directly, "that certain foul and slanderous rumors have been put abroad. Since we have all heard them,

I will not sully my mouth with them. Physician, how did my brother die?"

The man did not hesitate. "He died of a plague, Majesty. Of that I have no doubt whatsoever."

"Is it possible to administer any poison that would produce the same symptoms that he showed?"

The physician shook his head. "I have been treating all kinds of illnesses for many years, Majesty, and I know of no such poison."

"You see before you documents. Are you willing to swear by Amun, by Osiris, on the names of your ancestors, that Pharaoh died a natural death?" Hatshepsut cast a keen glance at Aset, who stood silently, her bird's eyes on the man's face.

He nodded confidently. "I will so swear."

"Do you fear me, Noble One?"

He smiled at her. "Majesty, I am an old man, and I fear no one now but Anubis and his judgment. My words are true. Horus died of the plague. It is that simple."

"Then sit, and affix your seal to all the papers. My heralds will deliver them to every city and town in the country. From this day any who speaks to the contrary will die." All saw her look meaningly at Aset, who shifted her weight and drew Thothmes closer to her. The judges nodded and murmured. She asked them if they were satisfied. They chorused their assent, bowing low to her, and went out. Aset, too, left without a word.

The funeral was almost an afterthought. Thothmes the Second went to his grave near Hatshepsut's lovely temple, leaving hardly a ripple on the surface of Egypt. Long before the cortege straggled over the sand, it was as if he had never been, but for the children who walked solemnly behind the coffin. Neferura and her mother, in mourning blue, were first; Aset and Thothmes were relegated to the rear, where the harem women wailed and tore at their linens. Mutnefert had been allowed to follow the coffin with Hatshepsut, and she cried pitifully all the way, her grief a distressing thing to see. Hatshepsut thought sadly that no one but Mutnefert brought true sorrow to the hole in the cliff and the pretty mortuary temple where Thothmes' likeness already waited for the offerings and prayers of his people. Mutnefert carried a great armful of flowers to lay in the tomb. Neferura also buried her head in her posy, her face expressionless and her thoughts hidden from the beautiful woman who held her hand and walked beside her so silently. As they waited while the coffin was stood upright and Menena came with the Sacred Knife to begin the Opening of the Mouth, Hatshepsut pondered all the funerals she had seen: her sister's, her mother's, her father's, and now her brother's. It seemed to her that she, and only she, would go on living, young and strong and unscathed, forever.

After the four prescribed days of ritual and mystery, she bent in the tomb to bid farewell to Thothmes. She looked about at all his belongings but felt no power emanating from them as she had upon Neferu-khebit's burial or her father's. She saw nothing on which her eyes could rest in memory or regret. In death he was as ineffectual and weak as he had been in life. When she saw Aset throw herself on the coffin in a flood of tears, she wondered whether the emotion sprang from true love or from fear of what the years would bring to her son without the benevolent protection of Pharaoh.

Over the next few weeks Egypt waited for the Queen to ratify Thothmes the Third's claim to the throne and declare herself Regent until the child had grown. Those closest to her were not surprised when the expected announcement did not come. The great wheels of government went on turning as always. The Queen held audiences and received ambassadors. She prayed and hunted, danced and feasted, as if Aset and her child did not exist.

Aset herself had spent the days following the funeral in restless terror, expecting at any moment to hear that she was exiled with little Thothmes. As time went by and her fears abated, she began to put out feelers, trying to discover the Queen's mind. On each occasion she found her way politely but firmly blocked. She retired to her rooms, mystified and uneasy. Hatshepsut had said nothing about putting her back under the ban, and so she paced her garden furiously, anger replacing fright. Still the Queen did not reaffirm her son's kingship. She decided to take matters into her own hands.

One morning, as Hatshepsut, together with Senmut, Ineni, and Hapuseneb, was beginning the correspondence for the day, Duwa-eneneh, her Chief Herald, burst in upon them. He was out of breath, wild-eyed. He had scarcely begun to stammer when Ipuyemre, Second Prophet of Amun, followed him. Menena sidled into the room, his hands crossed over his smooth paunch, an expression of pious joy on his oily face.

"Down, all of you!" Senmut roared. "This is not a beerhouse!" At his loud reminder all sank to the floor.

"Rise," Hatshepsut said equably. Her quick mind darted from one to the other, trying to find the reason for the interruption, but they still stood silently. "Ipuyemre, my friend, you seem to be the most composed," she said. "You may speak, seeing that I have sworn never to hold any conversation with the First Prophet of Amun."

He bowed, and as he spoke, she saw his hands tremble, though he tried to hide them. "There has been a great sign, Majesty, this morning in the temple. The Crown Prince was performing his duties as acolyte, together with the other boys and the High Priest, and Mighty Amun bowed to him!"

Hapuseneb sucked in his breath, hissing. Ineni dropped his scroll, its faint rustle echoing in the silence. Though Senmut felt his heart stop, he did not move. But his eyes were burning and fixed on Menena's face. The High Priest did not waver, but his lips twitched.

Hatshepsut also stood quite still, her hands frozen on the Seal, the sun picking lights on her golden collar as she breathed. Then she relaxed and smiled quizzically. "Indeed?" she purred, walking to Nehesi and handing him the Seal. "And what conclusions do you draw from this—this sign?"

"Why, that Amun is pleased with the Prince," the man stammered.

Her smile widened. "My dear Ipuyemre, you are ever faithful and loyal, but you fear me overmuch, as of course you should. Duwa-eneneh! I thank you for your hurried entrance, and now please tell me exactly what passed."

The Herald tucked his staff under one arm and bowed, his handsome lips compressed and his liquid eyes hard. "The Prince was praying, and he asked Amun if indeed he should be Pharaoh as his father wished."

"And then?" She seemed to be enjoying some private joke. Her mouth warmed, and her eyes twinkled, but behind it all Senmut sensed tension.

"Then, after a moment, Amun bowed his golden head." Duwa-eneneh spoke flatly and unemotionally. He could have been describing the food he had eaten that morning. He and Hapuseneb caught each other's eye and smiled.

"Amun bowed his golden head," she repeated, her fingers pyramided to her lips, as if she thought. "Duwa-eneneh, find the Prince and his mother, and bring them here immediately. Menena, get out. Wait in the hall. Ipuyemre, you may stay."

When the Herald and the High Priest had gone, she turned swiftly to the other men. "Well?" she asked, her eyebrows raised.

Ineni spoke. "It is, of course, quite true," he told her. "The sign has been given, else Menena and the priests would not be so public about it. But—"

"It is a trick!" Nehesi swore savagely. "The God bows to no one but you, Mighty One!"

"I know," she said, "for many bow to the God and do not bend their hearts with their heads."

"I also think it is a ruse," Hapuseneb said. "Who was with the boy when it happened?"

"Menena, of course," Senmut answered promptly.

"And the other boys," Ipuyemre reminded him.

"In that case," Hatshepsut said softly, "there are more anxious priests in the temple than we had thought, for if Menena was with the boy, who was behind Amun, in the sanctuary?"

They all looked at Ipuyemre, but he shook his head. "I do not know," he said helplessly. "I was without, in the inner court, with the holy dancers, and I saw the boy and the God only from a distance."

Duwa-eneneh returned with Aset and Thothmes. Aset was clearly excited; two spots of color burned in her cheeks, under the paint, and her body seemed tighter and more feline than ever. Thothmes was solemn. He went and bowed to his aunt-mother, giving her a whiff of the incense he had borne a short while ago.

"Greetings, Thothmes," she said. "I have heard of the favor the God accorded you, and I wish to know more. Tell me about it."

The child's clear eyes met her own. He had been warned by his mother that the Queen did not like him, that she wished he were not in the palace so that she could rule on her own. But he found it hard to hate this tall, lovely lady whose face was so perfect that he wanted to look at it for a long time.

"I was praying. I pray often, you know," he added defiantly.

She nodded. "Of course you do. It is right and good to pray." She encouraged him with a gentle smile.

He felt his courage rise. "I decided to ask Amun for his advice," he chirruped. Suddenly it seemed to the men listening that Thothmes had begun to parrot a lesson well-learned. "I held the incense high and begged him to tell me if I was to be Pharaoh."

"Did you? And what did he say?"

"He smiled on me, and then he bent his gracious head. He bent it very low, until his chin fell on his immortal breast. All those around me saw it."

"Hmmm. Tell me, Thothmes, who am I?"

He looked bewildered, and his lip curled. "You are the Queen of Egypt."

"And who else am I?"

"I—I do not know."

"Then I will tell you, seeing that your mother has seen fit not to do so. I am also the Daughter of Amun, his very Incarnation here on earth, fruit of his holy loins, his beloved, whom he loved before I was born. His thoughts are my thoughts, and his will is my will. Do you think that he would tell you that you could be Pharaoh without my knowledge?"

Aset made a half-strangled sound and stepped forward.

Thothmes shook his head, puzzled. "N—no, I suppose not. Then what did he mean?"

"He meant that he is happy with you. He wants you to work hard for him and for Egypt, and perhaps one day you may be Pharaoh. But not yet."

"Not yet?" His lips quivered, and he stilled them angrily. "But I am Crown Prince. That means that I must be Pharaoh!"

"When Amun tells me that he wants you for Pharaoh, then I will tell you, but it will not be for a long time. You are still only a little Prince, and you have much to learn before the Horus Throne can be yours. Do you understand?"

"Yes!" he snapped. "But, Majesty, I am a quick learner!"

She looked down into the mutinous face. "So you are, for you are in every way like your mighty grandfather, my father, Thothmes the First. Now go to your rooms. I want to speak more with your mother."

He left, his shoulders back and his shaved head held high.

Hatshepsut ordered Menena to be admitted again. She was holding her temper with difficulty, striving to be just in the face of this silly bid for power. When Menena took his place beside Aset, she found that she had gone utterly cold. "The God bends his head to no one but me," she said. "All Egypt has known this since the day I was born. You have tried a filthy, despicable trick on a little boy who believes in his God. You have dishonored Amun, but you have failed to do anything more than cause a small flurry in the places where men have nothing more to do than feed on gossip. If you thought to force my hand, then you are foolish and naïve. Did you imagine that I would rush to place the crown on Thothmes' head and then leave my country in the hands of such as you?" She smiled scornfully. "You are beneath my contempt."

Aset had listened restlessly, her hands fluttering in her linens. Suddenly she burst out, "My son is Crown Prince and the rightful heir to the throne! His father made it so!"

"And he is dead!" Hatshepsut flashed back. "While he yet lived, I was Egypt, and I am still Egypt! Little Thothmes would be as soft silver in your hands, and between you, you would milk my beloved country dry. Did you think that at your call the priests and soldiers would follow? Have you been wandering in blindness for the past seven years?" She flung up her hands. "This has been your last chance. My patience is becoming exhausted. I wish to hear of no more plots. If I do, I will have no hesitation in charging you with treason and having you both executed. You are a danger to the country you both profess to love. Now get out."

Aset would have spoken again. Her mouth was working and her eyes spat venom at Hatshepsut. But Nehesi moved forward, and they bowed hastily and went out.

"You are too lenient, Majesty," Senmut said. "Snakes should be trampled underfoot."

"Perhaps," she said wearily. "But I do not wish to deprive my nephew-son of his natural mother so soon after the passing of his father. I do not believe that Menena can do much without Thothmes to back him. Nehesi, make sure that the Followers of His Majesty keep them well guarded at all times. Senmut, I want the name of every priest serving in the temple, from the smallest acolyte to Menena himself, and the persuasions of each one. I have not yet made up my mind what I shall do, but I am loathe to give the crown to Thothmes yet."

20

It took her two years to make up her mind. In that time she ceaselessly tested her hold on Egypt, pulling gently on a rein here, snapping a trace there, drawing tighter a trailing leather strap. Then it was Mechir, when the earth was covered between the palms and acacia with a lush, waving carpet of green crops and the young birds struggled to fly from the nests along the riverbank. Canals new and old crisscrossed the swaying fields, full of calm water that mirrored the soft, late spring sky. The Nile hippopotami and their young lay contentedly in the mud, yawning now and then for sheer delighted ease.

The temple in the valley was complete. The last of the conscripted laborers had gone back to their villages and farms. The rubble had been cleared away, and the remaining mud huts had been razed. The lovely, liquid building glowed, shimmering in its hot stone cup, waiting for the feet of the Holy One to grace its gold and silver floors. Hatshepsut had commissioned the brooding Tahuti to construct another shrine within its walls, the shrine of Nubia, in secret, dark ebony, to commemorate her victory there. He had also designed inner doors of cedar and bronze, but it was in the creation of the great outer doors that he had displayed all his skill. They were of black copper, solid and a little forbidding, daunting those who would come in later years with anything but love in their hearts. They were inlaid cunningly with electrum, the amalgam of gold and silver so loved by Hatshepsut. Now they stood open, taking the light of the sun and transforming it into deep shafts of muted gold that pierced the trees, and she thought of them as she stood on her balcony on the morning of dedication.

The priests had chosen the twenty-ninth day of the month as the auspicious day. She stood, looking over the garden, saying her morning prayers. Behind her, in her bedchamber, her servants laid out the short kilt whose pleats were lined with gold so that as she moved she would spark light, and the ceremonial wig of gold and blue braids, and the belt of knotted gold rope studded with tiny carnelian ankhs. She watched the priests gather in the courtyard before the first tall pylon, milling in its shadow, their white linens dazzling in the sun. Though she caught a glimpse of Menena in his leopard skin, her words of praise to her God did not falter.

A sense of fate was on her this morning, a feeling that today her destiny would change once more. She felt the power fill her and mingle with the blood that coursed through her veins. She knew herself to be immortal, standing high above the world, naked, benisoned with the sun that poured unceasingly over her honey-colored skin. The treetops seemed to dip and toss in homage to her as her prayers took to the wind. At last she had finished. With a final sweeping glance over the grounds and the river and, across it, the Necropolis dancing on the heatwaves she walked into the cool shadows where the women waited to clothe her.

She stood still while the kilt was fitted around her waist and the belt and the heavy jeweled collar that swept down to her breasts were gently fastened. She held out her arms while her bracelets and bands were slipped on, her mind wandering over the years of waiting while, day after day, the stones and pillars were cut, polished, and erected and the times she had stood with Senmut and Thothmes while the terraces took shape. She thought proudly of the marvels she had seen with her father. Thus have I answered you, gods of the Plains. I give you my monument, a work far greater than any I have yet seen. I am content.

She sat, holding her hands palms upward so that they could be painted with the red henna. While they dried, she lifted her feet, and the soles and nails were painted also. Her golden sandals were put on, the jaspers on them already greedily sucking all light from the room and throwing it out again, as red as living blood. Her face was made up and powdered with gold dust that stuck to her lips and eyelashes and the thick black kohl that rimmed her eyes. As she gazed at her glittering image in the mirror, she was reminded again of her haughty ka. She smiled, thinking of him leaning negligently over her shoulder while the wig was lifted and settled on her head and the Cobra Coronet was slipped into place. She was changed into a Goddess, the golden, shining symbol of a golden, shining country.

Senmut and the others were waiting for her on the water steps. A hundred boats, beribboned and beflagged, waited also to take the court and the priests across the river. He was attired as the Prince he had become. His helmet was white leather embossed in gold. His bracelets and bands of office shone startlingly against his dark brown skin, and a great gold pectoral of linked chains and turquoise scarabs covered his shoulders, his neck, and his back. On the smooth, deep chest rested the emblem of the Erpa-ha Princes, the Hereditary Lords of Egypt. Before him his staff bearer waited, a white, gold-tipped stick in his hand. Ta-kha'et stood with the women, still cuddling the cat, which now wore a collar of crystal. She was in a filmy blue linen sheath. It was only when Senmut was about to embark that he noticed and wondered why she should wear the color of mourning on such a happy day.

One by one the boats were poled across the Nile, now a clear, swift-flowing river that was still sinking and would not reach its lowest ebb until high summer. On the opposite bank the crowds began to form into a procession, laughing and chattering under the vast canopies and flags that lined the road that had once been only a track. Hatshepsut took the lead. She had decided to walk, so all had left their litters behind. As she saw Senmut about to slip into line with Hapuseneb, Menkh, and her other glittering ministers, she beckoned him. He came quickly to the front of the ranks, a question in his kohl-ringed eyes.

"Where is Neferura?"

"She walks with the women, Majesty, surrounded by the Followers of His Majesty, and Nehesi walks beside her. The little one is on a litter. I thought it best that she should ride."

She nodded. "Good." Meryet-Hatshepset was only three, and such a progress, however slow, would tire her. Hatshepsut moved to one side, smiling. "This is your day as well as mine, Noble One. I have decided to share my glory with you. You may walk beside me." Shocked, he stepped to her side. She signaled for the horns to sound. "Without a doubt," she continued as they began to move, "your hand is in the temple as well as mine. I have thought on it, Senmut, and I want you to inscribe your name within the holy walls so that men may know how highly I have placed you and in what esteem I hold you."

He turned to her and bowed. They strode on, but his mind seethed. Such an honor was so rarely bestowed that he could think of only one other instance of it, and that was on the plain of Saqqara where King Zoser had allowed the God Imhotep to sign his mighty works with his own name. It was a gift that went beyond this world, for the gods would see the name on a place where only royal names were cut. They would judge him as a King. He knew where he wanted to put that name and the story of his life and his titles; he would put them behind the door of the inner sanctuary, where none would see them save the gods and the royal people who were the only ones allowed to enter the sanctuary and close the door, a privilege that not even the priests enjoyed. "You honor me indeed, Majesty," he said lightly.

She laughed, turning her golden head to meet his eye. "I have not finished with you yet, proud and mighty Prince!" They reached her first and only pylon and passed beneath it, joking and bantering all the way.

She stopped, drinking in her masterpiece with greedy, worshiping eyes, and the whole procession straggled to a halt behind her. Another hundred paces and the first ramp rose gently to the roof of the first terrace. Below it, on each side, the pillars stood in neat rows, letting the light flow between them and on into the echoing vastness of the first hall. With fifty paces more the second ramp rose. Again it led to the roof of another hall whose white pillars gleamed. It brought the eye to the final pillars of the shrines and on gently to the top of the hill, as if temple and valley and cliff were one, a strong and mellow harmony of natural stone and man-made melody.

No gardens were yet laid. The avenue that Hatshepsut had planned, which would run to the very edge of the river, was still only in her mind; but the rock and stone of the temple, in their unadorned simplicity, needed no addition to their powerful, gentle lines to make them more beautiful. She sighed, a gusty sound of satisfaction. She had had a golden likeness of Amun made to sit beside her own image in the center sanctuary, and she signaled for the litter bearing the God to go before her. The priests approached with their heavy burden. Young Thothmes had been chosen to walk beside Amun, bearing the incense. They started off again, Hatshepsut's eyes on the child's stocky brown legs beneath the little kilt. Slowly they reached the first ramp, where they stopped to pray. They flowed onto the second ramp, and the prayers were repeated, Menena's deep, musical voice carrying to those in the rear of the cavalcade and echoing from the sun-drenched cliffs. Hatshepsut entered the dimness of her shrine in a sober frame of mind, remembering how she and her brother had planned to enjoy this day together. Even now he watched through the magic eyes of his coffin, and she wondered what he was thinking of the most beautiful construction Egypt had ever seen.

Amun was settled on the raised throne that awaited him beside the gigantic, gold-plated statue of herself, its eyes seeming to pierce even the farthest corners of the temple. Young Thothmes placed the incense crucible in the tall copper stand made ready for it while another acolyte did the same on the opposite side of the shrine. Then all who had been admitted to the holy of holies lay on the new silver floor, making their obeisance to the two gods who dominated their lives. Menena strode through the prostrate bodies to stand beside Amun, and the rites of dedication began. The priests clustered in the sun on the roof of the first terrace, listening to the chants and the rattle of sistrums and menyts and charging their own incense burners. Below them, standing silently about the first ramp, the members of the court craned their necks to watch the smoke rising straight, spiraling to the cliff top in that sheltered place.

When it was all over, and Hatshepsut had walked in ceremony through every inch of her living dream, she knelt before Amun once more, saying her final prayers with a feeling that all was not yet finished. The Sun had changed his position, his long, silken fingers probing the floor of the sanctuary and exploring the inner pillars, reaching for the two statues. Those standing behind Hatshepsut saw her as never before, her golden head, her gold-powdered skin, her gold-decked, outstretched arms shimmering, haloed in fire. A silence fell. Thothmes bowed to Amun and recharged the incense. Menena gathered up his staff, and the nobles began to shuffle, thinking of the meal that was to follow, their throats dry from singing. But Hatshepsut continued to adore and to wait, knowing urgently that something must happen. As she sank to the ground for the last time, a pure, ringing voice issued from the lips of the idol, and the company froze.

"Rise and depart, Beloved King of Egypt," it said.

In the stunned quiet Hatshepsut's head jerked back. The memories, ambitions, frustrations, and dreams of all the years behind her flew to a point and exploded in a loud cry of triumph. She rose and wheeled about, her arms above her head. "He has spoken!" she shouted, every nerve taut with victory. Below, in the courtyards, the people heard the commotion and turned anxious eyes on one another. "I proclaim myself Pharaoh!"

"She cannot!" Yamu-nefru muttered sharply to his friend as they stood in the shadows, jolted from his usual cool languor.

Suddenly the nobles began to applaud. A ripple of claps ran around the sanctuary and turned into a river of sound. They were on their feet, cheering, calling for her. She pushed her way through them, Nehesi and Senmut beside her, her arms still extended and her face radiant. They burst into the open, and the acclamation became a roar as those outside took it up and surged toward her. The temple became a seething mass of white-clad bodies.

"I proclaim myself Pharaoh!" she shouted again.

The vibrant words echoed and reechoed, multiplied a hundred times as the crowds took it up. "Pharaoh! Pharaoh! Pharaoh!" they screamed.

Neferura watched with wondering eyes as her mother was lifted onto the litter that had so lately held the God and raised high over the upturned faces. Aset and Thothmes stood to one side; she was stunned and undone. They were swept forward by the press of excited bodies and found themselves behind the litter, surrounded by Followers of His Majesty. The tumult swelled around them as Hatshepsut was carried back to the river. She tore the little Cobra from her head, holding it high; then in one swift movement she leaned down and thrust it into Neferura's reaching hands.

She sat upright, smiling, and they took her aboard the Royal Barge and back to the palace, to a new beginning.

As she stood alone in the darkness on her balcony on the eve of her crowning, she thought, The years of work and worry and waiting have borne fruit. At last I am what my father intended me to be. There is no one in the whole of Egypt who can oppose me. Thothmes is gone. Aset and Menena have lost the race. My destiny is fulfilled. I am stronger than ever, more beautiful and more powerful than ever, the first woman worthy to be Pharaoh. She thought of Neferura, fast asleep on her little couch, the Cobra Coronet still held tightly in her hands, and of young Thothmes, his dreams of the crown now eclipsed by her brilliant presence, her unequaled strength, and her total control. Tonight none had reality but she and her God. They communed, there in the night, both looking back to the happenings that had brought forth this day. She was not tired. There were still deep, untapped wells of strength in her, waiting until her crowning to be unleashed. She felt as immortal as the stars that shone on her and the land that dreamed under her. She remained on her balcony for most of the night, sipping cold wine, watching the guards patrol her gardens, seeing an occasional, swift-moving dot of light as some priest hurried to the temple to perform his duties. When the night began to thin, she went to her couch, lying with eyes open, gazing at her blue and silver, star-spattered ceiling, her mind busy with all that she would do.

The barber came in the morning, carrying his sharp knives. She sat motionless while her lovely black tresses were cut, falling around her chair like a soft carpet. As Nofret carefully gathered each lock, she gazed at herself in the mirror. The man sharpened his razor and began to shave her head. He was silent and skillful and did not draw blood. She watched her face change under his hands. With a scalp now clean she looked sexless, the strong bones of her face standing out, the eyes seeming even larger and more luminous, the mouth more haughty, less able to smile. When barber had gone, Nofret lifted to her head the leather helmet that she would wear until the Double Crown took its place. Its wings sat on her shoulders, and its rim cut across her forehead, bringing a new severity and simplicity to her face. Nofret fastened the royal Eye of Horus around her neck; it hung heavily, hiding her breasts. Her guard opened the door and admitted Senmut, again arrayed in princely garb. He had Neferura by the hand. She was dressed richly, in gold and lapis lazuli. She had placed the Cobra on her shaved head, but her youth-lock hung awkwardly under it and set it at a jaunty angle. As she and Senmut prostrated themselves, it wobbled dangerously.

Smiling, Hatshepsut told them to rise. "No, dear one," she said gently to Neferura. "You are not yet a Queen. I hope one day to make you a King, but even so, you cannot wear the Cobra yet."

"But can I keep it in my rooms and look at it sometimes?" the child asked as she removed the coronet.

"If you promise not to take it outside or let Meryet play with it. Well, priest, are we ready?"

Senmut looked at the tall, glowing youth before him, at the male helmet and the Horus Eye and the royal rings. He bowed deeply. "We are. Your standards are without, and the flags fly high. The route is lined with people."

"And my chariot?"

He smiled. "In the courtyard, Majesty, and Menkh is impatient."

"He is always impatient! Then we will go."

Outside the sun was hot. She sprang up behind Menkh, straddling her legs and holding onto the chariot's golden sides as the cheering began. He twirled his whip, and the horses began to trot. But they did not move quickly, for Hatshepsut had decided to ride through the city so that all could see her. The glittering procession slowly wended its way up and down the streets. Children threw flowers, and their parents kissed the paving stones before the God who seemed to have shed the softness of her womanhood and stood as tall and as lean as a young male.

In the temple, when the time came, she herself removed the helmet and held out her hands for the crown, taking it from the gods who offered it. Senmut had a moment of shock at the sight of her naked head. Somehow it served to bring home to him for the first time the fact that she was indeed sexless and ageless within herself. As she slowly settled the smooth red and white Double Crown on her head and took the Flail and the golden Crook from Menena's hands, the fiery Uraeus, the cobra and the vulture of kingship, reared suddenly anew above features that were indomitably, distinctly the features of a Pharaoh. The heavy jeweled robe was draped about her.

After Menena had led her once more around the sanctuary, she turned and faced the gathering. "I take to myself all titles of my father," she said. "Herald!"

Duwa-eneneh stepped forward and recited them. "Horus, Beloved of Maat, Lord of Nekhbet and Per-Uarchet, He Who Is Diademed with the Fiery Uraeus, Great One of Double Strength, the Horus of Gold, Beautiful of Years, Making Hearts to Live, King of the South and North, Hatshepset, Living Forever."

Senmut noted that Duwa-eneneh had omitted Mighty Bull of Maat, and he smiled to himself.

She went on, lifting her chin high. "I also take to myself the title given to me by Amun at my first coronation. I am Maat-Ka-Ra, Son of the Sun, Child of the Morning. Usert-kau is my throne name, and I have decided that henceforth Hatshepset is no name for a King. I will be known as Hatshepsu, First Among the Mighty and Honorable Nobles of the Kingdom."

Senmut smiled again at this purely feminine vanity. His King had not become wholly male.

The Pharaonic beard was strapped to her chin. Instead of prompting laughter, it emphasized her power in a curious way as it could never have done on the chin of a man. Hatshepsu the First, King of Egypt, walked slowly out of Karnak into the spring sunshine, her lovely face, smooth and inscrutable as marble. She was expressionless before the homage of the soldiers. They had waited in the outer court to perform their own worship at the feet of the warrior who had led them into Kush and home again. She got back into the chariot and rode to the palace.

Before the feasting began, she sat on the Horus Throne, the Crook and Flail crossed on her breast, and her men gathered before her. In a moment of perversity she summoned Thothmes and made him sit on the steps at her feet. He obeyed, but she was keenly aware of his stiff back and his glowering, angry little face.

"Well," she said, smiling, "let us begin. How could I forget you, most faithful ones, on this my most holy day? Senmut, come forward!"

He crawled over the golden floor to her feet, and she herself got up and helped him to rise. The form was thus observed, but beneath the protocol of centuries her love for him shone out.

"For you, favorite of the King, Keeper of the Door, I have titles. I make you Overseer of all works of the House of Silver, Chief of the Prophets of Montu, Servant of Nekhen, Prophet of Maat, and last of all Smer, Revered Noble of Egypt."

One by one the cloaks of power dropped around him. The others, watching and listening, knew once and for all who shared complete power in Egypt; and they looked at Senmut's proud, closed face warily, feeling themselves cut off from him. He bowed and stepped to her side.

She beckoned Hapuseneb. "You with the secret," she said to him, "do you remember the day when I made you Chief of the Prophets of South and North?"

"I remember it well, Majesty. That was before you routed the inhabitants of Kush."

She nodded. "Nehesi, have Menena brought before me."

Hapuseneb knew what was to come. The others waited, breathless, until the aging High Priest had slid to the foot of the throne and made his homage.

Hatshepsut spoke mildly, but her eyes glinted at him frostily beneath the towering Double Crown. "Menena, a High Priest can be appointed only by the order of Pharaoh himself. Is it not so?"

He paled but bowed. "It is so," he said quietly.

"And I am now Pharaoh. I here appoint the Vizier Hapuseneb as High Priest of Amun, to take up the staff I gave him those years ago and to wield it now with authority. To you, Menena, I offer the thanks of the Hawk-Who-Has-Risen-to the-Sun, and I order you to leave Thebes before the end of Phamenoth."

She had finished with him. He bowed again and left, his composure as unruffled as always. Hatshepsut looked after him for a moment, remembering her father's unexplained hatred for the man, and her eye caught the glance that Senmut gave him in passing. Her Steward's face was full of loathing and fear. Startled, she filed the new information away for later reference. Senmut knew what she did not, and one day she must know, too.

She made Nehesi her Chancellor, an appointment that all expected and that followed naturally from his position as Bearer of the Royal Seal. Into Tahuti's hands she placed the distribution of all tribute. Puamra, the wanderer, she made Inspector of Monuments. Then it was User-amun's turn. She called him, and he approached her smiling. But after she had helped him to rise, she ordered him once more to the floor. "Many, many years ago," she said, "you bowed thus to me in mockery, irrepressible one, and I swore to you that one day you would repeat your words to me in earnest. Do you remember what they were?"

A ripple of laughter ran round the room as User-amun shook his head with difficulty, his nose against the paving. "Truly, Great Horus, my foolishness escapes my memory. May I beg your pardon most humbly?"

"Anen!" She was laughing now. "Read to me the words that I caused you to write."

The scribe got up from his position by her left foot, and solemnly intoned, "Hail Majesty! Your beauty is more dazzling to behold than the beauty of the stars. Ah! My eyes fail, and I cannot look thereon!"

"Now repeat!" she said, her shoulders heaving, and he did, his voice rising muffled from the floor. "Now you may rise," she said at last, and he sprang up, smiling broadly.

"Your Majesty has an infallible power of recollection," he remarked.

She nodded coolly. "Of course. And for you, bright bird, I have a tour of your father's Vizierate in the South, which you have neglected too much of late, preferring to chase my maids."

The granting of privileges and awards went on. At last the sun sank, and the horns sounded for dinner. She rose, visibly tired under the weight of the almost insupportable coronation robe. "Let us eat together," she said, looking deep into each of them in turn, "and then let us continue the work which we have begun in Egypt. No man shall say in future times that this land suffered under us!"

They went to the hall together, all crowding onto the dais to drink her health. Not one of them, with the exception of the wary Senmut, noticed that Yamu-nefru and Djehuty, with Sen-nefer, ate huddled in a corner behind a protecting lotus column. They did not laugh. Not far from them Thothmes and his mother stared with hard, bitter eyes at the bright company on the dais.

Toward midnight Hatshepsut shrugged off the heavy robe, clapped her hands, and the entertainments began. She had particularly wanted to see a troupe of dancers purchased by Hapuseneb in one of the coastal cities of the north. The men were acrobats as well as dancers, and they fascinated her with their leaps and somersaults, their gyrations always timed by their drums and their strange stringed instruments, which were not plucked like lutes but strummed. When they had finished and she had given them gold and made them repeat their performance, Hapuseneb gave them to her as a gift. She also delighted in a leopard that could perform tricks. It, too, was made hers. Until the small hours the best entertainers of the empire kept her enthralled while the wine goblets were filled and the slaves replenished the oil in the perfume cones on the heads of the guests. The banks and carpets of flowers were wilting in the heat from the lamps. Menkh, ever the fool, donned a dancer's thin linen and put on the girl's copper bracelets, prancing and mincing before Hatshepsut. She laughed but told him that she liked him better as her reckless charioteer. He retired, crushed, to his grinning comrades.

Hatshepsut rose for silence. "It is the time for rest," she said, "but before we go, I would like to hear a song from the great Ipuky, blessed singer of the gods. Help him, User-amun."

The old man came to the foot of the dais, leaning heavily on User-amun's shoulder. He was bent almost double now, hoary with age and often ill, but his voice had not lost its magic. Hatshepsut had given him a home and his own herb garden, a place where he could sit and smell the green things he could not see and end his days in peace of mind. He sat gratefully, settling the lute across his bony knees. They all waited in anticipation, watching the sightless eyes roll as his fingers sought the chords. At last he was ready.

At the first words Senmut turned to Hapuseneb in irritation. "It is the song dedicated to Imhotep!" he whispered fiercely. "Now why did he choose that one?" Hatshepsut hushed him crossly, and he retired to listen, mystified, as the solemn, awesome music flooded the great hall and fell in judgment on them all.

> Bodies pass away, and others remain since time of them that were before.
> The gods that were aforetime rest in their pyramids, and likewise the noble and the glorified,
> Buried in their pyramids.
> They that builded houses, their habitations are no more.
> What hath been done with them?
> I have heard the discourses of Imhotep and Hardedef, with whose words men speak everywhere.
> What are their habitations now?
> Their walls are destroyed, their habitations are no more, as if they had never been.
> None come from thence that he may tell us how they fare, that he may tell us what they need,
> That he may set our hearts at rest, until we also go to the place whither they are gone.
> Be glad, that thou mayest cause thine ear to forget that men will one day beautify thee.
> Follow thy desire, so long as thou livest.
> Put myrrh on thy head, clothe thee in fine linen, and anoint thee with the genuine marvels
> Of the things of the God.
> Increase yet more the delights that thou hast, and let not thy heart grow faint.
> Follow thy desire, and do good to thyself.
> Do what thou requirest upon earth, and vex not thine heart until that day of lamentation
> Comes to thee.
> Yet He with the Quiet Heart hears not their lamentation, and cries deliver no man
> From the underworld.

The last sad notes lingered in the heads of the drunken company, and there was no applause. Ipuky had expected none.

Hatshepsut stirred. "Thank you for the lesson, most wise one," she said. "Well it is for a King to remember such things on the day of his triumph."

He bowed his head quietly for a moment and got up, cradling his lute in both arms. User-amun helped him walk away from the dais, and then he disappeared into the shadows.

She dismissed them all and left them swiftly, shades of exhaustion under her eyes. They followed her, picking their way wearily through the mess of cushions, upturned goblets, and sprawling revelers to the quiet, torch-lit passages beyond.

21

She slept deeply for several hours, worn with the excesses of the day before. She woke easily a few minutes before dawn and sat up, waiting anxiously for the moment that would mean the culmination of all her strivings. She had Nofret place her chair so that she could see out her window to the eastern sky, and as she got off the couch and went to it, clutching her robe to her in the morning chill, she heard the High Priest, the Second High Priest, and the acolytes gathering outside in the corridor. At her order Nofret opened the door, and they stood reverently, Hapuseneb and Ipuyemre and little Thothmes and the others, filling the room with smoke. She sat motionless, gazing to the east as the rim of Ra trembled red on the horizon and the priests burst into the Hymn of Praise, glorifying her as his rays found her face: "Hail Mighty Incarnation, rising as Ra in the east! Hail, Emanation of the Holy One!"

She received their adoration, a tumble of pride and fierce, jealous possessiveness filling her. This was her birthright and nothing less: the throne, the land, the God. As the singing ended in a burst of praise, Ra lifted himself free of the clinging hands of night and began his daily journey. The doors closed again, and the priests went back to the temple to wait for her to come and perform the morning's prayers.

Nofret ordered her bath to be filled. One by one the guards admitted the princes and nobles who were permitted to watch Pharaoh at his ablutions. She slipped off the robe and walked past them, stepping down into the water, greeting each one and taking the opportunity to discuss the day's work while her slaves washed her. When the men had gone, she lay on her cedar board to be oiled, massaged, and scraped. Once dressed in kilt and helmet, the cobra and the vulture warning all she passed to touch her at their peril, she went to the temple to perform the rites for the first time as Pharaoh.

In the sanctuary, assisted by Horus and Thoth, she opened the shrine, taking the incense from Thothmes' hand and censing the God. She sprinkled him with water from his Sacred Lake, and laid his crown, insignia, and food before him. She listened to the priests' prayers for the health and safety of Pharaoh. As she did all these things, she was conscious of an undercurrent of supreme joy. She had always believed that this day would come. She had believed it mistily, with half-formed certainty, as a child. She had held onto the belief through the years of secret, subtle building, wondering for what purpose she squandered her talents while her husband lived like a butterfly. But now, locking the shrine and striding out into the sunlight, she knew.

Ineni sat in the audience chamber, where the day's dispatches were piled neatly on her table and Anen and the other scribes waited to take her orders for the day. He was looking drawn, the lines around the hawk nose and the straight mouth deeply etched. When she swept in, he bowed stiffly. He was troubled with aching joints and had pains in his hands; he did not pass her the first document as he usually did.

"What is it, my friend?" she asked him.

He bowed again uneasily. "Majesty, I can find no way of putting this. I want to resign my office as Treasurer."

She looked again into the worn face, noting its gray pallor. "Are you displeased with me, Ineni? Are my policies irksome to you?"

He smiled. "No. Nothing like that. But I grow old, and my duties are becoming too much for me. I will still build for you, but in my own time if you will permit it. As Mayor of Thebes I am already burdened more than my years can stand, and I want to spend more time at home with my family and to work on my tomb."

"You have served long," she admitted. "My father found you indispensable, and I must confess that I will sorely miss you here, for your knowledge is immense. Well," she sighed, "so be it. Retire with my blessing. Will you still dine with me sometimes?"

"As often as you wish!"

"Who will replace you? Can you recommend to me another Treasurer?" She had come directly to the point, but he had his answer ready.

"I suggest Tahuti. He is honest and very thorough, and though he is never troubled with flashes of genius, he plods steadily. Not one uten's weight will escape him."

"I agree. Tahuti, then. Duwa-eneneh, find him, and bring him here. He might as well begin immediately. Ineni, spend a month or two training him, and then I will let you go. Truly the old order changes!" She sighed. "While we are waiting, we might as well begin. What do we have this morning?"

Ineni selected a scroll. "There is a letter from Nubia, from Inebny, your Viceroy. He complains that his mines are working at their full capacity. When the taxes are collected, he can send no more gold than he has sent before. He says that he mentioned the matter to Your Majesty some time ago."

She frowned. "So he did. Years ago. I wonder how he has fared since then. Anen, draft a reply. Tell him that I thank him for his diligence and apologize for being so forgetful. Tell him also not to rape the mines; he can cut production for the time being. Prepare it, and Nehesi will seal it. Senmut, find someone to inspect the old mines in the Sinai Desert. It may be that there is still gold for the taking, though it has been many years since they were closed. Have a report for me within six months. And get me an engineer who can suggest the openings of new mines. What is next?"

The business was finished by noon, and she ate alone in her room before her afternoon sleep. She felt a little lonely, aware for the first time of the isolation complete authority brought her, but she would not have exchanged the Double Crown for a palace full of friends. She put her neck to her headrest and in the dim quiet closed her eyes with a prayer to Amun and a smile on her lordly mouth.

Before her first year as Pharaoh was out, she had redecorated the Pharaonic apartments, tearing down walls, pulling apart ceilings, and opening balconies. When she had finished, she moved into rooms that were bigger, higher, richer than before. She had left the floors alone, for they were plated in gold and quite free of all adornment. But she had her walls covered in solid silver into which Tahuti had beaten gigantic reliefs that ran from her blue-painted ceilings to the golden floors. When she lay on the great couch with its likeness of Amun at her head and its lion's paws at her feet, she could see her own face staring back at her from all three walls, her haughty chin bearing the beard of kingship, her eyes gazing levelly and with a cool superiority into the room, her forehead wide and serene under the Double Crown that bore the cobra and the vulture. Her doors were also of beaten silver, every one of them a solid plate from which the Eye of Horus looked out. In time she was surrounded by the dull, white gleam of that rarest of metals wherever she went. The polished silver in her audience chamber held other scenes. The walls were alive with motion, and from high on her throne she could see herself running, Flail and Crook in hand, while her enemies fled before her holy anger, or riding in her chariot, ax raised, while under the horses' hooves the inhabitants of Kush were ground to the dust. On the pillars in all the rooms of her suite were paintings of blue and pink lotuses whose stems wound to the roof and birds flying upward on red and yellow wings. She had more trees planted right against the sides of each of the rooms that opened directly onto the garden so that she could always smell the coolness and freshness of growing things.

Where the passage that took her from the banqueting hall to her apartments began and outside each of her doors, she set granite likenesses of herself, seated, her hands on her stone knees and face looking calmly down the halls, or standing, one foot before the other in an attitude of frozen movement. She deliberately left the stone unpainted, magnifying the impression of strength and divinity received by all who passed in and out of the heart of the palace.

She did not neglect Amun. His image glowed in every room, and before each image lay food and wine and flowers. Incense burned day and night before him, filling all the palace with misting gray smoke and the odor of myrrh.

She kept her architects, artists, stonemasons, and engineers busy. The avenue she had planned to run from the pylon of her temple to the river was laid, wide and smooth and solid. She ordered it to be lined with sphinxes, the holy lion bodies of the Sun-God, but the impassive faces that watched the worshipers going to and fro were all her own, beautiful and regal and aloof, framed in the flowing manes and topped with the tiny rounded ears of a lion. Pools and gardens were dug around the temple, and soon birds settled there. Butterflies, moths, and humming bees delighted in her flowers, but on her frequent trips across the river she felt that something was missing, that Amun was not altogether pleased with his Daughter's efforts to make his place of adoration more lovely than any other monument in Egypt. He had not yet told her why, and she waited contentedly, sure that she would know before long.

Tahuti made more gates for her. One she set on the western bank, at the arid and somehow desolate entrance to the Necropolis. Another, a vast plate of copper that had been consecrated and named the Terror of Amun, she erected in the temple at Karnak. All along the Nile the ravages the Hyksos had left were being lovingly restored under her direction. She had the pleasure of revisiting the pretty temple to Hathor at Cusae, walking through new gates into an outer court full of trees and paved paths and on into the sanctuary, where the smiling, gentle Goddess's priests once more lifted the censers. Hathor herself greeted her, repainted and restored to her rightful place before the white pillars of her sanctuary.

Puamra designed a new temple for her in Upper Egypt, this one to Pakht. He preened himself quietly when it was said that this building equaled the beauty of her beloved valley monument. On its walls she told the world of all she had done to build up that which was fallen in Egypt.

She began her biography on the long, sun-splashed walls of the terraces in the valley. The painters labored day after day under Senmut's watchful eye to record her miraculous conception, her royal birth, her crowning as Heiress with her father, and the mighty deeds of her life.

Senmut also spent much time in the rock-cut sanctuary, where his own artists painstakingly applied their brushes, setting down for all time his titles and his rise in the counsels of power. Senmut was not blinded by his success. He had quietly instructed the plasterers to inscribe his name under the layers of white plaster that preceded the paint, so that if ill times befell and his King lost the race that he felt convinced had only just begun, still the gods would know him. He stood watching in quiet satisfaction as it was done.

All over Egypt and far out in the desert Hatshepsut left monument after monument, stone piled upon stone. Everywhere her subjects looked, they saw her royal, dreaming likeness, reminding them that Pharaoh would never die; and the world marveled and worshiped her, the Son of the Sun.

In the painted, perfumed palace, in the towering temple, and in the fields, villages, and cities, Hatshepsut worked her will. With Hapuseneb as High Priest in the temple she had cunningly knitted together religion and government, sure now of no opposition from either.

Five years after her coronation Hapuseneb gave up his Vizierate to devote himself full time to his duties in Thebes. He still had not married. Many of Hatshepsut's women desired him, and many had made fools of themselves, coming up against his implacable, smiling gray eyes to be crushed in defeat. He treated them all with the same polite friendliness, but his many-pillared house, with its broad avenues sweeping to the river, remained empty of wives. Concubines he had, and some five or six children, but more often than not they never saw him. He moved quietly from temple to palace, and if he did go home, it was to recover, to sleep and to read.

In the same year that Hapuseneb resigned, User-amun's father died, and User-amun at last became Vizier of the South. He sobered quickly under the avalanche of work his father had been too ailing to do, but he had not lost his cheeky wit or his way with women. He was a terror and a delight in the palace, and Hatshepsut loved him.

One cold dawn Hatshepsut was brought the news that Mutnefert was dead. She was overwhelmed with surprise. She had forgotten the fat, lonely old woman who had never recovered from the death of her son and who had remained in her three rooms for the rest of her life. Mutnefert had never ceased to mourn Thothmes. Her tears and wailings had upset her harassed tiring-women for weeks, but slowly the loud cries of grief had given way to a silent, listless indifference to all save the memories of Thothmes and the prayers to the dead. She all but ceased to eat. Her jewels lay unworn and unwanted in their boxes, her rooms were no longer full of chatter and gossip, and no one visited her but Neferura, who came occasionally to sit quietly beside her couch and listen to the tales of long ago, when her father had been a prince and her mother a child. Mutnefert had always mistrusted Aset and had upbraided her son many times for bringing such a one into the palace. She had expressed no desire to see her grandson, but she had loved Neferura as well as she could love anyone in the twilight of her life, and for her the silences between them were full of comfort.

Neferura did not cry when her mother told her of Mutnefert's death. She just nodded. "My grandmother had died inside long before she died outside—because of my royal father," she soberly remarked to Hatshepsut. "Now she is happy, having her heart quietened by his presence. I will not mourn for her. She would be angry if I did."

So Mutnefert was laid in the splendid tomb prepared for her long ago by her husband, Thothmes the First, and Hatshepsut attended the funeral, still surprised that Mutnefert had lived on under the same roof as herself for so long and yet had been forgotten.

In the sixth year of Hatshepsut's reign, robbers were caught trying to break into her father's tomb. She was beside herself with anger. She sat in the Courts of Justice, white and fuming, while they were interrogated. Her thoughts flew to Benya, the only survivor of the excavation of the valley where her mother and her father and her brother lay. She sent for him and for Senmut, but she spoke to them privately, in her chambers.

"Six unhappy men are even now awaiting the executioner," she told them shortly. "They insist that none but they are involved in the desecration of the God my father, but how can I be sure?" She cast a dark look at Benya, pale and strained between his two guards, but his eyes met her steadily. He had grown into a handsome man and a mighty engineer, and she was the first to admit that there was none finer in Egypt. She turned to Senmut. "Many years have passed since my father saved your friend from death. How have his fortunes been since then?"

Senmut answered her angrily, aware that she was frightened and at a loss, but disappointed in her lack of trust. "Majesty, in all the years that have passed, Benya has been silent on this matter. If it were not so, then the God Thothmes would have been disturbed a long time ago. As for his fortunes, you had better ask him himself."

"I asked you. Do you give an impudent answer to your King?" But she was already sorry that she had summoned them, and she shook her head, mystified. "Benya's mouth is the only one still able to utter the words that would have sent these men scavenging like jackals. What else must I think?"

Benya had not lost his wits, and he answered her quietly. "What of those who followed the God to his tomb, Majesty? What of the women and the priests and all the others? Do you think that I would stoop to rob from the God who spared my life?"

"Oh, very well!" she snapped, waving her hands impatiently. "I did not think it was really you, Benya, and I am sorry that I had you arrested. Release him!"

The guards let him go and went out. He rubbed his wrists.

Senmut spoke. "Majesty, I advise you to move the body of your father and all his belongings. Put him somewhere safer."

Benya's face lit in a grin. "I will find him a true and proper tomb," he offered, his eyes sparkling. "Leave it to me." She gaped at him, astounded at his temerity, but after a moment they all laughed.

"The matter is serious, all the same," she warned. "Since you love to work so much, Benya, you may indeed see to it. I think that you should look to the cliffs behind my temple. There is much movement there, even at night, and none will dare to venture into a tomb that lies within earshot of my priests."

"A good idea, Majesty," Benya approved.

"And since you have presented yourself so precociously before me today," she went on, an imp of mischief in her face, "I have yet another task for you. I no longer wish to lie in the tomb Hapuseneb built for me. Tunnel from my shrine in the temple, Benya, far back behind my image and into the rock. There I shall lie close to those who worship me. I shall erect a likeness of my father to place in the shrine beside Amun's and my own. Thus can the people pray to all of us, for surely there is no mightier God than Amun and no greater Pharaoh than Thothmes and no more beautiful or able Incarnation of the God than I myself."

So Benya sweated once more in the valley that seemed to him to be consuming the better part of his life. He hewed the new tombs and soon the three statues stood side by side, their influence reaching far beyond their shrine, dwarfing all who stood before them.

The royal children thrived like healthy weeds. Thothmes became a priest, still serving every day in the temple, but all who looked on him doubted that he would remain there much longer. He was as stocky and strong as a young sycamore and already spent his afternoons in the barracks or watching the drills and exercises from the edge of the parade ground, his fists clenching and unclenching with frustration.

His mother was wisely biding her time. As she matured, Aset ceased to angle openly for her son's preferment; but her sly whispers, her sneaking innuendoes, her hints that young Thothmes would make as fine a Pharaoh as his grandfather had been fed softly into the ears of those who surrounded the young Prince. Though they shrugged, the seed brought forth a fruit that began, slowly and silently, to swell.

Hatshepsut dismissed all rumors of Aset's poisonous intrigues with a laugh. She was so firmly entrenched as Pharaoh that she believed herself to be at last immune, astride government and temple and holding on easily with knee and voice and whip. But Senmut, whose business as her Steward took him into many dark corners, was apprehensive, and Nehesi was more forthright.

"Majesty," he told her one day as they walked together from the audience hall to lunch on the grass by the verge of her lake, "it is time to take another look at young Thothmes."

"Another look?" she teased him, her red kilt swinging as her stride matched his own. "Why another? I see him everywhere: in the temple, eating everything in sight at my dinners, and kicking the dust and watching me as I take out my chariot. What else is there to see?" She laughed, and he saw the sunlight catch the gold embossing on her helmet as her head turned.

"He is growing," he replied tersely. "He tires of the everlasting chants of his fellows and the darkness of the sanctuary. He is restless, turning his eye to the soldiers who march in the sun."

"Pah! He is only twelve. You have been inactive for too long, Nehesi. Shall I make war so that you may fight again?"

"I know what I see," he replied stubbornly. "May I offer you my opinion, Most Divine One?"

She stopped suddenly in the middle of the path and turned to him in exasperation, her lips pursed. "If you must, and I see that you must."

"Already in the palace there springs a new generation of young ones: Thothmes and his friends Yamu-nedjeh, Menkheperrasonb, Min-mose, May, Nakht, and the others. Their blood is fresh and hot, and they have little to do but fidget in school and race around the grounds. Put Thothmes into the army, Noble One, and perhaps a few of his companions. Have him begin as a retainer, and work him hard. Do not leave him idle."

She searched his black face, surprised to see it full of expression. She often thought that his features lent themselves to sculpture as no others because of their supreme indifference, but now his eyes pleaded with her, and his hard lips were twisted. "Is this what you would do?"

His eyes slid away from her. "No."

"Then why give me advice you yourself would not follow? What would you do with my fiery little nephew-son?"

He moved abruptly. "Do not ask me, Majesty."

"But I must know! Tell me, Nehesi. Are you not my bodyguard and the Keeper of my Door?"

"Remember then, Holy One, that you asked," he said desperately. "If I were you, I would take steps to see that the Prince could nevermore be a thorn in my side, and I would send his mother right out of Egypt."

Her face gradually relaxed into an expression of watchful concentration, and her eyes probed him, sharp as the point of a lance. "Would you?" she said softly. "And do you not think, General, that the possibility has entered my head many times as I watch him spring up tall and fierce as his grandfather, able already though he is but twelve? But tell me, what would the God say of an action such as the one you suggest?"

"He would say that his Daughter has all law and all truth within her body because she is he."

She shook her head. "No, he would not. He would say, 'Where is my son Thothmes, blood of my blood? I see him not, at work or at play.' And he would punish."

"Majesty," Nehesi said, planting his feet squarely on the ground and meeting her black eyes, "you are wrong."

"Nehesi," she answered, challenging him with her gaze, "I am never, ever wrong."

They resumed their walk in silence, but before the week was out Thothmes, together with Nakht, Menkheperrasonb and Yamu-nedjeh, found himself a junior member of the Division of Set. He took to the training eagerly, as if he had been born to be a soldier.

Neferura also grew. She, too, was twelve, a willowy, pale, rather delicate reflection of her burning, vital mother, a good scholar, but a brooder who drifted in and out of the rooms of the palace on silent feet, her arms full of cats or puppies or flowers. Her youth-lock was gone, but somehow she stayed a child, her innocence mixed with an almost cold hauteur that made her difficult to know. All the deep and hidden affections in her, the dark-flowing rivers of love, went to her kingly mother and to the dark lord who was her Nurse. But more and more she wandered to the training ground to stand under her parasol in the heat and the dust, watching young Thothmes shoot the bow and throw the spear, hearing his laughter as he shouted to his friends, and seeing his taut young muscles flex under his tanned skin.

Neferura had no more to do with her sister than she could help.

Meryet-Hatshepset, at six, was a shrew, a demanding, fit-throwing, common child. She had burst in upon her mother one day, her face red with jealousy and rage, and accused her of favoring Neferura. Hatshepsut did not deny the charge but had her severely disciplined, and the little girl had gone to bed with her buttocks tingling and her head full of dark and bitter vows of revenge.

22

Hatshepsut reached the pinnacle of a glorious maturity and seemed to stay there, radiant in health and vigor and beauty. It was as if in her Godhead she was indeed immortal, drawing all men to her as she had all her life, imbued with every power and mystery of the God Amun himself. Often her servants knew she was approaching long before her Standard-Bearers came into view. The atmosphere around them would subtly change, as if a whiff of omnipotence went ahead of her; perhaps it was only her perfume, the heavy myrrh, carried on the breeze. More and more she was regarded with a superstitious awe, and the throngs of pilgrims seeking her shrine increased as the months went by.

But within she felt restless. As she lay on her couch during the stifling nights of summer, she thought of Senmut, his presence every day a reminder that here was a man who could satisfy fully the demands of her royal body if she would but say the word. For years she had declined to say it, aware of her position first as Thothmes' Consort and later as Pharaoh, one of a kind, destined to be alone. But she grew weary of her widowhood, and her sleepless nights and fevered dreams told her that it was time to put a final trust, once and for all, in the hands of the man she loved above all others.

One hot evening, as the purple streamers of Ra's Barque were pulled, sizzling, to the horizon, she had herself anointed with perfumed oils and arrayed in transparent linen. She sent for him. For this night she had put aside her helmet. After her coronation she had let her hair grow again, although not so long as it had been before, for she still had to keep her head covered at all times, as was the tradition for Pharaoh. It swept against her cheeks and framed her face, startlingly feminine with its pretty, kohl-rimmed eyes and red mouth. She put on a simple white and silver headband whose streamers hung over her bare shoulders. She ordered fruit and wine to be set out, and her best alabaster lamps, the stone ground so finely that the pattern of butterflies' wings could be seen glowing through them, flickered gently around the room. She dismissed Nofret and her slaves so that he should find her alone and unadorned, as he had at their first meeting, and waited, standing by the wind funnel so that she could feel the summer breeze coming down from the north.

The guard announced him, and she nodded for him to be admitted. As the silver doors closed quietly behind him, he bowed and strode toward her, a spark of surprise flaring in his eyes and as quickly dying away. He wore only a simple white kilt. His head and feet were bare, for he had been preparing to bathe in the river with Ta-kha'et. The oil and sweat glistened on his chest as he bowed again. Nothing of his chaotic thought showed on his face, but he rapidly assessed this new image: the filmy, drifting cloak; the wonderful, shining hair; the slightly languid, slightly provocative droop to the splendid eyes. Times without number he had wished to touch her, brushing by her in the audience chamber, smelling her warmth and her perfume at the feasts, seeing her limbs tense before she flung the throwing-stick. Time after time he had beaten back his blasphemous thoughts as Hapuseneb had advised him to do, so that over the years his face had become closed and a little hard, his gaze piercing, his manner lofty and uninviting to all who did not know the great Erpa-ha well.

She saw his eyebrows rise as she smiled and held out a hand. "It has been a long time since we have eaten and drunk together in privacy and spoken of anything but business," she remarked as he kissed her palm. "Come and sit, Senmut. Tell me, how is Ta-kha'et?"

He allowed her to lead him to the low table, and he sank onto the cushions in one graceful movement. As she settled herself beside him, he looked around for the slave that would serve them. "Ta-kha'et is well," he answered. "We live quietly when Your Majesty has no need of me, and I think it irks her a little. She loves plenty of entertainment."

Hatshepsut began to serve him herself, pouring his wine, offering him figs steeped in honey and melons soaked in wine. "Indeed? Then you should provide her with musicians and other delights."

"I have done so, but Ta-kha'et is of an uncertain temper. She says that no musician amuses her as I do!"

They smiled at each other, and the strange formality of this meeting began to leave them.

"Of course she is right!" Hatshepsut said, raising her goblet and looking at him over the rim. "I have told you before, you should marry her and make her a princess. That is what she wishes."

"Well I know," he said.

"Then why do you not? I will give her a good dowry. I know how poor you princes are!"

"It seems to me," he remarked lightly, "that we have had a similar conversation before. Is the King's memory so poor that he cannot remember?"

"Perhaps," she said simply, "for the years have flown since that time, Great Prince, and men's affections change."

"Some men's do," he answered lightly, "but mine do not."

"Would it bore you to tell me again why Ta-kha'et is still only a slave?"

He put down his golden cup and sat looking at it for a time. The room was filled with a waiting silence. She sighed softly, stirring on her cushions, the ribbons of her headband lifting from her neck now and then as the hot breeze found her.

At last he turned to face her. "No, it would not bore me. But, Majesty, you are now a King. I think that it is your place to speak on the matter, not mine, for though I no longer fear to be made ridiculous, I am afraid that my words would· fall on ears deafened by the years of which you spoke."

"Ah, Senmut," she replied softly, "why do we push words to one another as if to ward off something else? Do you not know that all my life there has been only one man to whom my love has been given and whom I shall love until I die?" Impulsively she reached down and found his hands, lifting them and burying her face in them, kissing them.

He bent toward her. "Now it is my turn to listen," he said. "Say it, Hatshepsu, say it!"

She groaned and let his hands drop into her lap, reaching out, almost blindly, for his face. "I love you, Senmut, I love you. I can wait no longer to be possessed by you. My body longs for you; my soul cries for you. I humble myself before you, seeking your love or your anger or your mighty indifference. But seeking. Hold me!" Her fingers trembled on his eyes, his cheeks, and she began to cry.

He lunged forward and caught her to him, crushing her fiercely against his body, whispering words of love that poured through his careful defenses. "Hatshepsu! My beloved, my sister." He took her chin in both hands, cupping her face, and she clung to him as if she was drowning. As they kissed, an aching tenderness quivered in their lips, and he felt her tears trickle through his fingers. "Are you sure?" he asked her gently. "It is no small thing, this, for a Pharaoh."

She nodded urgently. "I have been sure for a very long time," she answered softly, kissing his neck, his chin, his eyes. "Let us love while we may, my dear brother, for it is a sorry thing to grow older and see love shrivel and die for want of the sun."

She knelt quietly while his powerful, gentle hands touched her as they did night after night in her dreams, exploring the sweet, strong lines of her, the flawless curves of her young body. He gathered her to him with a great laugh that woke the shadows and rang to the roof, and she laughed, too. They rose and clung together, his arms tight about her waist and hers twined around his neck, and they kissed again, hungry, ready mouths pressed to suck at last all joy from one another.

His relationship with Ta-kha'et was a matter of physical need mingled with mild affection, two people rubbing along, needing each other sometimes, sharing bed and board amicably. But this burning, all-encompassing passion, this towering desire to become one with the woman he had worshiped and loved, day after day and year after year, surpassed every dream that he had thrust viciously to the back of his mind. He lowered her onto the cushions, handling the yielding, velvety flesh in an agony of happiness that hurt as well as blessed, forgetting her divinity, forgetting her royalty, knowing only that she was his true wife, the companion of his days, and the reader of his thoughts, the one who longed for him and wanted to please only him, forever. He took her slowly, patiently, his eyes on her face, watching the beautiful features loosen in ecstasy. Afterward they lay together, smiling, the hot wind cooling the sweat from their bodies, her head pillowed below his shoulder, his arms around her still, both thinking of the days and nights ahead that would glow with a new light.

"I cannot think why I have waited for this moment for so long," she said.

He laughed, contented and weary. "The time was not right, Majesty," he replied.

She tapped him on the chest with one sharp fingernail. "I pray you, Senmut, beloved, do not call me Majesty in private, nor yet Hatshepsu. Call me Hatshepsut, for in your arms I am no longer First Among the Mighty and Honorable Nobles of the Kingdom, but only Chief of Noble Women."

He grunted. "The only woman," he said. "You have always been the only woman."

"What of Ta-kha'et?"

He moved his head, but he could not look down to catch her expression hidden beneath the tangled hair. "Ta-kha'et is like the soft, yellow moon of harvest, and I come to her quietly," he said. "But you are the scorching, fiery sun of a summer noon. How can I go back to the embraces of Ta-kha'et after being so badly burned?"

"But you will not send her away?" In her own happiness, Hatshepsut wished Ta-kha'et to be content, too.

"No. That would be cruel. But I will not marry her, ever. That would be cruel to her also.

She was sleepy now, a warm languor stealing over her limbs. "Then you will never marry at all," she murmured. "I can share you with a slave, but woe betide the woman you call wife!"

"You are my wife, beloved," he said, and his grip on her tightened. "None shall ever tear me away from you, save with death."

In the dawn, Hapuseneb and the other priests came, as they did every morning, to sing the Hymn of Praise outside the silver door. But the couple within did not hear it; they were asleep.

Though no formal words were ever spoken, all in the palace soon knew that the mighty Erpa-ha had become the King's lover. Ta-kha'et accepted the new situation immediately, without grumbling. But she saw him less often, and it hurt her. She loved Senmut in her own way, and she delighted in his body. He still treated her with kindness, sitting with her in the afternoons while they talked of trivial things, but nothing could change the fact that he did not send for her to come to his bed anymore, and she was a trifle lonely. If she could have given him a child, she would have felt more secure; but she was barren, a reproach to any man. He told her that it did not matter at all, that he would never cease to hold her in high esteem and friendship, but she could not understand how any man could live without sons. Yet it was not in her nature to brood, and she soon found plenty to do: running his house for him, ordering his servants, hiring and dismissing his laborers. Still, it was not the same, not at all, and she was sorry.

During the days so full of responsibilities and worries, neither Hatshepsut nor Senmut treated each other with anything but the formality appropriate to the audience chamber or office. Their words were all of duties and policies. No one could put a finger on the changed atmosphere and say, "There, there is the difference." But difference there was, and no one felt it more strongly than Hapuseneb. Long before it was common knowledge in the kitchens, an unerring instinct told him that his King's relationship with her Chief Steward had changed. He had been expecting it, but all the same he could not help subjecting Senmut to a new coolness, and Senmut's quick intuition picked it out. He accosted Hapuseneb one morning in the temple. The High Priest had finished his ablutions and was going to lunch when Senmut stepped from behind a pillar and barred his way. Hapuseneb bowed, his eyes blank. He made as if to move on, but Senmut put out a brawny arm, and Hapuseneb was forced to stand. His acolytes were waiting beside him; he sent them away and turned to Senmut.

Senmut did not mince words. "What have I done to you, Hapuseneb, that you should show me a veil over your face? It is not like you to be so lacking in manners. I would have thought that since we had worked together so long, all such foolery was past."

Hapuseneb looked into the angry black eyes beneath the straight, dark brows and bowed shortly. "Your words are true, Senmut, but I do not apologize," he said calmly. "I am indeed lacking in manners, and I must confess that the lack surprises me, for I had always prided myself on being an impartial man, above all silly differences and serving only Egypt and the God."

"That has been so, and I have respected you for your wisdom. But now I find that I am losing a friend who was won slowly, with great difficulty; and I am not prepared to see you and me, Hapuseneb, fall out for a reason that is obscure to me. You owe me an explanation."

"I owe you nothing!" For the first time Senmut saw the gray eyes lose their steady gaze and harden. "Must I bare to you my heart, just so I can prove that I owe you nothing? Leave me alone!"

"What does your heart have to do with it?" Senmut snapped back.

Hapuseneb smiled wryly. "If you truly do not know, then I do apologize and say that I have misjudged you, Senmut. But I cannot say more. You and I are still friends and allies, but you must give me time to rediscover the respect I hold for myself." With another quick, twisted smile he was gone, his robes floating behind him as he passed through the pillars and went out the doors.

Senmut gazed after him, angry and bewildered. That night he mentioned the incident to Hatshepsut as they lay together on her couch.

She was silent for a long time. "Hapuseneb has a secret," she said finally, "but it is a private thing, between him and me. Even though I love you, Senmut, I will not betray his trust."

"This secret has never come between us before, and it worries me. How can I work closely with him anymore? He took me under his wing while I was yet apprenticed to Ineni, and he put his trust in me long before he knew the extent of my devotion to you. Why this sudden change of heart?"

"He is very astute, my Hapuseneb, and invaluable to me as a right judge of the characters of men. But remember, Senmut, that he and I grew up together, sharing all, and I knew him long before I knew you. I can say no more."

A glimmer of the truth came to Senmut, and he cried out, "But I did not know! I did not guess! Why did he not confide in me?"

"Because he is a proud man. Do not fear; all will be as it was. He is fair and just and does not want to make an enemy of you, but he is tormented. He needs time to conquer himself once more, as he has always done in the past. I love him, too, Senmut—as my oldest and dearest friend —and when he is hurt, so am I."

They said no more, both lying still, staring into the dimness, as Hapuseneb himself did on that night—all wrapped in their private thoughts.

The festival of her Myriad of Years approached, and Hatshepsut eyed the passing days warily, wondering how to celebrate this feast, which was so special because it would come only once during her reign. She remembered her father's jubilee, and the wild rejoicing that had gone on in the palace and the city. With one eye on the growing Thothmes and the other on her own many achievements, she decided to step up the day. She thought that by celebrating sooner than the time appointed by custom, she would press home to everyone the advantages her reign had brought and settle the crown more firmly on her head. Not that she felt she needed to be buttressed, but the name of the young Prince was cropping up on too many occasions for comfort. His prowess with the bow, his cool eye with the spear, his spectacular success in handling the chariot—all were discussed too freely for her liking. She wondered whether perhaps Nehesi had been right. She imagined the palace without him: herself entrenched without opposition, Neferura her Heir, and not a cloud in the sky. But after the first relief the vision afforded, her pleasure faded, and she saw herself alone before Amun, dumb and guilty. She finally rejected any idea of poisoning Thothmes. Poison was ruthless. It was the weapon of weakness, and she was not weak. Not yet. She would handle Thothmes in her own way.

When she held her reviews, she watched the solid, impatient youth whip his horses and thunder past her with the other troops. He was becoming more arrogant in his fourteenth year, swaggering about with his cluster of cohorts and demanding obedience from everyone whether he got it or not. He worried her. Seeing Neferura's secret, yearning glances, she decided that soon she would discuss a possible betrothal with her ministers and thus curb any immediate dark thoughts of sedition Thothmes might have. A betrothal was one way of promising much while delivering nothing. By the time he awoke to the fact that she intended the throne not for him but for Neferura, it would be too late. Neferura would inherit the powerful cabinet she herself had formed, and Thothmes, for all his blustering and threats, would then be rendered impotent.

But her Myriad of Years and the Anniversary of Her Appearing drew closer, and still she could not make up her mind on a suitable way to commemorate the day. It was at prayer that the idea came to her, as she sat on her balcony communing with the God. She left her view of the trees and went inside, sending for Senmut.

When he came, she wasted no time. "You are to go immediately to Assuan," she said. "Take Benya and whomever else you need. Quarry for me two obelisks, and bring them back before my festival."

"But, Majesty," he protested, "you have given me only seven months! It cannot be done in that time!"

"It can, and you will do it. Leave as soon as possible. And furthermore, set the workmen to tearing out the cedar roof my father put in Amun's house. You told me the other day that the wood was rotting, so rip it up. I will put my obelisks there instead. If any of the roof can be saved, it can be rebuilt around them."

"You have set me a formidable task," he remarked quietly. "If anyone can do it, I can, but this time I make no promises."

"It will be done," she said. "I have suspended work on everything else in Karnak, and you can take as many men from there as you like. While you are away, Hapuseneb can see to the roof if you so order. Senmut, I have asked a great deal of you in the past, but this is the greatest. Will you attempt it for me?"

He bowed to the smiling face. "As always, I am prepared to attempt the impossible for you, Majesty."

"Good. Then there is no more to be said."

She dismissed him lightly, and he left, almost running, feeling as if time was already snapping at his heels like a bad-tempered dog. He believed that the job could be done, but only just, provided there were no accidents. He shook his head and muttered a quick prayer to any god that would listen as he sent for Benya and ordered Ta-kha'et to have his clothes packed. It was a bad time of the year to stand in the baking, heat-seared quarries of Assuan. He wondered if any would die under Benya's lash before the stone was strapped to the rafts. It was not enough that this should be done, for the King had made it clear that she wanted hers to be the highest obelisks in the world. His mind was busy as he sent for his scribes. The floods were due soon, and if Amun wanted his Daughter's monuments, he would have to ensure that the water rose at the right time to float the enormous rafts Senmut would have to build. There was no point in wasting time constructing workmen's houses at the site, and he ordered the scribes to get hold of tents that could be erected or struck in a few minutes. His thought flew to tools, supplies, food, and even before the scribes picked up their pallets and scurried out, he was on his way to his litter and the docks, wondering where he could get enough precious timber to build a raft that could bear the great weight of such massive stones.

He, Benya, and the hundreds in the work force left before the week was out. There was much missing from the lists Senmut had compiled so hurriedly, but it could all be sent on. He and Benya stood in the bow as the rowers bent to the oars, the incense rising from the bank as the flotilla swung to midstream and began to buck the current. Hatshepsut stood watching until they were out of sight, and Senmut kept his eyes on her until she and her bright courtiers were hidden by a curve in the riverbank. He heard Benya chuckle.

"So she does work you once in a while, my friend! I had heard that she requires little of you now but your company."

"Well, you heard wrong!" Senmut barked, his mind already on the job ahead. "Since my father deposited me at the phylarch's door in the temple, I have done nothing but work for her, and well you know it. Go away, old friend. I am in no mood for joking."

Benya shrugged and left him, but before long he was back, chattering away as ceaselessly as ever. They drank together at sunset, while the rowers sweated on and the river slowly absorbed the last light of the day.

In two days they disembarked. Although it was late, just after noon, Senmut allowed no rest. He sent the men to pitch their tents in whatever shade they could find, warning them that the gates of the city were closed to them. While the supplies were unloaded, he and Benya paced the quarry, almost fainting in the intense heat.

"By Amun!" Benya swore. "We shall all die in this blistering! Well, I suppose I must gather my apprentices and begin to search the rock. Two obelisks. Two executioners, more likely. Curse the day I ever met you, O driver of men."

"Choose with care, and do not take too long," Senmut warned him. "We have little time. The men can work in shifts, and when the sun goes down, I have lamps to be lit."

Benya groaned, mopping his brow. "You to your job, then, and I to mine! Thank all the gods my tomb is ready."

But mine is not, and I am not ready yet to lie in it, Senmut thought as he watched Benya lope away. He swung to the boats, shouting for the burdened men to hurry.

With the knowing eyes and delicate hands of a master physician, Benya sounded the lowering rock and chose his veins. His apprentices marked out the two long, tapering shapes. At once Senmut ordered out the massive stone hammers, and the workmen began to pound, the dust rising in a vast cloud that whitened their skin and set them coughing. Senmut took his turn, grimly swinging the hammer while his sweat mingled with the sweat of the peasants. Day after day Benya strode up and down the lines of shining, muscled backs, shouting and cursing but never raising the whip that trailed from his brown hand like a thin snake.

In a month the obelisks began to emerge, though they still held firmly onto their bed of rock. Senmut ordered a day and a night of rest. He sent heralds north with reports of their progress and formal greetings. While the men slept and swam, he spent the hours pacing up and down the long, stubborn shapes, his eyes alert for any crack, any suspicion of a crumbling.

Soon they were back at it, sore and bone weary and dispirited. Almost unnoticed, the river and the humidity began to rise. The air became full of biting, stinging insects. Senmut took six men from the hammers and gave them whisks. They walked about, beating at the flies, while their friends worked.

In three months the hammers were put aside and replaced by the chisels. The pace was slower, the handling more delicate. Benya stopped swearing and peered over each man's shoulder, admonishing and advising. He begged Senmut to halt the work at night, for the lamps did not cast enough light. He was afraid of a sudden split, but Senmut shook his head firmly. If they rested each night, the job would not be done in time. So Benya retired, muttering, and the work went on.

At last the first stone was ready to be freed. The stonemasons waited by the bank to chip off the last threads and to polish its gently sloping sides. Senmut, his heart in his mouth, ordered the ropes flung around the tip and the nine-foot base. Benya checked the knots and adjusted the tension himself. When he was satisfied, he sprang away, looking over the logs that stretched to the river, the logs over which the obelisk would roll. Benya raised an arm, his keen eyes on the granite as it began to move slowly, ever so slowly. "Hold back!" he shouted. "Now more on the tip —more—not so fast, or it will slip! Pull together!" Senmut, perched nervously on the rocks above the site, watched the colossus grind to the logs.

All at once there was a scream of rage. Senmut left his vantage point and ran toward the sound. Benya was cursing and yelling, shaking his fists; and the workmen, shattered, dropped the ropes. Senmut looked down, gasping. In the base of the rock was a huge, jagged split, and even as he watched a piece of stone broke free and clattered to the sand at his feet. He bent and picked it up, stunned.

Benya was silent, trembling with disappointment. "Oh, God. Oh, God," he whispered. "This is my fault."

Senmut put a hand on his shoulder, determination hardening in him. "Not so. Well does stone love you, Benya, and do your bidding. No, we have been working long without proper light at night. It may be that we struck wrongly in the dimness." He straightened and tossed the piece away. "We begin again!" he shouted. "Now! This very hour! Benya, stop blaspheming and get up into the quarry. Try there." He pointed. "Find another suitable vein, and we will get out the hammers. Back to work! The King has commanded two obelisks for her festival, and two obelisks she shall have, though we all die under the sun!"

The men sullenly turned away, but they respected him for laboring beside them. When he snatched up the first hammer and strode to the rock face, which was hot to the touch, they followed him. Benya, sulking, gave his whip to an apprentice and retired to a small hill of sand, but he soon joined Senmut, restored to good humor by the sight of a Prince of Egypt stripped naked and sweating with the fellahin.

They were finished with four days to spare. When the mighty spires were settled aboard the raft, base to base, Senmut ordered wine all around and drank happily with Benya. They toasted each other and their men. On the river the engineers' boats circled warily, alert for any sign of shift. They had not all come through alive. Three men had succumbed to the heat, and their hearts had given out. Another six had been crushed when the unwieldy stone had slipped on them as they strained with the others to shovel out the sand beneath it. Senmut had them buried honorably, but he turned from the graves with satisfaction, giving barely a fleeting thought for the men who had been as he once was, peasants in the service of Pharaoh. He considered that on the whole a miracle, brought about by his own efficiency, had taken place.

It took thirty-two sturdy boats to tow the monoliths back to Thebes, even though Amun had sent the floodwaters hurtling between the straining banks, the water already spilling onto the land. Senmut, perched high in his little cabin above the raft, watched anxiously as the slack was taken up and slowly, ponderously, the boats caught the current and began to move.

They moved on, not stopping to tie up overnight, their nerves strained to the breaking point. Even Benya was silent for hours, his eyes on the hulks lying so low in the water, his hands white as they gripped the prow. Long before Thebes came into view, small crafts, fishing boats, and nobles' barges joined them, hugging the banks and ringed with excited, expectant faces. Early in the morning Hatshepsut saw them, a black tide on the breast of the river. She had summoned the army to the temple water steps, and they thronged behind her. Under the trees the temple gardens were thick with crowds from the city; they had been given a free day to see the giants dragged into the temple's outer court. As the raft neared the steps, dipping alarmingly as the sailors jumped down and waded ashore with the tow ropes, Hatshepsut ran to help. Hapuseneb, draped in his leopard skin, began the prayers behind her. Senmut left the high, tiny cabin and picked his way ashore. At his orders the muddied water became full of soldiers who leaped from the high banks to drag the stones up onto the waiting rollers. Inch by inch the obelisks neared the first pylon, surrounded by the excited, shouting crowd. Senmut paced next to Hatshepsut, his eyes narrow as he watched each labored step. Where the cedar roof had once been, he could see a broad stream of light pouring into the temple, illuminating the two mountains of sand onto which the stones would be dragged. They would be towed up bases first, then slid down the other side and into the square, notched foundations that gaped in the floor of the inner court. He went ahead swiftly, Puamra, the young architect, joining him. Together they checked every foot of the preparations. With a thunderous grinding the stones were hauled through the outer court. Senmut and Puamra stood to one side, where Hatshepsut strode to stand with them. They watched silently as the mighty shafts began to cant upward and swarms of slaves scampered up the hills of sand to guide them.

"Fingers to the Heavens," Hatshepsut murmured. "You have done well, Senmut. Did I not tell you that we could do anything?"

He bowed to her absently, his thoughts on the imperceptible shifting of the gray hulks. He saw Benya pacing backward and forward, shouting orders that echoed between the pillars as ropes mushroomed from the tips and hundreds of men leaned back, taking the strain. Senmut jerked his head at Puamra, and they went to stand beside the pits, under the shadow of the teetering bases. Out of the corner of his eye he saw Thothmes and two of his young friends, Min-mose, the apprentice engineer, and Menk-heperrasonb, his fellow soldier and architect, standing silently with their hands on their hips, their faces dark in the shadows and their expressions tense. Neferura drifted to her mother's side, whispering to her and pointing out Thothmes, but Hatshepsut was caught up in the drama of her moment and only nodded briefly.

There was a second of rest while men rubbed their aching arms and legs or squatted, exhausted, on the golden floor. Standing beside Senmut, his arm raised, Benya rallied them for the final effort. "Begin to lower! Slowly, you fools! Take the strain—easy—easy—don't let them swing!" He dashed forward, gesticulating madly. With a reverberating thunk the first obelisk sank, its base catching the deep notches, the slaves pulling on the ropes that steadied the tip and running back to draw it upright. Hatshepsut cried out, and Min-mose, smiling, muttered something to Thothmes.

The second base edged to its foundation, slid past the rim of the pit, and sank slowly. As it settled and the tip began to rise, it started to yaw.

Senmut shouted, "The notch! It has not caught the first notch!"

Benya screamed something unintelligible. Hatshepsut stepped forward, but Puamra barred her way. "Back, Majesty! It may yet fall!"

Thothmes and Menkheperrasonb had drawn closer, and Senmut had time to see the grin of pure delight on Menkheperrasonb's face before rushing forward, a nervous sweat running down his back.

With a grind the obelisk reared and steadied as all held their breaths, craning upward. It stayed proudly aloft, and Benya collapsed in a trembling heap. The overseers began to shepherd the slaves out of the court.

"Leave the sand," Hatshepsut ordered Puamra. "The two tips have yet to be plated, and the inscriptions must go on." She had wanted to coat them both from floor to tip in electrum, but Tahuti had withdrawn from the suggestion in horror.

"Majesty," he had said primly, "you are very wealthy, but even your vast treasury would be quickly emptied if you took so much gold and silver from it."

She had laughed at his reaction but bowed to his figures. She had contented herself with weighing out the precious metals for the tips herself, plunging her bare arms up to the elbows in the weighing baskets, the gold dust rising in a shimmering cloud and settling on her breasts and her stomach, and gently powdering the floor of the treasury.

Thothmes sauntered over to where she still stood with Neferura and Senmut. He bowed negligently, his black eyes impudently alight. "Congratulations, Flower of Egypt," he said, his voice holding the deepness of his approaching manhood. "Truly your monuments speak of a reign unending!"

Hatshepsut looked coolly into the blunt, haughty features, ignoring the undertone of sarcasm. "Greetings, nephew-son. I am glad that you approve. Where is your mother on this auspicious day?"

He shrugged. "She has a slight indisposition."

"She had better recover before my celebration. Shall I send her my physician?"

"That will not be necessary, dear aunt-mother. I do not think that her malady merits the hands of one who tends Pharaoh."

They were playing with each other, smiling with their lips but sparring with their eyes. Senmut listened apprehensively, feeling the air spark as the two forceful wills clashed. Thothmes was already a man to be reckoned with, and Senmut wondered why Hatshepsut persisted in dismissing him as a youth. He saw Neferura's eyes fixed solemnly on her brother's face, but King and Prince did not seem to know that she was there.

Thothmes waved an arm in the direction of Min-mose and Menkheper-rasonb. "Your fine obelisk almost came to grief," he remarked. "Perhaps you need the assistance of my engineer and my architect. It seems that your experts, Majesty, are getting old."

"Do you think so? Then recommend your men to me, Thothmes. What mighty works have they accomplished? Where may I see their skill?"

He flushed, his protruding teeth biting his lip. "As yet they have done little," he scowled. "But in time their works for me will equal and surpass all that I see here!"

"Then I suggest that you send them back to school, Prince, so that in time—" she stressed the words, smiling, "in time, they may attempt some small venture."

He was struggling between anger and admiration, and admiration won. He shook his head. "Oh, you are hard, aunt-mother. How the Double Crown suits you!"

"It would not suit you, Thothmes," she replied as they began to walk toward the outer court. "It is still too large for your head."

"The size of my head has little to do with it," he snapped. "It is what is within my head that is important."

"Indeed? Is it so? Then bring your oversized head to my Myriad of Years. I order it, Thothmes. You have been negligent of late, missing from the temple and from my feasts. I will not have insubordination. Also, I forbid you to criticize my ministers. Where are your own? Can they equal the selfless devotion, the many abilities of their betters?"

He did not answer, but bowed, scowling, and strode back to Menk-heperrasonb and Min-mose.

Neferura put a timid hand on her mother's arm. "Why do you make Thothmes so angry?" she asked. "Do you not like him?"

"I like him very much," Hatshepsut retorted. "He is full of the bull strength of your grandfather. But he is impatient, Neferura, and sometimes rude. He needs to be curbed like an unruly horse."

Neferura said nothing, but Senmut felt her warm hand steal into his own. He squeezed it, and they went to the palace together under the dry trees of summer.

23

The Myriad of Years was an extraordinary occasion, formal and daz-zling. Hatshepsut called all her advisers together in the afternoon and sat on the Horus Throne, the Double Crown on her head and the Flail and the Crook clenched tightly in her hands. In a short and pointed speech she reminded them of all she had accomplished as ruler even before the death of her husband, and she had her Scribe read to them the inscriptions the artisans were carving on the sides of her obelisks. While Anen spoke the words, her gaze traveled over them all.

Thothmes sat among them, his arms folded over his broad chest and his face raised to hers in pride and challenge. He listened, but it was only as Anen was concluding that he became restless.

"The God knew himself in me, Amun-Ra, Lord of Thebes. He caused that I should reign over the Black Land and the Red Land as a reward. I have no enemies in any land; all countries are my subjects. He has made my boundary to the end of heaven; the circuit of the Sun has labored for me. God has given all these things to me who dwells with him, for he knew that I would offer them to him. I am in truth his Daughter, who glorifies him. Life, stability, and satisfaction be upon the Horus Throne of her who lives, like Ra, eternally."

She met Thothmes' gaze and held it, mocking him, yet sad. He read a sympathy in the beautiful eyes. He smiled at her faintly and dropped his gaze.

Only that morning he had paced before her biography in the valley. He had stood before the calm, definite words astounded and angry, for since his last visit new inscriptions had been added. "I am God, the Beginning of Existence," he had read, and he had wanted to snatch up a hammer and pound at the plaster until the offensive line was nothing but a little pile of white dust at his feet. He knew that she spoke so surely from a knowledge that was deep within her and evident to all close to her, and he had stood there in the sanctuary, shaking his fist at her likeness in a fit of wild jealousy and something else, something perilously close to affection.

He looked at her far above him, gold-clad, magnetic, enigmatic, the woman his mother hated, the King who had taken his birthright from him. But her eyes, so steadily commanding his own, held warmth and complicity and a kind of understanding. He looked away, angry at himself for unbending to her and forgetting what she had done to him, even here in her audience chamber with the symbols of her godhead all around her.

The men crawled to her with gifts, and as the sun sank, the pile of fans, inlaid boxes, miniatures, and other rich knickknacks grew higher. Senmut, his worldly, cynical face framed in his massive black wig, came last, followed by Paere, his body servant, staggering behind him, bent under the weight of an enormous fur. Senmut caught it up and laid it at her feet. With a cry of delight she reached down, laying aside the Crook, and stroking the thick, shining pile. She had never seen anything like it.

"It comes from the cold mountains of Rethennu," he said, "and is very rare. I could find nothing else worthy to touch the body of Pharaoh." He retired coolly, ignoring the murmurs of surprise that fluttered around the room. Already its heat warmed her painted feet, and she looked to him and smiled, thinking of the winter nights when they would lie together, making love on its thick, blue-black back.

"I have heard," she said, "that in Rethennu it is very cold and that the mountains are very high and tipped with a white substance which is like a solid river falling from the sky. Is this so?"

He smiled a little sadly. "Truly Your Majesty knows her own land as well as the gods know the heart of every man, but it is a pity that Your Majesty did not travel north. There are lands full of marvels beyond the horizon. The white substance is called snow, and if one picks it up, then, lo, it melts away and leaves only a handful of water." He turned to her and smiled again, looking into her eyes.

Thothmes saw the private, meaningful glance fly between them, and a new rage began in him, but at fifteen he could not grope to its roots. When she rose to go to the feasting, he pushed his way out the door and ran through the halls. Not even the monotonous salute of guard after guard could soothe the wound throbbing within him.

That night, as he stood between the open double doors of the banqueting hall while his many titles were called and all waited to bow as he made his way to the dais with Hatshepsut, Senmut's thoughts were as dark as the evening sky glimpsed at the end of the long, brightly lit room. On this, the day when Hatshepsut celebrated her complete hold on Egypt, he felt that the time was fast approaching when his own hold on Thothmes and the affairs of Aset was slipping. He had always been able to get at Thothmes' servants and friends through his own spies. Without any compunction he had exiled, weeded out, warned, and threatened while Thothmes was still a child. But now Thothmes' friends were the sons of his own friends, and Thothmes himself was untouchable and growing in power. Walking slowly to the dais, seating himself, and bending with a smile to the King, Senmut saw dimly ahead, but too rapidly nearing, a time when she would be ringed, hunted, fighting desperately to keep her throne. A pharaoh could not lose a crown he had never had as she had lost the promise of the throne held out to her by her father and then snatched away by her petulant husband. A king could only lose his kingdom by losing his life.

The clamor of the feasting went on far into the night. The shrieks and laughter of the company echoed in every street of the city where the people also celebrated Pharaoh, but Senmut could not relax. Aset was there, covered in jewels, her thin face impassive throughout the procession of singers and dancers. Thothmes, too, was present, ringed by his friends, eating and drinking in a mood of sullen watchfulness.

Finally the noise abated, the merriment slowed and faltered as the dawn approached, and Hatshepsut removed the cone from her head and rose, dismissing them all. In an hour the Hymn of Praise would be sung, and the business of the day would commence. She wanted to bathe and put on a clean kilt before going to the temple for the morning's worship.

Senmut knew she would not need him until she summoned him to the audience chamber, and as she went out, preceded by her Fan Bearer on the Right Hand, her Seal Bearer, and her bodyguards, he edged to Hapuseneb and tugged gently at his kilt. The High Priest turned.

"Come with me into the garden," Senmut said in a low tone. "I need your advice."

Hapuseneb nodded quickly, and together they pushed their way through the throng. They went under the cloisters to the garden, where a few heated diners ambled in twos and threes, enjoying the cool breeze and talking softly while their runners lit their way with lamps and their slaves walked behind them. Senmut and Hapuseneb slipped away from them, gliding under the trees in the direction of the north wall of the temple. At last they stopped. There was no sound, and only the pale, cold glow of the setting moon showed them the black outline of the wall, looming above the tops of the trees. Senmut motioned Hapuseneb down, and they sank together onto the shadowed grass. Hapuseneb tucked his pleated linen around his feet and waited while Senmut crossed his legs and gazed at the red soles of his feet, letting the roar of the guests and the warm fumes of the wine he had drunk recede from his mind before he began.

He glanced quickly around the deserted garden. "Hear me, Hapuseneb, and then give me your thoughts, putting aside all our differences in the name of Pharaoh." The other nodded briefly in the darkness, and Senmut gathered his words, his tongue unwilling to give them life. "I am Chief Steward, and as such all the comings and goings of the palace are under my eye. I am also a Steward of Amun, and nothing in the temple escapes me. For long, under the King, I have controlled the business of the dispatches and the audiences absolutely; and I can say, as you can, that Egypt is under my hand as a carpet whose every thread was woven with my knowledge. But I feel as if I am losing my grip, Hapuseneb. Somehow there are cracks appearing in every corner of my control, and I am helpless, for the wedges driven are hammered in by the Crown Prince himself. I see the days of Pharaoh numbered." Hapuseneb stirred but did not speak, and Senmut went on, stumbling a little. "It is time to stop sneaking in the shadows, guarding the Horus Throne with spies, eyes that never sleep, eyes that grow weary in the face of a burgeoning strength." He passed his lean hand across his face. "I will say it plainly. If we do not do away with Thothmes immediately, then it will be too late, and Pharaoh and all she has worked for will be gone."

"It is already too late." Hapuseneb's deep voice broke the stillness that rushed in when Senmut stopped speaking. "I, too, have seen the seed sprouting in the women's quarters and on the training ground. I have cast about in my mind for something to wither it, but it is too late. If we had murdered Thothmes when he was still in his infancy, the deed would have gone unnoticed, for children die often, and of many diseases. But not now, not when he is healthy and strong as a running calf."

"Nehesi suggested it to me and to Pharaoh, but she forbade it."

"She would forbid it now if she were here. She is no greedy, rapacious, unscrupulous upstart like the Prince's mother. She is a noble woman, who rules with the blessing of the God but who also insists on staying within the law of the God. Thothmes is her own flesh. No matter what, she will let him live."

"She will go under."

Hapuseneb nodded quietly. "I think so. But she would rather perish than offend her Father, and murder is an offense that would reek in his nostrils."

"What of you and I, Hapuseneb? I care nothing for my life as long as I can serve her. Can we not do this thing in secret?"

"It would not be secret for long. How can you destroy a youth when he is full of vigor and the love of life and not have an accusing finger pointed? The finger would point straight at the One, and she would suffer, not us."

"We should have poisoned him years ago, in spite of her orders!"

"Then she would have been relieved and perhaps even grateful, but her trust would have waned, and eventually we would have been dismissed. No, she knows that in staying her hand she destroys herself, yet she will not move. She is a great, great King."

"Can we do nothing, my friend?" Senmut spoke softly, his voice dead. "Must we see Egypt in the hands of Thothmes after all? And what of Her Highness Neferura?"

"Neferura is safe. Thothmes must marry her to secure the throne, and that he will undoubtedly do. You know that the One plans to have them betrothed."

"To put off the hour of her defeat! But Thothmes will not be fooled. He is not as full of principles and mercies as she. Once he has Neferura—"

"Perhaps." Hapuseneb spread out his hands. "I just do not know. We can only serve as we have always done in the past, doing our best to lengthen her years. She has handled Egypt as if she was raising a beloved child. Even Thothmes must acknowledge her ability. Beyond that—"

"But if it were done and over with and Thothmes were dead, her anger might be swift and fall on us, but afterward—afterward—"

"She would feel the guilt, and Thothmes dead would finish her as surely as Thothmes alive. Face it, Senmut. It is not her will that her nephew-son should die. If it had been, the deed would have been done a long, long time ago, by you, by me, by Nehesi, by Menkh, by any one of us who serve her."

He was vehement, his words carrying to Senmut forcefully, but Senmut suddenly raised a hand and cut him off. They sat craning into the darkness, breath stilled and ears straining. There was a rustling under the trees to their right. Senmut put a finger to his lips and slowly began to stand, his arm shooting out and the shrubs waving frantically as he sprang. As Hapuseneb got up, he saw Senmut drag forth a small, scrawny figure. It was a little we'eb priest, his linen tucked around his thin waist, his face contorted with fear. He clutched half a goose in one hand, the other hand flailing the air as Senmut's grip tightened.

"What have we here?" Hapuseneb said grimly. Senmut released his grasp. The forlorn figure collapsed, shaking, into a heap on the ground. "One of my we'ebs, I believe. Get up, foolish one, and tell me what you are doing out here, far from your cell?"

Senmut felt a mist rise before his eyes. It was not Hapuseneb who spoke so quietly, with a soft threat in his tones, but glib and treacherous Menena. He felt again the sick fear as he had cowered behind the sycamore and the pain of the bark as it had scraped his cheek.

The lad got to his feet, cuddling the meat to his bony breast and looking at the two mighty men whose rings glittered wickedly in the moonlight and whose cold eyes were hard and angry.

"I know what he was doing," Senmut answered, his voice thick and his head whirling. "He has been to the God's kitchens, for a we'eb works from dawn until dusk and his belly is always empty."

"He must have heard all," Hapuseneb said slowly. "What shall we do with him, Senmut?"

The boy winced and uttered a muffled, unintelligible sound, but he made no move to run.

Senmut stepped to his side, his heart suddenly aching for the past, for the sunny days full of hope and promise, for the dreams of greatness, for the child he had been. "It is true, is it not?" he asked levelly. "You heard?"

The youth nodded.

"What are you going to do?"

"I do not know, Mighty One." The voice was ragged and nervous, but the bright eyes did not waver.

"You have courage! Tell me, whom do you serve?"

"I serve Amun, King of the gods, and I serve Pharaoh."

"And what of the Prince?"

"Him, too, I serve. But I do not serve men with murder in their hearts." The little chin rose defiantly, but the hands that held the goose shook.

Hapuseneb drew in his breath with a hiss. "He has sealed his death papers! If Thothmes hears of this, we are dead before our time!"

"I do not think so," Senmut said as he squatted, looking full into the thin face. "Do you want to go to Pharaoh with your story, we'eb?"

"I should, but perhaps Pharaoh knows of your plot and would kill me."

"Pharaoh indeed knows of our plot, for it is a very old plot, never finished. But Pharaoh will not let us do what we would like to do, so if you go to him, he will not harm you. Do you believe me?"

"No."

Senmut rose, still trapped in the memory of the youth who had gone back to bed instead of beating on the palace doors. Only now did he realize that that one failing had haunted him all his life. He reached his decision quickly. "Hapuseneb, I agree with you. We will have done with all plots. I must have been mad! Let all follow as it must, and may Amun's will be done." He turned to the we'eb priest, taking his arm firmly. "You and I, my little cock, will go immediately to Pharaoh, and you will tell her of all you heard."

Hapuseneb was motionless, but the boy gasped. "You will take me to the river and slit my throat!"

"I swear on the name of Pharaoh, Living Forever, that you will not die," Senmut replied. "Hapuseneb, I thank you for your ear. The dawn comes, and she awaits her hymn. Sing it with a clear conscience!" He laughed grimly and pulled the squirming boy away across the lawn, the darkness already giving way to the colorless, first light of morning.

Hapuseneb did not wait. He turned and went swiftly to his own entrance, beneath the frowning likeness of the God Thothmes the First, Egypt's avenger.

"It is too soon to disturb Pharaoh," Senmut said to the little priest. "We must wait until the High Priest has sung Ra into the sky. Come to my palace, and have breakfast with me. What would you like to eat? What is your name?"

"Smenkhara, Great One." He was bewildered and still suspicious. Senmut kept a tight hold on him as they crossed the broad avenue that ran to the royal water steps and went on under the trees to his own paths and his own gilded door.

"How long have you served in the temple?"

"Two years. My brother is a Master of Mysteries."

"Indeed? And what will you be?"

They passed the guards and entered the dark hall. Senmut led him to the right, through the audience chamber and into his private bedroom, calling for Paere.

The boy looked about, his curiosity edging out the fear. He had heard of the magnificence of Pharaoh's favorite and of his tentacles of power. He had seen him sometimes, walking into the temple with Pharaoh, both shining like gods. He was seized with a shy awe.

"I do not know, Mighty Steward. I would like to become High Priest some day."

"So you have ambitions, too!" Senmut released his grip and sent Paere for food and milk. He indicated the pretty carved cedar chair, and the boy perched nervously on the edge of it, watching as Senmut took off his wig. When Ta-kha'et ambled drowsily into the room, still in her sleeping robe, her feet bare, she found her lord deep in conversation with a grubby little priest who looked as though he had never eaten a good meal in his life. They were both stuffing hot bread and pieces of goose into their mouths, talking gaily all the while.

Hatshepsut received them an hour later. She was dressed and ready to go to the temple, but she sat obligingly, smiling while the boy stammered and blushed. He did not want to make trouble for the Chief Steward, a man who had fed him and spoken to him gently, with understanding; but

Senmut frowned at him and pushed him forward roughly, whispering to him that he must do his duty. The boy prostrated himself and told his tale, afraid to lift his eyes to the tall, graceful woman who wore the cobra and the vulture on her golden helmet.

When he had finished, Hatshepsut was no longer smiling. She told him to rise, seeking Senmut's eye over his head, a query on her lips. He nodded, and she returned to the little priest.

"Smenkhara, you have done well," she said. "We are pleased that you are a faithful servant and that you put your trust in us. I will look into this matter, for the charges are grave, but I must have your promise that you will never speak to anyone about what you have heard. I will punish in my own way and in my own time." The child murmured, "Yes, Majesty." "Now, what can I do for you? Would you like to carry my incense this morning, and we will worship the God together?"

He gaped at her, his face radiant, and she sent him to wait for her outside. When she and Senmut were alone, she turned on him angrily. "You were careless, and Hapuseneb also was foolish. Well I know your thoughts, Senmut, and Hapuseneb's and Nehesi's and all the others. I know, too, of Thothmes' thrusting eagerness, his will to ride over me and fling me aside. But I will have no murder!" She stood before him, emphasizing her words by beating her fist against her faience-inlaid collar. "I will not say it again. And if I find you implicated again in anything like this, I will have you disciplined as any common criminal." Her eyes bit at him, and she turned away in disgust. "Thothmes is my own blood. I will not have him harmed."

"Then at least send him away."

"And have him intriguing behind my back? No! Why did you bring the child to me? Why did you not deal with him yourself?"

"Majesty, may I sit down?" She nodded, startled, and he sank into a chair.

"I brought him because today the judgment of Amun is at last visited on a frightened, cowardly we'eb priest who did not do his duty."

"I do not understand."

He smiled wearily. "Once I, too, was a hungry priest, stealing from the kitchens of the God in the middle of the night. And like this little one, I heard something that it was not good for me to hear." She was suddenly still, her body tense. He noticed but went on. "Your sister, Her Highness Osiris-Neferu-khebit, did not die of a disease. Menena had her poisoned."

The weight rolled from him, and in the silence, broken only by her shallow breaths, he got up lightly and went to her.

She grew pale, and from deep within the murky depths of nights long gone a memory floated, hazy and jumbled. The fragment of a dream. Neferu with the body of the poor imprisoned little fawn and Nebanum standing with the key in his hand. But had it been Nebanum?

"I wanted to go to your father, to tell him all as this priest has told you all, but I was afraid, thinking that the One wished the thing to be done. While I struggled and agonized, the cup was prepared, and Neferu died."

Her shoulders slumped suddenly, and she sighed, unconsciously feeling for her amulet with her fingers. "At last, at last. I have seen you hate Menena, and I have long wanted to know the reason for your fear. Over all the years I myself have pondered her death and feared. Why, I did not know. But now all is clear. And you think that my father wished the death of his daughter?"

The memory surfaced and exploded. Not Nebanum. Of course not. The murderous red eyes of the Mighty Bull drilled her with pain.

"I still do not know, Majesty, but I think so."

"Why? Why would he bring harm to her? She wanted only to be left in peace!"

"Because even then he saw the Double Crown on your head, and if she had lived, on whose head would it be now? Thothmes your husband would have married Neferu and died in his turn, and his son would be calling you a name other than Pharaoh."

She put a hand on his chest, and he saw her eyes fill with tears. "It is so. I know it. I have guessed. Indeed while I was yet a child, a hint of this evil thing brought bad dreams to me, but it is a hard knowledge to bear, even now." She struggled proudly to control her face. "Go, Senmut. I am glad of your trust—and angry. I want only to go to the temple and say my prayers with this most fortunate boy. You could have slit his throat and cast him into the river, you know, just as he said." She smiled at him, a tiny, twisted grimace.

He kissed her hand and left her, a free man, striding to the officials who awaited him in the audience chamber.

Before the winter was over, Hatshepsut betrothed Thothmes to a glowing Neferura and then immediately sent him and his troops north on maneuvers. But she had made it quite clear to him that this was not marriage, only a promise.

He had sneered a little, standing before her in the throne room, his arms folded across his chest. "You have committed yourself, Majesty," he had said. "You may send me here and there on errands and expeditions, but sooner or later you must take Neferura to the temple and give her to me, for I am no longer a boy."

"I have eyes!" she retorted. "Oh, Thothmes, why do you prickle all over when we have dealings with each other? Did I not promise you this throne one day?"

"Yes, but now I do not believe that you ever intend to give it to me. When I was a child I was in awe of you. But now I am becoming a man, and still you shut me out of the audience chamber—my own chamber, the place where I as Pharaoh am entitled to sit. I think you intend the throne for Neferura."

"You are stupid if you really believe these things and yet shout your doubts all over the palace. What is to stop me getting rid of you? Then Neferura could indeed wear the Double Crown and marry some general to give Egypt heirs."

"Because you know as well as I that Neferura is sweet and gentle and kind and utterly unsuited to be Pharaoh."

"Then what of Meryet?" Hatshepsut was not amused. She knew now that his words were true. Neferura did not have the burning, eating ambition that she herself had had at that age. Although Hatshepsut loved her and desperately wanted the crown for her, Neferura could never control Thothmes or any other ruthless young noble who coveted the kingdom.

Thothmes laughed scornfully. "Meryet! She is full of spit and fire and already casts her eye over your younger advisers like the bitch she is. But as Pharaoh? She is shallow, like the river in summer. She cares nothing for you or Egypt." He shrugged, coming to stand close to her. "I will accept the betrothal, providing a marriage follows. I am content to soldier, for I love the bow, the spear, and the knife; and as you have so often said, I am still young. But do not wait too long!"

"You forget yourself! I am Egypt, and if I give you an order, it must be obeyed! Do not try my patience, Thothmes. You are arrogant and a fool, but because your school days are not yet over, I will forgive you. If your cheap mother had not filled your head full of rubbish while you were yet in her care, we might have worked well together. But before you could talk, she loaded you with hatred for me, and you cannot see past her spiteful words."

He mounted the steps and stood with one foot above the other, balancing easily on his long legs. "You have taken my crown from me and thus broken the law. My mother has nothing to do with it. And as for us working together, do we not do so? Am I not now a Captain of Retainers, and will I not go higher in the army at your command? Do I not sweat on the training ground for you, as all in the land sweat at your bidding?"

When he had gone she sat alone, cupping her chin in her hand, looking into the distance. Her silver walls were lit as the stray rays of the sun found them, and the breeze reaching her was scented with the flowers from her acres. Around her, her own likeness ran, indomitable, omnipotent, her enemies frozen in an attitude of eternal defeat. Still she brooded uneasily, the square jaw hidden in the painted palm.

"Ah, Thothmes," she breathed into the unaccustomed moment of silence, "would that you had been my son!"

24

That night, for the first time, she felt the press of the years. As she waited for Senmut in the twilight of her room, she held her mirror close to her face, searching for a wrinkle, the suspicion of a fold, telling herself that at thirty she could not expect the features she had had at fifteen. But the woman who gazed back at her had the limpid, clear eyes of her youth and skin as taut and flawless as ever. She stood, looking down at her naked body, the limbs flowing smoothly to her small feet, the well-muscled stomach, the breasts that did not sag.

All the intimations of age are in my own mind, she told herself, putting the mirror down and walking to the couch. My head is filled with endless decisions and policies. My thoughts are as cramped and bent as an old woman's.

She heard him come to the door and pause. The guard admitted him, and she saw him with new eyes, too: tall, spare, all the tight muscles kept trim by daily exercise at the bow and the chariot, the face haughty and all-knowing, the dark eyes ringed, the sensuous lips curving in a smile as he bowed. He was a man, he had been a man for so long, and she had loved him for so long. Then why the sudden searching for lines about the piercing eyes, for a fold above the jeweled girdle?

He sensed her mood at once and did not speak, going instead to the head of the couch and smoothing the hot forehead, massaging away the worries of the day.

She stroked the fur beneath her and smiled, feeling her body relax, but her mind raced on under the deft hands. She reached up, drawing him down to her, seeking his lips hungrily, but tonight the spending of her passion could not blot out Thothmes' face as he mocked her in the throne room. She slept unsatisfied, Senmut's arms about her, still feeling jaded in body and soul.

In the spring, when Thothmes returned from the north a Captain of Fifty, she sent him away again, this time into the desert to inspect the garrisons. She knew that she was hurting Neferura, who said good-bye to him with tears; but she also felt the quiet, almost audible crumbling, the minute changes in the air and at the table and in men's eyes. She ruthlessly told Thothmes' commander to do a thorough job and keep the Prince busy for six months. She wished that she, too, were going somewhere, anywhere. The palace had become oppressive to her, a hollow building full of smiling, bowing snakes; and she went more and more to the temple, where Amun waited for her in the dark, waited to share with her the secrets of his immortal mind. She went to her own temple, too, day after day, kneeling before herself and her father and the God as if she could wrest from the images more power, more time. Oh, more time. In the dark recesses of the shrines and on the roofs of the terraces her priests sang of her beauty and her omnipotence, the music falling about her like golden rain. She stood on the second ramp and looked down her avenue to the river, thinking of Mentu-hotep-hapet-Ra, whose temple had been partially razed to make room for her own. He had been like her, in love with the mystery and consecration of the valley and of the country. He had sent to paradise itself, to the home of the gods, for things with which to beautify himself and Egypt.

She almost ran to her litter, knowing now why Amun was still not satisfied with all she had given him. She flew to the palace library, where all the scrolls, new and old, valuable and worthless, lay piled neatly in vast wooden chests around the walls. The librarian left his cosy seat and prostrated himself, astounded.

"Punt!" she gasped as Nofret and her servants tumbled into the room after her.

"Majesty?"

"Punt! Punt! Find me the maps and writings of Osiris-Mentu-hotep-hapet-Ra, he that went to Ta-Neter, the holy land of the gods. Bring them to me in the audience rooms. Hurry up! Duwa-eneneh, bring Senmut to me, and Nehesi."

"Nehesi drills the Braves of the King, Majesty."

"Then send him when he has finished."

She swept out, rushing through the passages while her retinue hurried along behind her. She ordered the desk in the audience chamber cleared. She needed Ineni, and she sent Amun-hotpe to bring him from Karnak, where he was overseeing his latest work, pillared porticoes of sandstone lined with her statues.

Ineni and the librarian arrived together; Ineni still had stone dust on his hands and his kilt. A moment later Senmut strode in, and they settled themselves around the table. It felt like a council of war.

Hatshepsut laid her hands on the table. "Now!" she said. "Librarian, what do you have for me?"

"Very little, Majesty," he admitted. "Your illustrious forefather left only an account of his journey and a list of the marvels he brought back for the God."

"A map?"

"Of a sort. In your forefather's time a map was not needed, for Egypt and Ta-Neter traded often."

"So say the legends," Ineni reminded him. "For many, many hentis the name of Punt has been but a tale told to children."

"But before the Hyksos invaded us, did not our ships ply the shores of Ta-Neter?" Senmut broke in. "The ancient monuments are full of paintings showing such a journey."

"True." Hatshepsut nodded. "Librarian, what was the most important thing to be found in Punt?"

He smiled. "Why myrrh, of course," he answered.

She nodded. "Myrrh. The holiest of perfumes. I have another vision, Senmut. I see the gardens of my temple a sea of beautiful green myrrh trees. The fragrance of them will fill the nostrils of my Father Amun, and then he will be satisfied."

Senmut leaned forward. "Let me understand Your Majesty," he said carefully. "Do you mean to mount an expedition to seek the holy land?"

"I do, and you understand very well. The Hyksos are no more, and it is time to reopen the ancient route between Egypt and Ta-Neter." They looked at each other.

"I do not know," Ineni said slowly, "but I have heard that it is a long, long way. The ships may not return."

"They will go, and they will come back," she said decisively. "My Father has spoken. Myrrh he shall have, and men in times to come shall remember who it was that gave Ta-Neter back to Egypt."

Nehesi came in then, still hot and sweating from the sun that filled the training ground. He handed his bow and spear to the guard at the door, bowed, and took his seat at Hatshepsut's side, as was his right. "I apologize for my late entrance," he said. "Is the Seal needed, Majesty?"

She told him briefly what she was planning to do and took the faded map from the librarian's hands, dismissing him and rolling out the scroll so that they all could see the spidery marks upon it.

Nehesi shook his head. "My mother told me of this fabled land, but I know of no man who has been there and returned. She said that it was a sky land, from whence the gods descended."

"In truth the gods came from there," Hatshepsut said, "but it is no cloud country. Mentu-hotep reached it, and we will, too."

They stared at the map as if hypnotized. "It would take many months,"

Ineni said. He thought to himself that it could not be done, and he glanced at Senmut, but Senmut was tracing the outlines on the scroll with his fingers, musing. Nehesi's eyes were alight.

Hatshepsut waited until they had thought a little. "Senmut, I must spare you from your duties with me," she said. "You will go and command the expedition in my name. Nehesi, you also will go. For the time being Tahuti may carry the Royal Seal. Take the map and study it. Talk to the librarian, and then come to me with a plan. I can afford as many ships as you wish, and if they are to be specially constructed, I will put my docks at your disposal. Is there anything more to say?"

They shook their heads doubtfully, a little stunned by the swift change in their daily lives. She dismissed them peremptorily—all but Senmut.

When they were alone, she turned to him. He still sat at the table, his arms folded on its surface, his face carefully noncommittal.

"Well?" she said. "You do not approve; I can tell. What is the matter?"

"I think that the venture is a worthy one and will bring you great honor, but I do not want to go. Who will order your household while I am away? And with Nehesi gone, too, who will captain your bodyguards? Majesty, I implore you, send others. There are many capable sailors in Thebes."

"What you are saying is that you do not wish to leave me defenseless. Is it not so?" She smiled faintly. "Your words are true, of course. You and Nehesi are my right and my left hands. But I have other hands, Senmut, many of them, and this voyage is very important to me. I want success, and I can only ensure it by sending the best Egypt has to offer."

"What of Thothmes and his cohorts? Are you not afraid that with Nehesi and me gone, in all probability for many months, they may press upon you?"

"I do not know, but this is the time to find out. I can keep Thothmes busy in every corner of the country. You have been burdened with my affairs for a long time, Senmut. When was the last time you took a day to walk or fish or lie in your boat?"

"I care nothing for idleness," he replied harshly. "Permit me to say, Majesty, that it is madness to deprive yourself of your loyal men at a time when your fate hangs in the balance!"

"So that is how you see it?"

"Not only I. Every day Thothmes grows stronger, more brazen in his impudence. Let me stay, Hatshepsut! You need me!"

"I am a poor Pharaoh indeed if I must forever hide behind the broad backs of my officials," she retorted quietly. "And if that time has indeed come, as you say it has, then it were better for me to die. I will never be a figurehead, Senmut, an empty, pretty shell where there was once total power. Go as you are ordered, and do not fear. When you return, I will still be here."

He bit back the angry reply and rose. "I am yours to command," he said curtly. "I will go. I will consult with Nehesi, and you may expect progress within a few days."

"Good. I am content."

He bowed and swept out, calling for his staff bearer, and she heard them pass through the outer hall and the passage beyond. She called for her Fan Bearer and for Nofret, and while she waited for them, she thought of how life would be without him. She knew that he was right when he spoke of the foolishness of sending them away at a time when her grip on the Crook and the Flail was loosening. For a moment she was tempted to change her mind, to call him back, but she did not. She wanted to test her own words. Did she still control Egypt, or did Senmut? Her ka's warnings drifted through her mind, the voice muted but the tone still faintly amused: "He has great ambition . . . give him room to move or he will destroy himself and you!" She tapped the table absently with her fingers, frowning.

If he stayed, there would be more years of desperately holding on, clinging with breaking wrists and tired arms to the crown, bolstered by his ruthless love. Thothmes would grasp the crown, too, pulling and straining, until perhaps it would split in two, as it once had been, a divided crown, a divided kingdom.

Nofret entered and bowed, waiting. Hatshepsut sighed and got up. He would go, taking all laughter and joy and security with him. The last test she must face alone. If he came back and found all as it was—if he came back and found her gone—

She tossed her head and strode out of the chamber, her chin held high.

25

It took four months to build the ships, five of them, and equip the expedition. Senmen had organized the victualing. Hatshepsut had told him to take linen and weapons and other goods with which to trade, and day after day he had listed and gathered and checked. Menkh had begged her to let him go, too. But she had refused, making him her bodyguard while Nehesi was away; and together they had gone often to the docks, watching the loading. She and Nehesi and Senmut had spent long evenings poring over the only map left that might point the way to the mysterious country, and Senmut at last had rolled up the scroll and tucked it into his belt. They would sail north with the current to the delta, then cut east through the canal the ancestors had built and out into the Red Sea. To the north there was nothing, just a vast ocean; so they decided to go south, hugging the east coast. From the moment the prows broke through the canal, they would be on their own, with nothing but stories and legends to guide them. Nehesi sat patiently in the library with the old librarian, hearing the tales of Ta-Neter over and over, trying to fix in his mind any detail that might be useful. Senmut and Hapuseneb paced the temple gardens, laying out the policies Hapuseneb would follow, struggling to pierce the future, to see what the months ahead would hold, plotting dark strategies that might, or might not, be needed.

The summer was over, and high in the southern mountains Isis shed the Tear that would swell and multiply and become a good Inundation, carrying the ships away from Thebes and into the unknown.

Senmut bid Ta-kha'et farewell the day before he left. He was truly sorrowful, for he would miss her and think of her often. She clung to him, crying, incoherent, begging him not to go. He instructed Senmen to keep an eye on her, leaving with his brother the scroll with the words that would free Ta-kha'et and give her his wealth if he himself did not return. As he went down the passages of his home and out into his lovely, well-laid gardens, her sobs followed him. He did not look back. He was grimly determined to come back, even if he had to crawl every inch on his knees. He knew that he would sit under his sycamores again and play at dice with Ta-kha'et. But he was not so sure that Pharaoh would be waiting for him.

On the last night Senmut lay quietly with Hatshepsut in the dimness of her chambers. They had made love gently, speechlessly, as if they would never again hold each other. No intuitions, no presentiments gave him hope. In the silent, fleeting darkness he cradled her in agony, feeling as her husband Thothmes had done. Her whims, her fancies, her clear-sighted, peaceful policies, her deep love for Egypt—all were mixed together and totally undecipherable to any save her God.

When dawn came and the darkness ran away with sudden, unfeeling fickleness, they got up, and she knelt before him, kissing his feet. As she rose and embraced him, she whispered, "May the soles of your feet be firm." They were the only words spoken that night, words of farewell. He kissed her softly and let her go.

On the wharf the sailors, soldiers, engineers, and diplomats who were to accompany him were already stowing away their gear. The people of Thebes were drifting down to the river to see the ships cast off. Senmut went to Menkh's apartment, where he bathed, changed his kilt and his sandals, and put a simple brown leather helmet on his shaved head. He instructed and admonished his disappointed friend as he moved between bedroom and bathing room, talking feverishly until it was time to go.

With his staff bearer and his runners before and Ta-kha'et and his slaves behind, Senmut walked slowly through the city to the wharf, where Nehesi was already on board the first ship. Hatshepsut stood on the ramp, her face drawn and her eyes circled. She was arrayed in her coronation robes, for this was a solemn occasion. Amun sat beside her in his golden Barque, the priests having dragged his sledge to the very edge of the water. Hapuseneb stood near the God and the other priests, the incense clouding him. Thothmes had planted himself beside Hatshepsut, gazing impassively over the crowds and the river. Senmut and his household bowed to them all, and he passed up the ramp and into the body of the ship. He was shocked to see Thothmes there, back so soon from the southern garrisons, and he greeted Nehesi briefly, coldly, his eyes on Thothmes' brooding face. After a pause during which Senmen, papers in hand, his scribe trotting at his heels, went from ship to ship making a final, anxious check, the sacrifices to Amun and Hathor, Goddess of the winds, began. The sails filled, and the burdened vessels began to move into the current.

The crowds started to cheer, but Senmut hardly heard the confused uproar. A sudden and violent premonition shook his body, and his eyes met hers in a last burst of regret. Her face was calm under the red and white crown, shining in the sun, but with her big, dark eyes she told him of her love and her torment, and he could not look away. The shouting grew fainter, and the wind and the creaking of the ropes and the fluttering of the sails began to fill his ears. Long after Thebes faded from sight, he saw her, standing straight and proud while the wind whipped her kilt about her thighs and tugged the heavy robe borne on her slight shoulders.

"They look very beautiful, five white birds flying to places unknown," Thothmes said, edging closer to her elbow. "I wonder, will they ever come winging home?"

She started and turned to him slowly, as if waking from a deep dream. She looked for the sarcasm that always tinged his words, but he spoke evenly, with a friendly smile. I suppose, she thought, he feels that now he can cloak his overtures with affection, seeing me bereft of all support. "Of course they will return," she replied. "Amun sent them, and he will watch over them and bring them back to me."

"Ah!" he purred. "But when? It will take them almost a year to reach Punt."

"I know. If Punt is there."

"Do you doubt?"

"Not really. But I, like you, Thothmes, have my moments of fleeting indecision."

He raised his eyebrows, and once more the jutting Thothmesid teeth glinted at her. "I do not think that you can allow yourself any more such lapses," he said with a spark of his usual hostility.

She laughed. "Oh, Thothmes! Do you imagine that I shall spend my time closeted in the darkness, mourning for Senmut as the months fly by? I am Pharaoh, and there is much to do!"

The Sacred Barque began to move slowly back to the temple, and they left the wharf and followed it.

"Much for you, perhaps, but what of me? I have drilled and marched and inspected and I am sick of it. School is over for me. Look at me, Hatshepsu. I am nearly seventeen. Give me a post at court."

She shook her head vigorously. "Do you think I am mad or simple? Are you trading on my mercy, Thothmes? I have consulted the generals, and they all press me to make you a Commander. It seems that you are a brilliant tactician. So a Commander you are, from this day."

He sniffed. "And what does a Commander do in peacetime? Mend his harness? Polish his weapons?"

"Do what you like. The army is yours, as Crown Prince. I can find plenty for you to do, escorting caravans, disciplining tax evaders, and more inspecting, of course!"

"Delightful! A tame Commander, leading a tame army, for a tame Pharaoh who is not a Pharaoh!"

She stopped in the middle of the path and turned on him, gripping his forearm, her nails sinking into his skin. "I warn you, Thothmes," she said in a low voice, "subject yourself to me, or you will be sorry. I could have killed you a thousand times over, and do not forget it. And while we speak thus, let me make it plain that you are Commander under me. I at least have seen action. You have not. If I hear that you have led your troops outside the boundaries of Egypt, I will have you imprisoned and your troops will be disbanded and scattered among the other divisions. Is that clear?"

He made no move to free himself, and they glared at each other. "Yes, it is clear," he said. "Much is clear to me that is not clear to you, Pharaoh, Living Forever. Open your eyes!" She released him, and he strode away angrily, the marks of her nails still white on his arm.

Two months later word reached the palace that the fleet had arrived at the delta and was preparing to enter the ancient canal. Hatshepsut ordered more prayers and sacrifices, listening eagerly as Anen read the dispatch. She could almost see them, floating silently, moving quietly over the still, burning wastes toward the Great Sea. With Thothmes' eyes on her she took the private letter from Senmut and went to her chambers, breaking his seal and devouring the words with a pang of misery. He was well, and all was going as she would have wished. The canal was in a bad state of repair, and they had to run out the oars and pick their way with caution. He recommended that while the floods were high and the peasants idle, a force be sent north to strengthen the crumbling walls. He spoke of the wildlife and the beauty of the desert sunsets. At the end he broke down and told her that he longed for her as his sailors longed for water in the heat of the day, his soul crying for her. She put the letter in her ivory box, together with the trinkets and memories of all her years, and went to the temple, lying for a long time before the God, asking for his power to come through the months ahead unscathed, asking his blessing on the ships, asking a curb for Thothmes. When she rose at last, she forced herself to put all inner doubts away, and she walked on to yet another audience, where Menkh and Tahuti and User-amun waited for her in the glare of yet another hot afternoon.

Neferura came to her late one night as she was being prepared for sleep. The girl was announced and came swiftly across the golden floor, her bare feet making no sound. Hatshepsut motioned for Nofret to lay aside the sleeping robe and put down the comb, ordering her evening wine and dismissing her. Neferura stopped before her and bowed. She was dressed in a white, transparent sheath that showed the slim hips and budding breasts, and around her neck she wore a collar of pieces of square amethyst inlaid, like tiny tiles in the gold. A plaited, white and gold band circled her forehead, but her face was free of paint, and her black eyes met those of her mother uncertainly. Hatshepsut smiled and offered her a chair, but Neferura continued to stand, looking down as she nervously clasped her hands under her tiny breasts.

"This is a pleasant surprise!" Hatshepsut said. She had been so busy with the plans of the expedition that she had seen little of her daughter, though she had sent for the girl's tutor, as she did every week, to hear a report on her progress. Pen-Nekheb had wheezed and shuffled his way into her presence some months ago to tell her that he did not advise any military training for the girl; she was too frail. Hatshepsut had been deeply disappointed but had agreed that nothing must endanger the health of the Heiress. She anxiously watched the play of the lamps on the small figure, their flickering emphasizing the long, thin legs and the bony shoulders. Neferura always put her on edge of late.

"How have you spent your day? Standing in the sun while the troops went through their paces?" She teased Neferura gently, but Neferura did not smile.

"Mother, I want to talk to you about Thothmes."

Hatshepsut sighed to herself. Did not everyone want to talk about Thothmes? She sat in her chair while Nofret returned and began to pour the wine into the cup on the table at her elbow. Neferura hovered before her. "Speak then. You know that you may always tell me what is on your mind."

"He and I have been promised to each other for a long time now, but still you make no move to take us to the temple. Why do you wait? Have you changed your mind?"

Hatshepsut looked into the troubled, beseeching eyes. "Did Thothmes send you to me to plead on his behalf?"

"No! I spoke with him at noon, when we ate, but he did not have much to say to me." She blushed and looked at the floor. "He never says much to me."

"Do you really love him, Neferura?"

She nodded fiercely. "Yes! I have loved him for as long as I can remember! I want to marry him, and you have promised him to me. But the time goes by, and I wait and wait."

"You are both still so young. Only seventeen. Can you not wait a little while longer?"

"Why should I? How old were you when the Steward Senmut first caught your eye? Oh, mother, I am sick of being a pawn, pushed around by you, used by you. Can I not be myself and marry Thothmes?"

Hatshepsut quickly lifted the cup to her lips to hide the jolt Neferura's words had given her. Am I really so hard? she thought, dismayed. Am I losing all, even the love of my dear Neferura? She sipped the wine and put the cup back on the table. Then she rose and put an arm around the thin shoulders, stiff beneath her touch. "Is that how you see me, Neferura? Do you know what it means to marry a Crown Prince, and such a one as Thothmes?"

The girl defiantly shrugged off the arm. "Of course I know! And you put my marriage off because you are afraid that in marrying me Thothmes is immediately legitimized and can then topple you from the Horus Throne!"

"Quite right. And he would. You think you know him, Neferura, because you love him, but I see him through the eyes of state. I have known him since he was a baby, led through childhood by his scheming mother. I tell you that if you marry him, you condemn me to death. I am sorry, but there it is."

"I do not believe it! Thothmes is wild, but he is not ruthless!"

Hatshepsut went back to her chair and sank into it wearily, pushing the hair from her face. "It is true. I cannot take the chance. I am sorry again, Neferura, but you will never wed Thothmes."

"Then I will take him to the temple myself!" Her eyes blazed with fire, the spark born of Hatshepsut herself. Then Neferura's hands flew to her face, and she turned to leave. "No, I will not do that. I would never allow him to harm you that way, mother." Halting, she came back and stood beside the table on which lay the little Cobra Coronet. "You know, I do not want to be Pharaoh. That is what you wish for me, is it not? I would rather stay a Princess all my life. I would rather be at peace, like Osiris-Neferu-khebit. Do you not think," she offered forlornly, "that you might let us marry and then make Thothmes a vizier or a nomarch? We could live far from Thebes and from you. Then there would be no danger."

"My poor Neferura," Hatshepsut said quietly. "How long do you think Thothmes would be content to govern a small nome when he could rule a kingdom? Give me another year, one year, and after that time I will take you both to the temple. I promise this."

"No! I do not wish to cause your death!"

"It may not come to that. In a year Thothmes will see that I am no threat to him and will let me live in peace."

Neferura laughed, bending to kiss Hatshepsut on the cheek. "Oh, mother, you never give up, do you? Power is all you live for. Power and Egypt. Often they are one and the same to you. What will you tell me at the end of a year? Will you go to govern a nome and leave Egypt to Thothmes? I do not think so! And neither does he. I know that he does not love me, but it does not matter. I will be a good wife for him."

"I am sure that you will. In one year."

"By then Senmut will be on his way home." She laughed again, fighting tears. "I hate being First Daughter, mother. I hate this," she said, holding up the little crown. "I hate your plans for me, and I hate the needs of state that keep me from Thothmes. Let Meryet be First Daughter!"

"Neferura, Meryet's greed would tear this country apart if she ever became Pharaoh, and well you know it!" She had been about to tell Neferura that Thothmes would never have looked at her if she had not been First Daughter, but at the sight of Neferura's distorted, unhappy face she bit back her words.

O Amun, she pleaded, why did you not give me a spirited daughter and a lordly, capable son! What will happen to my life, my blood, my Egypt, after I have left to ride the Holy Barque?

"I know it," Neferura avowed, looking up at her mother. "I would rather Thothmes wore the Double Crown than that she should ever have the chance at the throne."

"So would I," Hatshepsut said. "I do not hate him, Neferura. He is of my own royal blood, and I have always treated him with affection. But he shall not take my crown from me as long as I live, that I swear." "It is not his! It never was! As the Incarnation of Amun the crown is and always will be mine, she finished fiercely."

"But after you, mother, what then?"

Hatshepsut lifted the cup again, studiously avoiding Neferura's contemplative stare. "Then if you do not want it, it must go to Thothmes."

"I do not want it."

"I am sorry." Hatshepsut glanced at her daughter as Neferura bowed and went out, the door closing softly behind her. She drank deeply, draining the cup to the dregs.

No further word came from the expedition, and Hatshepsut resigned herself to patience. Her thoughts were often on Senmut and Nehesi, charting unknown waters. As the months went by, she tried to imagine them, sunburned, hardened, sailing on and on. But somehow the picture distressed her, and she threw herself into her work. The God's feasts and her Anniversary of Appearing came and went with the customary celebrations, and she entered her thirty-fifth year with the same vitality that had heralded her twentieth. But Thothmes and his dogs snapped closer and closer to her divine heels, and it took every ounce of her control not to break and run from them, not to relinquish Egypt and hide.

A demon drove Thothmes, too, the same demon that had whipped at his grandfather and burst forth from Hatshepsut herself. Though he was careful to keep his troops within the borders, he was never at rest, dashing from nome to nome with his soldiers, lashing the horses that drew his chariot as he and Menkheperrasonb and his other fierce friends, young Nakht, Min-mose, May, Yamu-nedjeh, thundered like wildfire through the streets of Thebes and threshed the desert floor into clouds of red dust.

She watched it all calmly, her hands still curling stubbornly around the Crook and the Flail. She and Menkh and User-amun and Tahuti went about the business of government as usual, ignoring the constant comings and goings at the barracks, on the training ground, and even in the halls of the palace itself, where Thothmes strode, laughing. Hatshepsut had a palace built for him beyond her gardens. She insisted that he live there, and he and his friends retired to his new porticoes and chambers, galled because the nobles and princes still preferred to feast and gossip and pass the nights with Pharaoh, her thousand lights still playing on the water and the grass. Then he would be off again, racing south to the Nubian border, or west behind the Necropolis and into the desert, a madness of impatience on him. Hatshepsut knew that her years of power were running out.

She and Menkh went to the training ground one winter day to take her chariot around the circuit. She still drove as often as she could, sometimes alone, glad to be free of her worries for a while and concentrate on nothing more than the tug of harness and the whistle of wind in her face. As she and Menkh approached, they saw a crowd of soldiers gathered on the edge of the course. Her Standard-Bearer ran ahead to clear a path for her, and the soldiers parted, falling silently to the ground. She paced slowly through the crowd until she came to the circuit itself. A target had been set up, facing into the circuit, and a hundred paces to the right of it a line had been painted on the ground. Thothmes and Nakht stood behind Thothmes' bronze chariot, talking beside a young retainer who held two spears. She went up to them curiously, Menkh following.

"Greetings, Thothmes. What are you doing?"

They looked up, and bowed. Thothmes put on his helmet and reached for his gauntlets. "Greetings, Pharaoh. It is a new game that I have just devised."

"Then tell me about it!"

His servant handed him a spear, and he hefted it expertly, watching her. She was dressed in her usual white boy's kilt and white leather sandals, her white helmet, bearing the Uraeus, and a copper collar inlaid with jasper about her tall neck.

"If you like," he said. "I get into my chariot, and beginning at the target, I ride around the circuit, gathering speed. When I reach the straight, I am at full attack. Before I pass the white line, I must throw the spear and hit the target."

"Have you done it?"

"Not yet, but I am about to. What are you doing here?"

She indicated the golden chariot rolling toward them, driven by one of her Braves. "I come for exercise."

"Shall I take away the target and wait until you have done your circuits?"

"No." An idea came to her, a mettle rising in her as she looked at his grinning face. "Leave the target. I, too, would like to try your new game."

His smile grew broader. "Indeed? Then shall we have a contest, you and I?"

Her chariot came to a stop beside Thothmes', and the Brave of the King jumped down, throwing the reins to Menkh. Her eyes ran speculatively over the gleaming, burnished prow of it. "Very well. Give me a spear. Seeing that the game is yours, you may ride first."

He shook his head slyly. "Oh, no. As Pharaoh you may go first. But I think a contest tame without stakes. What shall we wager?"

"I have more gold than I know what to do with. Name your price, Thothmes." She realized as soon as the words were out that they had been foolish, for he went suddenly still, licking his lips reflectively.

He began to smile slowly. "If my spear finds the center and yours does not, you will give Neferura to me in marriage, in the temple, before this month is out."

A low swell of approval rose from the listening soldiers. Menkh whispered to her, "Majesty, do not agree. It is too great a thing to throw away on a wager."

Though she knew what he meant, she ignored him, gazing soberly into Thothmes' mocking eyes. She nodded decisively. "Agreed. And if my spear finds the center, you will give her up forever."

The small crowd was silent now, tensely, quietly watching the royal pair.

Thothmes nodded, his lips compressed. "Do we understand one another?"

"We do. Let us begin. I do not mind riding first. Menkh, my gauntlets." He bowed and handed the heavy white leather gloves to her. She drew them on, squinting up to see where the sun lay. She walked swiftly to her chariot and mounted, taking the reins from Menkh and drawing them tight in her hands. The little horses shuffled and tossed their heads.

She clucked to them, and as the wheels began to turn, the soldiers drew back. She trotted slowly once around the circuit, her eyes fixed on the small, round piece of wood painted a dazzling white. She stopped where she had begun, getting down to check the harness. She held out a hand for the spear, and the retainer gave it to her. With a last glance around she shifted the reins to one hand, winding them tightly about her wrist. She shouted to the horses, swinging onto the circuit and gathering speed.

Thothmes stood with his feet apart, his fists balled on his hips, his eyes narrow as he watched. The soldiers began to shout as she bent lower, already halfway around, the sun sparking from her wheels like flickering fire. They heard her call sharply, and the horses began to strain, their manes flowing, their hooves beating a thunderous tattoo on the packed, gray sand. She came around, wheeling into the straight, her spear sweeping in a glittering arc. They had a brief glimpse of her face, her mouth open and taut in deadly concentration, her eyes steady on the target. She whipped past them, and they saw the spear leave her hand, fly up, up, a black shaft against the blue sky. With a thud it was buried, quivering in the stout wood, and she yelled, leaning back to pull in the horses. With a cry they all rushed forward, milling about the target. As she trotted in a circle and came up to them, Thothmes strode up to the canting spear. Its tip had struck true to the center.

She leaped down, throwing the reins to Menkh, and went to look, laughing happily at the sight of Thothmes' scowl. "You did not think I could do it, did you?" she said. "You should have consulted my generals before agreeing so glibly to the wager! They had seen my skill long before you were born, Crown Prince!"

"Remove the spear," he ordered, and the retainer wrenched it free. "I have not yet run, Hatshepsu, so do not crow too loudly. You may yet lose."

"How can I? Mine was dead in the center!"

They walked to the edge of the circuit, and Thothmes mounted quickly, settling himself and snatching his spear from the soldier. Hatshepsut removed her gloves and handed them to Menkh. She shaded her eyes with her hand as Thothmes cantered onto the circuit and picked up speed. He was obviously not going to walk through it first. They heard him shout, and his horses stretched out. They all screamed encouragement, even Hatshepsut, caught up in the thrill of the careening chariot, the lithe, bending figure. His spear came down. He was cornering; he had reached the straight, slapping the horses with the reins clutched in one naked hand. The white line loomed suddenly, the target blurred. He threw with a gasping curse. Before the spear hit the target she was running, the soldiers behind her. He leaped from his moving chariot, pelted over the dirt, and came up, panting.

She was doubled up with mirth. "Embrace me, Thothmes! The gods took your spear and guided it! See! Where is my rent? Plugged by your tip! A perfect throw. Two perfect throws!"

Menkheperrasonb pulled out the spear, and indeed there was only the one hole, very slightly wider now than it had been before.

She burst out laughing again.

"Who wins?" he asked abruptly.

She stopped laughing and regarded him, feigning surprise. "Why, I do! I threw first."

"But if I had thrown first, I would have won!"

"Perhaps, but you did not. So I win."

"You do not! We both hit the center, and in agreement with the wager we both must win!"

"But, my dear Thothmes, that is impossible." Suddenly they were both sober, looking at each other with no thought now of the game. "We cannot both win, and we cannot both lose. One of us must leave the field, and it will not be I."

"Nor I."

"Then shall we run again?"

"No. This game can only be played once, and there is no going back. No second chances."

"I know. So I will take Menkh and my chariot and ride beside the river. You can stay here on the training ground and keep practicing!" Before he could retort, she was standing in the chariot with Menkh, and in another moment she had left them behind in her dust.

Thothmes watched her whirl away in the direction of the water; then he got into his chariot and raised his whip to the two sweating horses. "We will continue! My spear! Nakht, set up another target!" Nakht ran to do Thothmes' bidding, but the soldiers who had gathered to watch barely heard him. They were looking toward the little cloud of swiftly dissipating dust.

Thothmes spent the rest of the day in frustrated rage, an anger that had nothing to do with the outcome of the contest. He hated her, hated her. He seethed as he wrestled with Min-mose and threw him. He burned as he swam in the river and was still livid as he ate his evening meal in his own banqueting hall, surrounded by his friends. Her pretty, sundrenched face was before him, her low, teasing tones ringing in his ears. When he pushed his plate away and went into the garden, there she was, her mocking smile, trim waist, and slim thighs towering over him. He spat at the statue and turned from the impassive, uncaring face, wandering back to his trees and his paved walkways. The terrible hatred boiling in his veins suddenly turned into a devouring lust for the woman who rode her chariot like a man and could order the lives of anyone she chose. He sat down beside the nodding, sweet poppies, tearing one up by the roots and pulling at it absently. He saw her sway in her ridiculous, tiny kilts, her breasts jutting under the heavy golden collars she always wore, her eyes watching him unceasingly, always watching. He was seventeen. All his life he had hated her and admired her. Now there was something else, something born of his restless, growing, maddening dissatisfaction, a new channel opening in him, filled with his own blood and mixed with the fever that his father had sickened under and that Senmut and Hapuseneb and a hundred others had succumbed to as they passed in and out of the halls of power around her. He threw the mangled poppy away and drew up his knees, hugging his legs furiously. He was enraged and baffled by the calm, softly moving grasses, the slow dip and sway of the dark-branched trees, affronted that the world should be at peace while he was consumed. He groaned as he remembered the way she leaped into the chariot, her supple legs bending. He saw her pull on her gauntlets with long, eloquent fingers. He saw the generous mouth open to laugh, to laugh, always to laugh—at him.

He got up and left his garden, walking once more to the riverbank, taking the path that ran beside the water the whole length of the royal domains. He passed his own gates and came to his mother's gardens. But he strode on, passing her water steps and her gates. He came upon a group of guards. They questioned him briefly and let him through. His feet quickened of their own accord, and he began to run. He saw her lights twinkling gaily beyond him and to the left, and he turned up her wide avenue, trotting under her tall trees. He did not enter the banqueting hall but cut farther left and reached her own entrance.

A Follower of His Majesty stopped him. "Greetings, Crown Prince. A fine night. Do you seek audience with Pharaoh?"

Thothmes nodded, looking past the man to the silent silver passage and the torchlight. "Is the One within?"

"He is. You may pass." He stood aside and Thothmes walked in, slowly, pacing the empty corridors cautiously but smiling, burning. At her great double doors, beside her rough-hewn statues, he was stopped again. Two of her Followers barred his way.

Her herald rose from his seat and bowed to him. "Greetings, Crown Prince."

"Greetings, Duwa-eneneh. Is Mighty Horus gone to her couch?"

"I think not, but she is preparing to."

"I want to see her. Announce me."

Duwa-eneneh slipped into the room, closing the doors behind him, but he did not shut them fully. A ray of friendly yellow light streamed out onto Thothmes' feet. He heard soft conversation and then her light laugh. Duwa-eneneh came out, nodding to the guards. They lifted their spears and stood at attention. "You may enter," the herald said, and Thothmes walked past him and into the room.

He had been there before but not often. To his aroused senses it seemed that he was suddenly enveloped in her perfume; the myrrh seeped from her body, her couch, her hangings, even her silver walls. Far to the rear the darkness fought with the light from her lamps, and he caught a glimpse of black treetops beyond the balcony. He looked at her from just beyond the doorway. She was standing by the couch in her sleeping robe, transparent, smooth, white linen that fell from her shoulders to the floor. Her head was uncovered, the blue-black hair curling under her chin and catching the light as she turned to look at him. He glanced at the table beside the couch, where her helmet and her armbands lay, and looked beyond them to the gold and turquoise, heavily lined box that nestled the royal insignia, the vulture of Nekhbet and the cobra of Buto. They sparkled and taunted him from their blue bed. He shifted his gaze and bowed.

She inclined her head slightly in return. "Good evening, Thothmes! An odd time to be seeking audience! Do you want me to get dressed and come out to the training ground so that we may conclude our contest? Have you decided on other stakes?" She did not like the look of him. He seemed dazed, his eyes fixed on her. Deep within them an odd light flared steadily, as if he had been to the temple of Bast and drunk poppy juice.

He came closer, his step uncertain. "Majesty, I wish to speak with you alone. Be pleased to dismiss Nofret."

Hatshepsut shook her head slightly. "Thothmes, I do not think that I want to be alone with you. I mean you no disrespect, but I do not trust you. Nofret stays."

He spread out his hands. "I mean you no harm, Hatshepsu. I merely wish to talk. If you feel yourself in danger, you can always call for your bodyguards. Duwa-eneneh sits at your door to summon help if you need it." His lips curled faintly. "Do you fear me?"

"No, not you. But for the sake of my country I must not trust you. However, I am not a silly girl." She paused, considering. "Very well. Nofret, you can go. Wait for my summons in your own rooms." They were silent as Nofret bowed and backed to the door, opening it and disappearing quietly. "Now then. What do you want?" She was clearly impatient to hear him out so that she could dismiss him and go to bed.

He stood for a moment, irresolute, wanting to rush to her and take her in his arms. For just a moment he wondered what on earth he was doing, but she was smiling encouragingly at him, her eyebrows raised. He stepped nearer. "Can we not have wine while we talk?" he asked. "Will you keep me standing?"

She inclined her head. "There is wine on your right hand and a chair beside the wine. Did you come to chat, Thothmes?"

"Perhaps. I have a proposition to put to you." He turned and poured himself a cup of wine. He tossed it back with one gulp and poured another, feeling her amusement.

"Indeed? I am intrigued. Say on."

He sat down, pulling his long legs in under the chair. He wished that she, too, would sit. "I will come straight to the point, Majesty, and not keep you hovering by your bed for long. Here it is. We are agreed that you promised Neferura to me one day so that I may rule."

"Yes."

"But you will never give her to me, I know that."

"Well, I do not. Stop reading my mind, Thothmes."

"We both also know that I am almost full grown. When I am of age, soon, I can take with leisure what is mine, and you will be powerless to stop me."

"You may know that, but I do not. In the name of Amun, Thothmes, what are you up to?"

"Why can you and I not rule together?"

She slowly sat down on the couch, her eyes suddenly wary. "I do not yet follow your reasoning. Speak."

He waved an arm. "It is very simple. We can dissolve our differences in one swoop and both be satisfied. We will marry. Take me to the temple yourself, and I will have the Double Crown and be legitimized."

She looked at him blankly for a long time. He gazed back at her, his eyes filled with the fire that a moment before had been only pinpoints of yellow light. His handsome jaw was tight, the muscles flexing involuntarily.

"Is this a black joke?" She suddenly lifted her own cup, holding it out. He poured wine into it and sat down again. The room was very still.

"Not at all. I will not have to wait forever to have Neferura. You would thus be freed from the weight of all responsibility and all fear of me."

"It is not so simple," she said. "No, not at all. Your father came to me, Thothmes, with almost the same words you seek to woo me with. Because I was young and untried, I went with him to the temple, but I gave him a worthless crown and an empty rule. I am not such a fool as to believe that you are as soft and biddable as he was. I could never govern without your constant interference. By marrying you I would immediately cease to be Pharaoh and become only Divine Consort, battling you to no avail. You would have Egypt—and me—in the palm of your hand." She took a long sip of wine and rose, holding the cup in both hands and turning her hard eyes upon him. "Are you afraid to reach for the crown yourself? Do you see the bounds of my might as immeasureable? Do you quail? Can you not wait another few years and then tear the throne from under me?" She leaned forward suddenly. "It is because you slaver for the crown now, but you are still afraid of me! You fear me and cannot make a move!"

He rose in one swift movement, dropping his cup, the red wine splashing over the floor. In two long strides he was upon her. "It has nothing to do with the crown!" he snapped, teeth bared in a snarl. "If I wanted it, I could have it tomorrow!"

"You lie," she said evenly. "You are still not quite ready to make such a move, and you know it! Why are you here, Thothmes? What do you really want?"

He snatched the empty cup from her hands and threw it into a corner. He grabbed her arms and forced them behind her back, pulling her toward him. "You," he said savagely. "It is you that I want, proud Pharaoh." He lunged for her mouth, but she twisted desperately. He released one arm, jerking her head back to face him, his fingers entwined brutally in her hair.

"Look at me, Hatshepsu," he screamed. "I am a man, and your lover is far away. I will be baited and teased by you no longer. I will have you, and you will not cry out, for if you do, I will crack your arm like a rotten stick before your guards can reach you." He wrenched her, and she cried out sharply. He kissed her, grinding his lips into her mouth, pressing himself against her until she thought that her back would break.

She suddenly tasted blood, her own or his she could not tell. With a burst of insane fury she tore at his face with her free hand, raking his cheek, scrabbling for his nose, and he had to change his grip. In a flash she had sunk her teeth into his shoulder, and he threw her away, yelping with pain. She ran to her shrine and picked up a heavy copper incense stand, brandishing it threateningly at him. Her fingers gingerly felt her mouth and came away red.

"You mad bitch!" he panted, rubbing his shoulder, preparing to lunge at her again.

She took the stand in both hands and swung it over her head so that it whistled. "Touch me again, and I will dash out your addled brains!" she shouted. "Keep your distance! You craven whelp, to attack me when I am unarmed! Now I see your mind! But to secure the throne by such a clumsy seduction is well beyond your powers, puppy!"

They glared across the room at one another, both shaking with rage and exhaustion. He grabbed the wine jar and held it to his lips, drinking thirstily until it was empty. He wiped his mouth with a slow gesture and stood looking at her, his arms hanging at his sides. She still held the stand over one shoulder, her eyes following his every movement.

"I am sorry," he said stiffly. "I do not know what came over me. But you are wrong if you think that I want to take the throne in this crude way. I had no intention of forcing myself upon you when I entered your room tonight; I wanted only to marry you."

"Only?" She was panting. "What is this word?"

"I love you," he said, not meeting her eye. "I hate you more than any other, and I love you more than any other. But I think that from now on, I will give up loving you and hate you all the more. You are a deep and wily trap, as my father found, to his undoing."

"You do not know what you are saying. Your father and I loved each other in our way, and he was happy. It would distress him to see you standing there with your mouth bloody and the madness of lust still in your eyes. You speak of love, but you do not know anything about it. At seventeen love is a consuming fire in the body, but the heart is still locked shut. That is why I pardon you for laying violent hands upon me. That is why I will not have you thrown into prison. Love? Do you care about my thoughts or my plans or my dreams? Go away! You are only a mad Thothmesid after all."

He grinned slowly. "Nevertheless, I wager that it would be glorious to lie with you."

"That you will never know. Even if I did take it into my head to admit you to my bed, I would still never, ever, give you my kingdom. I would rather marry Senmut, for he is well-seasoned and a cunning and able man. I would rather give him the Double Crown." She lowered the incense stand and turned to set it back beside Amun. "I can still have children, Thothmes. Shall I marry Senmut and give Egypt a son?"

His breath stopped, and he began to choke. He could not tell from her expression whether or not she was serious.

"Do you hate me that much, Hatshepsu?" he asked quietly.

She walked to him and laid an arm around his shoulders, stroking him gently. "I do not hate you at all. How many times must I say it, and still no one will listen? You bring my anger upon yourself with your wild doings and your threats. Have I not promised you Egypt some day?"

"Yes, when you are dead!"

"If your father still lived, would you intrigue against him and plot to take his divinity from him?"

"Of course not. He would be Pharaoh within the law."

"And so am I, for I am the law. If—if you become Pharaoh in your turn, you will understand fully what that means. It is not a license to do what you please; it is a trust."

"You and your fine words! You have a silken tongue, aunt-mother. Well, I will slink away rebuked."

She suddenly embraced him, and he held her for a moment before they broke apart. "I wish that we were not enemies," she said sadly.

He bowed awkwardly, overwhelmed and ashamed, leaving her quickly without looking at her. She watched him go and turned back, breathing a sigh of relief. Her mouth throbbed, and the muscles of her back were sore. She washed her face before she called for Nofret, a creeping regret and a new fear budding within her, magnified by the silence of the room. She knew that Thothmes would never speak to her of love or trust or family affection again. From now on she would have to look over her shoulder every day and double the guards at her door at night. When Nofret came, Hatshepsut got onto her couch and reached for the fur Senmut had given her. After her night-light was lit and the other lamps put out, she lay holding it to her, the tears trickling slowly down her cheeks.

On a cold, still night in the middle of winter, the month of Choiak, Neferura came to Hatshepsut's bedchamber. She stood before her mother, her face white and drawn with pain. Hatshepsut awoke with a start to see the shadowy, swaying form above her.

Seeing that her mother was awake Neferura collapsed onto the couch and began to cry. "I have a pain, mother, a terrible pain, here." She rubbed the right side of her abdomen. "I cannot sleep."

Hatshepsut sent Nofret running for the physician and got up, tucking Neferura under her own covers. The girl moaned and writhed, sweat breaking out on her forehead, clammy to Hatshepsut's touch. She ordered the lamps lit and the brazier stoked. She looked at the water clock. It was only three hours since she herself had retired. Nofret returned with the physician, and while he examined Neferura, Hatshepsut had Nofret dress her. She sat in the little chair beside the couch, and Neferura groped frantically for her hand, drawing up her knees as the pain probed her. The physician straightened and drew the covers back over the thin body.

Hatshepsut snapped, "Well?"

He shook his head. "She is very swollen about the groin, and the flesh is hot to the touch."

"What will you do?"

"I can give her a tincture of arsenic and poppy to take away the pain, but little more."

"Magic?"

"A spell might work. I have seen this before, often. Sometimes the swelling goes down, but it comes back."

"Is poison at work?"

"No poison administered from without will cause a local swelling such as Her Highness's. You may set your mind at rest on that, Majesty."

She nodded, but she did not believe him. "Give her the drug, then. Nofret, send Duwa-eneneh to fetch the magicians. I want Hapuseneb here at once."

Nofret hurried out, and the physician measured the dosage, carefully giving it to Neferura from his tiny alabaster cup. The girl swallowed it with effort, in tiny sips, and fell back onto the pillow, closing her eyes. Hatshepsut hoped that she would sleep, but she did not. When Hapuseneb and the magicians came, bowing, Neferura still tossed from side to side, whimpering. They were shocked.

Hatshepsut rose. "Her body is in disorder," she said. "She has a swollen groin and much pain. Prepare an incantation to rid her of this devil." While they consulted together, she had a chair brought for Hapuseneb.

He sat beside Hatshepsut, looking at Neferura as she moaned softly. "Is this Thothmes' work?" he asked her quietly.

"I do not think so. The physician says not. Why would Thothmes destroy his ready tool? Neferura still means the Horus Throne to him."

The magicians came forward and stood about the bed, filling the room with their dreary music. Hatshepsut listened hopelessly, her mind wandering to Thothmes' death. Hapuseneb was motionless, his gray eyes fixed steadily on the Princess. Neferura soon lost consciousness as the drugs took their effect, but her sleep was uneasy. She babbled and cried, always moving on the golden couch. The hand still grasping Hatshepsut's was hot and dry, the forehead damp and cold under the physician's wary touch.

Someone bowed, and Hatshepsut looked up, startled, to see Thothmes straightening before her. He was still in his sleeping kilt, and his shaved head was bare, making his eyes darker than ever and his protruding teeth and high cheekbones more emphatically her father's.

"Is she very ill?" he asked.

She murmured helplessly, "I do not know."

"May I stay?"

She looked into his face but saw only the polite expression of a question. She waved for another chair to be brought. He sat and leaned forward, his elbows on his knees, his hands hanging.

The droning went on and on, a monotonous lullaby. From time to time the physician gently withdrew the covers and felt the swollen skin. The night wore on, and Neferura seemed to quieten.

When dawn came, she opened her eyes and smiled at them faintly. "Thothmes?" she whispered, her face lighting.

He knelt by the couch, stroking the hair from her face. "It is I, little one. Be at peace. I will not leave you."

"I feel a bit better now. The pain has gone."

The physician went to her immediately. When he rose, his face was grave. "The swelling has gone suddenly," he said. Hatshepsut ordered the magicians to cease. In the welcome silence they could all hear Neferura's short, rapid breaths, and Hapuseneb caught the physician's eye. The man shook his head imperceptibly, and Hapuseneb looked back at Neferura. She was smiling up into Thothmes' face. She placed her hands in his, and his fingers curled tightly around them.

"Am I very ill? Perhaps if I frighten mother, she will let us marry," Neferura whispered.

She turned her head to smile at Hatshepsut, but Hatshepsut saw something in those unfocused, drug-filled eyes, a flickering shadow of the Judgment Hall. As she rose with a cry and bent over her daughter, Neferura gave a little hiccup, just once, and sighed. She was dead. The eyes glazed rapidly; the smile became a lifeless grimace.

Thothmes gently withdrew his hands and stood up. No one moved or spoke. Sunshine crept across the floor, and the embers in the brazier died, but the people were frozen, stunned at the swiftness of the Princess's passing. At length Thothmes bowed and went out without a word.

Hatshepsut turned to Hapuseneb, her hands stretched forth, pleading. "She is dead. Dead!" she said unbelievingly.

He took the cold hands and warmed them between his own. "These things happen, Majesty," he told her quietly. "Only the gods know why."

She continued to stare at him, her eyes looking through him. "All of them gone. All of them!" She turned back to the couch and knelt, gathering the limp figure into her arms. "Come home, Senmut," she whispered into the damp hair that lay tangled on the pillow. "I have need of you now."

Hapuseneb left her cradling the body, rocking it softly to and fro. He went to the House of the Dead to summon the sem-priests. He could do nothing more.

Hatshepsut moved through the days of mourning woodenly, coldly, and Thothmes left her alone. All her hopes for a new line of female Kings had been pinned on Neferura, and with her death she felt another golden pin driven deep into the beautiful, huge quartz sarcophagus in which she felt she herself would lie before long. It seemed to her that the God had deserted her and that all the years behind her were full of struggles and deaths and defeat after defeat. She forgot the golden times: Senmut and her coronation and her close and loving relationship with a God who had given her her heart's desire. She saw only Amun, faithless Father, cruel depriver. She went to Karnak and strode up and down before him, reminding him of all the prayers he had not answered, but he did not speak to her as he often had done in the past. She went across the river to Osiris-Neferu-khebit, but here, too, there was no comfort. Neferu was dumb, smiling sadly at her with a pitying, uncomprehending stare. Hatshepsut went back to the palace to wait for the burial, knowing that she had been abandoned by gods and men.

The whole court attended the funeral. Ineni and Tahuti, Menkh, User-amun, Amun-hotpe, Puamra, Hapuseneb, even Anen, the Royal Scribe—men tired and dispirited, worn with the years of an awesome responsibility. She paced before them, her head down and her eyes on the small coffin, feeling as hollow and lifeless as her daughter's body. Thothmes walked beside her, swinging along silently. Somehow there was comfort in his easy vitality, the freshness in his springing knees. She felt the absence of Senmut and Nehesi like the sharp cut of a lance, needing them desperately as she at last entered the dark passageways of the tomb and stood while Neferura was lowered into her other coffins. At the other funerals—her father's, her mother's, Thothmes', her sister's—she had felt the pain of separation and sensed the sorrow of the furniture and belongings piled around. But Neferura's lovely things spoke to her of her own failures, the wasted years spent in fighting. For what? For a moment of deluded might? She stood by Hapuseneb and looked about her. There was Neferura's first doll, there her child's kilts piled neatly in her little tiring box, there her silver crowns, there her pretty blue sandals; even her pets lay with her in the dark.

And here am I, Hatshepsut thought grimly, still holding on, though I am so tired, so weary of myself and of Thothmes and everyone else. Am I, Son of the Sun, true likeness and Incarnation of Amun, never to die?

She left the priests to utter the final curses on any who tried in later years to force a way into the tomb and the workmen to begin the sealing of the stone doors as she went slowly back to the palace. She passed the mouth of her valley without so much as a glance, knowing that on this day the solemn, sphinx-lined avenue would be sleeping in the sun, empty of worshipers. She got into the royal skiff and sat with her head lowered, wondering for the first time in her life what she would do with the rest of the day, and the day after that, and the one after that.

A year had gone by since the five laden ships had left the Theban wharf, but that awesome, happy occasion already seemed to belong to an era long gone, a time of hopes and expectations in the midst of turmoil. That morning seemed to shine out like the last friendly glow of dwindling firelight on a cold desert night.

Before she had climbed the water steps, she saw that Thothmes and Meryet had already disembarked and were walking away through the trees. Hatshepsut paused for a moment to watch them glide away, their heads together, deep in conversation. So that was the way the wind blew. Of course.

She went to her couch and sent for Ipuky, and for the rest of the afternoon she lay with an arm across her face and her eyes closed, listening to all the old songs, the songs of conquest and laughter, the songs that belonged to other, less complicated ages, the clear, melancholy voice of the blind man filling her room like mellow water music and mingling with her own loud thoughts.

Two days after the funeral, Yamu-nefru, Sen-nefer, and Djehuty took their chariots, their tents, and their servants and went hunting lions in the desert. They journeyed for three days, sighting two beasts and bringing down another, returning each night to their camp under the shadow of the Theban cliffs to sit around the fire, their tents behind them, watching the spectacular sunsets. None were at ease. Though they had been friends since the days of their youth in the palace schoolroom, though they had fought and feasted together, a blanket of inhibitions seemed to smother them, separating one from the other.

It was only on their last night out that Yamu-nefru sent the servants to their own tent and poured their wine himself, balancing the jug carefully and studiously in his long, manicured fingers, avoiding their eyes. He sat cross-legged on his cloak, shifting his seat in the sand underneath. He cleared his throat delicately. "We have not had a merry hunting," he remarked to no one in particular. "Could it be that we have had more on our minds than just lions?"

"Say rather that we have had only one lion in our thoughts," Sen-nefer grunted. "I think that the time has come to speak frankly."

The others nodded, Yamu-nefru sipping his wine and watching them cautiously over the rim of his jeweled cup.

Djehuty spoke softly, his eyes on the orange sky. "The lion struggles fiercely in the trap, seeking knives with which to cut himself free. His bonds weaken. Soon he will burst forth of his own accord. Woe to those who did not assist him!"

"We do not fear his anger," Sen-nefer remarked. "It is not that that we must consider, but where our duty lies. We can no longer serve two masters in honesty, and honesty, my friends, can no longer be made to serve us."

"Have done with evasions!" Yamu-nefru snapped. "I at least will now speak plainly. Pharaoh's dreams have come to nought with the death of the Princess Neferura. For many years she has governed Egypt with a firm hand and a steady eye, but now she is bucking a clamorous successor. Thothmes maintains his right to the throne from the day his father died. Is he in the right?"

"According to law, yes," Djehuty replied. "We all know that. But we have served Hatshepsu for a long time. We have fought beside her and ruled our holdings under her, and she has treated us with all kindness and reward. She has been immensely successful as Pharaoh. Her peace has brought a precious security to Egypt, and if we leave her, we bring that peace to an end."

"It is coming to an end in any case," Sen-nefer said brusquely. "Thothmes means to take the throne soon, with or without her permission. If without, then you may be sure that blood will follow. If we support her still, we prolong the fight, for we have many soldiers under us, as has Thothmes. But if we go to Thothmes and offer him our help, she will be weakened, and her war swift. Her defeat will be almost painless."

"Painless for Thothmes!" Yamu-nefru retorted. "She will see any revolt as open treason. It is reasonable, for there is no doubt that she is indeed the God. I do not think that she will fight. All her life she has been bent on protecting her countrymen. If she thinks that Thothmes intends to fight and rend Egypt apart at the seams, she will give in rather than shed Egyptian blood."

"True," Djehuty nodded. "And in that case Thothmes will be Pharaoh before long. I am for him. He is able and strong and will make a good Hawk-in-the-Nest. Hatshepsu is losing ground. As she retreats, her power lessens, and Egypt suffers. Rather than see a government in confusion, I will put myself and my troops at Thothmes' disposal."

They drank for a moment in silence, considering Djehuty's words.

Sen-nefer spoke gloomily. "I go with you, but I am loathe to do it. She is a woman of great courage and resource. It will be a cruel blow to her to see us desert."

"It will be no desertion!" Yamu-nefru reminded him. "We serve Egypt, and Thothmes will soon be Egypt. It is very easy to discuss these things far from her presence, but can we stand before her in the audience chamber and repeat them?"

"Is there any need? Can we not go to Thothmes and then withdraw from court for a while?"

Sen-nefer was clearly distressed.

Yamu-nefru said disdainfully, "We are not cowards. If we throw in our lot with Thothmes, she must know it from our own lips, or I will not agree to go."

The sun had set, and above them the sky was turning slowly from flame to the palest of blues, the changing color revealing a round, clear moon and the silver dot of the evening star.

Djehuty turned his head slowly, scanning the vast horizon. He looked Yamu-nefru full in the face. "We all love her, the Daughter of the God," he said, "but it is time for a new Horus, a male Horus, and a new administration. It does not have to be tomorrow. Indeed, it is too soon, for Senmut and Nehesi will bring her a new glory from Punt, and Thothmes will have to wait yet again for the people's acclaim. I say hold back, but with minds made up."

Yamu-nefru carefully set his cup in the sand and fastidiously dusted off his fingers. "It all depends on whether or not Senmut brings home the fleet," he said quietly. "He may. Or he may not."

Sen-nefer disagreed. "In either case she is finished," he said brutally.

They gazed uncomfortably into the fire as the sky darkened to a rich royal blue and the desert stars appeared suddenly, flaming, hanging above them like Hatshepsut's wise, all-seeing eyes.

Senmut and Nehesi also sat in the sand, but before them the ocean rolled, a dark, heaving waste bordered as far as their eyes could see with lines of gray foam that dwindled and reformed as the waves broke. Behind them the jungle massed, a thick, humid tangle of fecundity, pierced by the tiny glimmers of Parihu's lights. The voices of their sailors and Parihu's subjects carried to them through the damp, hot air.

Nehesi sighed. "It is indeed a marvelous land, this Ta-Neter," he said, "but it is time to go home."

Senmut leaned back until the quivering palm fronds hid the sky. "Past time," he said. "This damp heat drains all life from me, and I feel as if I were about to sprout vines. How good it will be to smell the dry winds of the desert once more."

"The One will be pleased. She will be very pleased," Nehesi said.

They sat in a companionable silence, their thoughts full of the gracious halls and sweet gardens of Thebes and of the woman who waited for them patiently, leaning over the parapet of her balcony and staring with tired eyes into the southern sky.

In the spring Hatshepsut's desert police brought her word of more unrest in Rethennu. She reluctantly called a council of war, her heart not in it this time. Pen-Nekheb had died, and somehow the old spirit of cohesive force was missing from the men who faced her in the audience chamber.

But it was Thothmes who dominated the table, standing before them in his yellow helmet, his shoulders back, and his eyes flashing. One foot was propped up on a chair. "Rethennu holds Gaza," he said, "and Gaza is a mighty city and moreover a seaport. Give me leave, Princes of Egypt, to capture Gaza and thus not only put down these ever unsatisfied heathen but also acquire for us an outlet on the Great Sea."

"It is I who give or deny leave!" Hatshepsut warned him obstinately. "Speak to me, Thothmes, not to my advisers. Rethennu is ours and has been for many long hentis. Why should we do more than teach them a little lesson?"

Thothmes' eyes saw far into a future that she could not glimpse. "Because Gaza is the gateway to other countries, to other allies and conquests and riches. Though we in truth hold Rethennu, we do not hold it firmly enough. It is time to fill Gaza with Egyptian artisans, Egyptian traders, Egyptian vessels."

"But why? Why risk the army to take a city that can be fortified and held against us when we need only remind it to whom it owes tribute? We could do that with a small punitive force."

He looked down at her, incredulous.

The ministers were silent, even Menkh, who always had something to say, all knowing that their opinion here did not matter in the least and that they were seeing one more family squabble.

"Why? Because Gaza is a good testing ground."

"For what?"

"For me. For the army, which grows weary of feigned battle and long marches to nowhere. For Egypt, a chance to spring from Gaza and expand her borders."

"Pah! Our borders are already as wide as the sun's journey." She shuffled the dispatches waspishly, thinking not of proud and mighty Gaza but of proud and mighty Thothmes, who fumed and stamped from his palace to hers and out to the barracks and back again and up and down the country with his men. At last she rubbed the back of her neck under the black and white striped helmet, a headache lurking somewhere behind her eyes. "Very well. Take three or four divisions, and capture Gaza."

He looked at her in disbelief. "Just like that?"

"Just like that. Gaza has long been a thorn in our side, but as you know, I have managed to keep it from pricking too deep until now. If you think that Rethennu will lie quiet once Gaza has fallen, then by all means take it. But do not die, Thothmes, whatever else you do!"

They smiled at each other, still able to stand back and see their struggle from the angle of a sporadic family feud.

He bowed deeply. "Thanks, Mighty Pharaoh. Gaza shall fall, and I shall undoubtedly come home."

"Undoubtedly." Her mouth quirked in a half-smile. "But remember that the spoils fall to me."

He laughed. "I shall pile them at your feet." She dismissed him and turned to the uncomfortable, wary men, smiling at them quizzically. They stirred and smiled back with sympathy, listening while, outside, Thothmes shouted for the heralds to summon his generals.

They all left Thebes for the north: Thothmes in his golden helmet and silver Commander's armbands, Min-mose, Nakht, Menkheperrasonb, Yamu-nedjeh, May, Yamu-nefru, Djehuty, Sen-nefer, and fifteen thousand men, the Divisions of Horus, Set, and Anubis. Hatshepsut watched all morning while the glittering cavalcade swarmed along the river road. When the last baggage cart had disappeared, she left her balcony and went inside to a quiet, empty palace. She felt the anticlimax acutely, and thought of how she herself had marched happily away, leaving her husband to drift about the apartments at Assuan. Now it was Thothmes who spearheaded Egypt in the field, and she was left to pasture like an old horse, wandering peacefully in the sun. But it was good to wake up and hear Hapuseneb singing the hymn and to dress leisurely and go to the temple in peace, not having to worry about the day's endless grinding quarrels and Thothmes' subtle barbs. She did not relax her vigilance entirely, knowing that he would have left behind many spies. She continued to have her halls patrolled day and night, but she did not think that Thothmes would make a move against her unless he was in the city to snatch up the Crook and the Flail, and she allowed herself some measure of rest.

She was becoming anxious about the expedition, and in all the cities along the Nile she stationed messengers to bring her word if the ships were sighted. But day followed cloudless day, and still that word did not come. She spent more time with Meryet, trying to interest herself in the girl's constant, silly, spiteful gossip; but she shrank from the common, mean streak in her daughter. Hatshepsut knew that Thothmes and Meryet were becoming very close. She also knew that when the time came, Meryet would undoubtedly go cheerfully to the temple with him, applauding her mother's end. Hatshepsut sorrowed for the wistful and silent Neferura, who would at least have given her what support she could, frail though that would have been.

Meryet thought Hatshepsut cool and superior, and she obviously preferred the company of Thothmes' mother. Hatshepsut saw them often, walking together in the garden, arm in arm, aglitter with jewels, both thin and beautiful in a predatory, disturbing way, weaving slowly in and out of the trees, talking and laughing. Hatshepsut watched them expressionlessly, blaming only herself for Meryet's defection. It had not been easy, growing up under the shadow of a mother who was also an empire's Pharaoh.

Spring grew hot, became summer, and the day on which Senmut had sailed away two years before came and went without any message of her fleet's whereabouts. Hatshepsut regularly received dispatches from the army, now camped on the plain outside Gaza, preparing for battle. Sometimes Thothmes sent his own greetings, together with letters for Aset and Meryet. Feeling no compunction, Hatshepsut had the other letters opened and read them. But they contained no information about his plans for her. She did not think that they would, but she was coolly aware that the time of her overthrow grew ever nearer, and she took no chances, missed no loopholes. Thothmes' letters to Meryet were full of affection, but guarded. Reading them, Hatshepsut smiled grimly, knowing that Thothmes would not be foolish enough to endanger Meryet by any compromising words that might be construed, even at this late date, as treason. While Anen carefully resealed the scrolls she thought how, in spite of his blustering ways, Thothmes was deep, deep and wily. He made certain that nothing would go on papyrus that could be used against him in the unlikely event of a sudden change in his fortunes. She was pleased. Egypt would have a wise and far-seeing Pharaoh.

26

Egypt gasped and panted its way toward the Inundation, and at last Hatshepsut heard the words she had begun to doubt would ever be spoken. Duwa-eneneh came running toward her over the grass as she was walking to her lake to bathe. His face was alight, and she stopped and waited for him, anxiously, her hands clenched at her sides. He stumbled to a halt before her and bowed. She barely restrained herself from taking him by the shoulders and shaking him.

"They have been sighted!" he shouted. "Entering the river from the canal! The messenger is within!"

She turned and flew back the way she had come, her women after her. In the audience chamber the Medjay prostrated himself.

"Up! Tell me all! Are the numbers still five? How did they look?"

"Like five bedraggled swans, Majesty," the man smiled. "But moving swiftly for craft that must buck the beginnings of the flood."

"How long?"

"I would say about another five weeks, perhaps even six. They appear to be heavily laden and will soon have to slow as the water rises."

She turned to the shrine in the corner, a rush of new life welling within her, but she could not say her thanks. Amun smiled complacently, but it was Senmut's name that she whispered, half-dazed, in a trance of happiness. She dismissed the messenger and sent for Hapuseneb.

He came quickly, relieved at her radiant expression. When she told him that the ships had been sighted, he felt as if a great burden had been lifted from his shoulders.

"Thanks be to Amun! Are there letters, Majesty?"

"No, only the message. Soon there must be word from Senmut himself, but meanwhile prepare for a day of festivity, Hapuseneb. We will welcome him as no Pharaoh has ever been welcomed by his people before!"

"I do not understand." He had gone suddenly cold. His eyes, the color of gray slate, sought hers.

"Neither do I, but it may be that Thothmes will be cheated of the throne despite his strength."

Suddenly Hapuseneb knew. He stepped convulsively to her. "Majesty,

I beg you, I implore you as my Divine Ruler and my God, do not do this thing!"

"Why not? Why should I not marry him? He would be a powerful Pharaoh."

"Yes, but too powerful. Do you think that he would be content to take the titles while you kept the power, as it was with the God Thothmes? As your right arm he is mighty in his strength, but as your head he would leave you vacant. And how long would it be before Thothmes raised an army and marched to claim from Senmut that which he thinks is his? Then nothing would have been gained but time."

"Time," she murmured, looking about her long, echoing room. "Time. I am sorry, Hapuseneb. I sought only to avert what is to come, in a moment of weakness."

"It cannot be averted, Majesty. It can only be delayed. Forgive me, but it is beneath your divine perfection to attempt to prolong the agony in this cheap way."

"You offend me," she said quietly, her eyes closing and passively opening again, "but you are right. You are always right, old friend. There will be agony, will there not? Will I ever be ready for it? But let us put aside the future and dwell for as long as we can on the present. Arrange to bring Amun into the city on his Sacred Barque as before. We will greet the ships together. It will not be long."

He wondered whether the plan for Senmut had been taking shape in her mind for a long time, growing under Thothmes' jibes, or whether it was a sudden flash of rebellion. He had no wish to spend his last years in killing, and he had no doubt that if she moved as she said she would, then killing would be his destiny. She turned from him pensively, and he dared say no more about it. "It is a great achievement, this," he said. "No Pharaoh will be able to equal it."

She stood still and said coolly, without looking around, "Thothmes will."

Every day brought fresh reports from her lookouts, and the five ships struggled on upriver, battling the brown, muddy wrath of Isis's Tear. At last a tired sailor brought Hatshepsut a scroll bearing Senmut's own seal. She tore it apart in her eagerness to get at the contents. She had forgotten that Senmut knew nothing of what had passed since his departure and that for all he knew she was a prisoner and Thothmes was King. The words were polite, admiring, a subject's words to his lord. No hint of affection colored the pale pages. They were well and had lost no men. They had reached Ta-Neter and had stories to tell of its wealth and its barbarity.

Nehesi also sent his respectful greetings. She put it aside, near to tears, overwhelmed by the time that had gone by. She had scarcely finished reading it when another dispatch arrived, this time from Gaza. As she skimmed its contents, she began to smile and then to laugh hysterically. The scroll was from Thothmes. He had taken Gaza and was on his way home.

On the last night, when the fleet was anchored briefly twenty miles downstream, due to arrive the next morning, she did not believe that she would be able to sleep. But she did, deeply, dreamlessly, as she had in her youth. She awoke to the tips of the morning sun and the priests' high voices, feeling more vital and refreshed than she had in many months. She sent Hapuseneb to perform her devotions in her place so that she could prepare herself to greet the men who had gone so far and come back, almost as if from the dead. She was bathed and dressed carefully. She chose a short kilt, golden helmet, and beaded sandals, amethyst and carnelian, turqoise and gold and jasper about her throat and her arms, her fingers and her ankles. The palace also woke to a new vigor. The crowds already streamed from the city, shouting and laughing, milling about beside the jetties. The streets from the wharf to the palace had been festooned with flowers. Flags snapped from the tall wooden flagpoles, the Braves of the King standing beneath them in full, shining regalia. Their faces were solemn and inscrutable as they watched the comings and goings, missing nothing.

Amun was brought forth from the temple, and a great, awed hush descended on the motley city dwellers as the sun smote his hot, golden body. Pharaoh paced beside him, carrying the symbols of her authority crossed on her jeweled breast, her head high and a slight smile on her red mouth as the people swayed and lay before her on the stone streets. The nobles of Egypt came behind her, and the hush deepened, for many of the men following her were already legendary, their names on everyone's lips for almost twenty years. Avid eyes drank in every detail of their sober faces. There was something else in the air, too, a feeling of sadness mingled with the glorious joy of the occasion, as if it all was coming to an end in a final burst of majesty. The sun bathed them all in liquid light, a light that flowed mellow and molten, seeming to transform them into living flames from Ra's fiery Barque. The spell broke, and the cheering began again. Hatshepsut and her lords reached the river carried along by the deafening applause.

She sat, and the court gathered around her. She was motionless, gazing upriver to the bend still lying empty, a pool of brown water between the browner fields that spread to distant, rearing hills. Gradually all sound was replaced by an expectant, tense quiet. All heads were turned. All eyes grew tired from peering to the north. For an hour they stood thus, the spell holding them, a gathering of timeless statues.

Someone gave an excited, half-strangled cry, and pointed. Hatshepsut sprang to her feet, dizzy and faint from the sudden rush of fear and elation that coursed through her. They came, taking the bend with a ponderous slowness, oars dipping and rising, sails set to catch the prevailing north wind. Their decks were crammed with tiny black figures that began to wave and cry out, their voices carrying faintly to the seething city. Hatshepsut clutched the Crook and the Flail, hugging them to her, pressing her arms to her breast, impatient. The ships came on. Now two people were discernible, standing high in the prow of the lead ship, not moving. Her eyes flew to them and stayed fixed on them. The wash creamed back, and the oars dipped. She could no longer hear the cries of the sailors, for all around her a thunderous ovation rang out, swell upon swell.

After a moment of waiting and watching that seemed to last forever, she found his face, the eyes steady and warm. They looked at each other over the rapidly diminishing stretch of water, not moving or speaking, just drinking, drinking. They began to smile, and Hatshepsut flung out her arms, grinning uncontrollably, as the incense rose again, triumphantly, and the priests sang, and the people welcomed them home.

"Thebes and all Egypt salutes you, warriors and princes," she shouted as the lead ship nosed gently to her mooring, glad to be home. The ramp was run out. The other ships were maneuvering to tie up, their decks piled with all kinds of strange delights. The people gazed avidly at them, but Hatshepsut saw only Senmut. He came toward her, Nehesi at his side, swinging easily down the ramp, then lying prostrate before her on the warm stone of the landing stage. They rose and waited, watching as she gazed at them.

He had not changed. If anything he looked younger and fitter than when he had left. His eyes were clear and no longer shadowed. The lines of worry that had begun to form about his nose and mouth had been smoothed away; his muscles had regained their former taut appeal. Nehesi, too, had changed little. The smooth planes of his black face were perhaps tighter, his massive, strong body more compact and lithe. He greeted her with the same quiet respect and monumental indifference for the roaring crowds and eager courtiers that he had always shown. She handed the Crook and the Flail to User-amun and embraced them briefly, tears glittering on her long eyelashes.

Senmut turned to the boats and indicated their loaded decks. "Gifts for Amun and for you, Majesty," he said. Before she looked to the ships, she gazed across at him and smiled again, his voice sweet in her ears. Each deck was rigged with a canopy, and under each canopy the myrrh trees huddled, little, whippy young trunks and gay, waving branches. Their roots were sunk in the earth from which they had been dug, and they were bound lightly in wet sacking. More sacks were piled against them. "Myrrh trees for the gardens in the holy valley," Senmut said, "and sacks of myrrh ready for perfume and incense."

"Trees for Amun, just as he wished," she said, her eyes shining and her arms aching to reach out to him. "Oh, Senmut, this is truly marvelous! Have the sailors unload them immediately and take them across the river so the gardeners can begin to plant them. They will need much water. How many are there?" She could not tell by just looking, for they seemed to her to be a green forest, sprouting from the very decks of the ships themselves.

"Thirty-one. We have also brought cattle and much gold and other precious things."

For a while they stood and watched the trees being carefully unloaded. Amun was taken back to his sanctuary, and Hatshepsut and her court drifted back to the palace, chattering excitedly like a flock of bright peacocks. She mounted the throne in the audience chamber, and the nobles settled themselves around her, prepared to watch her receive the tribute. Senmut and Nehesi stood, one on each side of the golden throne, calmly watching as the gifts were carried one by one, according to ceremony, and placed at her feet. The sacks of myrrh came first, filling the room with their heavy, langorous scent. Tahuti and his scribes began to weigh them and note down their value.

Aset and Meryet stood with their retinues at the back of the room, awed in spite of themselves as the laden servants came and went. They had not believed that Senmut would return. Indeed, they had hoped that he would not and that Hatshepsut would be made to look finally and irretrievably ridiculous.

Punt was as full of gold as Egypt herself, and Tahuti soberly watched as the nuggets and dust and countless bands were divided and noted, Amun's share and the royal treasury's.

Nehesi leaned to her and said, "There are many of the thick bands, Majesty, because the people of Punt make them to cover their legs. You will see in a moment, for seven of the chiefs and their wives and families wished to sail with us. They wanted to assure Your Majesty of their joy at being reunited once more to Egypt and to pledge peace and prosperity between the two lands." He was smiling a little cynically, and she laughed quietly, not imagining for a moment that the chiefs of Punt had agreed to come of their own volition.

The gold was being piled on her right, and more servants were bowing, putting down a mound of ivory tusks and struggling under great slabs of ebony, black and gleaming dully. More slaves waited behind them, almost buried under animal skins: panther, leopard for the priests, and others. It was some time before she realized that not all the confused mass of hides belonged to dead animals, for twelve of her zoo keepers bowed with difficulty as they held onto leashed dogs, monkeys, and apes that set up an echoing rumble of barks and whimpers and cries, making her laugh. A cheetah was led forward, a lean, speckled, lordly beast that regarded them with a cold, unblinking stare. It sank onto its haunches and daintily began to wash its face. Senmut told her that this animal was a very special gift, sent by Parihu, the greatest of all the chiefs, for her exclusive use. He was a hunting cheetah, very swift and deadly. She took in her own hand the chain of golden links attached to his collar, and presently the beast got up and stood on the steps beside her, leaning its bony, warm body against Senmut's bare legs.

The presentations went on. There were many different kinds of wood, dark and hard, light and beautifully grained, sweet-smelling wood, wood to delight a carver. There were ostrich feathers, eye paint, and oil of myrrh. And Nehesi had thoughtfully brought back for her a selection of the flowers and strange plants of Punt so that she could add them to her own garden.

When it was over, she went among the gifts, helping to divide the tribute while the priests of Amun waited for their share, exclaiming and handling everything with the simple delight of a small child. After the hall had been cleared, she sat down again, and the seven chiefs were brought to her. She was surprised that they resembled her own countrymen, for they were fair-skinned and had long black hair and were slight of build. As Nehesi had said, they all wore rings of gold on one leg, from ankle to hip. They crawled to her over her gilded floor, and she bade them rise. The men were bearded, with thin, stern faces and inquisitive eyes, and their women and children were dressed as they were, in short kilts much like her own. She welcomed them, speaking softly as she stressed her respect for them as the dwellers of the land from whence the gods had come and told them how she wished for only peace and good barter between their two countries, as there had been of old. They listened impassively, their dark eyes fixed on her painted face. One of the men stepped forward and bowed, praising her in a hurried, broken voice. The children crowded close to their mothers' legs, silent and big-eyed.

Suddenly, Hatshepsut knew what was wrong. She held up a hand, and the man stopped speaking. "I have made you welcome," she told them, "and a great feast has been prepared for you. We will eat together. But you do not feel welcome. You are in fear, lest having been taken from your homes, you will not return. I make this promise to you: Stay in Egypt for as long as you like, and when you are ready, I will send you back to Ta-Neter with an escort of soldiers and many gifts. I swear this on my own name, King and Pharaoh of Egypt."

The people of Punt relaxed and began to chatter among themselves in their own strange tongue. Hatshepsut rose. "We go now to the temple to give thanks to Amun and to show him his tribute," she said. She left the audience chamber with Senmut by her side and Hapuseneb leading them. Her canopy bearers stepped forward to shield her from the sudden glare of the hot sun as they paced solemnly to Karnak. Before the open doors of the sanctuary, Hatshepsut was at last able to say the prayers that had died on her tongue during the two long years of waiting. Thothmes was still far from Thebes, and all around her was the evidence of her eternal beauty and power. She prayed fervently, first lying on the floor, then rising to address the God publicly.

"I will cause you to know that which was commanded me. I have hearkened to my Father Amun, who bid me to establish for him a Punt in his name in Egypt and to plant the trees of the God's land beside his temple, in his garden. I was not neglectful of that which he needed." The clear voice rose emphatically, defiantly. "He hath desired me as his favorite, and I know all that he loveth. I have made for him a Punt in his garden, just as he directed me." She listed all the gifts that she was presenting to him, her mighty Father, silently apologizing for her lack of faith, her bitter doubts and angry words to him. "Ye shall fulfill according to that which I have exacted," she reminded him, and only Senmut heard the hint of pleading behind the arrogant words. "Your lifetime is the life of my mouth. I, in my Majesty, have given a command that the offerings to him who begat me should be made splendid." She made her homage again, kneeling on the floor.

From somewhere behind the God, the oracle's voice floated over the company. "The God gives you thanks, Daughter of his body and King of Egypt. Go in peace and in every good gift. Punt has come to Egypt, and Amun is glad."

The rituals were over. The assembly drifted to their couches for the afternoon sleep, but Hatshepsut went into the garden with Senmut. They sat under the cool shade of a spreading sycamore, a restraint between them. Though they held each other, watching the drowsy insects crawl and bumble over the grass, they found it difficult to look into each other's face.

"Tell me of Punt," she said at last. "How many times in the past months I have dreamed that I stood beside you in the ship and watched with you the unfolding of horizons which I shall never see!"

Hapuseneb had taken him aside on the way to the audience chamber and hurriedly told him of the death of his young charge and of Thothmes' steady pressures. He was still shocked. Hearing the note of sadness in Hatshepsut's voice and seeing in her a new fatalism, a listlessness, though outwardly she was as lovely and gracious as ever, he realized what inroads the hand of fate had made in the last two years while for him destiny had seemed to stand still and draw back. He felt its rush again, this time a sweeping juggernaut ready to fling him into the abyss that had gaped before him, every step of the way, from the time of his apprenticeship with Ineni. Looking into the black hole of his future, hovering on the edge, he felt the fierce wind at his back. He did not speak of Neferura, and she was glad.

"We turned south when we emerged from the canal," he said, "but that you know, Majesty. We hugged the coast for many months, always seeking the place of which the librarian and the elders spoke. We had almost despaired of finding it when we anchored one night and were greeted by Parihu, he of whom Nehesi spoke. He feared us, seeing our bows and axes; but we spoke of peace, and as we looked at the cast of the features before us, we knew that we had indeed found the dwellers of the blessed land. Parihu was astonished at our skill, thinking that we had fallen from the sky!"

She laughed a little, her throat tight with the pain and pleasure of his voice, his warm arm around her, remembering. "Such a moment! Such a blessed moment!" she said, beginning to cry, relief and strain taking their toll.

He could not remember a time when Pharaoh had cried like this, quietly, for nothing. He wondered how Menkh and User-amun and Tahuti had fared in his absence, faced with an unsteady government and a hunted woman. He tightened his hold on her and went on as if her tears were not falling into her lap, reaching from time to time to wipe them gently away. "Parihu's wife, Ati, was the most enormous woman I have ever seen in my life, and she was borne to the beach on the tiniest donkey I have ever seen in my life. The inscrutable Nehesi almost spoiled the expedition by his efforts not to laugh. It seems that such fatness is regarded as a sign of great beauty by the people of Punt, and Ati was a fair queen indeed! They live in palm houses raised high above their river, on stilts, and all around them is thick jungle. . . ." He went on softly, stroking her hair, talking and talking as the heat increased and the gardens became hushed and still, trying to fill her mind with images other than the dark and desperate phantoms that ate at her thoughts. He felt her limbs loosen and her breath slow. When at last he ran out of words, she put her head on his shoulder and sighed. Looking down, Senmut saw that she was asleep, and he kissed her eyes. He smiled to himself and leaned back against the trunk of the tree, pulling her with him, but he did not slumber. He rested, his eyes on the heat-dancing acres before him, the events of his short life passing slowly through his head with a kind of sad, lost aura, tinged in a faraway, sunny glow.

Hatshepsut slept on, curled against Senmut, until dusk, when the horns blared from the temple walls. In the banqueting hall the slaves moved quickly to and fro, putting final touches to the gilt and flower-strewn tables for the feast of the chiefs of Ta-Neter.

She awoke with a start, bolting upright and looking around to see where she was. Senmut touched her arm, and she turned around, focusing on the face she had loved for so long, touching a dream that was real. He was home at last.

It was a special night. Something of the magic of days gone by permeated the vast, lamplit halls and colonnaded passages, something of the time when Thothmes had been no more than a child and Hatshepsut's feasts had gone on until the dawn. But also there was a sense of a beautiful pageant coming to an end. The guests and servants thronged the rooms, their laughter and gossip filling the myrrh-laden air. The swish of white linen and the twinkle of jeweled sandals were everywhere. The cool night wind, still without the cutting edge of a winter just begun, blew freshly, dispersing the aromas of rich, hot food and perfumed oils as it floated lazily between the lotus pillars of the banqueting hall.

A mood of almost hysterical gaiety hung over the group gathered on the dais. The gusts of laughter and light, incessant conversation wove in and out as the loin-clothed servants glided in and out through the open double doors, bearing wine and platters heaped with steaming delicacies and flower garlands.

Hatshepsut had known, in the deepest part of her, that tonight would be the last of her great feasts. She had dressed as sumptuously and as carefully as if she was going to her death. She wore the Double Crown, wondering if Nofret would ever place it on her head again. She wore the royal collar of gold and the hanging, heavy pectoral of her coronation, the Eye of Horus. The ankhs, symbols of life, gripped her arms, and on her fingers great rings glittered, gold and blue and purple and green. Each ankle was encircled by thin silver bands adorned with little likenesses of Hathor that joined at the fingertips. Her sandals were red leather decorated with lotuses picked out in red gold, and her kilt was beaded with tiny golden globules that clung to the soft linen like raindrops.

She sat among the men who had formed the most cohesive and indestructible power party in Egypt for the last twenty years: Senmut, her beloved, arrayed as a Prince, his kohled eyes meeting her own over the flowers; Nehesi, the black one, General and Chancellor, once more carrying the great Seal at his plain leather belt, his face set impassively under his blue helmet as he looked to the guards around the walls; Hapuseneb of the sane, steady eyes, his priestly linens wrapped under him and his curved fingers in the water bowl; Tahuti, still frowning as the long lists of tribute unrolled in his head; User-amun, black eyes flashing and hands gesticulating wildly, a grin on his pert face as Menkh leaned closer to hear the end of the joke; Puamra, toying with his food, his closed face musing and his cats prancing stiff-legged around him; Inebny the Just in earnest conversation with her Viceroy for Lower Egypt, their heads bent and their thoughts engaged on some matter of diplomacy, both oblivious of the uproar around them; Duwa-eneneh at his post on the bottom step of the dais, his handsome face alive as he ate and watched the naked dancers, his herald's staff on the floor beside him; poor, polite Ipuyemre, her Second Prophet, poor, inarticulate but devoted Ipuyemre; staid Amunhotpe; Senmen the Mighty; Amunophis, her Steward. Names, faces—history now, living history—voices soon to be stilled, quick brains used up, their days come and gone like pieces of dry leaf upon the bosom of the river. So she thought, looking from one to the other while her goblet was filled and she drank again. The chiefs of Punt ate silently, their inquiring eyes upon her. She missed Yamu-nefru, his easy drawl and mincing, languid gestures; and she missed Djehuty and Sen-nefer, for they had always brought to her a sense of timelessness, their families and hers stretching back into the dimness of the early time of Egypt, a cord holding past, present, and future together.

Ta-kha'et sat down among the princesses and nobles wives, the gray cat curled asleep in her green lap, her auburn hair flaming among so many black, coronetted heads. She had finished her meal and was watching Senmut steadily, her eyes never wavering. He had come to her in the dusk, before he had dressed for the feast. She had flung herself on him and wept. He had brought her gifts; he had not forgotten her. They had sat for a while in his quiet study, drinking beer and talking, but she knew that she would sleep alone tonight as she had done for so long now. But as always she did not complain, even to herself. He was back, he was home, and they would again play board games together in the long afternoons, beside his ornamental pool under his sycamores. She stroked the cat absently. It began to purr in its sleep, but her gaze never left her master's face as he smiled and inclined his head, talking quietly with Pharaoh, two crowned heads above the others.

There was music and wine, and the story of the journey told by Ipuky's son, and more wine and dancing, and more wine. The noise and clamor increased as the moon waned. The halls, the gardens, even the temple, were full of celebrants, and the shouts and cheers and hoarse laughter drifted over the river to the night fishermen silent in the distance. They woke to listen, bemused, turning their faces to the powdering of lights that dusted the royal precincts. The revelers poured into the gardens and ran and shrieked and staggered over the grass and among the flowers.

Hatshepsut drank and laughed, too, as years became months became weeks became days. The days collapsed into minutes and the minutes into seconds, precious, precious seconds, more vital, more lovely, more enduring than all the gold in her treasuries. At length she looked at Senmut and he at her. They left the confusion of the hall, threading their way through the groups in the garden, swiftly walking along the avenues, leaving the sounds behind them until there was only moonlight flooding her bedchamber and the half-heard padding of the guards beyond the door. She sighed, a gusting heave of her breast, and took off the Double Crown, laying it reverently and unsteadily in its casket. Senmut moved to light the night-light, but she stopped him, catching his arm and throwing it around her neck. They kissed, the years of separation dissolving as if they had never been. In darkness and silence they probed each other slowly, rediscovering the hidden delights of each other, trying to pour into the moment every inexpressible emotion they had stored and treasured from the time of their first meeting, trying to break down every last invisible wall. The stones of kingship and lowly birth gave way, crumbled, and were no more. Words were not necessary. With their hands and lips and oil-bedewed limbs they spoke of love and death, of kingdoms fought for and won and lost, and of sunshine and worship and children and the sheer joy of being alive. When it was over and they lay side by side on the warm fur, they both knew that never again would such an experience come to them. It was a final blessing. Nothing lay ahead but the darkness.

They drowsed for half an hour, hearing from far away the departure of the guests and nobles, a dim bustling, a few shouts of command, the patter of a running slave's feet. For an hour the predawn hush enveloped them.

Hatshepsut stirred and raised herself on her elbow, stroking his chest as her hair fell over his face. "Senmut, have you achieved all that was in your mind when first I summoned you to the lake? Is there anything more, before—before—" She could not say "the end."

He brushed her hair from his eyes and smiled up at her. "Nothing more, Hatshepsut. I have been and done far more than I ever dreamed of in those days."

Her fingers paused. "If I asked for marriage now, would you deny me?"

He sat up suddenly, looking at her. She tossed her head defiantly. "What is in your mind?" he demanded.

She jumped up and ran to her table. "This," she said, holding up the Double Crown. "This. For you."

For a long, long moment he stared at her and at the solid, smooth-sided thing she was caressing. Within him his other self, so cool, so collected, so calculating, sidled close and whispered, "Take it. Have you not earned it, son of the earth?" But other thoughts followed, sad and vicious thoughts, and he shook his head slowly as he felt his luck leave him, and glide out the door. "No, my dearest sister, no," he said. "I know myself, and I know you a little, though you are deep and well nigh impossible to fathom. If Thothmes were not breathing hard at your heels, would you still be offering it to me? Suppose I take it now and set it on my head. Suppose I become Pharaoh Senmut the First. Thothmes will fight, and I will be forced to defend an Egypt that will not serve me. Do you hope to lengthen the hour of your triumph at my expense? Will you use me, too, even now?"

She flung the crown onto the table and buried her head in her hands. "I love you, I love you. That is all I know!" she sobbed. "I do not want to die, not now, not ever. I do not want to leave you, and the pleasant fields of Egypt, and those who have made my life a delight and a perfume in my nostrils! Give me your strength, O my beloved!"

He went to her, saying nothing, trying with all the might of his arms to stave off the black, snaking shadows of eternity.

5

27

Thothmes came swaggering home a month later, the army behind him, laden with the spoils he had promised her and a host of prisoners to be put into service. To her paining, oversensitive eyes he seemed to have grown, filled out, and she received him with tight lips and a cold greeting. He seemed not to notice. He stood beside her as the treasures of Gaza were piled at her feet, his deep voice reciting the highlights of the campaign and the siege. She went with him to the temple, where he paid his respects and gave his thanks to Amun. He was already planning immense additions to the temple, and Menkheperrasonb, his architect, and Minmose, his engineer, walked with him as he inspected every inch of the temple courts. She left him to it and went to find Senmut, wanting to know the mood of the people. She found him with Hapuseneb.

"How has Thebes welcomed the Crown Prince?" she asked them.

Senmut told her, his eyes willing her to stand her ground and not falter. "From the delta to Thebes the army was followed by crowds of fellahin and city dwellers, shouting his praises," he said brusquely. "They called for him, and when he left his chariot and went among them, they called him Pharaoh and kissed his feet. They love you, Majesty, and they always will, but they have forgotten your peace and your prosperity. They want only conquests."

"The mob is always fickle," she murmured, "and ever people want what is not good for them. If they want war, then Thothmes will undoubtedly give it to them. How it angers me!" she said, "that all I have done to fill the chests of the temple and the treasury with gold and to give my subjects a little peace in which to grow will be set at nought because the horns of war stir their simple hearts!" She bit her lip and left them abruptly. Senmut wisely did not follow her. The final acceptance, the last hard laying aside, she would have to face herself.

Two months later, in the middle of the night, Hapuseneb's frightened acolyte woke him, whispering breathlessly in his ear that the Crown Prince was without. Hapuseneb fought off his dreams and struggled from his couch, thanking the boy and telling him to summon Nehesi and the

Followers of His Majesty immediately. He let the lad out of his own little door, the one that led directly into Amun's sanctuary, locking it behind him. He shrugged on a thick robe and splashed water on his face. He wished now that he had chosen to sleep in his own house downriver instead of in the apartments of the temple, but he wasted no time in foolish regrets. When his doors were flung open, he was seated in his chair, his hands folded in his lap. His cold gray eyes greeted Thothmes across the dimness.

Thothmes was alone, but at the end of the passage two of his soldiers stood guard. Hapuseneb had no idea where his own temple guards had gone, but he could guess; gold was a strong magnet. He did not rise and bow, but only bent his head slightly. Thothmes advanced until he was looking down on the High Priest. Then and only then did Hapuseneb rise, and the two men were face to face. Hapuseneb, as was correct, waited for the Prince to speak. Thothmes had been drinking, but he was not drunk. Hapuseneb could smell the beer on his breath as he opened his mouth, and Thothmes' earrings swung as he shifted his weight, planting his feet firmly on the floor and bringing his fists to his hips in a characteristic gesture, his eyes fighting savagely for possession of Hapuseneb's own.

"I will waste no time," Thothmes said. "I want to sleep as much as you, High Priest. I have a proposition to put to you." He waited for Hapuseneb to reply, but the gray eyes went on smiling slightly, so he continued, his jaw thrust forward. "My aunt-mother is finished as Pharaoh. She knows it, and I know it, but she will not move. I have had enough of waiting. There will be changes in the palace, and I need not tell you what they will be. I am sure that you know."

"I know," Hapuseneb said, his heartbeat quickening. "We all know."

"Of course you do." Thothmes stepped away suddenly, swinging about the room. There was an aura of impatience around him, a palpable, restless, brute force. Hapuseneb shivered a little and drew his hands in under his woollen robe, seeing Thothmes the First, the Mighty Bull of Maat, stalking in his room in the faint yellow glow of the night-light. "You have served her long and most faithfully, High Priest. Your father, the Vizier, served my grandfather with the same laudable devotion, and that is why I come to you in person and do not summon you to a public audience." He wheeled abruptly. "Do you serve Egypt or Hatshepsu?"

Hapuseneb answered him levelly, though his mouth was dry. "You know already what I will say, Prince. I serve Egypt as embodied in Pharaoh."

"You evade me, and I am tired, so I will put it more plainly. Will you serve me as High Priest, or will you continue to align yourself to a pharaoh who has never been Pharaoh?"

"I serve Pharaoh," Hapuseneb said stubbornly, "and Pharaoh is Hatshepsu. Therefore I will continue to serve her as long as she lives."

"I am offering you more than your freedom. I am giving you a chance to continue in the temple and in the courts as you have always done, remaining Pharaoh's confidant and adviser. I need you, Hapuseneb."

Hapuseneb smiled faintly. "I cannot desert her as long as she rules Egypt."

"And after that?"

Their eyes met, and Hapuseneb struggled against the overwhelming magnitude of Thothmes' will. "I am hers. I cannot put it more clearly."

Thothmes stalked to him, frowning. "Come, come, Hapuseneb. You are not a baseborn upstart like Senmut. You are of an ancient and aristocratic family. Side with me, and live in every good blessing."

Hapuseneb shook his head emphatically, his hands trembling under the robe. "I will not betray her who has heaped rewards and affections upon me from the time of our youth together, even if it means my death. She is Pharaoh, Prince, and has been since her father's rising to Ra. If there is any treason, then it will be found in those who support your claim."

Thothmes blinked and stepped back, irritation making his cheek muscle twitch convulsively. "You are a fool. I ask you once more and then never again. If you feel you cannot serve me, will you accept exile and agree never to cross the borders of Egypt for the rest of your life?"

"I will not run away. I will not leave her friendless, with no defense. I would rather die." The gray eyes faltered momentarily and looked away. Hapuseneb sat down. His knees would hold him up no longer.

Thothmes sneered and walked quickly to the door. Hearing him come, his soldier opened it and stood waiting. "It may come to that," Thothmes said loudly. "Yes, it may. Reflect on your words, and if you have changed your mind before morning, bring me word." His hand was on the door.

Hapuseneb regarded him mildly. "I am sorry, Prince, but my mind is not swayed by every wind of good or evil that blows. It will never change."

"Die then!" Thothmes exploded, the door crashing shut behind him.

Hapuseneb got up stiffly and went to stoke the brazier. He was shivering violently and was very cold. He had scarcely flung fresh charcoal onto the embers when his door burst open again and Nehesi strode in, knife in hand. Behind him four Followers of His Majesty ran, fanning into the room, eyes quickly scanning every corner. Hapuseneb smiled tremulously and held out his hands to the new blaze. "Thank you for coming, Nehesi."

"I wasted no time." Nehesi sheathed the knife and went to Hapuseneb. The guards retired at his nod. "I thought to find you wounded or dead. I saw Thothmes and his cohorts crossing the outer court, all armed to the teeth."

"He came only to talk. We talked, and then he went away."

Nehesi glanced at the High Priest. "You are pale."

In truth Hapuseneb was sweating profusely. He was still trembling, but he had begun to recover his customary aplomb. He led Nehesi to his table and poured wine, drinking thirstily. "I suppose I am. Thothmes is preparing to move—I think within the next day or two. He came to offer me safety."

Nehesi laughed grimly. "Indeed? I can guess the price—and your answer. Where were your guards?"

"Lured away, I suppose. I doubt if I shall see them again. We must go immediately to Senmut and warn him. He is probably in the royal apartments." He shrugged helplessly. "What can we do?"

"Nothing but die like men," Nehesi said indifferently. "At least we can say that we have lived like men. We will be justified before the gods. Our end will be swift, but what of Pharaoh?"

They looked at each other hopelessly, the cups still in their hands, angry that now, at the last, they were as impotent as newborn babies. They left Hapuseneb's rooms together, knives drawn again, gliding warily through the night, the Followers of His Majesty behind them, their eyes straining, searching the darkness.

Senmut and Hatshepsut were asleep when Nehesi sought admittance from Duwa-eneneh, but before the herald knocked softly on the door, they were awake, listening to the urgent whispers outside in the passage. Duwa-eneneh found them on their feet, robes clutched tightly around them.

"The High Priest and the Chancellor request audience," Duwa-eneneh said with a bow. Seeing his face, Hatshepsut felt a stab of panic. It had come. And so soon, so soon!

She nodded, meeting Senmut's encouraging smile. "Let them in. And stay with us, Duwa-eneneh. I think that what they have to say concerns you as well."

He opened the doors, and Hapuseneb and Nehesi entered quickly. He closed the doors quietly behind them, making sure that the Followers of His Majesty had taken up their positions outside and at either end of the long, twilit passage.

"Speak," Hatshepsut said briefly, "and do not be afraid to spare me. The time is here. Is it not so?"

Nehesi went and sat by her table, under the small window. Hapuseneb approached, telling her as gently as he could of Thothmes' proposal. She listened without comment. When he had finished, she went up to him and touched him softly on the shoulder.

"For your own sake, beloved, you must leave Thebes tonight and flee to the north. I will not have your blood on my conscience."

"I will not go. My place is here, and here I stay. Nehesi and Senmut and your other ministers will say the same."

"I have taken everything from you, Hapuseneb, even your heart. Must I take your life also?" Her voice was a private, low murmur, and the other men heard only its tone, pleading, begging. "I will give you gold and soldiers. You can easily find peace in Rethennu or Hurria. Please, Hapuseneb, go from me!"

He fingered his badge of office, shaking his head slowly from side to side and smiling at her as she spoke. "No and no and no," he said. "How could I live then, knowing that I had left you to your fate?"

"Fool! Fool!" she said angrily. "What can you, any of you, do if you stay? The tide runs against me, and nothing you can do will avert the flood!"

"We can die." Nehesi's voice floated to them from the other side of the room. "We can die." She let out a cry of frustration and flung herself back to the couch, sitting tensely on its gilt edge. "We can show Thothmes what true loyalty means, and we can make the ultimate sacrifice of our devotion. No soldier could ask more," he went on, speaking as if he were discussing the outcome of the day's dispatches from the nomes.

She chewed on her lip, thinking furiously. "How long do we have?" she asked them.

Nehesi left his perch and came into the circle of the lamplight. "No time at all," he said. "Now that Thothmes has shown us his hand, he will move fast. He will strike at you first, Senmut, as the most powerful prince in Egypt. Then he will eliminate Hapuseneb as the highest official of the temple, and then me as Pharaoh's bodyguard."

"I think he will try to do all at once," Senmut said. The conversation had the quality of a deep, unpleasant dream for him: the dull, yellow light; the stiff figures; the night wind moaning faintly in the shuttered wind catchers; and over them all the swiftly falling shadow that would never lift to show the skirts of day again. His voice was as lifeless and heavy as his limbs. "He will strike quickly and completely, between one day and the next, fearing that if he gives you time, Majesty, you might yet muster a force and defeat him."

"How little he knows me," she answered. "He himself, if he were in my position, would not hesitate to pour out the blood of the army just to hazard a try, but I will not. I will not kill."

A heavy silence settled over them, an almost apathetic mood of defeat.

She stirred and sent Duwa-eneneh to summon Nofret and her slaves. "We will eat and drink together as Ra rises," she said, "and we will speak of these things no more. You know what is in my heart for all of you. If I can do no more than plead your justification before the gods, then that I will do. In later times we will laugh together as we walk the green fields of paradise with eternity before us and remember it all as a game."

They did not move or look at her, each of them struggling with emotions that ran too deep for words. Nofret came in and was sent away again for food and wine and lights. When these things arrived, they sat on cushions on the floor and ate and drank to each other, talking softly of all that they had done together since the far-off, shining days of their first offices, holding each moment up to the light of memory, exclaiming quietly over its beauty or its terror or its humor, smiling at each other, resignation and love in their eyes. Then it was dawn, and while she knelt before them, her black hair falling over her face, they sang the Hymn of Praise, arms around each other, voices breaking finally, tears coming unbidden as Ra saw them through the high window and bathed them in his limpid glow.

She got up and embraced them, holding them to her fiercely before she let them go, crying with them in the dawn silence. One by one they prostrated themselves and kissed her naked feet, slipping away into oblivion, taking with them the days of strength and happiness they had given her and vanishing like wind ripples on the placid water. She turned to Senmut, her face white and drained and somehow younger in the spreading light. "Let us go onto the roof," she said, taking his hand. They left the bedchamber, mounting the stairs that clung to the palace wall and coming out finally on the flat roof of her audience halls. They sat, still holding hands, and Senmut knew that he was looking his last upon the lordly pylons and obelisks of Thebes. Far to the west a band of night still hung, a gray cloud clinging to the tops of the cliffs and hazing the sun. The broad reaches of the Nile lay glinting in the new day, its waters dimpling and sparkling, the reedbeds and tall palms an oasis of cool green. Closer in lay the gardens and lawns, statues and wide avenues and twisting paths where he had walked and dreamed and laughed and wept. Now they were empty in the hush that preceded the clamor of the day, the grass glittering with dew, the Imperial flags fluttering in the morning breeze. In the distance he saw the dip and glance of the sun on the golden prow of the Royal Barge, resting at anchor beside the water steps. He drew in a deep breath, inhaling all the perfume of Egypt, muddy water and sweet lotus, the freshness of living trees and a waft of myrrh.

He turned to her slowly. "Thank you, beautiful God," he said quietly. "Thank you, Divine Incarnation, Living Forever. I shall not forget." He gathered her gently into his arms and kissed her while the winter mists blew away and Ra's fingers grew hot on their tired faces.

28

Senmut went back to his palace and spent the day unobtrusively putting his affairs in order. Before the noon hour had passed, he bundled Ta-kha'et and most of his servants onto his barge, ordering his captain to take her north to his parents' farm. She protested loudly, sensing danger, but he kissed her lightly on the cheek.

"Do not argue!" he said firmly. "Go to my father, and stay there until I send for you. It will not be long. See! I have even ordered my musicians to go with you! Please, Ta-kha'et, make no more fuss, or I shall call for my Steward, and he will beat you!"

She looked up into the gently smiling face and stopped shouting. "Very well, Senmut, I will go. But if you do not send for me before the end of winter, I shall come sailing back! What are you going to do?"

"Something very hard," he replied. Suddenly the cat sprang from her arms and hissed at him, its eyes frightened and staring in the sun. It struck out at his ankle, baring its claws, and sprinted up the ramp to disappear within the ship.

"You have upset him," she pouted as he hustled her up the ramp and nodded to his captain.

"Not I," he said. He kissed her again and left her, standing on his little wharf as the gay red and white boat pulled away and the oars were run out. She waved once and went into the cabin, still angry, but he did not move until the barge's stern vanished around a bend and the water ceased to heave with the wash. He walked slowly up the water steps and along his deserted avenues. The sun was hot, but not with the usual, heavy, drugged weight of summer. He went to his pool and sat cross-legged on the grass, gazing into the brown depths as the fish darted and the dragonflies hovered, his mind a careful blank. Though he tried, he could not shut out the sound of his own rapid breathing and the beating of his vigorous heart. Even as he forced it down, a great love of life swelled within him. He groaned and covered his face with his hand.

His Under Steward touched him on the shoulder. "Master, how many will be dining tonight?"

Senmut looked up at him, startled. He laughed. "Why, no one, my friend. I hold no feast tonight, so you may go to your quarters as soon as you will. Dismiss the servants before dusk, and see that the slaves are far from my rooms. I will need no one, I think, until the morning."

The man bowed, perplexed, and left him. He continued to watch the busy blue and green and violet fish, but he felt light, light and free, and not until the shadows of his trees touched his back did he get up and walk quickly in under his pretty, colonnaded cloister.

They came just after the temple horns had sounded midnight. He was waiting for them, sitting beside his couch, reading in the steady glow of his night-light. From the darkness of his reception hall he heard their furtive, quiet steps turn into the deserted passage. They paused and came on more slowly. He smiled at their hesitation, laying aside the scroll and rising to his feet. No doubt they had expected a host of guards and a palace full of lights and waiting soldiers. Someone tried the door softly. There was a hurried, whispered question followed by a brusque command. Senmut stood motionless, fighting for control as the white-hot fingers of panic groped for him. The tall cedar, gold-inlaid doors began to inch open. Senmut still did not move. In the shrine behind him the plume of incense wavered suddenly in the fresh draft, and the scroll lying on the couch rustled dryly, but his eyes were fixed on the gulf of blackness widening in the wall. His senses began to shriek within him: Fly! Run! Live! Live! A brown, ringed hand appeared, cautiously feeling the edge of the door. Senmut closed his eyes for a split second and swallowed, sweat drenching his kilt and running down his naked back. With a reverberating boom the door crashed back against the wall. Two men rushed at him, raised knives glittering yellow and cold in the friendly, soft light. He saw their faces, wild under the blue helmets, their eyes fierce, their teeth bared. For a moment, one long, frozen moment, when they seemed to glide toward him with sickening slowness, time seeming to merge with eternity, he looked up to his walls and saw her face, brooding and forever untouched under the Double Crown, the golden eyes fixed upon him in mild authority. He smiled at her. And then They were upon him, and in the agony of his dying he screamed, falling, the sound of his own fear in his ears, his own blood gushing into his mouth. Above him his blue ceiling, strewn with silver stars, shook and dissolved into a deeper, wider blackness, a mouth of ice that swept down to devour him.

They struck Hapuseneb as he walked alone in the moonlit silence of his garden. He died minutes later on the wet grass, wounded in the stomach and chest.

They got Nehesi as he strode between the palace and his own quarters, overpowering his two guards and thrusting a knife through his neck while he struggled with ferocious strength to shake them off and run back to the palace. He staggered on for three paces, then fell face down on the cold stone path. It still lacked four hours to the dawn.

Hatshepsut was still up when Paere burst in upon her. Nofret lay on her mat at the door, dozing fitfully, but Hatshepsut had begun to walk her floor, her arms folded under her breast, her head down, unable to rest and go to her couch. The little servant came staggering through her private entrance, a Follower of His Majesty behind him. She turned and ran to him, horror-stricken. He was weeping and babbling, shivering. His hands and one cheek and the front of his kilt were smeared with blood. He was trying to speak, waving something in front of him with frantic despair. At a half-strangled word from her the soldier picked up the water jug standing in the corner and threw the contents over Paere's head. He shuddered and gasped, still crying. Suddenly he collapsed onto her chair and began to sob, still clutching the thing in his bloody hands.

"They have killed him. They have murdered him!" he shouted brokenly.

She stepped forward, her feet numb, and wrenched the object from his grasp. It was a scroll, sticky with blood. It bore her own seal, opened long ago. As she unrolled it slowly, nervelessly, her other door was flung open, and Duwa-eneneh ran in.

"Majesty, Hapuseneb! Nehesi! Both dead! So soon! What shall I—?"

But she ignored him, staring at Paere with an expression of absolute terror and grief on her face. The scroll was Senmut's own, the very first plan of her temple in the valley that he had submitted to her. Across its neat, lovely lines she had written, "Authorized and approved by myself, for the architect Senmut. Life, Prosperity, and Happiness!"

In the morning, after a sleepless horror of a night, when she had tried to comfort Paere and speak rationally to Duwa-eneneh, all the while wanting only to walk to the top of the temple and fling herself off, she had Nofret array her in white and silver and put the Double Crown on her head. The ravages of the past hours were impossible to erase, but the woman did her best, laying the rouge heavily along the cheeks and ringing the swollen eyes with the blackest of kohl. Hatshepsut took Duwa-eneneh and strode to the audience chamber. She marched to the throne, mounted the steps, and sat upon the smooth, icy gold, her anger and sorrow invisible on her proud face.

The bodies of Hapuseneb and Nehesi had been quickly taken to the House of the Dead, but no one knew where Senmut lay. His room had been sealed by her order until her police could begin an investigation, but as the hours went by and servant after servant came to her with negative answers, she had begun to fear that she would never find him. Knowing Thothmes as she did, she thought that it would not be enough for him to destroy the living flesh. He would rend and separate and bury deep, so that the gods could not find him to welcome him to paradise. She understood very well Thothmes' insane jealousy, his hatred for Senmut as her right hand; but this senseless, demonic spite was beyond her. The fear of him began to grow inside her. Hapuseneb. Nehesi. Senmut. . . . There was no one left to speak and act for her. She was alone.

She awaited his coming patiently, sitting back on the throne, her arms lying along the lions' backs, her feet together on the ivory footstool that was carved with the likenesses of her dead foes. Duwa-eneneh stood motionless beside her, holding her standard, and the palace began to move into another day.

He came at last, striding down the long hall, his sandals beating a loud, dominating rhythm. It was all she could do to keep silent and watch him approach, for she saw only his hands wet with the blood of her faithful ones. She read a defiant guilt and a new awakening to power in his eyes. She loathed him—and she feared him.

She saw Yamu-nefru and Djehuty and Sen-nefer walking behind him. She rose to her feet in disbelief, the unbearable weight of this pain upon pain tearing into her. She sucked in her breath in agony, and the three came on and at last halted, bowing. Thothmes lifted his eyes to hers, and they looked at each other for a long moment. Somewhere a horn blew. A hawk flew past the window. Outside, in the garden, a servant walked, singing. They faced each other in a deadly and vicious silence until Hatshepsut lowered herself slowly onto the throne.

"You killed them."

"Of course I killed them! What else did you expect? Did you think that I would let the months and years go by and do nothing?"

"No."

"I had no choice. Surely you see that!"

"There is always choice. You gave the coward's answer."

"I gave the only answer!" He shouted at her, his voice ringing to the silver ceiling.

She regarded him impassively, turning her gaze to the three men who stood behind him. "Come forward, Yamu-nefru, Djehuty, Sen-nefer." She said their names slowly and deliberately.

They left Thothmes and bowed at the foot of the throne. Their faces were bland, expressionless, and their very indifference hurt her intolerably.

"Did you have aught to do with these despicable murders?"

Yamu-nefru put out a hand in shock. "No, Majesty, I swear on your name! We only knew this morning that Senmut and the others were no more!"

She read his eyes and nodded, satisfied. "You may thank the gods for that. Thothmes or no Thothmes, I would have punished you with my own hands. Do you have anything more to say to me?" She could not believe that they had changed allegiance without a word.

They exchanged glances, and Yamu-nefru spoke again, his bronze bracelets clinking as he gestured. "We have loved you, Flower of Egypt, and we have served you with our own blood. We have fought beside you and governed honestly in your sight and in the sight of the God. But now the Crown Prince puts forth his claim, and under the law we cannot ignore it. We do not move through fear."

"I know that."

"We move in the belief that Thothmes is indeed the Hawk-in-the-Nest, true inheritor of the Double Crown."

"By what law?"

"By the law that states that Pharaoh shall be male."

She passed a hand over eyes burning with weariness and waved them aside. "All right! All right! I understand your reasoning and your strange, cunning honesty. I have loved you, too. And now you may go. Or do you wish to stay and see your Pharaoh lose her crown?"

Thothmes nodded, and they turned and strode away.

When their footsteps could no longer be heard, Thothmes said, "They wish to avoid bloodshed. That is all. Their thoughts are hidden from me as well."

"You think nothing of bloodshed!"

He walked closer, and Duwa-eneneh stiffened. "I have not come to rake up dead ashes. Yesterday is over, and tomorrow is mine. Come down from the throne."

"No."

"Come down, Hatshepsu, or I will call my soldiers and have you thrown down!"

She wanted to scream at him, "Do it then! Do it!" But it was a senseless defiance, a silly little gesture. With a shrug she walked slowly down the steps, cold fury in her eyes. "There! The throne is yours!"

"Take off the crown."

For a moment her will faltered, and she paled.

As he looked into the big black eyes Thothmes saw a pleading, a terrible defeat that suddenly tore at him, filling him with sympathy. He saw a death in those eyes, a wrenching, awesome falling apart. He almost put out his arms, but a flash of obstinacy reached him, and all sympathy fled.

"Take it off!"

"You will have to come and get it yourself. Put the knife away, Duwa-eneneh. There has been enough killing."

The Chief Herald miserably sheathed his knife and looked away. Thothmes stepped to her and in one easy movement lifted the heavy crown from her head. Her hair fell around her face, freed from its bonds. Suddenly she was Hatshepsut again, a woman, a Queen. He turned as she laughed, the old mocking note infuriating him.

"Well, well! We have a new Pharaoh! But what about your legitimization, Thothmes? Meryet is panting to take you to the temple and become Queen."

"I do not want Meryet," he said harshly. "I want you."

She was stunned. "Me? You want me as your Queen?"

"Of course. Meryet will be useless as a consort, but you could rule actively with me. We would be invincible, you and I."

"Do you mean to stand there with the blood of my dearest flesh still warm on your hands, and offer me marriage?" It was too much, and she sank to the steps. "I suppose that when I die, you can then marry Meryet and go on securely ruling Egypt. Oh, you are deep, Thothmes, deep and unscrupulous!"

"Not so!" he answered roughly. "I do not need you, for as you say, I have Meryet. But I want you."

"Why?" she said. "In the God's name, why? I am nearing forty, and you are only just reaching for your majority. A pretty match, Thothmes!"

"Well, what am I going to do with you?" he snapped in exasperation. "I cannot leave you to wander wherever you please, stirring up trouble!"

"That, Pharaoh, Living Forever," she said, smiling faintly, "is your problem." She jerked her head at Duwa-eneneh and went out of the audience chamber to her own silent, empty rooms, leaving Thothmes standing there, frowning angrily, with the crown in his hands.

She needed desperately to rest, but she found she could not. Every time she lay down and her body became still, her mind began to churn with ghastly pictures: Senmut lying in his own blood, Hapuseneb dead under the moon, Nehesi on the damp paving stones of the avenue with a knife through his throat, his eyes staring into nothing. She finally left her bedchamber, and taking Nofret with her, she went to Meryet's apartments. There was no doubt about the new atmosphere in the palace. As she walked quickly down the passages, between the pillars of her halls, and around corners, the soldiers and slaves and nobles bowed to her with the same reverence, but their eyes were inquisitive and scared. All around her she heard their whispers. Little knots of people gathered outside the ministers' doors, talking rapidly and excitedly. She sensed rather than saw the milling confusion of minor officials who ran here and there, uncertain whom to approach with their questions, standing nonplussed with sheafs of papers in their hands or wandering aimlessly from room to room. On the way she had to pass Senmut's office. She glanced in as she walked by. The doors were open, and his table lay empty of scrolls. His big chair was drawn up to it as if at any moment he might walk toward it, arms full of papers, calling to his scribe. She quickly averted her head and strode on.

Meryet was standing on a reed mat, her arms held out, as Hatshepsut walked through her door. A slave was winding a dripping piece of linen around her and under her shoulders. Water pooled on the floor and spattered Hatshepsut as she approached, the words of greeting dying on her lips.

"Meryet, what on earth are you doing?"

Meryet-Hatshepset looked at her mother with guarded, surly eyes. "I am being fitted for a new sheath. If the linen is wound around me wet, it then shrinks to my figure as it dries. In the end it is most becoming. It is the latest fashion."

"The latest. . . . Do you know what has been happening in the palace? Do you know about me?"

Meryet's slave fastened the sopping linen under the Princess's arm with a large bronze pin. Meryet stepped carefully off the mat, holding out her feet so that the girl could slip on her sandals. "Of course I know, and I am sorry, mother, but it is all your own fault. If you had bowed to Thothmes a long time ago, then none of it would have happened. You have only yourself to blame."

Hatshepsut looked into the hard, sullen eyes of her daughter. She was speechless. She turned on her heel and walked out the door. Meryet called after her, asking her what she had wanted, but Hatshepsut stalked on. When she reached the branching of the passage, she stopped and whirled around. Meryet was standing outside her door, looking after her. Hatshepsut shouted back, "You are worthy of Thothmes, and he of you! I wish you joy of one another!" Before Meryet could answer, she was running into the garden, running anywhere, her tears blinding her and making her stumble over the grass.

Thothmes decreed the customary seventy days of mourning for Hapuseneb and Nehesi. Day after day their bodies lay under the hands of the sem-priests who wound the stiff limbs with bandages and prepared them for their last journey. But of Senmut, Thothmes deliberately did not speak. "He deserves no mourning," he told her contemptuously, "and no burial. He was a traitor." She had to grieve on her own, lying before the image of Amun in her own lonely room, saying the prayers for him without priests or acolytes to hold the incense and make the responses. She hurt now without respite, the pain growing within her until she was one long, howling, unbearable ache. She refused to walk in the funeral processions, showing her disgust by her absence, but she stood on the roof and watched them form, the blue mourning garments of the harem women shining in the early sun and the golden sledges glinting by the water, bearing away all that was left of her life. She whispered prayers to them as the barges were poled across the river, but she cried no more. There were no more tears to be shed. All that remained was a great, endless tiredness and an impossible loneliness that filled the vast halls of her palace with echoes from the past.

Two days later Thothmes and Meryet went to the temple, and the crown was officially placed on Thothmes' head. Meryet received the little Cobra Coronet, gloating and smiling, triumphant. That night the feasting went on until the small hours, the ebb and flow of the merrymaking wafting to Hatshepsut as she lay on her couch, Nofret beside the door. She could not sleep. She had not gone to the temple, either. Thothmes had threatened and wheedled and finally shouted, but she just looked at him silently and shook her head.

"Will you at least help me with the problems of government?" he had begged.

At last she had shrugged and turned away. "If you like," she had said indifferently. "Certainly Meryet will be no use, and it will give me something to do." She wanted to fill the days with something, but after two months Thothmes told her that he could manage without her, and she retired to her apartments with the same glacial calm.

It hurt her to give up the leadership of the Braves of the King to Thothmes. He had finally demanded the Commander's silver armbands, sending her own second-in-command to fetch them. His petty probing in the wound of her defeat made her angry, thus taking some of the sting away as she handed the bands to the uncomfortable, unsmiling soldier. She embraced him, thanking him for his service, and sent him away.

Thothmes had appointed Menkheperrasonb, his architect, High Priest of Amun. She could never get used to seeing him in the leopard skin, waiting before the God's sanctuary when she went to make her devotions. She had to steel herself to meet his gaze day after day, and more than once, walking to the temple in a mood of abstracted brooding, she had expected to smile into Hapuseneb's face, and the presence of Menkheper-rasonb shocking her.

It was only one of many, many changes. One day she called for Duwa-eneneh, waiting with a message for her new Steward, but it was Yamu-nedjeh who entered her room and made his bow.

"I sent for my Chief Herald, not you," she said sharply. "Where is Duwa-eneneh?"

Yamu-nedjeh did not smile. "The noble Duwa-eneneh has been called to his estates in the south," he said, his face carefully composed. "Pharaoh has appointed me Chief Herald in his absence."

Hatshepsut looked sadly at the tall young man with the thick, straight eyebrows and square shoulders. She could not answer. It was no use to fight, to scream, to demand the immediate recall of Duwa-eneneh. She knew that he would never come back. She sent Yamu-nedjeh away, and Nofret carried the message instead.

As the weeks went by and each new day brought fresh and wrenching proofs that her total lordship was over, she channeled her gusts of energy into furious physical exercise. She hunted with a ruthlessness that was new to her, killing every day. Killing mindlessly in the wilds beyond the palace walls and bringing back carts laden with the carcasses of animals and birds, quarry that she turned from at the end of the day without a backward look. She spent hour upon hour with her bow and arrows—draw and loose, draw and loose, target after target being taken down, cratered with jagged holes. Though she rose in the mornings with stiff muscles and an aching shoulder, the frustration and fury did not leave her, as she dimly hoped they would.

Menkh rode with her, held her quiver, ran with the dogs after her stricken prey. He seemed not to have changed. He chattered ceaselessly, laughing and capering before her as he had done all his life. He ignored the ever-present soldiers that Thothmes had set to guard them both, who trudged after them wherever they went. But when she met his eyes, Hatshepsut saw the bleeding of a quiet wound as deep as her own, a flow of pain he was unable to staunch. In all the loud babble of his nonsense she noted no reference to past or future, as if he were holding off not only herself but also all the years behind him. His only defense was the brilliant gloss of the courtier's wit coupled with his own zest, a defense that must fall at last and let in the hard glare of reality.

Thothmes had noted their daily forays, as he noted everything. He weighed, pondered, and finally moved, dissolving their crazed partnership with brutal speed.

Menkh met her under the trees by the barracks, dressed not for hunting but for travel. His pack rested at his feet, and a cloak was over his arm. When she came up to him, he bowed; but as he straightened, she saw a tormented face. Overnight, the lines of laughter around his eyes had become cruel reminders of encroaching age. She glanced at the soldiers behind him and turned swiftly to look again into his eyes.

He did not wait for her to greet him. "My humblest apologies, Divine One, but I cannot hunt with you today—or tomorrow either. I am to go away."

"You?" she said, shocked.

His face worked for a moment, grief and anger and something else, alien and frightening, fighting for control of him. "Pharaoh has need of a charioteer to augment a new squadron he has formed. He is building another garrison within the borders of Nubia, and I am to go there." He smiled at last, bitterly. "It is a long, long way."

"How far?" She was almost speechless. How could Thothmes, even with his vast suspicions and dark speculations, ever imagine Menkh capable of fomenting plots with her when his sunny soul, like User-amun's, lay open for the world to see?

"So far that I do not believe I shall ever come back. This garrison is out on the desert, surrounded by the men of Kush. But the years are longer than the miles. In a word, Majesty," he finished bluntly, "I am banished."

Her mind refused to function, her thoughts darting away from her grasp. Not you, Menkh! My last friend, my last living memory! If you are to go, then who will tell me of my childhood in these days when there is nothing else left to me? Thothmes knows this. How implacably thorough of him, how typically full of spite. Is it not enough that he has my throne?

"What of Ineni?" she snapped. "Surely Thothmes will listen to him."

Menkh shrugged. "My father went to Pharaoh. Thothmes gave him all deference and honor, but it did no good. Father is old, and his hands shake. There is no oil of persuasion now on his long tongue. He was told that if his son chooses to associate himself with a traitor, then his son must pay the price."

Her eyes narrowed. "And if I go to him?"

"What good would it do? Forgive me, Majesty, but you would only fan his hatred."

"And you would suffer. I know him! But what more suffering can you endure than this, dear friend of my youth?"

He looked about him slowly, savoring the day, squinting into the sun. The trees rustled above their heads, and the strident whistling of the birds was like a tuneless music. "I have lived all my life in paradise," he said. He laughed. "Now I must tread the underworld. A hot march it will be, and without hope. Yet, Majesty, I do hope." He spoke lightly, trying to cheer her, but she was not deceived.

Something within her coiled tightly and broke. "Amun, Amun," she cried. "Have I not been dutiful? Have I not been your faithful Daughter? Why this, too?"

Her voice echoed back to her from the other side of the training ground, bringing to her other words than the ones she had spoken. And have I not given you your heart's desire? Did you think that the price would not be heavy?

She bit her lip. "Hope if you will, dear one, but I fear you will die of it. I, for my part, have had done with all hopes and all delight."

He stepped closer to her. "Farewell, Hatshepsu, Pharaoh, Living Forever. We have done much together. How much more would have been possible without the intervening hand of fate." He spoke not as servant to lord but as friend to friend.

Although she searched his eyes she could find no trace of the youth who had danced at her feasts, who had twirled his whip so gaily over the heads of her proud horses, who had laughed at her on the battlefield for her sweat and grime and anger. She silently said good-bye to the laughter, the lighthearted foolishness that had warmed them throughout the years. The man who stared back at her so intensely was not Menkh. He was a deeply serious stranger, all frivolity gone forever, replaced by a calm that was neither healthy nor natural. She had a premonition that the gods would strike him down long before the men of Kush could ever raise their bows.

She leaned forward very slightly and kissed him on the mouth. "Speak no more of fate," she said harshly. "Remember me, Menkh, when the desert nights are long, as I shall remember you."

He bowed and picked up his pack, slinging it over his naked shoulder as the soldiers closed about him and prepared to march. "So be it," he said. "Perhaps you will find another charioteer, Majesty, but none with my grace, I swear!" The smile was ghoulish, a parody of his easy grin.

She did not reply but stood still and watched until he and his guards had vanished among the thick trees beside the water.

She never hunted again.

Thothmes' ruthless reorganization went on. Tahuti was spared because of his knowledge, but he was relegated to the post of Under Treasurer, and the wild Min-mose, with his loud laugh and reckless manner, was appointed Treasurer. May became Royal Fan Bearer at the Right Hand of the King. Hatshepsut's own Fan Bearers were dismissed, and she sorely missed the men who had walked beside her, their scarlet fans waving over her crowned head. Her women had to carry her fans instead, but she walked proudly and disdainfully in spite of this new emblem of humiliation walking beside her, for the position was always given to men. Nakht, the chariot driver who had never lost a race, became Thothmes' Royal Messenger, and his bronze wheels flashed up and down the country, busy for the Pharaoh whose stony eyes turned ever north, to Rethennu and the lands beyond. Suddenly the halls of government were filled with warlike men, the cohorts of Thothmes' military days; their thoughts were arrogant and quick, filling Thebes with the tumultuous words of battle.

Hatshepsut moved quietly among them, winning their grudging admiration by her silent, lithe grace and the wisdom of her few words. But she fled them often, for the palace was no longer a peaceful, well-ordered place, and even her own servants spoke of nothing but Thothmes' might and the enjoyable prospects of war. She would cross the river in the early dawn and pace the stones of her temple avenue alone, her sphinxes watching her passage with calm, uncomprehending eyes, not recognizing their creator in this slow-moving, quiet woman. She would walk up the ramps in the sun's radiance and wander through her shrines, followed by her worshiping priests, allowing the unchanging peace and beauty of the pillared halls to comfort her.

She never stopped to read her biography or Senmut's, either. The words were forever engraved on her soul in flaming hieroglyphs. She did not need paint to remind her who she was and from whence she came. Thothmes or no Thothmes, she was still God and always would be. As she walked under the green shade of her myrrh trees and dipped her fingers in the sacred pools, it seemed to her that Senmut walked beside her, his strong arms waiting to embrace her.

How short a time it has been, she thought, looking back down the terraces to the hot silver ribbon of the river. It seems as if only yesterday I parted the reeds to see him standing there in his coarse linen, his head bare and my throwing-stick clutched in his hand. Little we'eb priest! Tomorrow I will see him, walking and talking with Ineni as they ponder some odd problem. The day after that he will come and feast with me and pour my wine and press the sweet, blue lotus to my face. Great Erpa-ha, Prince of Egypt for all time!

I remember thinking once that only two things really mattered to me, the people and the power, but I was wrong. Behind the people and the power are two far greater mysteries. The God. And the love of Senmut.

Epilogue

After twenty years of struggle to rise, struggle to rule, struggle to hold onto what was hers, there was no longer any need even to think, and the grayness of uselessness threatened to engulf her. Far better, she thought, listening to the silence, that my days should have ended with Senmut, under the assassin's knife, in a burst of blood and sudden fear.

In the soft lamplight the door was flung open. Her stepson strode into the room, the guard groveling behind him, uttering polite little noises of protest. But Thothmes shut the door in his face and came forward. His body glistened with the perfumed oils of the feast, and his eyes were rimmed with kohl. The ankh on his breast shot golden fire into the duskiness, and on his head reared the symbols of his kingship, the cobra and the vulture. He stopped by the couch, his hands on his slim hips, and she waited.

"This room is cold," he said. "Where are your servants?"

"I have one left to me for the night, two for the day, as you well know. Even my scribes and my faithful Nofret have been dismissed. What do you want?"

"To talk of Kadesh. Were you asleep?"

"Almost. I have had difficulty sleeping of late. Now what of Kadesh? Do you seek my advice?" Her tone was caustic. It had been long since he had looked to her for counsel.

"No. But the envoy and his entourage have just decided to leave tomorrow—and in high dudgeon. Soon I must follow."

"War?"

"War."

"Then you are a fool. Is it not enough that our borders are secured and our land at peace? Can you not be satisfied with an occasional foray for slaves, a salutary warning or two?"

"No. The time has come to teach our enemies that Egypt is the center of the world. I am going to build an empire that all men will speak of to the end of time. I am, after all, a soldier. You made me one."

"Yes, I did. To command under me, to follow my wishes. No matter what you do, proud Thothmes, you cannot hide the fact that you took my throne from me."

He leaned over her suddenly, his black eyes alive with anger. "Speak not of treason to me, usurper! For twenty long years you kept my crown upon your own pretty head. But now I am at last the stronger, and I have taken what has been mine since my father died. I have captained for you in Rethennu, in Nubia. I fell upon Gaza at your command with all the might of my army and took it. Now I captain for myself. I am Pharaoh. I!"

They glared at each other, trembling on the verge of more bitter words, but Hatshepsut reached up and laid a hand on his cheek. He smiled and sat beside her on the couch.

"We have said all this many times before," she remarked, "and always we arrive at the beginning again. I am getting too old for such open strife. Tonight I left the feast because my daughter, your shallow, simpering wife, refused to speak to me. Me! Goddess of the Two Lands! Would that Neferura were still living!"

"Well, she is not!" he replied harshly. They fell silent. "Touching Kadesh," he began again, "I am going to mount a full-scale campaign in the near future. I will be away from Egypt for some months—"

As he hesitated, she jumped in. "And who is going to govern while you are away? Your featherbrained wife?"

"Thebes is a city full of able and loyal advisers and administrators," he said slowly. "But of one thing I am sure. You, dear aunt-mother, are not to put one finger on the reins of command. Do you understand?"

"Of course I understand. But who, dear nephew-son, is better able to direct the country than I?"

"You make things very difficult for me. I cannot take you with me, and I cannot leave you here, for I know, as surely as Ra rises triumphant each day, that I would return to find my Viziers dismissed and you seated firmly on my throne once more. Let go, Hatshepsu, let go." His fingers closed about her arm, and he bent lower still. "You have lived as no Queen has done before. You have pressed out the grapes of power. You have tasted the joys of the gods, and still you are hungry. I have seen it in your eyes. I see it now, the hope that I shall go and once again it shall be as you wish. But it can nevermore be. The traitor Senmut is dead. There is no one left to bind your wrists with golden chains to the kingship that was never yours. No more scheming, aunt-mother, no more secret whisperings and plottings."

She wrenched her arm away, and as the fur slipped from her breasts, she struck him on the mouth. "I should have ended your life when I had the chance," she hissed at him, "but I would not. It would have been so easy when you were a child, dependent on my good will. The priests and all my ministers would have turned their backs and pretended not to see.

But no! I spared your life! The good Senmut spared your life! Have a care, Thothmes. The old queen bee can still sting!"

The Lord of All Life rose and put a hand to the corner of his mouth. "Do not threaten me," he snarled. "You are in no position to do so, and such reckless courage will only bring you death. I say it plainly. You are in my hands, and the glory of Egypt comes before all things, including you. If you must die for the good of this country, then do not be mistaken, you will. You make it hard for me, Hatshepsu. I cannot make a decision, and that is unlike me. I tell you plainly, for four years you have been on the brink of death, and I have stayed my hand. Why, I do not know."

"I do," she said softly. "It is a debt. You loved me once as a young man loves for the first time, blindly, passionately, with great single-mindedness. And as with a young man's first love the fire quickly died, but the memory burns still." She shrugged. "Forget it, Thothmes. Do what you must. I am ready."

High up in the walls, a faint gray light began to seep through the windows, and she could see him more clearly. He, too, had not slept this night, and he looked tired, the heavy-lidded eyes veiled. The lamplight sank to a sickly yellow glow, and the cold silence of early morning enveloped them as they waited, watching another day start to invade the room.

Hatshepsut spoke, quietly, without emotion, her hands limp and motionless beneath the beautiful fur. "Morning is here," she said. "Soon the High Priest will come. Perhaps he is already on his way, with the Second High Priest and the censers and the acolytes. They will all gather outside your room, with the Royal Fan Bearer and the Keeper of the Royal Seal and the King's Sandal Bearer and the Chief Herald and—there are so many of them, are there not? They will begin the Hymn of Praise. 'Hail, immortal Incarnation, rising as Ra in the east! Hail, Life-Giver, Living Forever!' How does it feel, proud Thothmes, to know that you are not worthy of their praise? How does it feel to know that it is I, not you, who am the right and true Incarnation of the God, chosen by him before I was born, named before I was born, given the crown by my earthly father long before you opened your eyes in the women's quarters to see a common dancer as your mother? That is all that really matters, is it not? You cruelly slaughtered Senmut, and you may silently poison me, but that— that you cannot change! Never! You may destroy my name, you may forbid the records of my deeds, but your own unworthiness you cannot obliterate with the stonemason's ax. Now go. Go and receive the adoration of the priests. Go and fight your wars. I am tired unto death. Go!"

He heard her out in silence, the anger building up behind his eyes and his face becoming taut. When she had finished, he strode to the doors and flung them open with such force that they crashed back against the walls. "You are an extraordinary woman, Hatshepsu, extraordinary!" he shouted. "And beautiful still, and cruel. So cruel still. See how I repeat myself! You have angered me!" He straddled the doorway, his chest heaving. "Do you fear nothing?" He turned on his heel and was gone.

"Mighty Bull of Maat?" she called after him. "Pah!" And she began to laugh.

She lingered beneath the fur, unwilling to get up, smiling to herself as the light in the room became golden and she felt its new warmth lick her upturned face. When Merire knocked, she bade her enter, still lying with the soft, thick pile bundled under her chin. As Merire approached and bowed, Hatshepsut regarded the fat face and small, beady eyes with the same wave of revulsion she felt every morning when the plump little spy waited for her orders. How long? she thought in a sudden mad repudiation of the useless, senseless hours that stretched before her. How long has it been since Nofret greeted me with a smile and answered my questions as she extinguished my night-light and helped me into my bath? How many dead years?

"This morning I shall eat in bed!" she snapped at Merire. "Send slaves with fruit and milk but no bread; then come back in one hour to fill my bath." The silent woman bowed again and waddled out. Hatshepsut gave an exclamation of disgust and closed her eyes. To die with that face at one's elbow!

She dozed a little until Thothmes' Under Steward knocked. She sat up to receive his obeisance, and the slaves arrived, bearing her breakfast. They set it before her on her table and went out.

"How is Pharaoh this morning?" she asked the man.

He stood stolidly at the foot of her couch and answered without smiling. "Pharaoh is well," he answered. "He has gone to answer the dispatches."

Why does he not smile? she wondered as she sipped the milk and began to peel an orange. Every morning he smiles, but not this time. Not today. Why? "Is it a fine day?"

"It is."

"How is my grandson?"

"The Prince Amunhotep is likewise well. He attended school for the first time yesterday."

"Did he?" Her bright tone revealed none of the pain and pleasure his words brought to her. She had not held the baby since the day he was born, for Thothmes carefully kept her away from him lest he should become fond of her. In all the four years since his birth Hatshepsut had seen the little Prince only three times. "Then he will do well," she added, "for he is young to begin to learn."

The Steward continued to stand awkwardly, eyes downcast and hands behind his back.

Hatshepsut sighed and dismissed him. "Are you not going to ask me if there is anything I need today?" she called after him.

He came back, blushing with embarrassment and something else, something she could not understand.

"Forgive me, Majesty. I grow forgetful."

"A bad omen for my day," she said lightly.

He stiffened and gave her an agonized look. "Accept my apologies for spoiling your day, Majesty."

She bit into the orange, sucking the juice thirstily. "You will not spoil my day, my friend, but Pharaoh will. Is it not so?" She shot a dark, penetrating look at him.

He lost his control. He bowed clumsily, fell beside the couch to kiss her hand, and then ran out the door.

She suddenly went still, the orange falling from her fingers, her appetite leaving her.

So it would be now, today, upon her with no warning after all. Although night after night she had steeled herself for the end that might overtake her before another sunset flooded her walls, she knew finally that she was not ready. She would never be ready. She swung from the couch and went into her antechamber to get her little ivory box. She carried it back into the other room, sat in her chair, and lifted the lid, sifting the contents with tender, wistful fingers. Here was the little ostrich fan that Neferura had given to her on a New Year's Day long gone; she stroked the wispy feathers slowly. Here a letter from Senmut, the one he had sent by messenger as his ships left the delta and turned into the canal on their way to Punt. She began to unroll it, but her courage failed her, and she dropped it with a light whisper. And here, right at the bottom, beneath the bright jewels of yesterday and the scrolls and pressed flowers, the ribbons and trinkets bringing back to her a sweet breath of days gone by, was the thick golden ring that Wadjmose had worn on the night he died. It was still black from the fire that ate his body. She drew it out and turned it over and over in her hand for a long time, seeing Nehesi's face when he laid it on her shaking palm. She slipped it over her thumb. Wadjmose. A brother she had never met. How many faces she had never seen, how many places hid delights she would never know! Solemnly she took off the ring and laid it back in the box. She closed the lid and locked it, for Merire was tapping on the door and it was time to dress.

It had been a long time since she had worn kilts. Merire looked at her dumbly as she pushed the soft sheath aside and ordered her to find one of her old garments. They were piled in a chest behind the door, neatly folded, just as Nofret had left them. Hatshepsut pulled one out while Merire stood, still gaping, and wrapped it on. It fitted as perfectly as if she had taken it off the day before, and she clasped a jeweled belt around her waist and put on a yellow helmet. Merire found her electrum collar with the flowers of amethyst and jasper and fastened it around her neck. While she pulled on white leather boots, she told Merire to find Per-hor and have him harness her chariot.

Merire went out, but before she went to the stables, she visited Thothmes' Chief Steward. Hatshepsut never drove her chariot in the morning, and Pharaoh would want to know. The man sent her away again and had his scribe take down a message for Thothmes.

He was sitting in his tent on the outskirts of Thebes, his generals around him and his army spreading over the plain. As he read it, he was strangely still. "She knows," he muttered.

"Your pardon, Majesty?" Nakht said.

But Thothmes shook his head and ordered more wine. It would not be long now, and he must wait. In the morning they could march. In the morning. . . .

The racing circuit lay shimmering in the sun, a blinding dazzle of hot earth. Per-hor was waiting for her, standing in the golden chariot while the horses pranced and shuffled to and fro. When he saw her coming, he jumped down and handed her the reins.

She smiled and greeted him as she stepped up, drawing on her gauntlets. "Stand behind me today, Per-hor," she called. He sprang up obediently behind her. "We will not go round and round," she said, gathering up the slack. "Today we will go out onto the desert for a while."

The horses snorted and began to trot. Per-hor kept his balance easily, the breeze freshening in his face. "Pharaoh will not like that, Majesty," he shouted in her ear.

She turned briefly and grinned at him, flicking the horses with her whip. "Pharaoh can rot!" she called back, her words caught away by the wind. They thundered down the river road and presently veered east, careening under the cliffs and out to the flat land beyond.

All morning she slashed at the horses, galloping mile upon mile through sand that stung their faces and silted in their nostrils and mouths. The wind grew fiery with the full blaze of the midday sun, burning the sweat from them and drying their skins. Per-hor gripped the sides of the chariot and hung on grimly, marveling at her sudden burst of strength, for in the brief three years he had known her, she had always been so calm, almost cold, a slow-moving, quiet enigma. Up and down they fled, scoring the desert, driving finally in their own red, choking dust. When he was wondering desperately whether, perhaps, he should seize the reins and end this madness, she wheeled savagely and started for the cleft in the rocks and the safety of the river. He closed his eyes and breathed a prayer of relief. The horses staggered to the barracks and stood, sweating and dejected. He got down stiffly, holding out a hand to assist her, but she stood still for a moment, her gaze slowly traveling from the low stone buildings to the grove of trees by the training ground and on to the edge of the river. When she at last put her hand on his and jumped to the ground, he saw that she had been crying, the tears running down her cheeks, making rivulets in the sand that caked her face.

"Wash and change your clothes, Per-hor," she ordered him. "And then report to me in my chambers at once." He bowed, and she left him, walking wearily through the gates and along the avenue to her door. He wondered what was on her mind, for she seldom asked for him before sunset.

Her apartment was deserted and silent, cool in the midafternoon furnace that beat upon its thick walls. Without calling for Merire she took off the helmet, the kilt, and the gritty jewels, tossing them carelessly onto the couch. She went to her bathing room and washed herself in cold water, then walked back to her bedchamber with the water still dripping pleasantly from her brown body. She opened all her chests and with the utmost concentration selected other clothes: the blue kilt tissued in gold that had been made for the occasion of Neferura's Purification, a belt of gold and silver links, plain gold bracelets, golden sandals, a small coronet of gold with the plumes of Amun rising from the back, and a wide collar of gold, a single sheet studded with turquoises. She went to her shrine and said her prayers quietly, eyes squeezed shut, deliberately thinking of nothing more than the presence of her Father.

She rose at last and called for Merire, sitting before her copper mirror and waiting while the girl assembled her pots and jars. "Paint my face carefully," she said. "Use the blue eye color, and sprinkle it with a little gold dust, and be sure to make the outline of the kohl smooth to my temples." Merire's touch was light, and Hatshepsut watched impassively as the cool paint glided onto her skin.

If only my body had changed. If only my face had become lined and pouched. If only the blood did not still sing through my veins like water, laughing and bubbling over clean stones. If only—yes, if only. . . .

As Merire took up the comb and ran it through the heavy black hair, Hatshepsut picked up the coronet and set it on her brow, taking one last long look at the dull, gleaming reflection of her matchless face. She put down the mirror with a snap. "It is enough," she said. "Go and tell the Chief Steward that I am ready."

Merire hesitated. "Majesty, I do not understand."

"No, but he will. Go quickly, for I am impatient." The servant bobbed and went out.

Hatshepsut left her cosmetic table and walked through the room out onto the sunlit brilliance of the balcony. She heard Per-hor enter quietly behind her, and she called to him, "Bring me a chair."

When he had brought it, she sat in the bright afternoon, looking out over the gardens and trees to the river and the copper-colored hills beyond. "Ra is westering," she said.

He nodded and did not reply, leaning over the balustrade, his taut young face a careful blank. They stayed thus, in a deep and companionable silence: he, wondering when she would tell him why he had been summoned; she, sucking up the gay, sun-dappled glory of the scene below her, letting go the cords of living one by one and feeling her grasp slacken as the pieces slipped away and went snaking into the past.

When the Chief Steward knocked on the door of the room far behind them and came padding out onto the balcony, silver tray in his hands, she looked up at him in awe, as if she had never seen him before. "Your afternoon wine," he said, bowing and setting the tray on the gray stone beside her chair.

Per-hor suddenly sprang to life, striding across the balcony with a cry. "But you take no wine before the evening meal, Majesty. I know it!" he said urgently, his eyes darting from the silver goblet to the Chief Steward's expressionless face. And, as he looked into Hatshepsut's smiling eyes, he understood.

"I do today, Per-hor," she said evenly. "Steward, you may go."

"I am sorry, Majesty," he said uncomfortably, "but I have orders from the One himself not to leave your side."

Per-hor straightened angrily and advanced on the man, but Hatshepsut nodded briefly, as if she had expected no other answer. "Thothmes still fears that even yet I might wriggle out from under him and somehow bring him to ruin," she laughed. "Poor Thothmes! Poor, poor, insecure Thothmes! But I beg you, Steward, to withdraw and wait without, in the passage. I will not jump over the balcony and run away. If you like, you may send a Follower of His Majesty to sit with me, for I had rather go forth in the company of an honest bodyguard than with one of my nephew-son's minions!"

The Steward whitened. "That will not be necessary, Majesty," he said stiffly. He turned on his heel and strode out the door, closing it and locking it behind him.

Per-hor knelt before her, and she took his hands in her own. "Do not drink it, Majesty!" he begged her. "Wait. The tides of fortune may yet change!"

She shook her head sadly, bending to kiss his dark head. "They run too swiftly for any more change," she said. "Many, many times they have flowed for me, bearing me on waves of triumph, but not again. They heave for Thothmes and will not carry me on their bosom anymore. Now get up and fetch me my lute."

He did as he was told, going and getting it, cradling it in his arms, and handing it to her gently.

She stroked the tight strings pensively. "Do you remember the song he would sing to me when we sat together on the grass and watched the waters of the lake ripple, and the birds swooped here and there over our heads, crying their song with him?" He shook his head mutely, and she smiled. "Of course you do not remember. How could you?" Her fingers found the chords, and she began to sing softly, her eyes on the far distance where the sun was sinking.

Seven days from yesterday I have not seen my beloved,
And sickness has crept over me,
And I am become heavy in my limbs
And am unmindful of my own body.
If the master physicians come to me,
My heart has no comfort of their remedies,
And the magicians, no resource is in them.
My malady is not diagnosed.
Better for me is my beloved than any remedies,
More important is she for me than the entire compendium of medicine.
My salutation is when she enters from without.
When I see her, then am I well;
Opens she her eyes, my limbs are young again;
Speaks she and I am strong;
And when I embrace her . . . when I embrace her. . . .

Her voice faltered and broke. She could not finish the song. She lay down the lute and reached for the goblet, staring into its red depths. Per-hor was motionless, sitting at her feet with his arms clasped tightly about his knees, his face turned away. She drank steadily, tasting the sweet coolness and the hint of something else, something bitter. She set the goblet back on the silver tray with a little sigh. "Hold my hand, Per-hor," she said, "and do not let it go."

Convulsively he reached for her, grasping her fingers tightly.

She leaned back in the chair. "My blessing be upon you, son of Egypt," she whispered. "Senmut, Senmut, are you there? Are you waiting?"

Per-hor felt the lean hand quiver, but his grip did not loosen. He heard her murmur once more, wearily. He sat there for a long time while Ra dropped slowly to the black rim of the cliffs, the light on the balcony flooding red and streaming behind him to engulf her bedchamber. When the evening wind sprang up, lifting the hair from his forehead and stirring the golden hem of her kilt so that it brushed his arm, he tried to rise, but his muscles would not obey him. He sat on, her cold hand pressed to his face and the last shreds of her Father's shining garment lighting the jewels on her feet.

Also from Chicago Review Press

The Eagle and the Raven
Pauline Gedge
Foreword by Donna Gillespie

"[Gedge] gives us the daily life and landscapes of Celtic Britain with an almost psychic immediacy."
— *Toronto Star*

"A novel of majestic sweep, splendid assurance and controlled imaginative power."
— *Publishers Weekly*

$18.95 • 978-1-55652-708-1

"A big, other-worldly and beautiful novel. Gedge . . . has brought another age pulsating to life."
— *San Francisco Chronicle*

$16.95 • 978-1-55652-441-7

The Egyptian
Mika Waltari
Foreword by Lynda S. Robinson

"*The Egyptian* contains the ingredients Americans relish: war, women, intrigue, romance, wassail, horror, and lavish scenes of violence, indulgence, suffering, and death. Waltari has successfully combined research, imagination, and the cunning of a good tale-teller in bringing the generation of Akhnaton to life."
—*New York Herald Tribune*

"A grand immersion into an epic tale." —*Philadelphia Inquirer*

CHICAGO REVIEW PRESS

Available at your favorite bookstore, by calling (800) 888-4741, or at www.chicagoreviewpress.com